Flowers in Her Hair

Flowers in Her Hair

Mark Wisnewski

"
There are places the heart remembers long after the body has forgotten the way." – MW

For the wanderers, the dreamers, and the brave —
may you always find your way home to yourself.

Special thanks to Karin Konyari.

1

It was just before sunrise when David sat in the open doorway of his Kombi, legs dangling, toes brushing the dirt. Salt drifted in from the sea, the faint rhythm of waves carrying the first breath of day.

Across the horizon, gold and pink unfurled upward, the ocean catching each new crest of light. Seagulls called, trees rustled behind him, and the tide whispered its slow refrain.

He loved this hour — the air cleaner, the world unclaimed. Those still cocooned in bed would never know how quickly night surrendered to blue.

From his perch he watched Bondi shift from shadow to colour. A few early surfers paddled out, fishermen set their lines, and one or two revellers slept off the night. The waves rolled steady, their foam tipped with morning fire.

He breathed in. This was the beauty of living this way — no walls, no alarms, just the world waking with him. Freedom was worth more than any wage packet.

Nearby, a young couple sat beside their Kombi, wrapped in a blanket, sipping tea from mismatched mugs. Down on the sand, joggers left fresh trails, surfers hoisted boards, and early swimmers waded out laughing as the chill bit their skin.

As the sun cleared the horizon, Bondi came alive. David stood, smiling. The day was perfect — and the road was calling.

He packed his things, nodded to the couple, and slid into the driver's seat. The Kombi rattled to life. Winding down the cliff road, he eased past cars parked haphazardly along the verge. Campbell Parade was quiet, kiosks shuttered, waiting for the rush.

He rolled past the Gelato Bar and Bates Milk Bar — pink Laminex booths, chequered lino, mixed grills and milkshakes already in his mind. He'd miss that place.

At the Pavilion car park, longboards leaned against the walls. Local surfers lounged nearby, waxing boards and chatting.

"Hey, Davey!" one called. "Heading out already? Saw your board still strapped to the van."

David grinned. "Nah, mate. Festival up north. Music, people, the whole scene."

"Ourimbah?" another asked. "Heard it's meant to be the Aussie Woodstock."

"Bit of everything," David said. "Gotta be there to feel it."

"You reckon you'll come back?"

"Maybe. Bondi's got good energy. But the road — it's alive."

"You never did play that six-string of yours down here," someone teased.

David laughed. "Next time."

They clapped him on the back, wished him safe travels.

"Don't forget us beach bums when you're living the dream."

David walked backwards toward the van, grinning. "Never. Catch a wave for me."

The Kombi sputtered, then roared awake. With a honk and a wave, he pulled away — Bondi fading in the rear-view, the open road ahead.

2

David gripped the wheel of his old Kombi as it rattled along the Pacific Highway. The engine whined, but the morning felt fresh, his spirit lighter after leaving Bondi behind. Ahead lay the Ourimbah music festival — whispered about for weeks in Sydney's underground scene. First stop: Stanmore, to collect Lisa. They weren't a couple, not yet, but this weekend might show whether they could be something more.

The Kombi wasn't much — faded blue paint, a scatter of dents — but it was home. His guitar lay in the back with the camping gear, a sketchbook, and a bag of food. Patchouli clung to the van, mixing with bitumen and rubber as the city thickened around him.

Bare feet on the pedals, denim bell-bottoms, tie-dye shirt thin as gauze — he looked every bit the drifter people assumed he was. He didn't mind. The road didn't care.

Parramatta Road swallowed him whole — tyre shops, used-car yards, smoky pubs, trucks grinding through gears. Fading ads for

Resch's and Coca-Cola blurred past as pedestrians dodged traffic along the narrow footpaths. He drummed the wheel, humming along with the Beach Boys drifting from the radio. *Surfer Girl.* That song always took him back.

He remembered the first time Lisa walked into Ashwoods, the record store where he'd lucked into a job. No experience, no patter — just *I love music, man.* She'd slipped past him every Saturday for a month, polite smile, never buying a thing. Then one morning she stopped at *Bookends.* He'd walked over, heart hammering.

"That's a great album," he'd said. "Especially 'America'."

She'd looked up, smiling slow and warm. That was the spark. And now he was driving to her house, wondering how far that smile might carry them.

Stanmore shifted around him — factories giving way to terraces and Federation homes with iron-lace verandahs and small tended gardens. Bougainvillea spilled pink over pale façades; jasmine threaded the air. Among the Holdens and Fords, the odd Kombi hinted at another way of living.

He checked house numbers, nerves twisting. This was a world of swept driveways and tidy gardens — beautiful, but far from Bondi's wild ease. He could almost feel Lisa's parents judging already: bare feet, dented van, patched shirt.

A curtain twitched. Then the front door opened.

Lisa stepped out first, sunlight catching her hair. A scarf held it loosely back; her floral dress swayed around her legs. She looked like she'd stepped straight from one of his sketches.

"Ready?" she asked, fingers clasped.

"As I'll ever be," he said, giving her hand a quick squeeze.

Her father followed — tall, broad-shouldered, greying hair neat. His eyes measured David in a single glance.

"Mr Gardener," David said, offering a hand. "Good to meet you, sir."

The handshake was firm, assessing, then eased. "David, is it? Come in."

The house smelled of roast lamb and furniture polish. Wooden floors gleamed; a brass lamp caught his eye.

"That's a beautiful lamp," he said. "My folks had one like it."

Peter's gaze softened. "My mother's. Been here forever."

They sat at the kitchen table with cups of tea. Peter's questions came steady — work, travel, plans. Then the one that mattered.

"She's my only daughter. You understand?"

David held his gaze. "I do, sir. I care about her. My life might look unconventional, but I'd never put Lisa in harm's way."

A pause, then a slow nod. "Good. That's what I wanted to hear."

He stood. "Come on. We'll have a proper talk down the road. Pub's calling."

* * *

The Annandale was heaving. Cigarette haze hung thick as low cloud, the jukebox crooning through The Easybeats before being swallowed by the roar of Parramatta Road. Old blokes hunched over form guides; glasses clinked like loose change.

Peter claimed a table by the window. "I like a Resch's. What'll you have?"

"Same. Thanks."

"Peter," he corrected, weaving toward the bar.

David sat, palms flat on the table to still the shake. Through the fogged window he watched buses growl by, a kid on a dragster weaving between parked Holdens.

Peter returned with two middies. "Cheers." He drank deep. "Twenty cents now. Was fifteen not long ago. Robbery."

David laughed. "Records at Ashwoods were four-fifty when I started. Now you're lucky to get one under six."

"And people still buy them?"

"Place is packed. Music's like air lately."

Peter studied him — measuring, not unkind. "I'd have thought all this new noise would scare people off. Beatles went from suits to..." He gestured vaguely. "...whatever that is."

David smiled. "Maybe the world's cracking open. Doesn't mean it's falling apart."

Peter snorted. "That yours, or off a poster?"

"Bit of both." David sipped. "Truth is, I don't need much. A van that runs, a guitar that mostly stays in tune, a few good people. Stack enough sunrises in a row — that's a life."

"And a job?"

"I work when I'm in one place long enough. Not allergic to alarm clocks — just prefer waking because the light's good."

Peter turned his glass. "Freedom's a fine word. Responsibility's the one that keeps the lights on."

"I reckon both can fit in the same van."

Peter held his gaze, then lifted his glass. "We'll see."

* * *

The Gardener home greeted them with warmth and the smell of roast lamb. Lisa appeared from the kitchen, flour dusting her dress. Alayne followed — sharp-eyed, warm, assessing.

"So this is David," she said, wiping her hands.

"Lovely to meet you," he replied.

"Welcome, then."

The dining table shone beneath the pendant light — polished cutlery, steam rising from serving bowls. The roast sat proud in the centre, potatoes crisp, peas glossed with butter. For David it was a glimpse of childhood, Sunday dinners that once held a family together.

"Saturday roast," Alayne said, carving. "Don't get used to it — you're a special case."

Conversation flowed easily. Peter poured wine from a flagon; Alayne asked about the Kombi and the paintwork. David spoke of tune-ups done with borrowed tools and stubborn luck. When Alayne asked about his sketches, her tone softened — genuine interest replacing scrutiny.

Stories rolled around the table — burnt sausages, childhood adventures, family lore. Lisa laughed, cheeks warm, eyes bright.

Then Alayne rested her chin on her hand. "So tell me, David — what are you chasing up there? Why the road?"

He set down his fork. The house quieted.

"I want to see the world before it closes its doors. Music, beaches, people — I want to feel it, not just read about it. And if Lisa comes, I'll make it safe for her. It's not about running from responsibility. It's about living with it — wide awake."

Alayne studied him, then smiled. "That's a good answer."

Peter grunted, but without argument.

Dessert followed — apple crumble and cream. By the time coffee was poured, the edges of tension had worn smooth.

"You'll be heading off early?" Alayne asked.

"First light."

"Make sure my daughter eats something proper," she said, mock stern. "And don't let Peter talk you into more beers."

Peter chuckled, clapping David's shoulder. "One more wouldn't hurt."

Lisa rolled her eyes, but her hand found David's under the table — warm, certain.

Later, with plates cleared and the night stretching, Peter lingered at the table.

❀

"You've done all right tonight," he said quietly. "Don't let it go to your head."

David grinned. "Wouldn't dare."

Outside, cicadas hummed. The Kombi waited under the amber streetlight, paint dulled but patient.

Alayne pressed a small paper bag into Lisa's hands. "Snacks. Apples, sandwiches, tea. Don't live off greasy chips."

Peter turned to David. For a heartbeat his face was unreadable. Then he reached out, grip firm.

"Keep her running straight," he said — and David knew he meant both the Kombi and the girl.

"I will, Peter."

Something eased in the older man's gaze. He patted the Kombi's panel, then slipped an arm around Alayne.

Lisa kissed her parents goodbye and climbed into the passenger seat.

The engine coughed, caught, settled into its familiar rattle. As David eased the van into gear, he glanced back. Peter and Alayne stood together at the end of the driveway, framed in the streetlight — small, solid, proud.

He lifted a hand. Peter raised his in return.

The Kombi rolled away, painted flowers flashing once beneath the lamps before the curve of the street took them out of sight.

3

The Kombi rattled over a rise, suspension groaning before settling back into rhythm. Behind them, the lights of Stanmore — and the weight of family — slipped into memory. Ahead stretched the Pacific Highway, long and open, shimmering in the late-summer heat.

Lisa sat with her bare feet on the dash, knees hugged loosely, David's flannel shirt draped around her shoulders. The window was cranked open; the breeze tugged at her hair as the city thinned to bushland.

For a while there was only the hum of tyres and the clatter of loose panels. Then Lisa spoke, voice low over the rush of air.

"Did you really go for a beer with him?"

David kept one hand on the wheel, the other on the gearstick. "I did."

"And?"

"He cares — more than he lets on. Maybe more than he knows how to show."

She tucked her chin to her knees. "Did he say anything?"

David smiled. "He said you were always brave. Even when you were little. Running into the garden, coming back with stories about fairies and tunnels under the lemon tree."

Her eyes softened. "I didn't think he remembered that."

"He remembers everything."

They drove in silence, trees flickering past, the sun climbing higher. Then David said quietly, "He didn't give me permission, Lis. He gave me responsibility. That's heavier."

She leaned her head back, gazing at the endless sky. "I just needed to know he didn't hate all of this."

"He doesn't. He's scared — but not angry."

Her hand found his thigh, light but certain. "Then I can breathe again."

By mid-morning they pulled into a servo. David filled the tank while Lisa wandered through the shop, returning with a Cherry Ripe and a packet of Fantales. She tossed one through the window.

"Bribery."

"Accepted," he said, unwrapping it.

Back on the highway they traded lollies, sticky fingers and small stories — the music they'd grown up on, the teachers they'd hated, the places they still wanted to see.

The city gave way to sway and colour — eucalypts bowing in the wind, paddocks flashing gold, hills rolling green. The Kombi hummed along, its painted flowers catching the light like stained glass in motion.

Lisa pressed her palm to the glass, watching the world unspool. "It feels different already. Like we're not just leaving Sydney — we're leaving everything."

"That's the idea," David said, drumming the wheel to the radio.

An EH Holden wagon rumbled past, surfboards strapped to its roof. The driver flashed a peace sign. Lisa leaned halfway out the window to wave back, laughter scattering in the slipstream.

Hand-painted signs began to appear on trees and fenceposts:

OURIMBAH FESTIVAL – 10 KM PEACE AND MUSIC THIS WAY

Lisa leaned forward, excitement sparking. "This is it. We're close."

David downshifted as the highway narrowed to a dusty track. "This isn't just a left turn, Lis — this is the whole road."

She looked at him, eyes wide. "Do you think we'll be different after this?"

He held her gaze a heartbeat longer than the road allowed. "I think we already are."

The Kombi rattled onward, the bush closing in. Faint at first, then clear, came the roll of drums on the wind. Smoke curled above the treetops; a pulse of music slipped through the eucalypts.

Lisa reached across, lacing her fingers through his.

And just like that, the weekend began.

4

Gravel crackled beneath the Kombi's tyres as David followed the hand-painted signs nailed to trees:

WELCOME HOME PEACE LIVES HERE TUNE IN. DROP OUT. LET GO

The track wound between tall eucalypts, late-summer air thick with dust, woodsmoke, and something sweet drifting through the leaves. Lisa leaned forward, palms on the dash, light catching her bare knees.

"I can hear music," she whispered.

The trees opened — and the world changed.

A valley pulsed with colour and sound. Vans sprawled in crooked rows, painted in swirls of blue, red, citrus yellow — peace signs, flowers, spirals, slogans scrawled in handmade brushstrokes: *Make Love Not War, Be Here Now, Love Is a Revolution*. Quilts hung like flags. Sarongs fluttered.

Patchouli, frying corn, woodsmoke, and the unmistakable curl of cannabis drifted above the crowd. From the far stage came a ragged guitar snarl, a rolling bass line, drums cracking after it. Cheers rippled across the paddock.

Lisa pressed to the windscreen, pointing at everything — crochet vests, shirtless boys painted in stripes, girls spinning barefoot, children racing past with flowers in their hair.

"Oh, David…"

He slowed the Kombi, gripping the wheel as if anchoring himself in the storm of colour. "Bloody hell."

She kissed his cheek mid-laugh. "You brought me here."

He found a space among the vans and cut the engine. The sudden stillness felt unreal against the roar outside. Lisa unlatched the door before the van had even settled.

Their bare feet hit the grass. Music and laughter throbbed through the earth. Hot wind tugged at Lisa's tie-front top and whipped David's shirt against his back. They stepped into the chaos — two wide-eyed newcomers swallowed by the river of bodies.

They drifted through the swirl: girls in bikini tops and long skirts; boys in beads; couples tangled in shade; toddlers painted like tiny warriors; old men cross-legged rolling smokes. A girl with stars painted across her shoulders moved like she'd been born to the rhythm.

Lisa clutched David's hand, breath catching — ready to laugh or cry or run.

Then she saw them.

Under a wide gum tree sat a Kombi painted in flowers and spirals, door open to a nest of blankets. A woman with long dark hair — Shelly — strung beads, wrap skirt loose around her legs. Beside her, two barefoot twins leaned on each other, giggling. A man rested a bongo on his knee — sun-browned skin, loose curls, bare chest above frayed shorts. Rhythm radiated from him.

Shelly looked up and smiled, warm and certain, like she'd been expecting them.

"Hey there," the man said, voice warm as smoke. "First time?"

Lisa nodded. David squeezed her hand.

"Shelly," the woman said. "And that's Gypsy."

"Autumn," one twin said.

"Winter," the other added.

"David," he said. "Lisa."

No more was needed. They were already being welcomed in.

By sunset the paddock swelled louder. Guitars howled. A harmonica bled. The crowd answered in a single wild voice. Yet beneath the gum, within this small constellation of blankets, life moved slower — firelit, human.

Gypsy tapped his bongo — not performing, just breathing rhythm. Shelly threaded beads. Lisa leaned into David's shoulder, whispering astonishments into his ear.

A cobalt-painted girl drifted past with a joint. Lisa blushed and shook her head. David followed her lead. The girl smiled and moved on.

The fire popped, sparks lifting like fireflies. The sky softened to velvet blue.

"There are so many," Lisa whispered.

"They were always there," David murmured. "We just couldn't see them."

Shelly placed a finished string of beads in Lisa's palm. "For you. First night."

Across the paddock, a voice rose into *Turn! Turn! Turn!* and was answered by bells on ankles.

They spread a blanket near the circle and slept under the hum of distant guitars and the soft echo of Gypsy's hands on skin.

Morning began without clocks. Kettles rattled. Guitars tuned lazily. Birdsong stitched through the gum leaves.

A kookaburra laughed overhead, setting a few hungover campers groaning. Smoke from breakfast fires drifted low — billy tea, toast, onions frying in cast iron.

Lisa rubbed sleep from her eyes, tank top slipping off one shoulder. Someone pressed a tin mug into her hands — herbal tea steeped sweet. Autumn and Winter bickered over beads, dissolving into giggles.

"Morning, lovebirds," Shelly said. "First night survive you?"

Lisa laughed. "I don't think I've taken it all in yet."

"You don't have to," Gypsy said, stretching. "Just breathe it."

By mid-morning the paddock had become a wild market. Makeshift stalls sold macramé belts, beads, incense, patched jackets, vinyl in dusty crates. Children chalked peace signs into dirt. Smoke hung low — sweet and hazy.

A wiry man with painted spirals held a brush. "Sun for your arm? Price is kindness."

Lisa looked at David.

He grinned. "Art's on the house?"

"Always," the man murmured.

A sun bloomed in gold across her forearm.

They queued at a yellow Kombi for vegetable curry and chai, served by a woman in denim shorts and an oversized shirt knotted at the waist.

"Left a desk in Melbourne," she said. "Burned the rulebook. Haven't missed it yet."

They ate cross-legged under a tree, Lisa's ankles sandy and bare.

Later, a bearded poet stood on a milk crate declaiming nonsense about love and shovels. A heckler yelled, "Try rhyming love with shove!" and the poet bowed.

"Everyone's performing," Lisa whispered.

"Maybe that's the point," David said.

Not everyone glowed. A gaunt man hunched against a Kombi smoked a rollie to the filter, eyes darting.

"Scene's all pretend," he muttered. "Everyone's still running."

"We're not running," David said.

"Yet," the man snorted, drifting away.

The truth stung, but didn't dim the sun on Lisa's arm.

They were swept toward the stage as a blues band ripped into *Baby, Please Don't Go*. Lisa danced — shy at first, then fearless. David stepped into the rhythm beside her.

They lost track of time.

As dusk settled, a low growl rolled from the trees. Conversations faltered.

A black Harley burst through the dust. Tall rider. Inked arms. Leather vest marked **IRON CHIEFS**.

He dismounted — calm, watchful.

Lisa leaned closer to David.

Gypsy stepped forward. "Right on time."

They clasped hands.

"Everyone, this is Ryder."

He crouched by the fire, set a billy to boil, and said nothing else.

Gypsy's guitar lifted into *Catch the Wind*, Shelly humming harmony. Autumn and Winter curled together, dozing. Ryder stared into the flames, quiet gravity wrapped in denim and ink.

"I want to come with you," Lisa whispered suddenly. "To Byron."

Gypsy smiled. "You'd be welcome, little sister."

"It's gentle there," Shelly said. "Musicians everywhere. A sun that forgives."

David looked at Lisa and saw the road unspooling behind her eyes.

"We'll go back first," he said. "Talk to your parents. Then... Surfers. Byron."

Relief lit her face.

Ryder poured tea. "You look like a man who knows the difference between a broken engine and a broken heart."

"Only fixed one," David said.

"Same tools sometimes," Ryder muttered.

Lisa whispered, "If we go back to Sydney... will it feel different?"

"It should," David said. "We're changed."

By the third morning the festival's rhythm had settled into their bones. Lisa wore a borrowed crocheted top as she danced, sun on her skin. David watched her glow.

Not every moment sparkled. A drifter tried reading her palm for a kiss; David stepped between them with a smile that wasn't one. Lisa learned something about boundaries that day.

Later they found Ryder carving driftwood — a shape half-woman, half-weather.

"For someone I knew," he said.

By twilight the louder acts faded. Poets took the stage. Gypsy's voice broke gently through the hush. Fire circles drew them inward.

Lisa looked around — Shelly threading wildflowers into her hair, the twins plaiting bracelets, Ryder silent, Gypsy warm as firelight — and she knew this wasn't chaos. It was order built from trust.

The festival looked softer at dawn. Flags drooped. Tents leaned. Smoke hung heavy and low.

Lisa and David packed slowly. The twins hugged her tight.

"Find us," Autumn murmured.

"We're always where the sound is," Winter added.

Shelly pressed a bracelet into Lisa's pocket. "For courage."

Gypsy stood with the sun behind him. "The world's only as small as the fences you let others build. Make your own gates."

Ryder lifted two fingers from his mug — a farewell, an approval.

David started the engine. Lisa watched them fade into dusty light.

"You brought me here," she whispered. "To something I didn't know I needed."

He laughed softly.

The highway unfurled ahead — wide, bright, waiting.

Behind them, Ourimbah settled into memory.

Not an end.

A beginning.

5

They pulled away from Ourimbah with the music still humming in their bones. The festival slipped into the rear-view — smoke thinning, colours folding back into bush and sky. The Kombi rattled along the highway, windows down, warm air spilling over their faces. Lisa sat sideways in the passenger seat, knees drawn up, wearing denim shorts and a bikini top beneath David's old flannel shirt. Gum trees flickered past like frames in a film.

The radio finally found its sweet spot — The Beatles, Cream, a scratchy bit of Dylan — each song stitching itself into the golden thread between them. Lisa laughed suddenly, her voice spilling out with the music.

"If Byron's really like that — the music, the markets, people just living free — what would it be like for us? You and me?"

David kept one hand on the wheel, the other tapping time on his thigh. "We'd meet all sorts. Musicians, dreamers, people with nothing but the road in their pockets. Some good, some a bit... out there."

She hugged her knees, hair wild in the wind. "I want to see it. Even the strange parts."

He glanced across. Sunlight caught in her eyes, fierce and bright. "Yeah. I do."

She kissed his shoulder. "You're too steady, David. I'm already gone in my head — bracelets jangling, toes in the sand. I want all of it."

The road unrolled, their laughter blending with the radio's crackle. Behind them the festival was already turning into memory; ahead waited a promise neither could quite name

The Kombi hummed along the bitumen, the engine weaving through bursts of static. The Doors climbed out of the speakers — Morrison's voice thrown down the highway like a dare. Lisa sat cross-legged, hair streaming out the window, restless in the best way — fingers tracing circles on the glass, knees brushing his arm, turning toward him again and again as though the road was only half as interesting as the man steering her through it.

"What do you think it'd really be like?" she asked over the music. "Not just visiting Byron — actually living there. Waking with salt in your hair, guitars outside your tent. Everyone... free."

"Depends what you call free," David said. "Some people up there have nothing — no money, no place to go back to. Just the road and whatever turns up."

Her eyes sparkled. "That sounds perfect. Doesn't it? People who aren't stuck in the same patterns every day. Musicians, poets, people who just... believe in something else. We'd hear their stories, share ours. Like being part of a tribe."

"A tribe can be messy," he said. "Arguments, jealousy. Not everyone wants to share. You ready for that?"

She leaned closer, cheek warm against his shoulder. "If it means music by a fire at night and swimming in rivers by day? Yes. A thousand times yes."

He chuckled. "You're already gone, aren't you?"

"Completely." She flicked her head, a strand catching on her lip.

David brushed it away with his thumb, touch lingering just long enough to make her heart trip. "You'd fit right in."

"And you?"

"I'd rather build something than drift," he said. "But maybe building can happen there too — just... different."

Creedence rolled in, steady as tyres on tar.

"So how long would we stay?" she asked. "A few weeks? Months?"

He didn't answer straight away. Sunlight strobed across his face until he said, "As long as it works. As long as it feels right."

She kissed his temple, light as breath. "You're steady. That's why I trust you. But me?" Her smile brightened. "I want to see everything — even the strange parts. Especially the strange parts."

The Kombi rolled south, but their words tugged north — to Byron, to all the unknowns waiting there. The van carried two dreamers only just beginning to understand how wide the world could be.

By afternoon the highway narrowed. Trucks roared past, trailers rattling, hot air buffeting the Kombi. The open-sky feeling of the festival gave way to something tighter. Roadhouses and paddocks bled slowly into suburbs. Powerlines appeared, then shopfronts, then the familiar sprawl of Sydney tugging them back toward its centre.

By the time they hit Parramatta Road, the spell of Ourimbah had thinned, replaced by traffic lights, exhaust, and the jab of horns. The Kombi felt smaller here, boxed in by sedans and delivery vans.

Lisa grew quieter as the city closed around them, laughter folding back into her ribs. She rested her head on David's shoulder, watching pubs with peeling paint, neon fish-and-chip signs, billboards for soap and toothpaste. The world of colour and music they'd just left already felt like a half-remembered dream.

David noticed but didn't press. At a red light he squeezed her hand. She gave him a small, brave smile.

As they turned into her street in Stanmore, the sun dropped low, washing the weatherboard houses in honey light. Gardens spilled over fences; a tricycle lay on a path. Somewhere a dog barked. Neighbours chatted over driveways as though nothing in the world had tilted.

Ordinary. Steady. The world Lisa had always known.

David parked outside her parents' place. The EJ Holden sat in the driveway like a sentinel. The Kombi coughed into silence, the engine ticking as it cooled. For a moment neither of them moved.

"It feels different now," she murmured. "Coming back."

"That's because you're different now," he said.

Her smile wobbled. "Do you think they'll understand? About Byron. About... us."

He touched her cheek, thumb steady and warm. "We'll find out."

They climbed out together. The evening smelled of roast, lawn clippings, and something else — possibility pressed up against fear. As they walked up the path, the dream of the road north folded itself carefully away, waiting for its time, while they stepped back into the world of family, questions, and decisions that could no longer be postponed.

6

The front door creaked open and the familiar scent of roast chicken drifted through the hall — Alayne's doing, always eager to have a proper meal waiting when Lisa came home.

"Lisa?" she called, bright but cautious, as if half-expecting silence.

Lisa barely set her bag down before hurrying into the kitchen. Alayne turned from the oven just in time to catch her daughter's arms around her neck. The hug was tighter than usual, held a heartbeat longer. When Lisa drew back, her cheeks were flushed, eyes bright in a way Alayne hadn't seen before.

"Did you have fun?" Alayne asked, already smiling at the answer written across her daughter's face.

Lisa laughed, breathless. "It was incredible, Mum. The music, the colours, the people — it was like stepping into another world."

Alayne brushed a strand of hair back, studying her. Something had shifted; Lisa seemed lit from within.

Peter appeared in the doorway, tea towel slung over his shoulder. Lisa hurried to hug him, and he chuckled, patting her back.

"You're home two minutes and glowing like you've seen the sun for the first time," he said.

"It felt like the first time," she replied. "Everything was new. The music never stopped. People danced barefoot, strangers talked like friends. It felt... free."

David stepped quietly into the hall. Peter shook his hand — steady, measuring — while Alayne offered a warm, assessing smile. She noticed how Lisa's eyes flicked toward him, that soft magnetism she hadn't learned to hide.

"Well," Alayne said, ushering them toward the table, "you can tell us everything over dinner."

They had barely begun to eat when Lisa blurted it out, the words falling like they'd been waiting all day.

"Mum, Dad — David and I want to go to Byron Bay. Not just for a weekend. For a while."

Forks hovered. Peter's brow lifted. Alayne glanced between them.

"That's quite a leap from a few days at a festival," Alayne said, laying her fork down.

"It's not just the festival," Lisa said quickly. "It's the way people live. Everyone's so open, so alive. It felt... right. Like where I'm meant to be."

Peter cleared his throat. "You've never lived away from home. Not more than a few nights."

"I know," she said softly. "But I didn't feel lost. I felt found."

A look passed between her parents — quiet, startled, worried.

David spoke then, calm and deliberate. "We're not talking about running wild. I'll find work — cafés, farms, workshops, whatever I can. We'll take care of each other."

"And money?" Alayne asked.

"We'll live simply," he said. "Like people up there do. We don't need much."

Lisa reached across and took her mother's hand. "Please, Mum. I don't want to wake up one day and wish I'd been brave enough."

Peter leaned back, studying her. "And if it goes wrong?"

"Then I come home," she said. "At least I'll know."

Silence settled, the hum of the fridge filling the kitchen. Then Alayne's shoulders eased; a small smile softened her mouth.

"You came home glowing. I don't want to snuff that out," she said. "We'll talk more — but we need to understand what this really means."

David nodded. Lisa squeezed her mother's hand. The idea of Byron was no longer a whisper; it was real, sitting right there on the table with the roast and potatoes.

After dinner the house grew quieter. The smell of gravy lingered. Lisa helped clear plates, though she barely noticed what she carried.

"You really do look different," Alayne said, watching her.

Lisa grinned. "Different good or different worrying?"

"Both," Alayne admitted. "There's a light in you. But Byron's far. What if you get lost in it?"

Lisa rested her head on her mother's shoulder. "I didn't feel lost up there. I felt like myself. And David's steady. You saw that."

Alayne's mouth softened. "That's what I'm holding on to — him keeping your feet on the ground while your head's in the clouds."

"Maybe it's time I had both," Lisa whispered.

Later that night Peter stood on the verandah, cigarette glowing in the dark. David joined him, hands in his pockets.

"She's never been this alive," Peter said. "But she's never been this far from us either."

"I know," David said. "I won't let her get hurt. Not by anyone. Not by herself."

Peter eyed him. "Responsibility's heavy. Can you carry it?"

David met his gaze. "I don't know everything, but I know how to work and stand by her. That's a start."

A thin smile tugged at Peter's mouth. "You remind me of me. Full of plans and stubborn certainty." He offered the cigarette, then chuckled. "No — keep your lungs for the music."

David grinned. "That's the plan."

"Keep her safe," Peter said. "And bring her home if it falls apart."

"I promise."

Over the next few days the house hummed with small preparations. David repaired a loose fence paling while Peter held the nails. Their rhythm was easy, companionable.

"You've got a knack for this," Peter said.

"Work's work," David replied. "I can pick up odd jobs on the road. Mechanics, labouring — whatever keeps us moving."

Inside, Lisa helped with bills, her neat script marking numbers. "We can camp most nights," she said. "Buy from markets. Maybe I can make macramé to sell."

Alayne's worry softened into pride. "And when you're tired or lonely?"

"Then we come home. We're not running — we're just going to see."

By the weekend they'd saved fuel money, mapped the route, and set out a loose plan. Peter leaned over the atlas with them.

"So... Newcastle, Port Macquarie, Coffs, then Byron?" he asked.

"Pretty much," David said. "I'll find work along the way. We'll keep costs down."

Lisa doodled a flower in the margin. "We don't need much. Just each other. And we'll write every fortnight."

Peter didn't smile, but something in his shoulders eased.

At night Lisa and David sat on the back step, the hum of Parramatta Road drifting over the fence.

"I think they're warming to you," Lisa murmured.

David smirked. "Your dad's testing me. I'd do the same."

She nudged him. "You're doing fine

The Gardener house shifted with David's presence. He wasn't a guest anymore — he rolled up his sleeves and asked, "What needs doing?"

Peter found him one morning oiling the gate hinges. Another afternoon he had his head under the bonnet of the EJ Holden. By week's end Peter caught himself smiling — not at the car, but at the young man willing to learn.

Lisa, meanwhile, was a whirl of energy. She hummed while she folded washing, chattered about the music and the firelight and the people she wanted her parents to meet one day. Alayne listened, torn between fear and delight.

Evenings found them around the dining table with the road atlas spread wide. Peter tapped the route with a pen; Lisa added doodles; David made practical notes. Responsibility and dreaming, side by side.

Alayne rested her chin in her hand. "What about work here? You've prospects at home."

David placed a plate in the drying rack. "This is part of my path too," he said. "I want to see things before life ties me down. And Lisa deserves that with me."

His honesty disarmed her. "You're both so young," she said. "But maybe that's when you're meant to be brave."

By week's end the mood had shifted. David was no longer the boyfriend; he was the young man fixing fences, carrying groceries, earning quiet trust. Lisa was no longer the girl underfoot; she was a young woman glowing with something new.

At dinner, Peter finally said, "If you're set on this, at least you're not walking in blind. You've thought it through. That counts."

Lisa clapped her hands. "So you'll let us?"

Alayne smiled softly. "We'll let you. But this is still your home."

Lisa hugged her tight, relief and excitement flooding her.

David caught Peter's eye and gave a steady nod — a promise understood.

The house became a flurry. Lisa darted between her room and the hall with armfuls of clothes — shorts, skirts, tops, sandals.

"Do you think I'll need the red skirt? Or is that too much for camping?" she called.

"Take it," Alayne said, folding what Lisa dropped. "But you'll want a jumper too. Nights can turn cold."

Outside, David lay beneath the Kombi — changing oil, tightening belts, checking bolts, dirt smudged on him the same way responsibility was settling into him. He worked with the quiet confidence of someone who understood what depended on the machine running true.

Peter stood in the doorway, arms folded, watching the young man under the van.

"You've done this before?" he asked.

"Plenty," David said. "Better to catch something here than halfway to Port Macquarie."

Peter exhaled, almost smiling. It wasn't just about engine work. It was foresight. It was care.

Inside, Lisa's voice floated through the house — excited, nervous, hopeful. Out front, David tightened the final bolt. Two halves of the same journey: her radiant anticipation, his steady preparation.

Maybe, Peter thought, just maybe... this could work.

7

Morning light spilled across the front yard as the Kombi idled at the kerb — packed, rattling, faded, and suddenly noble, as though it knew it would be carrying more than luggage. Lisa hovered by the door with her suitcase, denim shorts and a cotton top beneath her open flannel shirt, excitement too big for her body to hold still. Alayne fussed over last things — a jumper tucked in, a toothbrush checked twice — stretching the moment before letting her daughter go.

Peter came last, keys jangling in his hand. He looked at Lisa, then at David, then at the Kombi. David took the suitcase and stowed it carefully — no jokes, no rush — steady in the way that anchored Lisa's flurry. The side door thudded shut, the sound of home giving way to road.

Lisa hugged her mother tight. Alayne whispered something into her hair — a braid of pride and worry — and let go a moment later than she meant to. Peter clasped Lisa's shoulders, memorising her face.

"Go on, then. But write. Don't make us wait to know you're safe."

He turned to David and offered his hand. David met his eyes, gripped firm. Peter's mouth twitched — the smallest admission of approval.

Lisa scrambled into the passenger seat, hair tugged by the morning breeze. David slid behind the wheel. The Kombi rumbled, coughed, caught. As they pulled away, the house shrank in the mirror; Peter and Alayne stood arm in arm, not waving, simply watching — proud, fearful, hopeful — until the curve swallowed them from view.

Lisa found David's hand across the gearstick and squeezed. "We're really doing this," she whispered.

And they were.

❊

Parramatta Road gave way to open sky. Traffic thinned. The Kombi found its rhythm — a rattle here, a hum there, the engine singing its old, stubborn song. Through the radio fuzz, George Harrison slipped into the cabin: *Here Comes the Sun.*

Lisa lit up. She leaned back, eyes closed, knees pulled up, bare feet pressed to the dash. Bracelets chimed softly as she tapped her toes and let the sunshine into her bones. Wind turned her hair into wild ribbons. She sang — unpolished, free — her voice flying out the window with the morning.

David shook his head, smiling at her joy.

California Dreamin' drifted in next. She pointed out cows like they were rare wonders, then collapsed into laughter. When *Spirit in the Sky* kicked in, she howled the chorus, grabbed his arm, and made him nearly veer. Her kiss on his cheek was quick, warm, alive.

Past Brooklyn the Hawkesbury flashed like broken glass under morning light. They rolled into Mount White, the roadhouse flat-roofed and cream-green, the forecourt dusty and sun-washed.

Inside, bacon and diesel thickened the air. Truckies hunched over Formica tables. A jukebox wheezed through Creedence under the rumble of heavy boots.

Barefoot, Lisa skipped across the gravel without flinching. "Come on, I'm starving!" she said, tugging David's sleeve.

They ordered the kind of food that came on heavy plates: bacon and eggs for him, buttered toast and sweet tea for her.

"Feels like everyone's on their way somewhere," Lisa said, nose to the window. "Do you reckon they're off to do something amazing? Or just back to work?"

"Bit of both," David said. "Not everyone's chasing what we are."

She turned to him. "And what are we chasing?"

David looked past the forecourt to the highway stretching away. "Freedom. A different way of living. Something bigger than this."

She nudged his leg. "Then let's not stop too long."

Outside, she flung her arms around his neck and planted a quick kiss that made him laugh, half-shy. Truckies shook their heads — amused at the barefoot girl and her whole-hearted joy. Lisa didn't notice. Or didn't care.

The Kombi rattled back onto the road. Newcastle waited ahead, but the feeling of arrival had already begun.

By the time the highway folded into Newcastle, the Kombi wore a veil of dust and a satisfied hum. Lisa pressed her forehead to the window, pointing out everything — old farmhouses, slashes of Pacific between the hills, Golden Fleece billboards peeling toward the sun.

Hunter Street buzzed with life: art deco façades beside tired brick shops, sailors mixing with locals, pubs spilling music onto the pavement. Uni kids with guitars. A woman in a miniskirt clutching textbooks. Barefoot surfers leaning on railings with boards at their feet.

"It's like a city — but not Sydney," Lisa said. "Smaller, louder. Like everyone's in on something."

"A working town," David said. "Feels honest."

At a red light she kissed his temple. "Thank you for bringing me."

They rattled past a barbershop, a bakery, a bookshop with paperback covers fading in the sun. Two boys strummed guitars on the footpath; Lisa's laugh turned heads and left strangers smiling without knowing why.

They found Nobbys easily. The lighthouse swept white arcs across the late afternoon. Surf broke in silver lines. The ocean breathed in and out like a living thing.

"David..." Lisa whispered, spinning barefoot in the salt wind. Her cotton top fluttered against her skin. He leaned on the Kombi and watched joy move through her — unfiltered, unafraid.

Music floated from a pub tucked behind the dunes. Lisa caught it first — head tilting like a bird.

"Let's go," she said, taking his hand.

Inside: cigarette haze, beer-sweet air, sticky floorboards. A local band ripped through *Friday on My Mind* and the whole room sang it back. Lisa was swept in immediately — clapping, laughing, pulling David into the crush. He let the beat loosen him; her grin loosened the rest.

A slower number softened the crowd. Lisa leaned into his chest and they swayed as though the pub had fallen away. He kissed her hair without thinking.

Later, they walked back beneath the slow blink of the lighthouse. They curled in the Kombi overlooking the dark water, the white beam sweeping through the cabin like a soft pulse. Lisa whispered fragments of song into his shoulder until sleep found her. David watched silver light wash over her face, the steady surf keeping time.

For the first time in his life, he thought — *this is freedom.*

Dawn spread pale gold across Nobbys. David slipped out with his board; Lisa woke to the creak of the Kombi door and propped herself on her elbows. Wrapped in the blanket, she watched him wade in.

He paddled out, turned, caught the wave and rose with it. For a moment he belonged wholly to the ocean. Spray caught the light. Lisa cheered despite the roar.

Dripping and salt-streaked, he came in.

"You didn't tell me you could do that," she teased, brushing hair from his eyes.

"I can do a few things," he said — and bolted when she splashed him. They ran laughing through the shallows; her top plastered to her ribs, his shorts dripping. When he caught her, the sea folded around them like a welcome.

Later they wandered the rocks, reading the tide-pool hieroglyphs. She held shells to the sun; he watched the way wonder lived so easily inside her.

At midday they shared fish and chips on the seawall, vinegar sharp as memory.

"This," Lisa declared, licking salt from her thumb, "is how I want to eat. Outside. Salty. Messy. Happy."

"That's the plan," David said.

That evening they found a quieter pub with a folk trio in the corner. Candle stubs flickered in bottles. Chairs creaked. Voices braided Dylan and Donovan into something warm. They walked back beneath sharp harbour stars, her hand warm in his.

Morning arrived with coffee and sea air. In a dusty record bar, posters curling on the walls, Lisa found a worn copy of Simon & Garfunkel.

"This one feels like us," she said.

David bought it, thin wallet and all.

By late morning the road tugged again. The Kombi coughed, then settled. Lisa hugged the paper bag to her chest, watching Newcastle hand them back to the highway.

"Do you think we'll come back?" she asked.

"Maybe. But even if we don't, we'll carry it."

Nobbys shrank into sea haze behind them. She leaned over and kissed his cheek — a quiet farewell — and turned to watch the Pacific glimmer.

The highway found its rhythm again — forest tightening, loosening, revealing water in silver flashes. The radio did small wonders: *The Letter*, *Spirit in the Sky* (again), *Ob-La-Di, Ob-La-Da*. Lisa's bare feet drummed the glovebox; she threw her head back in joy.

"Feels like flying," she said.

"Flying at fifty-five," David teased.

She smacked his arm. The Kombi wobbled like a laugh.

Raymond Terrace. Hot pies under a Coke-red awning. Bulahdelah. Sawdust and Saturday, farmers rolling sleeves. Nabiac. Milkshakes sweating in tall glasses — strawberry for her, chocolate for him. Taree. A river breeze and a new vinyl in a brown paper bag.

Port Macquarie glowed soft at dusk. They ate fish and chips by the river, slept near Town Beach with the Kombi a small lantern against the dunes. Morning brought wax on David's board, Lisa heckling, the sea applauding with lace around their ankles.

Coffs Harbour. A market stitched with fabrics bright as flags. A busker nudging *Catch the Wind* somewhere warm. Lisa's anklet chimed each time her foot changed its mind. A hostile stallholder dimmed her for a moment; David leaned his forehead to hers.

"Don't let him take the day," he murmured.

She didn't.

The Big Banana. Milkshakes. Lollies. A jukebox crooning *Bus Stop*. A jetty walk under moths and sodium light, her head settling on his shoulder like it belonged there.

Yamba. A vanilla slice reckless with custard. A pineapple doughnut held up like treasure. The lighthouse turning the world into a wide white compass.

"We're really doing it," she whispered into the wind. "Just us."

"Wouldn't do it any other way," he said.

Ballina smelt of bacon and morning. *Mrs Robinson* hummed from the café. David closed his eyes at the first mouthful of breakfast.

"You'll have to roll me into Byron," Lisa warned.

"You'll dance it off," he said, certain.

Beyond Ballina the coast unbuttoned itself. Hills leaned toward the sea. Eucalypts whispered. The ocean flashed in and out, shy and brilliant. They didn't talk much — the music took over: *The Sound of Silence* unfurled and left room for quiet awe.

They crested a rise — and there it was.

The pale spine of the headland. The white blink of the Cape Byron lighthouse — slow, steady, ancient. The eastern edge of everything.

Lisa put both hands to the windscreen. Her breath caught — the sound people make when longing becomes landscape.

"David..." she breathed.

"I see it." He kept his eyes on the road, but he felt it too.

She cupped his face, kissing his temple, cheek, the corner of his mouth — a map of gratitude and promise.

"We made it," she whispered. The salt might have been the sea. It might have been her.

The lighthouse blinked again — flash, breath, flash — a metronome older than both of them.

The Kombi hummed, rolling down toward a town that hadn't been waiting for them exactly, just for the version of them shaped by every mile behind.

Lisa pressed her palm to the glass, blessing their arrival.

"Hello, Byron," she said softly. "We're here."

8

The Pacific Highway shimmered in late-afternoon heat, the Kombi rattling north with windows wide. Every few bends the trees fell away and the ocean flashed — dazzling blue that made Lisa gasp.

A sun-faded sign, half eaten by vines, announced:

BYRON BAY – 10 KILOMETRES

"David, look!" she cried.

He grinned, steady on the wheel. "Told you we'd make it."

She couldn't sit still. She flung her arms around his shoulders and kissed his cheek, his temple, anywhere her lips could land. The Kombi lurched, tyres skimming gravel.

"Careful!" David laughed, wrestling it straight.

"I don't care! You got me to Byron!"

Salt thickened on the air; cicadas gave way to gulls. They rolled off the highway and the town opened like a secret.

Fibro shops in peeling pastels lined the street: a milk bar with kids licking ice creams on the steps, a surf shop with boards stacked in a line, a record store spilling music into the air. Barefoot locals carried baskets of fruit; surfies slung towels; girls in shorts and crocheted tops drifted past, laughing at nothing at all.

"It's everything," Lisa whispered to the glass.

Bitumen softened to sandy track as the town's hum fell behind, replaced by the hush of leaning trees and eucalyptus on the breeze. Music floated from somewhere unseen — voices, a guitar, the steady thump of a drum.

A ute rattled past, the men inside leaning to stare, words lost in the engine's growl. Lisa shifted closer to David, a tightness in her shoulders.

Across the road, outside a squat white station, a uniform leaned against a patrol car. Senior Constable Rand. Arms folded. Watching. He didn't move. He didn't need to.

Lisa shivered despite the heat.

"Let them stare," David murmured, squeezing her hand. "We're here. That's all that matters."

Beyond Rand's shadow, Byron waited.

They parked near the dunes; the Kombi settled with a tired sigh. Sand crunched underfoot as Lisa stepped out, the wind rushing over her — salty, clean, new.

"It feels like this is where everything changes," she said.

They climbed the dune, and at the crest, she stopped.

Tents — patchworks of canvas, sheets, weathered tarps — scattered along the beach. Driftwood frames, palm-frond roofs, spirals painted in ochre and bright dyes. Bonfires flickered like fallen stars. People sat cross-legged or sprawled together, guitars passing from hand to hand, drums pulsing low and steady. Painted bodies danced barefoot in the sand. Children and dogs bounded through the dusk. Smoke, salt and incense braided the air.

"This is what I thought freedom might look like," David said.

"Do you think we'll fit in?" she asked quietly.

"I think we already do."

They stepped down into it, fingers twined.

"Well now… look what the tide brought in."

A woman swept from the firelight, arms wide, patchwork skirt flaring.

"Shelly!" Lisa cried.

Shelly wrapped her tight. "You made it, sweet soul." She pulled David into a hug too. "You're home now. Whatever you need, you'll find it here." She turned and shouted, "Gypsy! Two new hearts at the fire!"

Gypsy rose from the circle, scarf loose at his neck, bongos slung over his shoulder. His grin was wide and knowing.

"Look at you — glowing like you've walked through something," he said. "Come. You're hungry."

They followed him in. A pot of lentils bubbled beside the fire; mismatched bowls were stacked in the sand. Music drifted; laughter rose; warmth wrapped around them like a second skin.

Lisa warmed her hands on a painted bowl — and saw her.

A flash of gold on the edge of the firelight. Glitter on her cheeks. A flower tucked behind her ear. Laughing, telling a story with her whole body.

Willow.

She turned, caught Lisa's gaze, winked, then spun back to her tale.

Heat climbed up Lisa's neck; her heart tripped and stumbled.

The night deepened. Stories turned into songs. Songs softened into humming. The lighthouse swept its slow arc across sky and sea, steady as breath.

"Stay close tonight," Shelly said later, touching Lisa's arm. "A nook by the Kombi — quiet and shady come morning. Family looks after family."

"Sleep well, road-hearts," Gypsy added.

They spread their blankets behind a crooked tea-tree. Lisa curled into David, their fingers laced. The Southern Cross burned sharp above them.

"This doesn't feel like running away," she whispered. "It feels like being found."

"That's because it is," he murmured.

Waves rolled. The fire cracked. And for the first time since leaving Sydney, she felt entirely, beautifully home.

9

The fire circle was already alive when they returned from their walk. Lanterns swayed from branches, their light drifting like fireflies through the smoke. Someone played guitar, fingers loose, while the twins danced barefoot in the sand.

Lisa clutched David's hand as they stepped closer. She felt it before she saw it — that shift in the air, like a note held a little longer than it needed to be.

The yellow Mini Moke was the first thing David noticed, tucked half into the shadows at the edge of the clearing. Its bonnet was covered in hand-painted flowers and fading stickers — peace signs, moons, *love is enough* scratched into the paint.

She was sitting just in front of it.

Cross-legged on a woven mat, a short length of cord in her hands, Shay looked as if she'd been there forever. Long sandy-brown hair spilled from beneath a weathered Akubra. A loose olive shirt slid off one shoulder, showing the strong line of her collarbone. Her tanned legs folded easily beneath her as she twisted the thread around her wrist, head tilted in concentration.

Lisa stopped walking.

Firelight reached Shay in fragments — glancing off her hair, catching her eyes when she finally looked up. The camp's noise thinned.

"Welcome," Shay said, voice low and honey-thick. She didn't smile until Lisa's breath caught; then her mouth curved, slow and certain. "You look like you've been searching for something."

David chuckled, charmed without meaning to, but Lisa only nodded, heart thudding. She wasn't sure what she'd been searching for, but in that instant she thought maybe Shay knew.

Shay patted the earth beside her. "Then you've come to the right place."

Lisa slipped off her sandals and lowered herself onto the mat, cross-legged like Shay, movements quick and uncertain. David followed, but it was clear the moment belonged to Lisa.

"First days here?" Shay asked.

Lisa shook her head. "We only just arrived a little while ago."

"You still carry the road in your shoulders," Shay said gently. "Tense — waiting to see if it's safe to let go."

Lisa blinked. "I suppose I am."

"Don't suppose." Shay's tone softened further. "The body knows before the mind. And yours is still listening for footsteps behind it."

Lisa swallowed.

"What if I told you," Shay went on, "that here, the only thing following you is the tide? Comes in, goes out — always returns, never the same."

Lisa exhaled, smiling. "That sounds... nice."

"It is," Shay said. "If you let it be. Most people carry their cages with them, even out here under the stars."

Her words landed heavier than the firelight suggested. Lisa could only nod, her chest full.

David rubbed the back of his neck. "You've got a way of making things sound simple."

"Life usually is," Shay said. "It's people who make it complicated."

For the first time since Sydney, Lisa felt she wasn't just passing through something — she was stepping into it.

The fire hissed as someone tossed on another branch, sparks chasing skyward. The guitar softened to a lullaby. Within the small circle of the mat, the world moved to Shay's rhythm.

"Do you know the story of the fisherman and the merchant?" she asked.

Lisa shook her head.

Shay told it simply — a fisherman resting beneath a palm tree, a merchant urging him to work harder, build a fleet, retire rich. The fisherman smiling and saying, *And what do you think I'm doing now?*

Lisa breathed out slowly. The tale felt like a hand pressed to her heart.

David chuckled. "Simple truth, isn't it?"

"Most truths are." Shay looked at him, brim dipping to shadow her eyes. "You've got salt in your veins, don't you? The sea tells on you."

He blinked. "How'd you know that?"

Shay rose, fluid as water. The firelight turned her hair to gold. She nodded toward the surf.

"There are boys down there who know the waves like brothers. You might like them, David — your tribe, even if you don't know it yet."

David stood, curiosity tugging. Lisa couldn't look away from Shay's easy grace.

Shay's gaze found her again. "And you, love — don't mistake still-ness for weakness. Sometimes the strongest thing you can do is let yourself be carried."

The words settled deep, like seeds.

"Come on," Shay said, tipping her hat back. "Byron doesn't wait — and neither does the tide."

10

Moonlight silvered the path to the beach. Behind them, the camp's laughter faded. Ahead, the sea breathed steady.

On the sand sat a half-circle of surfers, boards planted upright like totems. They were lean and salt-carved, passing a joint hand to hand, voices rolling with tales of swells and wipe-outs.

Shay stepped forward without hesitation. "Evening, brothers."

Smiles answered her. She gestured to David. "Sydney boy — ocean in his eyes."

He blinked. "I never said—"

"Didn't need to. The sea tells on you."

Laughter rippled through the circle. "Sit, mate. Tell us where you ride."

David settled in, words awkward at first then easy — Bondi mornings, crowded breaks, stolen waves. The surfers groaned in sympathy and swapped stories.

Lisa watched from the edge. Not just David, though he looked more alive than ever — shoulders loose, eyes bright — but Shay, crouched near the glow, one hand tracing lines in the sand. Shay didn't interrupt or boast; she simply listened, presence grounding the group, reminding them the ocean allowed no masters.

After a while Shay turned to Lisa. "You see it, don't you?"

"See what?"

"How he shines with his tribe. How the sea gives him back to himself."

Lisa's eyes softened. "I do."

"That's love," Shay said quietly. "Letting someone be more than just yours. Letting them be theirs."

The words unsettled and soothed all at once.

Shay rose, brushing sand from her palms. "Tomorrow you'll taste Byron proper — markets, music, fire. But tonight, let the ocean sing you to sleep."

The surfers murmured goodnights. Shay led the way up the dunes, stride unhurried, the sea whispering behind them. Lisa walked half a step behind, fingers brushing David's, eyes fixed on Shay — on the sway of her hair, the quiet power in her shoulders, the mystery in her words.

And somewhere inside her, something new began to stir.

11

The fire had burned low, leaving only a soft scatter of ash and a faint smell of smoke drifting through camp. Morning light crept across the dunes in pale gold, gentle as a hand brushing hair from a sleeping face.

Lisa slipped out of the Kombi, the cool sand waking her feet. The echoes of the night before clung to her — laughter, music, the warmth of David leaning into her, and the sudden, bewildering sweetness of Willow's kiss.

It played behind her eyes like a memory she hadn't decided how to hold.

She wandered toward the water, the tide rolling in slow breaths. Each wave tugged at her thoughts, washing them forward, pulling them back. She felt... opened. Not broken. Not guilty. Just newly aware of something inside her that hadn't had a name until now.

The sea breeze lifted her hair. She closed her eyes.

"Morning."

Shay's voice came soft from behind her. When Lisa turned, Shay was standing at the edge of the sand, hands tucked into the pockets of her loose cotton pants, Akubra tipped back just enough to see her eyes.

"Didn't sleep?" Shay asked.

"Not much," Lisa admitted. "Just... thinking."

Shay nodded like she already knew the shape of those thoughts. "Big nights have long shadows."

Lisa hugged her arms around herself. "I'm not sure what last night meant."

"It meant you felt something," Shay said simply. "Everything after that is just weather."

Lisa breathed out a shaky laugh. "You make things sound easy."

"They are," Shay said, smiling. "When you stop trying to fight the tide."

They walked back together in companionable silence — the kind that didn't press or pry. By the time they reached the camp, kettle hiss rising, birds bickering overhead, the world felt steadier beneath Lisa's feet.

Shelly waved her over. "Come here, love. You look like you've been arguing with the moon."

Lisa sat beside her as Shelly handed her a bowl of papaya and muesli.

"Eat," she said. "Life makes more sense when your belly's not empty."

Lisa smiled and obeyed, the familiar warmth of the camp gathering around her — people moving slowly, voices rising, the smell of salt and tea and the lingering kindness of music still humming in the air.

She wasn't ready to untangle everything yet.

But she wasn't afraid of it anymore either.

Whatever came next, she would meet it as she was — open, unsure, unfolding.

And somehow, that felt enough.

12

The fire had dwindled to a low glow, but its warmth still seemed to follow Lisa as she stepped barefoot out of the Kombi. Mist drifted through the trees like soft cloth. The camp was quiet, except for the twins' distant laughter and someone humming something tuneless and joyful, as if the night had spilled into their dreams.

David slept on his stomach, hair mussed, one arm stretched toward the space she'd left. She watched him a moment — how safe he looked, how simple it had always been with him — and felt that familiar ache again. Simple didn't mean easy anymore.

She walked toward the surf, the sand cool under her feet. Every step brought back pieces of last night: Willow's laughter in the firelight... Shay's calm eyes... the kiss that had barely been a kiss and yet lived in her chest like a small, bright flame.

What's wrong with me?

The thought came soft, not unkind — more curiosity than shame.

She wasn't running from David. She wasn't running toward Willow. She was just... opening. That scared her in ways she didn't have words for.

At the water's edge, the tide gathered around her toes, tugging, teasing. The wind smelt of eucalyptus and possibility. She imagined telling David everything — the kiss, the feeling, the confusion — but the words felt heavy, unformed.

Not yet, she told herself. *Not until I understand it myself.*

Back at camp, Shelly waved her over. "You look like you've been talking to ghosts. Sit — papaya before you float away."

Lisa sank beside her and accepted the bowl. "Just thinking."

"Mmm." Shelly stirred her tea knowingly. "Thinking's how Byron gets inside you. Starts rearranging the furniture."

A smile tugged at Lisa's mouth. "I'll survive the décor."

"I've no doubt," Shelly said. "But if you're restless, the small market in town's setting up. Go take a wander. Sell some bracelets if you're feeling brave."

She slipped a handful of macramé cords into Lisa's palm — bright and soft like promises.

Across the clearing, Shay leaned against the Kombi, arms folded. She didn't speak, just nodded — a quiet, patient *I see you. Take your time.*

Lisa set off along the sandy track, her satchel bumping lightly at her hip.

13

The market spilled across the park in a joyful tangle — bright stalls, rows of fruit, steam from coffee carts twisting into the morning light. Music drifted from three different buskers at once. Children wove between legs, turning everything into a game.

For a while, Lisa wandered and let the noise carry her. She touched dyed skirts, smelt soaps that reminded her of the Sanctuary, bought peaches so warm from the sun she ate one on the spot. She felt... almost steady.

Until the world changed shape.

A stallholder — narrow eyes, a mouth pinched inward — stared at her bare feet and beads.

"You people again," the woman muttered. "Selling nonsense and calling it art."

Lisa blinked, taken aback. "I'm just browsing."

"Then do it clean," the woman snapped. "Some of us work for a living."

The words landed like grit. Colour drained a little from the morning.

Before Lisa could answer, a voice sliced through the air.

"Everything alright here?"

The uniform was the first thing she saw — khaki shirt, badge polished like a mirror.

Senior Constable Rand.

He looked at Lisa as if she were litter he intended to pick up later.

"Markets are for locals," he said mildly, which somehow made it worse.

"I... am," Lisa managed.

His gaze dragged down her clothes, her wrist, her bare feet.

"Funny. You don't look like one."

The stallholder smirked.

Rand leaned closer, tone still conversational. "Let's keep the peace, miss. Byron notices things."

He waited just long enough for fear to settle, then walked on.

The noise returned slowly — coins, chatter, a guitar tuning. Lisa's hands trembled.

A young potter at the next stall offered her a small, apologetic smile.

"Don't let him stick to you," he said gently. "He only knows one song, and it's flat."

Lisa tried to smile back. "Thank you."

But the warmth of the morning had shifted. The market felt different now — edges sharper, shadows longer.

She bought nothing more. The satchel at her hip felt heavier as she turned back toward the track that would lead her home.

14

By the time she returned to camp, heat shimmered off the sand, the cicadas already screaming noon. Shelly saw the stiffness in her shoulders before Lisa could hide it.

"Markets lose their charm?" Shelly asked.

Lisa swallowed. "A policeman stopped me."

Shelly's face tightened. "Rand."

Lisa nodded.

"Tall, tidy, smells like shoe polish and judgement?" Shelly clarified.

Lisa huffed something like a laugh. "That's him."

Shay wandered over, offering a cup of tea. Her voice was calm, grounding. "You alright?"

"I think so," Lisa said. "Just... shaken."

"That's his trick," Shay murmured. "Fear makes people small. Don't give him any of yours."

Shelly nudged her knee. "You're one of us now. He can glare all he likes. We've weathered worse."

The words helped. Not everything, but enough.

Later, Lisa sat beneath the Kombi threading beads, her hands moving on instinct. David arrived, smelling of salt and sun, and crouched beside her.

"Shelly told me. Did he touch you?"

"No," she said. "Just words."

"Words bruise too," David muttered.

Lisa's jaw tightened. "I'm tired of men deciding how big I'm allowed to be."

That made him smile — proud and soft. He caught a bead before it fell and pressed it back into her palm.

Willow arrived with water, dust on her shins and fire in her eyes. "He won't win," she said. "You stood your ground. That's what matters."

They sat in a quiet triangle of shade — something protective humming between them.

When Gypsy called for firewood, the three rose together without speaking.

They gathered driftwood until their arms were full. When dusk came, the fire sparked back into life — warm, bright, alive. The twins drummed, Shelly hummed, Chook tortured his harmonica. Shay watched from her usual place — silent, steady.

Lisa sat between David and Willow. Not planned — just instinct.

"Better?" David murmured.

"Better," she said — and realised it was true.

The fire glowed. The night breathed.

Belonging wrapped itself around her like a blanket.

And though the world beyond the dunes still held Rand, and fear, and whatever came next, here in the circle of light she wasn't small at all.

15

Dawn slipped through the gums like a secret being told slowly. Birds began their morning argument overhead, and the sea rolled its applause against the sand. David stepped from the Kombi, blinking into the soft wash of light — then he saw the hammock.

It swayed gently between two trees.

Lisa and Willow tangled in sleep, hair messy, limbs draped in the easy way of people who trusted each other.

Peaceful. Uncomplicated. Beautiful.

David smiled, not jealous, just quietly struck by it.

Shelly, already stirring embers, said, "Two possums after a feast."

"Think they'll wake before noon?" he asked.

"Not unless the world ends."

The hammock rustled. Lisa blinked awake first, smiling before her eyes were fully open. Willow mumbled something incoherent, stole the first sip of Lisa's coffee and called it "tax."

It was all so easy — the laughter, the warmth, the way fear seemed to have loosened its grip during the night.

Camp moved slowly around them. Gypsy strummed a half-song he'd forgotten the end of. The twins argued about spoons. Shay drifted past with her hat low and her calm like something she'd borrowed from the ocean.

They drove into town together, dust rising behind the wheels. Willow rode shotgun; Lisa leaned out the window so her bracelets chimed like declarations of freedom. They bought bread, fruit, and gossip. David secured a trial shift at the record shop — a hint of roots waiting to take hold.

Lisa wandered into the post office. The air smelled of ink and dust, postcards lined up like tiny doorways. She chose one of the lighthouse and wrote her parents a gentle note about markets, the beach, David's job. She thought of adding more — firelight, Willow's spark, Shay's quiet gravity — but some truths were better carried than mailed.

Willow was waiting outside, tossing her hat and catching it.

"Send them proof you haven't joined a cult yet?" Willow asked.

"Mostly," Lisa laughed.

"Good. Let's go misbehave."

They wandered with ice creams melting faster than they could eat them. Willow picked the rainbow one because of course she did. Lisa stuck to chocolate. Their laughter filled the grocery aisle too brightly for a town still deciding what to make of people like them.

Later, on the sand, the breeze warm and the clouds drifting slow, Lisa found Shay sitting with her arms behind her, face lifted to the sky.

"We kissed," Lisa said.

Shay didn't look startled. "Willow?"

Lisa nodded.

"How did it feel?"

"Like... someone opened a window I didn't know was shut."

Shay tilted her head toward the drifting clouds. "Clouds look heavy from below. But from above, they're always in sunlight. You don't need to decide what this kiss means while you're still standing under it. Let yourself rise a little first."

Something inside Lisa loosened.

"I want to feel everything," she said quietly. "To live."

"You are," Shay said, smiling. "More every day."

Twilight found Willow by the fire pit, nudging embers with a stick. Lisa sat beside her quietly.

"I've been thinking about last night," Lisa said softly. "I don't want to pretend it didn't happen. It mattered. It changed me."

Willow looked at her hands, then at Lisa. "Then it was worth it."

Lisa reached for her fingers in the sand. Willow's found hers halfway.

They kissed again — slower, certain, true.

Afterwards they sat shoulder to shoulder, sharing breath and silence, the fire murmuring in front of them and the lighthouse blinking its steady approval behind.

The next market day in Byron was bright, noisy, and easy for a while. Shelly sold, Willow charmed, Lisa found her rhythm. Bracelets caught sunlight. People laughed. It felt like the town might be softening.

Then the afternoon cracked.

They were fetching bags from the Kombi when a police Land Cruiser tore into the car park, gravel spitting. Rand stepped out as though the ground belonged to him.

"Oi. You. Show me your ID."

"I didn't do anything," Lisa said.

"Did I say you did? Or are you hiding something?"

He grabbed her arm. His fingers pressed too hard.

Willow stepped between them before thought existed. "Back off."

He smirked. "Sweetheart, don't make this cute."

Ryder rose from his motorbike, slow and enormous. "She's with us. Let her go."

Rand puffed up like a rooster that had forgotten its own size.

"That's it. You're under arrest."

He cuffed Ryder roughly, satisfaction all over his face.

Ryder didn't resist. "Easy," he said, eyes on Lisa. "You okay, kid?"

She nodded, trembling.

Willow wrapped an arm around her shoulders. "Don't let him in your head. You're safe."

The Land Cruiser roared away, dust swallowing its tail-lights.

The world felt different now.

Less innocent.

More real.

16

The fire was burning again by the time Ryder returned.

The Land Cruiser had long gone, leaving only tyre tracks across the sand and a sour taste in the air. Word had spread fast through the camp — not shouted, just passed quietly from one tight jaw to another. The night felt stretched thin, like the silence before a second storm.

Ryder's wrists were red where the cuffs had bitten, but he carried himself like nothing had happened. He dropped onto a log beside Gypsy and Shelly, smoke curling between them.

"Did he charge you?" Shelly asked, handing him a chipped mug of tea.

Ryder snorted. "Nah. Too many people saw him lose his temper. Sergeant pulled him back before he could make it stick." He flexed his hands. "Still, the bastard enjoyed himself."

Gypsy leaned forward, elbows on his knees, staring into the flames. "He's not going to stop. They never do, once they've decided we're the problem."

Shelly stirred the pot absently. "He'll come again. Next time it won't be words."

Ryder nodded, jaw set. "Maybe it's time we think about moving on. Further north, or inland. Find somewhere quieter before he finds another excuse."

Gypsy didn't answer straight away. The fire popped, sending a line of sparks upward.

"We could," he said finally. "But running's a kind of surrender. Rand's not the world — he's just what's wrong with it. If we keep moving every time the wind changes, we'll never grow roots."

Shelly sighed, half worry, half pride. "You and your roots," she murmured. "Sometimes I think you're part tree."

Gypsy's grin was brief but real. "Maybe. But even trees bend before they break. We'll see what the days bring."

* * *

A few paces away, the younger ones had formed a smaller circle — quiet voices beneath the hum of the sea. Lisa sat between David and Willow, knees drawn up, fingers twisting a bracelet she hadn't realised she was still wearing. Shay watched the fire, calm and steady as always.

David's expression hadn't softened since they returned from the car park. "He grabbed you," he said quietly. "I should've been there."

"You can't protect me from everyone," Lisa replied.

"I can try," he said too quickly. "Maybe we should go home. Back to Sydney. Your parents—"

"No." The word came stronger than she expected. "Don't you dare."

Willow leaned forward. "She's right. That's exactly what he wants — to scare us back into boxes. You think leaving fixes anything? It'll just make him sure he was right."

David looked between them, jaw working. "I just don't want her hurt."

Lisa touched his arm, gentle but firm. "You can't keep me safe by making me small."

For a long moment, only the surf filled the silence. Then Shay spoke — her voice soft, even, and somehow large enough for all of them.

"Fear's natural," she said. "But it's not a compass. Gypsy knows that. He's led people through worse. If he thinks we can hold our ground, I believe him."

Willow nodded. "Same."

David stared into the fire, shoulders loosening a little. "You really trust him that much?"

"Not blindly," Shay said. "But faith isn't about certainty. It's about staying when things get rough. If we leave every time someone in uniform growls, we'll never learn what peace feels like."

Lisa exhaled, feeling something inside her settle. "So we stay?"

Shay smiled. "We stay smart. We stay together. That's enough."

Willow raised an imaginary mug. "I'll drink to that. Except we're out of beer."

Lisa laughed — small but real. "Shelly's got tea."

"Then tea it is," Willow said.

David reached for Lisa's hand. She let him take it. Their fingers laced quietly, the day's fear slowly draining out of her with the tide.

* * *

The sky deepened to indigo. Crickets took up the night's rhythm. A single headlight appeared along the track, gliding toward the camp like a wandering star.

Ryder looked up. "We expecting company?"

Gypsy shook his head. "Not that I know of."

The light drew closer, then dimmed. A panel van rolled to a stop near the trees, engine ticking as it cooled. A tall, lean man stepped out, guitar case over one shoulder, a half-smile under his sun-faded hat.

"Evening," he called. "Didn't mean to intrude. Just looking for somewhere to camp for the night."

Gypsy stood, brushing sand from his trousers. "You're welcome here, mate. Fire's warm. Kettle's on."

The stranger smiled, eyes catching the glow. "Name's Ross."

Shay glanced at Lisa, her half-smile carrying that curious, quiet knowing. "Seems the road sends who it needs," she murmured.

Ross opened his guitar case and sat by the fire. Conversation softened around him. The camp seemed to breathe out — as if the storm had finally passed and something gentler had walked in to take its place.

He tuned once, twice, then strummed a chord that shimmered through the trees.

The camp fell quiet.

Ross played a slow, wandering melody — no words at first, just music that caught the edges of grief and smoothed them. When his voice came, it was low and warm, running like water over stones.

I've been chasing morning through a hundred towns of rain... But tonight the wind is warm and the fire knows my name...

The words hung in the dark, luminous as sparks.

Lisa felt something unclench in her chest. The fear, the anger — it all loosened under the music. Willow leaned lightly against her shoulder. David breathed out beside her. Even Chook, sitting cross-legged in the shadows, held his harmonica still, listening like the song was teaching him something.

When Ross finished, the fire crackled as if answering.

"Beautiful," Shelly whispered. "That sounded like the road missing someone."

Ross chuckled softly. "That's about right. The road always misses someone."

* * *

Gypsy lifted his guitar, strummed, found a key. "Mind if I borrow your tune?"

Ross grinned. "Take it anywhere you want."

They played together — easy, instinctive, a conversation without words. Chook slipped in with his harmonica, the twins clapped along, Shelly tapped a wooden spoon against her mug. Soon someone began to dance, skirts catching the firelight.

The storm that had rattled them earlier felt distant now — replaced by warmth, rhythm, laughter. A kind of healing only music could manage.

Ross and Gypsy ended on a long, shimmering note.

Chook whooped. "Best bloody noise I've heard since Nimbin!"

Laughter rose like a wave.

Ross wiped his brow, smiling softly. "You've got a good mob here."

Gypsy nodded. "They're family. Not by blood — by fire."

Ross considered that, then said, "Mind if I stay a few days?"

"Stay as long as you like," Shelly answered before anyone else could. "Music earns its place."

Lisa sat back, feeling the night settle into her bones. Willow gave her a slow, warm smile. Shay nodded once, her eyes soft in the glow.

The storm had not broken them.

The storm had made space for a song.

And as the ocean rolled steady beyond the dunes, Lisa realised the truth the Sanctuary had been teaching her all along:

Some things you face alone. But the things that matter? You face together.

17

Dawn found them where the music had left them.

The fire was a low cradle of coals, breathing smoke that smelled of last night's laughter. Guitars slept against the logs. Beyond the dunes, the sea murmured steadily, keeping time like it always did.

Lisa woke first. Her hair smelled of smoke and salt. For a moment she couldn't tell whether Ross's melody was still playing or simply echoing in her chest. That line about the fire knowing his name hummed through her like something half-dreamt.

Gypsy was already up, coaxing the kettle to life.

"Morning, little one," he said, voice rough with sleep.

"Morning," she murmured. "Did we really play till the stars went out?"

"Till they clapped," he said with a grin.

Across the clearing, Ross sat cross-legged, tuning his guitar again. The sound was softer now — almost private, a tune meant for daylight. He nodded as Lisa wandered over.

"Couldn't sleep?" she asked.

"Didn't want to," he said. "Morning's a good listener."

He began to pick a few slow notes. The melody was new but carried the same bones as the night before — gentler now, sunlight instead of flame. Gypsy joined with a quiet rhythm. Shelly added the clink of spoons against a pot.

One by one, the camp woke to it: Willow stretching, Shay tipping her hat back, the twins blinking sleep from their eyes.

Ross sang under his breath, the words soft and unforced:

There's smoke after the storm, and a song beneath the sea, If you follow it at sunrise, it might lead you home to me.

The lines drifted through the gums like morning mist.

Lisa closed her eyes, letting the sound wash through her. The fear that had chased them the last few days felt small now — embarrassed by the light.

When the song faded, Gypsy poured mugs of tea and passed them around.

"That's a keeper," he said.

Ross shrugged lightly. "It just... turned up. Like the morning did."

Shay smiled. "Maybe the road's still writing through you."

Gypsy nodded toward the ridge where smoke curled thin from a farmhouse chimney. "We'll move soon," he said quietly. "Rand's shadow won't stretch this far forever, but I reckon it's time to find new ground. Somewhere near the mountain — river water, room to grow."

Shelly nodded. "A sanctuary."

The word settled warmly between them — not hope, but intent.

Lisa looked from Ross to Willow to David, still half-asleep beside the Kombi, and felt something rise in her chest — a mix of belonging and forward motion. The song had found them, and now the day would too.

* * *

Morning stretched golden and generous. By the time the mist burned off the dunes, the camp was alive with sound: gulls arguing over scraps, waves collapsing on the shore, Gypsy coaxing smoke from the first fire of the day. Wet sarongs hung between trees, colours shifting like stained glass in the breeze. Tea steamed in enamel mugs, sweet and earthy.

Ross sat in the Kombi's shade with his guitar across his lap, drifting through lazy chords. Every so often he caught a phrase worth keeping, hummed it once, then let it go again. Music seemed drawn to him naturally, like a tide finding shore.

Down at the waterline, Lisa, Willow, Shay and David stood ankle-deep in the surf, half deciding whether to talk, half deciding whether to dive.

"You sure you can handle the waves today?" David called.

Lisa feigned offence. "You forget who taught you half your moves."

"I reckon the ocean did that."

Willow elbowed him lightly. "You two can argue about who's Neptune later. Race you in!"

They splashed into the shallows, laughter mixing with salt spray. Shay hesitated a moment before running after them — her rare laugh chiming bright as wind-bells across the sand.

Gypsy ducked under a breaker and came up shaking his hair like a dog.

"Water's warmer than last week!"

Ross lifted his guitar in salute. "So are the harmonies, mate!"

For hours, time forgot its duties. Boards skimmed across waves, salt clung to sun-warmed skin, and the sea glittered like hammered glass.

Lisa and Willow floated out past the break, lying on their backs, staring at the endless blue. Their voices drifted over the water — tiny jokes, whispered secrets, soft admissions that dissolved into the wind.

When they paddled in, dripping and breathless, David was waiting with towels and that look he sometimes tried to hide — the one that noticed Lisa before anything else.

She flopped beside him, burying her toes in the warm sand.

"Think I finally understand why people never leave this place," she said.

He brushed a damp strand of hair from her cheek. "Because they forget where else they were going?"

"Exactly."

He leaned close. "Don't get too attached. Ballina's calling."

She laughed. "You and your plans."

"Shay says the camping's good there. Quieter beaches, water you can drink, stars bright enough to knock you over."

"Then we should go," Lisa murmured, watching Willow and Shay already debating what to pack. "Soon. But not today."

"Deal. But I'm still driving."

"You always are."

Behind them, Ross shifted into a proper melody — a rolling, sun-drunk tune that made bodies sway without thinking. Gypsy joined with a hand drum, Shelly clapped along, bracelets flashing like sunlight. Even the twins swayed, eyes half-closed, lost in the simplicity of it.

When the song wound down, a hush remained — the sweet stillness that only comes when everyone is breathing in time.

Ross tapped his guitar gently. "Called that one 'Wings I Never Chose'."

Gypsy raised a brow. "What's it about?"

Ross shrugged. "Freedom, maybe. Learning to stay light enough for the wind to carry you."

Shay nodded from where she sat cross-legged in the sand. "You'll have to play it again tonight."

"If the tide allows," Ross said, tipping his hat.

* * *

The day ended the way good days always should — slowly, without anyone noticing it had begun to fade. Surfers drifted in on long glides of glassy water, boards tucked beneath their arms. Gulls quarrelled over fish heads by the rocks. The air smelled of salt, sunscreen and smoke.

Gypsy and Ross played soft, wandering tunes on the sand. Shay sat cross-legged, braiding a necklace from thin twine. Willow and Lisa lay side by side on a towel, watching the light slide off the water.

David stood knee-deep at the edge of the tide, gazing north. "Ballina's only an hour," he called. "If we leave after breakfast, we'll be pitching tents before sundown."

Lisa lifted her head. "Can we stop for ice creams on the way?"

Willow laughed. "She's already planning the lunch break."

"Someone has to keep morale high," Lisa said. "Adventure runs better on sugar."

When the sun finally kissed the sea, they walked back up the track to camp — barefoot, hair tangled, the kind of tired that felt clean.

Shelly waited by the fire, sleeves rolled, a pot of stew simmering.

"You lot look like boiled prawns," she said fondly. "Sit before you fall down. You'll want to eat before I start my lecture."

Gypsy groaned. "Not the safety speech again."

"Yes, the safety speech again," Shelly said, pointing her spoon like a weapon. "New town means new dangers. Don't trust every smiling face. Don't swim drunk. Don't eat anything Chook finds in a paddock. And write home when you can."

Lisa kissed her cheek. "We'll be fine, Mum."

"That's exactly what worries me."

Ross wandered over with his guitar. "They heading out tomorrow?"

"Ballina," Gypsy said. "Good swimming. Quieter."

Ross nodded. "Sounds right. Sometimes the road asks for a change of key."

Firelight swayed against the trunks of the gums. Willow leaned close to Lisa.

"We'll bring back stories," she whispered.

"And maybe a tan that doesn't end halfway up my knees," Lisa murmured.

Ross tuned his guitar and struck a slow chord. "One for the road," he said.

Gypsy slid in beside him, and soon the camp filled with their voices blending — low, bright, timeless. Sparks climbed into the dark like newborn constellations.

When the song faded, Ross looked around the circle, eyes glinting. "You all have wild names," he said. "Gypsy. Ryder. Willow. Chook. I feel like I wandered into a poem."

Gypsy chuckled. "Maybe you did."

"But seriously," Ross said, shifting closer to the flames. "What are your real names?"

Willow exchanged a smirk with Lisa. Ryder kept his eyes on the fire.

"Names are masks," Gypsy said. "I was Daniel once. Didn't fit."

"Leanne," Willow admitted softly. "But Willow bends."

"Jacob," Ryder muttered.

Ross nodded thoughtfully. "There's something powerful about knowing the name someone doesn't say anymore."

A wild giggle erupted from the darkness. Chook burst into the firelight, spinning in loose spirals, arms spread wide like wings. His eyes shone strangely in the glow.

"Hey, Chook!" Ross laughed. "What's your real name?"

Chook froze, struck a dramatic pose. Then he pointed skyward.

"I... am..." he began, voice low and theatrical.

The camp stilled.

"I am Pegasus!" he cried, voice cracking open the night. "Feathers in my bloodstream — thunder in my chest!"

Willow blinked. "What in the world—"

"Let him fly," Gypsy murmured.

Chook swept his arms wide. "I fly without leaving... I burn without flame... I am Pegasus!"

He collapsed backward in the sand, laughing wildly, then rolled onto his back, staring at the stars. "That's my name, man. I am that."

Ross stared, stunned. "That was... brilliant."

"That's just Chook," Lisa said, shaking her head.

Chook shot upright again. "I am Michael — I am Joseph — I am Pegasus!"

The camp erupted in laughter. Even the twins clapped.

Ross strummed a chord, a melody forming. "I am Pegasus... that's a song."

He shaped it softly; Gypsy joined him, harmony sliding in like tidewater.

The night swelled with sound — laughter, flame, sea breeze, and starlight.

None of them knew they were watching the beginning of something that would outlast them all.

And above them, the stars leaned low, listening.

18

Morning rose golden through the gums, soft and forgiving after the wildness of the night before. The fire had collapsed into a pale bed of ash that still breathed smoke and seaweed. Dew clung to the grass like quiet applause.

Lisa stood beside David's Kombi, a mug of tea warming her hands. The side door yawned open, stuffed with blankets, food tins, macramé cords and all the clutter travellers accumulated without meaning to.

"You sure we need all this?" David asked, eyeing the pile.

"Absolutely," Lisa said. "Half of it's from Shelly. Apparently we're preparing for the world to end or for Byron to run out of tea."

"Both would be tragedies," Willow said, tossing her pack into the van with a flourish. She tied her sarong at her hip, barefoot and bright-eyed. "It's going to be tight in here."

"Tight is an understatement," Lisa murmured.

Willow winked. "Depends where we put all our parts to make it fit better."

David made a strangled sound somewhere between a laugh and a cough. Shay shook her head, smiling. "You'll keep, Willow."

Gypsy sauntered over, raising a lazy salute. "See you on the road. Don't let the world tame you."

Shelly hugged them one by one, her arms warm and her words half blessing, half instruction.

"Drive careful. Keep your water topped up. Watch the tides. Don't swim drunk. Don't eat anything Chook finds in a paddock. And write home when you can."

Lisa kissed her cheek. "We'll be fine, Mum."

"That's exactly what worries me."

They piled into the Kombi — David at the wheel, Shay with a map across her knees, Lisa and Willow tangled in the back among blankets and optimism. The engine coughed, sputtered, then settled into a steady hum.

"Next stop, Ballina," David said.

"Freedom, here we come!" Willow whooped, arm out the window as the wind tangled her hair.

The radio crackled before settling into Russell Morris. Their laughter spilled out into the early sun as Byron shrank behind them — the lighthouse, the firelit nights, the Pegasus moment — blurring into memory softened by distance.

The highway unfurled south, a long ribbon between forest and sky.

"Here's to new beaches," Shay said.

"And to not killing each other before we get there," David added.

"You'll love every minute, Davo," Willow said, leaning on Lisa's shoulder.

The four of them slipped into the rhythm of the road — passing sugarcane fields, small towns with names that tasted like summer, jacaranda petals drifting like purple confetti. They waved at passing cars, earning peace signs, honks and looks of bewildered delight.

Lisa rested her chin on the window frame, hair whipping in the salt wind. Willow leaned halfway out the open door, calling, "We love you too!" at a truck driver who honked twice in reply.

Four tiny dots on a long stretch of Northern Rivers road — small in the sweep of cane and sky — and yet it felt like the whole world had opened its arms.

* * *

The bridge into Ballina arched over the river like a lazy stretch of muscle, steel glinting in the sun. Below, the water turned slow circles — brown in the shadows, silver where the current caught the light.

David exhaled as they rolled across. "Smell that? River and salt."

Lisa leaned out the window. "It's like the ocean, only quieter."

They found a patch of grass where the river met the sea — half shaded by casuarinas, half open to sky. David parked the Kombi under a crooked tree and stepped out like someone relieved of a burden.

"Home for a few days."

Willow stretched. "Finally. I was fusing to that seat."

They settled in easily. Shay staked the tarp with her neat knots. David unrolled their swags. Lisa unpacked Shelly's provisions — tea tins, bread, honey, and the candle that didn't smell like goats.

"Told you she knows everything," Lisa said.

By afternoon, the river-mouth waves were calling. David paddled into small sets, Willow heckling until she wiped out. Lisa floated beside Shay in the shallows, listening to the low hum of the world rearranging itself around them.

Later, they lay in the shade eating peaches, juice running down their wrists. Pelicans glided low. The smell of salt and mangroves wrapped around them like a blessing.

When the sun fell, they built a small fire ring of stones. Driftwood caught quickly; flames painted them in copper and rose.

"Tomorrow we find that waterfall Ross mentioned," David said. "The one behind the banana farm."

"We'll get lost trying," Willow said.

"Wouldn't have it any other way," Lisa murmured.

David sat beside her, squeezing water from his hair. For a second the fading light caught something tight in his jaw — unspoken, uncertain — before he smoothed it away.

* * *

The next days unwound like a holiday the world had forgotten to end.

They wandered barefoot down River Street — past bakeries smelling of sugar, fishing shops with faded bait posters, and boats clinking softly against their moorings. An elderly Greek man at the milk bar slid them extra chips and told them how he'd stayed for "the light and the space." Willow nearly charmed him into free milkshakes for life.

They swam in the river mouth and let the tide push them gently toward the bank. Willow threw her skirt at David mid-swell, declaring she couldn't swim in "this thing." Shay sat higher on the sand, sketching the dunes, tracing the shadows that moved across them.

At night they sat around the fire with mugs of tea, the river breathing beside them. No one spoke of Rand or the trouble behind them. Just wind, laughter, and the steady hush of water folding itself into shore.

For a while, Ballina felt like peace made tangible.

* * *

Then, one evening, a sound rose from beyond the trees — low, resonant, ancient.

A didgeridoo.

Its drone curled through the air like smoke, settling into bone and breath. Lisa felt it as much as heard it — part heartbeat, part history. Willow went still, eyes wide. David leaned forward. Shay's smile was soft and knowing.

"That's a yidaki," she said.

The music stopped. Silence deepened.

A figure stepped into the firelight — tall, lean, hair tied back with a leather cord. Earth-coloured clothes. Calm eyes reflecting flame and river.

"Evening," he said. "Hope I'm not breaking your peace."

"You've just given it a heartbeat," Shay said, rising.

He nodded. "Jundamurra. I belong to this Country. Thought I'd offer a song to it — and to you."

Lisa stepped forward, voice soft. "It was beautiful. It felt like the land was alive."

"It is," he said. "The yidaki doesn't make music. It wakes what's sleeping."

He sat with them and played again. The sound rolled through the clearing — deep and steady, like wind moving through stone. Each breath carried memory: rain on dry ground, footsteps in red dust, stories older than language.

When the final note faded, the silence that followed was full — warm, reverent, alive.

"That's how we greet the land," Jundamurra said. "A way to say: we're still here. Thank you for holding us."

He told them of Bundjalung Country — of rivers, mountains, pelicans, trickster winds, old stories carried in footprints. Willow had him laughing with questions about "cheeky girls who steal blankets."

Lisa absorbed every word as though the world were expanding inside her.

By the time the fire burned low, they were stretched around it — Shay curled near Lisa, David half-asleep, Willow mumbling jokes into her arm. Jundamurra sat nearby, eyes on the river, peaceful.

When dawn arrived, wrapped in mist, he was already awake, coaxing coals into life. He handed them damper and tea, soft steam curling into the cool morning.

"The land here," he said, "remembers everything. Walk lightly."

They listened.

Then they packed the Kombi.

Jundamurra walked beside them.

* * *

The river road shimmered with heat as they drove north. Cane trucks lumbered past. Holiday cars trailed laughter. The air smelled of eucalyptus, diesel and sugarcane.

Willow pressed her chin between the seats. "So what's this waterfall we're chasing?"

Lisa leaned forward. "Unicorn Falls. Right?"

Jundamurra nodded, listening to something beneath the engine hum.

"Long before fences or towns, a spirit followed the rain everywhere — mountain to sea, sea to cloud. One day she fell to earth in a storm. Her hair became rivers. Her tears became waterfalls. The biggest hid deep in the forest. They say if you find it and your heart is honest, the falls will show you what you've lost — or what you still need to find."

Lisa's breath caught. "Does it really exist?"

"Everything believed in exists somewhere," he said.

David smiled. "Then let's go find it."

The road wound upward, into hills glossed with silver-green light. When they crested the ridge, the ocean returned — vast, blue, breathing.

"The sea and the falls," Jundamurra murmured. "They're part of the same song. You just have to listen for the echo."

Lisa smiled at him, wind whipping her hair.

"Then maybe that's what we're doing."

And as the Kombi rattled north, windows open, river behind them and the unknown ahead, it felt — for a fleeting, perfect moment — as though the land itself was singing them home.

19

The Kombi rattled its way back into Byron just as the sky bled out the last of the afternoon light. The horizon burned orange and rose, the sun slipping behind the western hills and leaving the world rimmed in gold. Salt air rolled through the open windows, thick with seaweed and woodsmoke. The surf's distant thunder drifted across the dunes, blending with the lazy beat of someone's radio down in town.

Jundamurra walked beside them for the final sandy stretch, his long stride matching the van with unhurried ease. Every so often, Lisa leaned out the window to wave — not to call him closer, but to anchor herself to the quiet certainty of him, making sure he was still there and not just a figure stitched from river mist and myth.

By the time the fire was lit, the camp was alive again.

Kombis and canvas tents clustered under the trees like old friends, smoke curling into the deepening indigo sky. Gypsy tuned his guitar, plucking aimless notes that somehow already sounded like memory.

Shelly flitted between the fire and her makeshift kitchen, enamel mugs clinking as she poured tea and muttered about people who believed billy water boiled faster if they stared at it.

Chook was, predictably, trying to prove her wrong.

"Just keeping an eye on the bubbles, Shell," he said, crouched beside the flames.

"You keep an eye on your manners," she shot back, waving a spoon like a warning.

Willow's laughter burst across the clearing, bright and unrestrained, setting Ryder to grumbling.

"Bloody hell, woman — you could wake the dead."

"They'd probably have more fun than you," she teased.

Then Jundamurra stepped into the circle.

The hum shifted — not to silence, but to a deeper, watchful quiet. His presence carried its own calm gravity, like a ripple across still water. He nodded once, acknowledging everyone without fuss, and lowered himself beside the flames, the didgeridoo resting across his knees.

Gypsy's grin bloomed wide. "Brother," he said. "The river's sent us a gift."

Jundamurra's answering smile was modest, but his eyes glinted. "Met these four travellers on the road," he said. "Thought I'd walk with them a while."

Shelly stepped forward immediately, pressing a steaming mug into his hands. "Well then, sit closer to the fire. You'll freeze out there with nothing but that stick for company."

Ryder snorted. "That stick's not for firewood, Shell."

Jundamurra lifted the didgeridoo slightly, humour flickering in his eyes. "This one holds more fire than you think."

Willow leaned across Lisa, whispering, "Told you he'd fit right in."

Lisa smiled, drawn to his quiet steadiness — something in him made the night feel older and wider.

The circle settled. Gypsy began to play, low and steady. Jundamurra raised the didgeridoo, and the sound that followed seemed to rise from the earth itself — a deep, breathing rhythm that met Gypsy's guitar halfway. Together, the two instruments stitched something ancient into the night, a song older than language and somehow brand new.

Even Chook, moments from launching into a drinking contest, dropped to the sand in reverent silence — though not before whispering, "Told you I was the entertainment," prompting Shelly to swat him with a tea towel.

* * *

As the night deepened, the music gave way to stories.

Jundamurra spoke of Fingal, where the river met the sea and the rocks held the spirits of ancestors. He told of the mountains inland that guarded the dreaming tracks, and of songs that carried the names of rivers like prayers. His voice moved slow as tide, shaping the air, each word falling into place like stones in a riverbed.

Lisa listened with her chin on her knees, eyes wide, heart open. David sat beside her, steady and still, taking it all in. Shay leaned back on her elbows, eyes closed, a small, knowing smile at the edge of her mouth. Even Willow — usually unable to sit still — folded into the story with quiet awe.

When he finished, the fire had burned low, embers glowing deep red. For a long moment, no one spoke. The surf boomed faintly beyond the dunes — a heartbeat answering their own.

Gypsy strummed a soft chord. "Looks like the Sanctuary grows stronger."

Lisa smiled at the word. Sanctuary. It felt right — this place, these people, this fragile moment of safety and possibility.

Shelly pushed herself to her feet, brushing sand from her skirt. "Alright, tribe. There's stew left if you can still hold a bowl. But if I find that billy tipped over again, I'll be handing someone over to the police."

Laughter rolled around the circle — warm, tired, genuine.

Jundamurra lifted his mug in quiet salute. "Good fire. Good mob."

Gypsy nodded, eyes reflecting the glow. "You're one of us now, brother. Sanctuary's yours too."

A wave crashed hard on the dark shore, its foam hissing through the wind like applause.

The fire cracked one last time, sending sparks spiralling into the star-freckled sky. For a heartbeat, the whole camp seemed to hold still — bound by story, song, and the ancient pulse of the land beneath them.

20

The late afternoon sun melted gold across the canvas awning strung between the Kombi and two leaning eucalyptus trees. Smoke from the small fire drifted upward in loose threads, blending with the scent of tea tree oil and sea salt. A line of hand-painted seashells clinked softly in the breeze, keeping rhythm with the distant hush of waves.

Lisa sat cross-legged on a woven mat, a coil of twine in her lap. Her fingers fumbled through the beginnings of macramé, knots slipping whenever she tried to tighten them.

Beside her, Shelly was patient as ever — bare feet tucked beneath her skirt, a turquoise bead threaded through one of her long braids.

"Left over right," Shelly murmured, guiding her hands. "Under and through. Now right over left."

Lisa bit her lip, tongue caught in concentration, and tried again. The knot came out crooked.

"I think I did it backwards... again."

Shelly chuckled softly, sunlight catching the fine lines at the corners of her eyes. "That's the beauty of it. You pull the thread and start again. Nothing's ruined — it's all part of the journey."

They were weaving a bracelet: driftwood, shells and soft twine threaded with promise. Nearby, the twins plaited feathers into each other's hair, laughing about something Ryder had said earlier. Gypsy sat by the fire, coaxing his guitar into tune, the low hum drifting like smoke between the trees.

Lisa glanced at him, then at her work. "Do you really think anyone would buy this? It's kind of... wonky."

Shelly lifted the half-finished bracelet, turning it with gentle fingers as though it were precious. "They won't buy it," she said. "They'll feel it. You've breathed yourself into it. That's worth more than anything you can price."

The words warmed something small and tender in Lisa, and she tucked them away like a charm.

"Mullum markets are next week," Shelly added. "I'll take wall hangings and anklets. You should bring a basket of these bracelets. We'll set up together."

Lisa studied the pattern in her lap — uneven but honest. Pride bloomed softly in her chest.

"I'd like that," she said.

* * *

By twilight, the world had dipped into purple. The fire crackled softly, throwing slow-moving shadows across the mat where Lisa now had three bracelets laid out, each one a little neater than the last. A shallow dish of beads and charms caught the fire's glow like treasure. Shelly hummed while threading a dreamcatcher. The twins twirled barefoot in the sand to music only they could hear.

The sound of tyres on gravel announced David's return. He crossed the clearing with the easy grin of someone carrying good news — hair wind-tossed, shirt half untucked, a paper bag of oranges in one hand and two LPs under his arm.

"You're back," Lisa said, looking up from her knots. "How was it?"

He dropped beside her, stretching his legs toward the flames. "Think I've found my groove. The record store's got a spare spot — part-time, cash in hand, and the owner's a legend. We spun Zeppelin all afternoon." His grin widened. "I even sold two Cat Stevens albums to a bloke who swore he only came in for a map."

Lisa laughed softly. "Sounds like a great gig."

He nodded toward her handiwork. "And you've been busy."

She held up one of the bracelets, suddenly shy. "Look what I made."

David turned it over, smile softening. Then he slid it onto his wrist. "This is brilliant."

"It's a little crooked."

"That's what makes it perfect." He nudged her gently. "Guess we're artists now."

Across the fire, Gypsy began to strum the opening chords of *For What It's Worth*, the melody drifting into the dusk like a quiet protest disguised as peace. Lisa leaned against David, her head resting on his shoulder — the bracelet snug against his wrist, the scent of oranges mingling with the night.

Around them, the camp breathed. Shelly tended the stew, humming. The twins argued over whose turn it was to stir the pot. Jundamurra watched the fire, silent and steady, as though listening for something only he could hear.

The world beyond might still have its rules and cruelties, but here — under gum trees, by the sea, hearts open and unguarded — they were shaping something new. Not just rebelling.

Becoming.

Shelly stepped behind Lisa, peeking over her shoulder at the row of bracelets. "You're a fast learner," she said warmly. "Tomorrow we'll start on wall hangings — proper macramé work."

Before Lisa could answer, Willow appeared with Jundamurra in her wake. Her hair was still wet from the surf, catching the last gleam of firelight.

"Those lessons," Willow said, hands on her hips, "can they wait?"

Shelly raised an eyebrow. "Why?"

"Because," Willow said, grinning, "Jundamurra wants to take us to find the waterfall."

Lisa's breath caught. "The one you told us about?"

"The very same," Jundamurra replied. His voice was low and smooth, the fire reflected in his eyes. "Unicorn Falls. If we leave at first light, the forest might still remember the path."

The flames cracked, throwing sparks into the deep violet sky.

David met Lisa's gaze, smiling slowly. "Guess the lesson can wait."

Beyond the dunes, the sea answered with a long, rolling hush — as if it already knew what they would find.

21

The sea was a dark mirror by the time they settled in again. Waves folded softly against the shore, and the first stars blinked awake above the gum trees. The Sanctuary breathed its familiar rhythm — smoke and salt, murmured conversations, the faint thread of guitar drifting through dusk.

Jundamurra sat beside Gypsy near the fire, both tuning their instruments in easy silence — Gypsy with his paint-freckled guitar, Jundamurra with the didgeridoo resting across his knees like a sacred weight. When they began to play, their sounds met in the firelight: deep drone against shimmering strings, ancient pulse answering wandering melody.

The music rose toward the dunes, swelling and thinning with the tide. It wasn't a performance; it was a conversation between land and sky. The didgeridoo grounded the night, the guitar lifted it, and between them something old and bright seemed to stir.

When the final chord faded, a reverent quiet settled over the circle — the soft hush that follows beauty. For a breath, nobody moved.

Then the twins clapped too loudly, Willow whooped, and the spell cracked into laughter.

"Bloody hell," Ryder muttered. "You two could start a religion."

Gypsy smirked. "We did. It's called Wednesday."

Shelly flicked a twig at him. "Don't get clever. You'll ruin the magic."

But her eyes shone. Everyone's did.

Willow lay back on the sand, hair spilling around her like a halo. "You ever notice how the stars look different after days like today?"

Shay smiled. "They don't look different. You just start seeing them properly."

Lisa sat nearby, arms loose around her knees, firelight softening her features. "Feels like we brought the river back with us."

Jundamurra nodded, gaze fixed on the horizon. "You did. The river remembers who listens."

A gentle quiet followed — not empty, but full of everything they didn't need to say aloud.

David poked the fire. "Shelly says the Mullum markets are on this weekend. You taking your macramé, Lis?"

Lisa tucked a strand of hair behind her ear. "If I get it finished. Still learning not to tangle the whole thing."

"She's a natural," Shelly said. "Fastest student I've had."

"Markets'll love that," Willow added. "Half the town lives on bracelets and herbal tea."

Jundamurra chuckled — warm, low, unhurried. "Mullum's good country. The markets there hum different — full of stories. You can feel the land breathing under your feet."

"Will you come with us?" Shay asked.

He considered the stars, then nodded. "Aye. For a bit longer. The Country wants me near the coast awhile yet."

The fire cracked, sending sparks spiralling into the dark.

Gypsy leaned back. "It's settled then. Byron tonight, Mullum soon. The road keeps moving, and we move with it."

Lisa looked around the circle — the glow on familiar faces, the flicker of flame in their eyes, the ocean's patient heartbeat folding in from beyond the dunes. It felt like home, yet also like standing on the edge of something just beginning.

Gypsy played again — softer now, almost a lullaby. Shay rested her head on her knees. Willow hummed along, lazy and content. David's hand found Lisa's in the dark, his thumb brushing hers gently.

Jundamurra watched the flames, the stars reflecting in his eyes. "Tomorrow," he murmured, almost to himself, "we'll wake to a new song."

And as the fire burned low, nobody doubted him.

22

Dawn crept in on soft feet.

Mist curled low over the dunes, threading through the paperbarks like smoke that had lost its way home. The surf murmured somewhere beyond the trees, a steady heartbeat promising good things.

Lisa woke first. The world was pale blue and silver, the air cool against her skin. David lay half-asleep beside her, hair wild, one arm flung across his eyes. She brushed a stray curl from his forehead, kissed it lightly, and slipped quietly out of the Kombi.

Outside, Shelly was already up — apron tied over her nightdress as she coaxed the billy into a boil. The smell of tea and woodfire hung in the crisp morning air.

"You're keen," Shelly said. "Off chasing waterfalls before breakfast?"

Lisa laughed softly. "That's the plan."

"Well, take care. Jundamurra knows his country, but the bush still bites if you don't pay attention." She handed Lisa a small bag of fruit, bread and a flask of tea. "And tell Willow to keep her shoes on. I'm not digging spinifex out of her feet again."

Willow's voice rang from behind the Kombi. "Too late for that, Shell! My feet are one with the earth!"

Shay followed her, shaking her head. "One with the dirt, more like."

Jundamurra appeared soon after — tall, quiet, his shadow long in the early light. He carried a small pack slung over one shoulder, the didgeridoo strapped diagonally across his back.

David staggered from the Kombi with a yawn. "We ready?"

"Ready enough," Jundamurra said. "The road's short, but the track's not for hurry. The falls don't like noise."

They loaded into the Kombi — Lisa in the front, Willow wedged cheerfully between her and David, Shay folded comfortably in the back. Jundamurra chose to walk the first stretch, guiding them toward the hinterland.

Morning unfurled in soft colours — lemon light through gum leaves, pink wildflowers along the verge, dew trembling on every spiderweb. The radio caught a station out of Lismore, fading into an old Crosby, Stills & Nash track. They sang loudly and badly, Willow conducting with a hairbrush while David drummed the wheel. Even Shay joined in, her laughter bright against the engine hum.

Traffic thinned as they moved inland. Cane fields ran in neat green rows, farm dogs barked from ute trays, kids on bikes waved at the colourful van. A timber truck groaned past, and the group slipped easily into their road-trip ritual — inventing stories for every stranger they passed. Even Jundamurra cracked a smile.

By mid-morning, the bitumen surrendered to gravel. The Kombi rattled and groaned, mirrors trembling like nervous wings.

"This is it," Jundamurra said. "We leave her here."

They pulled over beside a gate half-swallowed by lantana. Beyond it, a narrow track disappeared into a wall of green. The air was cooler here, rich with fern and damp earth.

"Unicorn Falls," Jundamurra said quietly, "isn't on any map. She moves when she wants to. If we're lucky, she'll let us in."

They followed single file — David with the pack, Lisa close behind, Willow humming, Shay watching their tracks with careful eyes. Birds flitted through the canopy; the ground was soft underfoot. The deeper they walked, the more the world shifted. Sunlight filtered down in pale shafts. The air thickened with unseen magic.

Lisa caught up to Jundamurra. "Why's it called Unicorn Falls?"

He smiled gently. "Old story. Long before settlers, there was a white spirit — part woman, part horse — who guarded the waters. She could walk between worlds. Wherever she drank, the land healed. The word for her sounds like Yoonikal. Somebody heard it wrong, and the name stuck."

Willow's eyes lit up. "So we're off to meet a spirit horse?"

Jundamurra chuckled. "Maybe. Or maybe you'll meet the part of yourselves you haven't met yet."

The track dipped. The sound of rushing water grew louder. Ferns brushed their legs. The air tasted of moss and spray. Lisa's heart thudded — not from exertion, but from the sense they were stepping into something sacred.

Then the trees opened.

The falls spilled from a basalt ledge into a deep green pool, mist catching the sunlight in drifting veils. Rainbows shivered in and out of existence. The water's voice filled the clearing — endless, soft, alive.

"Unicorn Falls," Jundamurra said simply.

No one spoke. Even Willow fell quiet. Lisa stepped forward, letting the fine spray kiss her skin. Shay's fingers brushed hers, grounding her gently.

"This place..." Lisa whispered. "It feels alive."

"It is," Jundamurra said. "Everything that listens long enough becomes alive."

He studied them with quiet fondness. "In our stories, water isn't just for washing. It's for remembering. Everything alive learns to begin again."

Lisa turned to him. "How do you begin again?"

A soft grin tugged at his mouth. "Some say to be reborn in the old way, you must enter the waters as you came into the world — nothing between you and the sky."

For a heartbeat, silence.

Then—

Willow threw her dress over her head and whooped. "Sounds like an invitation!"

She splashed into the pool, pale limbs flashing in the green light. "Come on, slowpokes — your turn!"

David raised an eyebrow at Lisa. "You heard him."

Lisa blushed, then laughed — the kind that loosened old knots — and peeled off her clothes before plunging into the cold water. Willow cheered and splashed her.

Shay remained on the bank, arms folded. "Somehow," she said to Jundamurra, "I doubt that's written anywhere sacred."

Jundamurra laughed, warm and deep. "Sacred? Maybe. But mostly it's just a good place to cool off after a long walk."

Willow snorted; Lisa covered her face; David nearly inhaled river water.

Shay sighed dramatically. "Well, I can't be the odd one out."

She slipped her dress over her head and stepped gracefully into the pool. They cheered as she dove beneath and surfaced, flicking water from her hair.

Laughter echoed through the clearing, bouncing against stone and spray. The falls roared like applause.

From the bank, Jundamurra lifted his hand in a quiet blessing. "Now you're part of the country," he called. "She's got your story now."

Lisa floated on her back beneath the shimmering curtain, watching light refract and break across the water. For a moment, she couldn't tell where she ended and the river began.

23

The sun rose slow and amber over Mullumbimby, drawing gold lines through the mist drifting between paddocks and gum trees. Market day. Traders arrived early—sun-lined faces unloading woven baskets, carved timber, jars of herbs, fresh mangoes beaded with dew. Incense curled from clay bowls. Someone fried banana bread on a hotplate. The air tasted warm before the day had truly begun.

Lisa sat in the back of the Kombi with her knees drawn up, a basket of jute-and-shell bracelets beside her. She had barely slept. Every knot she'd tied felt exposed—a small piece of herself offered to the world.

Shelly crouched beside her, painting tiny blue flowers along her cheekbones. "Don't hide your glow," she murmured. "Let them see you. The ones who matter will know it's real."

Lisa nodded, breathing deep. She wore a flowing white dress, bare feet, and an old denim vest stitched with peace signs. Unsure—but alive.

They arrived early. Gypsy eased the Kombi into a paddock car park beside rainbow vans and battered utes. Music floated from the centre of the reserve—flutes near the chai tent, bongos rolling across the grass.

Lisa helped Shelly spread woven mats, pinning the corners with driftwood. They arranged the bracelets in a crescent of colour. Behind them, Shelly's wall hangings swayed in the breeze. The twins flitted past selling painted stones, their laughter drifting like confetti.

By nine, the market pulsed—farmers, surfers, tourists weaving through stalls. Tarot readers, herbalists, soap-makers, juice vendors. The whole place throbbed like something half-alive.

Lisa's first sale came from a red-haired girl with freckles and an Irish lilt. "This is beautiful," she said, lifting a bracelet. "You make it yourself?"

"I did," Lisa replied, shy but steady.

"I'll take two."

She wandered off slipping one onto her wrist. Lisa turned to Shelly, stunned. "I actually sold one."

"You sold two," Shelly said, beaming.

Pride bloomed inside her like a small sun.

* * *

Near midday, the hum shifted—a quiet rolling inward, like breath held.

Thomlin had climbed onto a wooden fruit box beneath the big flame tree. Magenta vest. Peacock feather in his cap. Bare chest glowing.

He lifted one hand.

The market stilled.

Then he spoke—velvet and thunder:

"Children of rhythm! Waltzers of wonder! You, who sing in silence and sway in sunlight— come close, come closer—don't blink! You'll miss the moment where magic unzips the sky!

"I speak now to the barefoot believers, the tie-dye troubadours, the stardust sisters, the tambourine boys and girls with sunburnt shoulders— you brave the grind with bells on your ankles while the world tightens its tie and forgets how to feel.

"They call you drifters— I call you seeds. They call you bludgers— I call you brave. They call you dirty— I call you earth-bound. And when they call you lost, laugh softly, and say: I am finding my way by starlight.

"Let the markets ring with barefoot commerce! Let the bankers tremble at your hand-carved beads! You trade in truth. You sell stories knotted in string. You make anklets of rebellion and bracelets from breath.

"Beware the man who clutches rules with both hands— he has never danced. Pity the woman who scowls at painted cheeks— she has forgotten the language of wonder. And if a policeman should squint at your colours, smile wide. He cannot arrest joy.

"You are not the fringe. You are the future peeking in from the edge. You are not the wrong generation— you are the right frequency. And if they try to write history without your name, paint it on walls. Sing it from fruit boxes. Etch it into the smile of the stranger you just met."

Then he bowed—directly to Lisa.

"To the flower girl with the hopeful hands— weave your knots like spells. Sell your truth with grace. The world is watching. Make beauty unavoidable."

With a grin and a spin, he leapt from the box and vanished into the crowd like a trick of the light.

Lisa stood frozen, chest fluttering.

Around her, the market breathed again.

* * *

By mid-afternoon, heat softened everything. Laughter thinned. Shade became precious.

Then came the strange, heavy quiet.

Sergeant Alan Greaves arrived.

His patrol car rolled in slow, gravel crunching beneath the tyres. He stepped out immaculate and metallic in the sunlight, sunglasses low, posture tight enough to crack. He observed without speaking—but everything about him judged.

When he reached Lisa and Shelly's stall, he paused. "Morning."

"Morning, Sergeant," Lisa replied.

He scanned the bracelets, the wall hangings, her bare feet, painted cheeks. "You've done well," he said—as if surprised. "Markets've always been part of this town. Just keep things respectful. Clean up. No trouble."

Then, softer: "Don't forget where home is, Miss Gardener."

He moved on.

Shelly muttered, "The stars must pity that man. He's never danced a day in his life."

Lisa released her breath slowly.

Thomlin's voice echoed: *Smile wide. He cannot arrest joy.*

* * *

Dusk arrived warm and slow.

Back at the Sanctuary, firelight flickered across faces tired in the loveliest way.

Lisa lay back on a woven mat, bracelets beside her, fingers still threaded with twine. Thomlin had reappeared briefly at twilight, pressed a folded scrap of paper into her hand, and vanished again.

David arrived barefoot, sun-flushed. "You sold out," he said.

"You survived Wade's record dungeon," she replied.

They exchanged tired, proud smiles.

Gypsy played a lazy rhythm. The twins danced barefoot. Shelly hummed a lullaby from another lifetime. Jundamurra watched the fire with quiet knowing.

And for one perfect moment, the world felt whole—stitched together by hands, song, sunlight, and the quiet courage of being exactly who they were.

24

Dawn crept gently through the canvas awning, painting soft gold over the camp. The last of the night's smoke drifted in thin blue ribbons, clinging to the cool air. Lisa stepped barefoot across the sand, hair wild from sleep.

Willow was already awake, perched on the bonnet of her battered blue Mini Minor, sipping from a chipped enamel mug. The rising sun turned the faded paint almost violet.

"Couldn't sleep either?" Lisa asked, climbing beside her.

Willow handed her the mug. "Didn't try. Too much noise in my head."

They sat in quiet, shoulders brushing, watching the tide creep toward shore.

"You coming with us?" Lisa asked softly.

Willow nudged her. "With the group? Or with you?"

Lisa's laugh puffed warm. "With us — to Fingal."

Willow squinted at the glowing horizon. "Depends if your old Kombi decides to cooperate. My Mini might be towing you the whole way."

"Be serious."

"I am," Willow said, smile softening. "If you're going, my little flower, then I'm already halfway there."

Lisa's heart warmed until it felt too big for her ribs.

* * *

Down near the fire pit, Shay knelt beside her canary-yellow Mini Moke, a box of mismatched tools scattered around her. David joined her, rubbing sleep from his eyes.

"You'll come with us, won't you?" he asked.

Shay didn't look up. "The road takes me where the wind blows. Plans and I aren't on speaking terms."

"Could've fooled me."

She passed him a mug of tea, eyes amused. "This life's mine. Ours, sometimes. But nothing in life is forever — just moments strung together like shells on a cord."

"That sounds... poetic."

"It's freedom, preacher boy. Scary when you fight it. Beautiful when you don't."

* * *

By the time the camp fully woke, choices had settled quietly like tide marks in sand. Some would stay. Some would drift. But for Lisa, Willow, Shay, David and Jundamurra, the road north was already humming.

Shelly bustled about with her sleeves rolled up. "Food first. Water. And don't forget a tin opener this time."

Willow winked. "We'll live on love and daisies."

"You'll die on love and daisies," Shelly muttered, stuffing tins into a crate.

Jundamurra crouched by the fire pit, murmuring in language, giving thanks to the land. The twins chased each other through the trees, garlands bobbing in their hair. Ryder leaned over his motorbike while Gypsy lectured him on "mechanical patience."

Lisa looked around — the colours, the warmth, the life of it — and felt the ache and excitement of leaving coil inside her.

* * *

Engines rumbled awake one by one. The tribe gathered in a loose semicircle as Gypsy climbed onto the Kombi step and raised a hand.

"Listen up, tribe! Some stay, some wander, but the road binds us. Wherever we end up, we'll meet again in song."

Cheers rose.

Lisa hugged Shelly tightly. "Thank you."

"For what?"

"For teaching me knots. And maybe untying a few."

Shelly's smile flickered. "Go, before I start crying."

Willow sniffed dramatically. "Too late, Mum."

They climbed into their vans. Jundamurra walked beside the convoy until the trees thinned.

"Ngalingu yiradhu, Bundjalung jagun," he said.

Lisa leaned out. "What's it mean?"

"May the land watch over you."

* * *

The convoy rolled north in a bright, ragged ribbon — Kombis, Minis, Triumphs. Shay's Moke darted ahead, honking wild greetings. Chook zoomed past in his ex-postal van, tin windmill clattering, shouting that he had "aerodynamic enhancements."

Fields unfurled on either side — cane, cattle, bananas. The air smelled of eucalyptus and warm road.

Lisa twisted to watch Byron fade behind them. The lighthouse shimmered in the distance, a memory turning its last page.

David squeezed her hand. "You alright?"

"I don't want to lose what Byron gave me."

"You won't," he said. "It's in you now."

At Mooball they stopped beside a leaning post box. Lisa slipped a letter inside.

Dear Mum and Dad...

She imagined the small journey it would take — from this wild road back to the quiet street she'd come from.

"You ready?" David called.

Lisa turned, sun on her cheeks. "Ready."

* * *

The highway climbed gently toward the border. As the sign appeared:

Tweed Heads 12 km Fingal Head 18 km

the convoy erupted in cheers. Willow leaned half out of her Mini, hair flying.

"Goodbye, Byron! Love youuu—"

Her farewell was drowned out by cicadas screaming from the trees.

"Nature just shushed you," Shay yelled.

Jundamurra watched the land with softened eyes. "Country gets louder up here. Ancestors walk close."

Lisa's pulse fluttered. "Is that good?"

"It means you're coming the right way."

* * *

The land changed as they neared the headland — darker rock, brighter green, the smell of salt thickening in the air. Jundamurra guided them down a narrow track until they reached a hollow sheltered by dunes and banksias.

When they stepped out, the world felt different — heavier with meaning.

"This is Fingal," Jundamurra said quietly. "My people's place. The old stories breathe here."

No one spoke. Even Gypsy removed his hat.

He showed them where to set camp. Shay stretched a tarp between two banksias. David coaxed a fire to life. Willow gathered driftwood, skirt fluttering like a blue sail. Lisa laid blankets, hands gentle, reverent.

"Feels like we're guests in someone's dream," Lisa murmured.

"Maybe we are," Shay replied.

A short time later, figures appeared along the headland — Jundamurra's people. Elders. A young mother. A boy with clapsticks. They approached without haste, without hostility. Just presence.

The Elder woman lifted a smoking branch. Her eyes held no judgement — only deep, ancient knowing.

"This ground is not yours," she said.

Lisa's breath caught.

"But you have come the right way. Through one who knows it."

She swept the smoke over them — not welcome, not warning, simply recognition.

"Sit. Listen. The land will feel you."

And as they lowered themselves to the earth, Lisa felt a slow, quiet shift inside her — as though Fingal had opened a door she didn't yet know how to walk through, but somehow understood she was meant to.

25

Lisa woke to the sound of the sea breathing against volcanic rock—long, slow, steady. The Kombi was warm with shared sleep: Willow curled behind her like a soft tide, David half out of his blanket, Shay leaning against the door with dawn silvering her hair.

She slipped out quietly, sand cool under her feet.

Jundamurra was already awake by the rekindled fire. He stirred the ashes with a stick, the land holding him instead of sleep.

"Morning," he said softly.

Lisa sank beside him, pulling her shawl around her shoulders. "Feels different here."

"Because it is," he said. "You don't step onto Country. Country steps into you."

She nodded, the river stone warm against her ribs. She didn't tell him. She didn't need to.

* * *

Breakfast unfolded slowly—bread, oranges, Byron honey, mugs of tea passed hand to hand. Willow shuffled out of the Kombi with hair in wild tangles.

"Morning, spirits of the land," she yawned. "Is there tea or should I start crying now?"

David handed her a mug. "Please don't cry. Nobody here is emotionally prepared."

She winked at him. Shay snorted into her drink.

The camp moved like a heartbeat—steady, unhurried, alive.

When the group finally gathered at the edge of the river track, Jundamurra lifted a hand.

"Today we walk the old path," he said. "Beside water that remembers."

* * *

They followed him single file along the river where mangroves met sand. Dragonflies skimmed the surface, wings flashing green and blue. The river mirrored slow-drifting clouds.

Gypsy and Shelly walked ahead, the twins pestering Chook, who claimed he was composing a hit single called *Reeds of Destiny*. Ryder rode further inland, his Triumph rumbling like distant thunder.

Lisa, Willow, Shay and David walked together, bare feet sinking into warm sand.

"It feels alive," Lisa murmured.

"Everything that listens becomes alive," Jundamurra called back.

Lisa touched the stone beneath her shawl, feeling its faint pulse. She hadn't told anyone about the birthing water. Not yet. It didn't feel like a story meant to leave her chest.

Willow skimmed a pebble across the river—one, two, three skips. "Think it heard that?"

"It did," Jundamurra said. "It'll remember."

"God, I hope it remembers me in a good mood."

Shay laughed. "Rivers like mischief."

* * *

By mid-morning the river widened into shallow pools, sunlight trembling gold on the surface.

"This is where freshwater and salt greet each other," Jundamurra said. "Step in with a quiet heart."

Willow didn't wait—she was in the water before he finished speaking, skirt hitched up, squealing at the cold.

"Come on!" she called. "Don't let me be the only brave one!"

David waded in with a grin. Lisa followed, the cool water wrapping her legs like silk. Her skirt billowed, a white bloom drifting in the current.

Behind them, Shay lingered beside Jundamurra.

"You made that bit up, didn't you?"

He chuckled. "Mostly."

"And the point was...?"

"To see who was listening—and who was simply eager to take their clothes off."

Shay threw her shirt onto the bank and stepped in, water rippling around her like she belonged to it.

Willow cheered. "There she is!"

For a while the world became nothing but light, laughter, splashing, and the scent of warm river stone.

No patrol cars. No judgement. No weight. Just sunlight and water and renewal curling around their ankles.

* * *

After the swim they ate bush fruit from woven pandanus leaves and followed the track as it climbed toward the headland. Eucalyptus thickened the air. Each step took them higher until Fingal unfurled in a long sweep of coastline—cliffs, black rock, white surf.

Lisa stopped, breath catching. "It's... beautiful."

"It's sacred," Jundamurra said. "The place where the ancestors breathe closest."

The wind pressed against them warm and sharp, carrying the scent of salt and stone.

Shay slid an arm around Lisa's shoulders. "Feel it?"

Lisa nodded. "It's like the world's breathing."

"Then breathe back."

They stood together—a small tribe on the lip of something vast—each one altered in quiet, unseen ways.

* * *

They returned to camp under a soft afternoon sun. Gypsy reignited the fire; Shelly sliced fruit; Willow draped herself across the sand complaining of "river hair"; the twins danced; Chook claimed he'd discovered a new chord called *D Philosophical*.

Shay sat sharpening a stick, glancing occasionally at David with a sly, unreadable smile. David pretended not to notice, though he noticed everything.

Later, as dusk pressed in, the sea curled against the rocks in long hushed breaths.

Lisa sat by the fire, the hidden stone warm and steady against her heart. The tribe moved around her like a constellation—shifting, glowing, connected.

She didn't know what the next days would bring. Only that something inside her had shifted—not like a door opening, but like a path revealing itself one breath at a time.

The land was listening. And she—for the first time in her life—was listening back.

26

Night settled over Fingal like a long, low song—velvet-black, humming with the breath of river and sea. Waves folded themselves against volcanic rock with patient rhythm, as if the coastline were exhaling stories older than language. Above, the stars shone sharp and innumerable, bright enough to make a person whisper without knowing why.

Small fires dotted the headland—tiny orange hearts scattered across the dark. The tribe had grown again: familiar Byron faces, new wanderers drifting in with the tide, and several of Jundamurra's mob who had come to sit with the land. A quiet sense of ceremony threaded through the clearing—not demanded, simply present.

Gypsy tuned his scarred guitar near the main fire, Shelly beside him weaving flowers into twine. The twins spun circles around Chook, pestering him as he strummed his half-strung mandolin and claimed it was "tuned to the moon's emotional state." Ryder and two Iron

Chiefs leaned against their Triumphs at the edge of the clearing, silent sentries in the silver-blue dark.

Lisa sat cross-legged near the flames, shawl around her shoulders, the warm river stone resting steady at her heart. Firelight flickered across her cheeks.

Willow dropped beside her with a grin and nudged a tin cup toward her. "You look like you're carrying a secret."

Lisa smiled softly. "Maybe I am."

"Well, if it's love, pass it on. I'm parched for it." Willow clinked their cups. "To Fingal—and whatever magic rolls our way."

Across the fire, Shay spoke quietly with Jundamurra. There was a steadiness between them—a grounded ease Lisa admired. Shay seemed even more centred tonight, warm as fire and sharp as starlight.

Gypsy strummed a low chord, gathering the murmur of conversations into a hush. His voice drifted through the glow:

"There's a fire on the headland, and it burns without name... Calls the dreamers and the drifters back to where they came..."

The didgeridoo answered—Jundamurra's deep, ancient hum threading under the melody until it felt as though the land itself was singing. Drums rose, soft at first, then swelling as hands joined in. Willow whooped. The twins clapped wildly. Chook found a harmony that was almost music.

Lisa laughed, heart lifting.

* * *

When the rhythm eased, Jundamurra rose.

Silence fell—immediate, instinctive.

Four Elders stepped from the shadows, faces lit by fire, calm as carved stone. The woman from the birthing water walked at their centre, her shawl marked with ochre and white lines that glimmered like constellations.

She raised her hands. "Ngalingu." *Welcome.*

Her voice carried the tides—strong, gentle, certain.

She spoke in language first, words rolling like surf, then continued in English:

"Tonight we honour the walking ones—those who came from far away, and those who belong to this land. The Country has watched you. It knows your feet. You have listened. And so it remembers you kindly."

A soft murmur rustled through the circle.

She looked to Jundamurra. "My son, you brought them well."

"They walked with open hearts," he said.

The Elder stepped closer to the fire. "The sea watches us tonight. Let it see your joy. Let it hear your truth. Dance if you have feet. Sing if you have voice. This is how we remember."

Drums rose again, deeper, layered with the heartbeat of the land. Sparks whirled into the night.

Jundamurra moved first—grounded, ancient, each step a story. Others followed: Shay with her quiet grace, Gypsy's easy sway, Shelly weaving petals through the air with every turn. Their movements weren't rehearsed—they simply belonged.

Lisa felt her pulse slip into the rhythm.

Willow grabbed her hand. "Come on. No one's watching."

Lisa stepped into the circle—cool sand under her feet, dress rising with each turn. She spun once, breath hitching with joy. David reached for her hand, laughing, drawing her into step beside him.

Firelight braided their shadows into one.

* * *

When the drums softened, they collapsed onto the sand—breathless, glowing. Someone offered water. Someone else passed fruit. The Elders watched, eyes soft with approval.

Lisa lay back with her head in Willow's lap. The stars wheeled above—bright, sharp, endless. She felt the hum of the earth beneath her spine.

"This," Willow murmured, tracing circles on Lisa's arm, "is what forever should feel like."

Lisa couldn't speak. She only smiled.

Nearby, Shay leaned lightly into David's shoulder. "See?" she said quietly. "Moments like this—that's all any of us get. Little fires in the dark."

David nodded slowly, eyes on the stars. "Then I'll keep mine burning as long as I can."

"That's all any of us can do," Shay murmured—soft, warm, with just a hint of teasing.

* * *

The night stretched long. Songs rose and fell. Laughter softened. The sea whispered its endless hymn along the rocks.

Lisa drifted toward sleep as Jundamurra stood alone near the fire—starlight framing him, smoke curling around him like an unfolding story.

She breathed in salt, fire, night, belonging.

And beneath the cliffs, as though the world itself leaned close to listen, the sea exhaled one long, patient breath— a reminder that some songs have no ending.

27

The sun fell slow, spilling warm orange across the shallows. The day gave itself to dusk in lingering strokes, and the whole coastline glowed as though dream-painted.

Willow padded across the sand with a carton tucked under one arm. "Traded some of Shelly's herbs," she announced. "Pretty sure we accidentally cured a man's marriage in the process."

She cracked a can. They sat in the cooling sand, toes buried deep. Laughter bubbled through the air—light, easy, careless.

Music drifted from Gypsy's distant fire. Lisa, Shay, Willow and David sang half-remembered lines, mangling harmonies until they dissolved into giggles and let the waves finish the chorus.

Willow was the first to spring up and sprint toward the sea. "Moon owes me a dance!"

Lisa hesitated—then followed, white dress flashing once before she disappeared into warm water. Shay waded in with the ease of someone who knew the tides intimately. David, laughing, stripped off his shirt and dove in after them.

The sea wrapped them in silver and salt—dunking, floating, splashing, shouting nonsense at the stars.

Sometimes a touch lingered—fingers at a waist, a breath at a neck. No one named those moments. Naming made things smaller.

* * *

They climbed back up the beach, skin shimmering with salt. Moonlight draped the river mouth in gold. A small driftwood fire crackled, warming the night.

"To everything we don't need to name," Willow toasted, passing cans around.

They drank. Something in the air shifted—quiet, inevitable.

Gypsy played a lazy melody. Shelly passed warm mugs of honeyed tea. Sparks drifted into the sky.

"It feels like the end of something," Lisa murmured.

Shay glanced over. "Or the beginning of the bit that scares you and excites you at the same time."

Ryder tossed a branch into the fire. "So what's next for the merry band? Some talk of Nimbin. Some of Surfers."

Willow propped her chin in her hands. "Surfers Paradise. Musicians, dreamers, people who pretend to be trouble but aren't committed enough."

Shelly snorted. "You just want a new crowd to adore you."

"Obviously."

David poked the fire. "Nimbin commune sounds interesting. People building something real."

"Sounds like work," Gypsy said.

"Sounds like freedom," Lisa murmured.

Heads turned. A steadier girl now—roots winding, wings stirring.

Jundamurra nodded once. "Freedom's good. But don't run so fast you forget to listen."

* * *

Conversation softened. The ocean whispered. Someone hummed. Someone else harmonised without thinking. The night settled warm around them.

Lisa leaned into David's shoulder. Willow watched her with a soft, knowing smile. Shay added a log to the fire—sparks whirling up like tiny comets.

Gypsy plucked one last note. "Tomorrow," he said, "we'll see where the road wants us."

For a moment, it felt as though the stars agreed.

* * *

Later, inside the Kombi, the world shrank to candlelight and breath. Windows fogged. Salt clung to the air. They lay close—too close not to feel the truth of it—and laughter softened into something warmer, quieter.

The candle guttered. Shadows shifted. Trust rose like a slow tide.

No one spoke of love. No one needed to.

Sleep found them like waves—warm, slow, pulling them gently under.

28

Dawn slipped through the Kombi's louvres in a thin wash of silk-blue light.

David woke first, drifting up slowly from a warm, weightless dream. The Kombi breathed around him—soft, close, alive with shared warmth. Lisa lay curled against his side, her hair a salt-tangled halo across his chest. On his other side, Shay slept with her head resting over his heart, an arm draped loosely across both him and Lisa—her hand lying exactly where his pulse beat the fastest. And behind Lisa, Willow slept in a gentle curve around her waist, her breath warm against the nape of Lisa's neck.

David didn't move. He only listened—to the soft rhythm of their breathing, to the ocean folding itself against the rocks, to the faint hum that lingered from the night before.

It wasn't confusion he felt. It was awe.

Shay stirred first. Her hair brushed his chin as she lifted her head, eyes heavy with sleep before softening with quiet understanding.

"Morning," she whispered.

"Morning," he murmured.

Lisa blinked awake next, stretching gently. For one heartbeat she looked between them—Shay pressed lightly to David's side, Willow warm along her back—and something peaceful flickered across her expression. She smiled, small and steady, then sat up.

No one asked questions. The moment carried its own truth.

They slipped outside into the early light. The sand was cool beneath their feet; the air held the mingled scents of salt and last night's fire. Gypsy's cooking pit smouldered as Shelly coaxed the coals into a clean, bright burn.

"Morning, sleepyheads," Willow rasped, arms stretching above her head. "Dream sweet?"

Lisa laughed softly. Shay smiled long and slow, like someone who'd heard the sea whisper secrets.

Gypsy lifted his guitar in greeting. "Tea's nearly on. Damper soon. And if anyone needs redemption, the river's just over there."

A ripple of laughter warmed the morning air.

Shelly handed Lisa a mug of billy tea, touching her wrist gently. "No need to thank me, love. Just breathe."

Breakfast moved slow and easy—waves rolling in, eucalyptus leaves rattling somewhere inland, enamel mugs settling into sand. Every so often Lisa caught David's eye. Neither looked away too quickly. Shay hummed under her breath. Willow wove a thin crown from blades of grass.

The morning didn't rush. It unfolded.

* * *

Later, the four wandered to the river, sunlight scattering coins of gold across the water. Shay trailed her fingers along the surface, sending ripples outward.

"Feels different today," David said quietly.

Shay nodded. "It is. You can't step in the same river twice."

Lisa walked beside him, her skirt brushing his hand. "Something's shifted," she murmured.

He didn't answer, but he didn't need to. Her smile filled the silence.

By mid-morning they crossed the dunes toward the sea. White sand stretched wide, the water bright enough to squint.

"Last one in makes dinner!" Willow shouted, taking off.

Lisa chased her, laughter lifting like wings. David followed. Shay strolled after them at her own serene pace.

They crashed into the waves in a spray of silver—shrieks, splashes, breathless joy. Willow grabbed Lisa's hand and spun her through the shallows until they tumbled laughing into the next wave. Shay joined in with surgical precision. David tried to splash them and was immediately ambushed from both sides.

"Truce!" he sputtered.

"Never!" Willow crowed, diving under.

They floated between sets, the ocean rocking them like a cradle. Small touches—a shoulder brushing, fingers grazing—held no tension now, only ease.

What had been unnamed last night simply lived here now, gentle and unspoken.

When the sea grew rougher, they let the waves herd them ashore. They collapsed in a warm line on the sand. Willow rolled onto her stomach.

"Same time tonight for another sleep-in?" she teased.

Lisa nudged her with a sandy foot. "You're impossible."

"Resourceful," Willow corrected, preening.

Shay closed her eyes, content. David looked at the three of them with the soft astonishment of someone finally exhaling.

The edges between them had blurred—not into chaos, but into harmony, like a chord settling into itself.

They stayed until the tide touched their toes, then wandered back toward camp where Gypsy's guitar drifted on the wind and the smell of Shelly's damper hung sweet in the air.

No vows spoken. No labels needed. Just four sets of footprints weaving together until the sea gently took them.

29

The winter sun sat low but warm, spilling honey-gold light across the Tweed camp and turning the grass to copper. Smoke drifted from the fire in pale ribbons, carrying the scents of damper, tea and sweet wood ash.

Lisa sat cross-legged beside Shelly, threading beads onto hemp cord. David lay nearby, sketching steadily in his notebook.

The quiet cracked open with the groan of an engine labouring up the track—uneven, impatient, unmistakably Chook. A battered Holden rattled into view, coughing blue smoke.

Before it fully stopped, Chook tumbled out—hair wild, shirt half-buttoned, eyes wide.

"I've seen him," he blurted. "Rand. Down near Fingal Beach—then Chinderah. Felt like he was sniffin' around."

Gypsy laughed, warm and rolling. "Mate, we've got fires every night. If he wants us, he doesn't have to sniff that hard."

Lisa smiled, though something cold curled in her belly.

Shelly snorted. "You're an idiot, Chook. Wastin' petrol, runnin' around like a kelpie without a farm."

Chook paced tight circles, muttering about shortcuts. The breeze shifted, carrying the sweet, earthy scent of cane burn. Even Ryder paused, blade mid-sharpen.

Gypsy lifted a hand. "We'll talk tonight. No sense borrowin' fear before it arrives."

Lisa returned to her beading, but her fingers slowed. Rand moving quietly beneath these hills felt like smoke coiling around her shoulders.

* * *

That night the group gathered close around the fire. The cold crept through the grass; cane smoke drifted across the valley like a ghost. Lisa felt the river behind her—steady, grounding.

Shay spoke first, calm as deep water. "Chook might add colour to the story, but trouble doesn't care if we believe in it. Safety's in numbers—and listening."

Gypsy nodded. "We move," he said quietly. "Mount Warning way. Close to the river. More cover."

Ryder grunted. "I'll scout it at first light."

Shelly huffed. "And we'll make Chook head of security. Give him a badge and a torch."

Chook brightened. "Badge is good. But I want a spear."

Laughter cracked over the cold night, though unease glowed beneath it.

* * *

Two nights later the fire burned higher—restless flame, restless eyes. Jundamurra stood at the edge of the glow, tall and still, didgeridoo at his side.

Gypsy rose. "We've been guests here," he said. "This is Jundamurra's Country. They let us drink their water, walk their tracks. We don't leave without thanks."

Shay and Shelly stepped forward with a woven basket lined in cloth. Inside lay gifts gathered over weeks—beaded pieces, macramé, carved shells, jars of Shelly's preserves. Lisa recognised her own knots.

Jundamurra's gaze softened. "My mob see you," he said. "You walked light here. The river knows your steps."

He lifted the didgeridoo. A low note rolled out like the earth shifting under stars. Lisa felt it in her bones. The river breathed. The cane fields sighed somewhere beyond the valley.

When the last note faded, Gypsy clasped his shoulder. "You'll be missed, brother."

David shook his hand. Lisa hugged him tightly. "I'll never forget dancing under the stars with you."

"You'll hear me on the wind," he murmured.

He slung the basket over his shoulder and walked into the dark. Moments later the didgeridoo's distant song rose again, travelling through the valley until it dissolved into night.

* * *

Morning came silver and cold. Dew clung to the grass. Ryder returned from scouting with a single nod—everything ready.

Engines coughed awake. The convoy wound through cane fields and quiet back roads, ash drifting like black snow across the windscreens.

Lisa leaned into the window. Ahead, Mount Warning rose like a sleeping giant catching first light.

By late morning they reached a river bend Ryder had chosen. The bank was green, gums tall and sheltering. The mountain stood sentinel above them.

Children splashed into the water. Kingfishers flashed blue. Laughter echoed across the clearing.

Lisa and David unrolled rugs beneath the gums and hung a line for Shelly's beads. Gypsy eased the Kombi into its nook. Lisa paused, letting the river shine across her skin.

For now, the mountain was their guardian, the river their song, and the drifting smoke just another breath of the world.

30

The day had been cool and bright, the kind of winter sunlight that sharpened every colour in the Tweed Valley. Lisa spent most of it on a rug with Shelly, knotting macramé cord while Shay threaded beads into an anklet, her bare toes curling into the grass. The air was still. The mountain watched.

By the time the fire caught, cold had crept in. Mist clung low along the riverbank. Somewhere far off, a dog barked, another answered.

It was Chook who noticed first.

"Look," he breathed, pointing.

On the horizon a dull red glow rose steadily, as though the sun had decided to set again. Smoke unfurled across the sky, lit from beneath like the belly of a storm. The air shifted—sweet, charred, thick enough to taste.

"Cane burn," Gypsy said.

They drifted to where the land dipped, giving a long view of the valley. Behind them the fire cracked softly; before them the wavering line of flame crawled through the stalks. Smoke rose in twisting columns until the wind smeared the sky copper.

"It's like black snow," Shelly murmured as flakes drifted around them.

Shay caught one on her palm. "Burns don't melt."

Lisa watched the horizon, something tightening in her chest. Rand moved through her thoughts like a shadow. Fire travelled fast. Trouble faster. Yet something in the sight steadied her—the way flames cleared what needed clearing.

A ute rattled up the track, tray stacked with sacks. A weathered local climbed down.

"Thought you mob might like some fresh-cut," he said, thumping a sack onto the grass. Cane stalks gleamed inside. "Sweet as it comes."

Gypsy poured tea for him. He spoke of burns and wind, of how flame ran sharpest through the dry patches, of how the glow could stretch across the whole valley.

Lisa bit into a stalk and gasped at the burst of sweetness. David laughed and thumbed the juice from her chin.

Ryder tapped a rhythm on an upturned tin. Gypsy's guitar answered, low and rolling. Someone hummed; then Shay's voice slipped into the melody—soft, earthy—wrapping itself around the firelight.

Lisa lay back on her elbows. Ash drifted like dark snow. The mountain rose black against the glowing horizon. The taste of cane lingered—sweet, sharp, fleeting.

You'll hear me on the wind.

Tonight the wind carried fire and music, river-breath and warmth, earth and smoke. She wondered if Jundamurra felt it from wherever he walked.

For a long moment the whole valley seemed to breathe with them—firelight flickering, guitar notes humming, ash settling like soft confetti. Surrounded by her tribe, Lisa felt something new forming inside her.

Not fear. Not restlessness. Change.

And the mountain watched over it all.

31

The morning mist still hugged the river when Lisa woke. She heard boots in the grass—Ryder already up—and the soft hiss of the billy steaming over the fire. The scent of tea drifted through camp, mingling with damp wood, ash, and the sweetness of riverbank air.

Behind the Kombis came the shuffle and murmur of the tribe packing. Shelly wrapped jars of preserves in cloth. Lisa folded her macramé carefully, smoothing the knots with her thumbs. Shay tied a small bundle of beaded anklets and leather bands, her breath puffing pale in the cold. The gentle, practical rhythm of it settled the morning, weaving purpose into the crisp winter air.

By the time the sun pushed the mist off the water, the Kombis were loaded and ready. Engines coughed awake one by one, exhaust pluming white.

The convoy wound along the narrow road into Murwillumbah—Mount Warning never far from view, its dark outline rising in the corner of every window. Fields flashed green and gold, broken by blackened patches where cane had already burnt. Even with the windows cracked open, the sweet, smoky tang lingered—sugar and ash drifting on the breeze.

The market sprawled along the main street—bright awnings catching the morning light, locals in jackets and felt hats wandering between stalls, baskets swinging from their hands. The air was thick with the smell of hot pies, fresh bread, and frying onions.

They set up near the end of the row.

Shelly arranged her jars in tidy pyramids. Lisa strung her macramé between two poles, the knots swaying gently. Shay laid out her anklets and bracelets with deliberate care, beads glimmering like tiny river stones.

Within minutes, curious eyes turned their way.

A woman in a wool coat paused to buy a jar of quince jam. She lingered. "Where've you all come from?" she asked.

Lisa smiled—warm but careful. "Up from Byron. Just following the sunshine."

The woman nodded politely, though something flickered beneath her expression before she moved on.

Two stalls down, a farmer selling sacks of sweet potatoes gave them a friendly wave. The man beside him—older, jaw set—barely looked their way.

Lisa heard the mutter as he handed over a bag. "Bloody longhairs."

The words bit sharper than she expected. Heat climbed her cheeks.

David leaned close, voice low. "Let it go."

She nodded, though the sting stayed.

By mid-morning, the street throbbed with life. Children darted between stalls, faces sticky with fairy floss. Coins clinked; chatter rolled across the bitumen; a busker near the bakery strummed an old guitar, singing lines that drifted like warm smoke.

Lisa sold two wall hangings to a young couple setting up their first flat. The woman traced the knots with her fingertips, as though reading them. "These feel like home," she said.

The words warmed Lisa deeply—a soft bloom in her chest.

But not every gaze carried kindness.

Conversation slowed. A hush rolled up the row like a cold front.

Sergeant Greaves.

He walked the stalls with deliberate steps, boots clicking, hat brim low. His gaze swept across displays, traders, strangers—a slow, un-blinking searchlight.

He paused at their table.

He didn't speak. He only looked—at the jars, the bracelets, and finally at Lisa. His eyes were cool. Measuring. A stone skimming still water.

With the smallest nod, he moved on.

But the chill he left behind did not move with him.

No one spoke until he vanished into the milling crowd.

"Just doing his rounds," Gypsy said, though no one believed it.

By early afternoon their baskets were lighter, their pockets heavier. The tension of Greaves' visit loosened, sinking beneath the hum of a day well lived.

Back at the Kombi, they folded cloths, packed jars, tied bundles. The scent of baking bread lingered as they rolled out of town, Mur-willumbah shrinking behind them.

Lisa glanced back once—at the colour, the sound, the bright awnings lifting in the breeze.

Then the road narrowed again, the valley closing gently around them with its tapestry of cane and quiet river.

But a thought gnawed softly at the edge of her mind:

If Greaves had found them this easily, then Rand was only ever a step behind.

By the time they reached camp, the river's hush wrapped itself around her. The day's noise faded like a dream dissolving at the edges.

But Greaves' gaze—cold, assessing—clung to her like smoke that refused to lift.

32

Night came down fast in the valley.

The last of the daylight slid off the cane fields, swallowed by the dark outline of the mountain. By the time the fire was coaxed to life, cold had thickened along the riverbank. Mist curled low through the grass, catching the flames and turning them to honeyed smoke.

Lisa sat close to the warmth, knees drawn to her chest, watching sparks drift upward and vanish. Around her, the camp had softened. Voices were muted, laughter brief, movements slower. Even the river seemed to hush itself.

Sergeant Greaves' quiet scrutiny at the market clung to the air like burnt sugar—sweet at first, bitter by the end. Behind him, in thought if not in sight, walked Rand.

Shay broke the silence. "He wasn't just passing through," she murmured. "He was watching."

Ryder's whetstone rasped along the edge of his knife in steady strokes. "He'll be back. Blokes like that always come back. Badge or no badge—it's all the same underneath. Control."

Gypsy stared into the fire, fingers plucking muted chords—not quite a song, more a thought stretching itself. "Fear makes men like him foolish," he said softly. "They see peace and mistake it for weakness."

Shelly set the billy beside the flames, snorting. "Or they see freedom and think it needs fixing. I reckon we're doing more good here than half the churches and councils put together."

Shay stretched her legs toward the fire, beads around her ankle catching its light. "They don't understand us, so they fear us," she said. "Same story everywhere."

Gypsy's fingers stilled. His voice dropped lower. "Then we show them. Properly. No hiding, no shrinking. Let them see what we are."

Ryder lifted an eyebrow. "You mean a gathering?"

"Yeah," Gypsy said. "A big one. Anyone who's drifted through—travellers, sleepers along the river, musicians, wanderers. Bring 'em all. Fire, stories, music. Let the valley know we're here."

Lisa frowned. "Won't that bring more attention?"

"Probably," Gypsy replied with a crooked smile. "But trouble finds us anyway. Might as well give it something beautiful to trip over."

A ripple of laughter moved around the circle—fragile, but real. Even Ryder's mouth twitched.

Shay leaned closer to the flames, voice steady as river stone. "If we do this, we do it our way. No fear. No anger. Just light."

Shelly nodded. "And something warm in people's hands. No one's ever picked a fight with a full stomach."

Gypsy tipped his head toward the silhouette of the mountain. "It's time the valley saw what's growing here."

A hush settled over the camp, deeper this time, shaped by purpose rather than dread. The fire burned lower, its amber glow dancing across thoughtful faces.

Lisa leaned gently into David. Their shoulders touched, a soft anchor in the cool dark.

"Do you think we can handle something that big?" she asked.

He hesitated only a moment. "Maybe. But I think we're meant to."

A gust rolled down from the mountain—cool, sharp, carrying cane ash and river damp. It swept through the camp like a whisper. Not warning. Not promise. Something poised between the two.

Gypsy shifted his guitar and began to play again.

A slow, steady tune. One that climbed toward the dark ridge overhead, as though the mountain itself needed to hear it.

A song for the gathering ahead. A song for courage. A song to hold back the shadows.

33

The plan began with Gypsy leaning against the Kombi, arms crossed, eyes half in the distance.

"We've been breathing the same air too long," he said. "Time to stretch the legs. Take a drive inland—Nimbin way. Maybe Tyalgum, maybe Uki. Be back before the next market."

By mid-morning, they'd loaded two Kombis with the essentials: rolled swags, baskets of food, Shelly's jars of jam "in case we meet someone worth sharing with," and a bag filled with Lisa's macramé and Shay's jewellery for trade. Someone tossed in the battered enamel billy. Chook shoved in a half-open bag of potatoes. Willow added a handful of wilted daisies she insisted were still good luck.

The road out of Murwillumbah wound like a lazy river through the hills, each bend opening into a different postcard—moss-thick paddocks, wire-patched fences, timber farmhouses perched on quiet rises. Mount Warning followed them for a time, dark and patient, before the ridges swallowed it whole.

Shay sat sideways on the Kombi's bench seat, legs folded beneath her, weaving coloured thread into her hair.

"Wait till you see Nimbin," she told Lisa. "It's... different. Even for us."

Willow grinned. "Different's my favourite thing."

* * *

Uki was their first stop—a scattering of timber shops and a single pub casting deep shade across the footpath. The main street smelled of woodsmoke and warm bread. Inside a café, they drank strong tea surrounded by old tools, enamel signs, and a black-and-white photograph of Mount Warning from decades earlier.

The owner spoke with slow, considered words, nodding toward Lisa when Gypsy mentioned Nimbin.

"Tell her she's got a heartbeat you can feel under your feet," he said with a knowing smile.

Outside, Shelly bought a loaf of still-warm sourdough, and they ate thick buttered slices beside the Kombis before heading further inland.

* * *

The road tightened as it climbed toward Tyalgum, curling through green hills dotted with cattle and the occasional goat chewing at a fence line. The village was small but somehow louder—not in noise, but spirit. Music spilled from an open hall where a fiddle player kept time with a barefoot woman stamping rhythms into the boards.

Willow dragged Lisa inside without warning. They stayed for three songs, the timber floor trembling beneath a mix of boots and bare feet. Shay clapped along, sunlight caught in her hair, laughter woven into the melody.

Outside, Shelly traded a jar of quince jam for a hand-dyed scarf the colour of late afternoon sky, settling it around Lisa's shoulders with a satisfied nod.

"Every traveller needs something from the road," she said.

* * *

The drive toward Nimbin twisted through valleys so lush they seemed painted. Eucalypt shadows stretched long across the bitumen; a whipbird cracked the silence clean in half. Lisa leaned into the window, the cool air biting her cheeks, her hair snapping free in the wind.

When they crested the final rise, the town unfurled before them—a ribbon of weatherboard shopfronts painted in colours the sky had forgotten how to make. Murals climbed every wall: rainbows, peace signs, faces from record sleeves Lisa half recognised. The main street pulsed even in winter—bare feet, beads swinging from necks, incense drifting like a casual spell.

They parked at the edge of town and stepped into it as though crossing an invisible border. Willow vanished instantly into a shop selling flowing skirts and tie-dye shirts. Lisa and Shay lingered at a stall stacked with hand-painted flutes and tiny drums.

A woman in a velvet coat offered tin cups of chai from a dented teapot. "On the house," she said. "Welcome to Nimbin."

They wandered the day away—music, colour, incense, laughter drifting through warm air.

* * *

When the shadows lengthened, the creek found them before they looked for a campsite. Clear, cold water. A flat patch of ground. Enough space for all of them.

Gypsy built the fire while Willow and Shay chopped vegetables for stew. Stars gathered fast—crowding the sky, bright and unfiltered. Somewhere up the hill, a stranger's guitar spilled notes that tumbled down like water over stone.

Shay sat beside Lisa, quietly braiding her hair while Willow told a story about dancing barefoot in a paddock until dawn. Shelly passed around the last of the chai they'd saved from town, cinnamon and clove curling into the cool night.

When Lisa finally lay back in her swag beside the creek, the sky full and silver above her, she felt a fullness she hadn't known how to name—something travel alone couldn't give. Belonging, shaped softly by roads and laughter and the quiet certainty of the people around her.

* * *

They wound home over the week, stopping again in Uki and Tyalgum to trade bracelets for bread, jam for stories, and laughter for anything people were willing to give. Their baskets were heavier by the time they rolled back through Murwillumbah's streets, each trinket a breadcrumb marking where they'd been.

Mount Warning rose ahead, its shoulders carved against the sky.

The road had bent and twisted, offering new corners and new faces, but somehow it had still brought them back to where they were meant to be.

* * *

They reached camp just as the sun slipped behind the mountain, honey-gold light spilling across the grass. The Kombis eased into their places like old dogs finding their patch.

Lisa stepped out barefoot, her toes curling into the cool earth. The river smell hit first—water, reeds, yesterday's smoke—then the softer scent of damper clinging faintly to the air. It felt like walking back into a story she'd set down for a while, only to find it had kept going without her.

They moved slowly, shaking the road from their bones. Ryder stacked logs for the night fire. Shelly checked her jars for cracks. Shay wandered down to the river to trail her fingers through the water, hair falling over one shoulder. David followed—not in a hurry, just drawn there.

Lisa watched them, warmth blooming quietly in her chest. They moved so easily together, as if the river carried them into the same rhythm. It wasn't jealousy she felt—just awareness. Like noticing a new colour in the sky.

She hung the blue scarf Shelly had traded for in Tyalgum, its fabric catching the last of the light. Willow came up beside her and tipped a handful of smooth river pebbles into her palm, a gift that needed no reason. Lisa smiled and slipped them into her pocket, feeling their cool weight settle against her leg.

* * *

By the time the fire caught, the sky had deepened to violet. Gypsy strummed a slow tune that sounded like the road itself—long and unhurried. Shelly passed mugs of tea; the steam curled into the cold.

Lisa leaned into David's shoulder, his arm resting loosely around her. Across the flames, Shay sat cross-legged, eyes half-closed as if listening for something the fire might say. Willow lay back, watching the first stars appear.

From where Lisa sat, they looked like pieces of the same constellation—unnamed, shifting, bound by something she didn't yet know how to describe.

* * *

Winter's gold sharpened into clearer, brighter days. Mornings were for stepping out barefoot into dew and letting the sun climb your legs. The camp breathed with the season. Rugs and swags lay open all afternoon, and bright clothes hung between trees like flags from some invented tribe. The river ran quicker now, full of new rain, its voice an ever-present undercurrent.

Lisa found a spot by the water—a smooth rock that stayed warm all day. From there she could see everything: Shay and David rigging a new tarp frame, moving easily together; Willow crossing the paddock with a crown of wildflowers; Shelly slicing peaches for preserving.

Willow dropped cross-legged beside her and tossed a handful of daisies into her lap. "You look too serious," she teased.

Lisa laughed, the sound skipping across the river like a bright stone. Willow looped a daisy chain over her wrist, the flowers cool against her skin.

Lisa stared at the white petals and felt something flutter quietly inside her. Maybe it was the river. Maybe it was Willow. Maybe it was the soft truth that she didn't have to understand everything to feel it.

* * *

By midday the cane trucks rumbled along the distant road, dripping stalks as they went. The smell of cut cane mixed with sweet ash from burnt fields—a perfume that clung to skin and cloth.

When the work paused, they drifted toward the fire. Gypsy oiled his guitar, Shelly hummed over her peaches, Ryder tinkered with the Kombi's rear light. Lisa sat with her knees drawn up, watching the river shimmer through the trees, thinking how easily the days had begun to fold into one another—each one stitched with sunlight and small laughter.

It was almost dusk when word reached camp.

A man passing along the river track said he'd seen a patrol car crawling through town twice that afternoon, the driver taking his time looking at anyone who didn't fit the picture of a local.

The fire didn't dim, but something in the air shifted—subtle, but real. Shay's eyes met Gypsy's. Ryder's hands stilled. Lisa felt David move a little closer without thinking, and Willow's grin faltered just enough to notice.

The days might have been stretching brighter, but the shadows were stretching too.

* * *

The next morning cracked open cold and clear. By midday they were stretched out in the grass, tea cooling beside them, too content to move. David and Shay were back under the tarp, tying down a section that flapped loose. Their hands brushed once, twice—accidental but unhurried. Lisa noticed the way he smiled, and the way Shay tilted her head so the light caught her cheek.

She didn't feel replaced. Just... tender. As though her heart had grown a few extra rooms she hadn't realised she needed.

Lisa sat by the river with Willow beside her, their knees touching. Willow threaded another daisy chain and looped it over Lisa's wrist like a second bracelet. Lisa's laughter came easy, bright enough to scatter the birds.

From where she sat, the whole scene looked like a painting that hadn't settled on a single story yet—Shay and David under the tarp, Willow beside her, Gypsy's guitar threading music between them. The map of who was closest to who shifted each time the breeze changed.

When the mountain swallowed the sun, Gypsy built the fire higher than usual. The flames painted gold over their faces, and the smell of damper mixed with cane smoke drifting from the valley.

Shay and David came back from the river carrying driftwood. Their hands brushed as they dropped the pieces onto the pile; the look they shared was quiet, real. Lisa watched them, twisting the daisy chain on her wrist.

Willow slipped in beside her, shoulders touching. "You've been quiet," she murmured.

Lisa smiled gently. "Just thinking."

"That's dangerous," Willow teased, nudging her.

Gypsy began to play—slow, wordless—and something in the sound pulled them closer to the fire. Shay sat across from Lisa, her eyes reflecting the flames. David settled beside her. The air between them felt alive, like the space before thunder.

Shelly pulled the damper from the coals, and everyone drew in. Warm bread passed from hand to hand, butter melting across fingers. Laughter folded over itself until no one remembered what had started it.

Willow leaned close to whisper something, and Lisa laughed with her mouth full. Across the fire, Shay met David's eyes over the rim of her mug. The fire popped, a scatter of sparks climbing into the dark, and for a heartbeat it seemed every invisible thread between them glowed at once.

The night went on like that—songs, shared mugs, touches that lingered a little longer than they needed to.

The mountain watched. The river murmured. And somewhere beyond the cane fields, the rest of the world kept turning.

34

The morning broke without hurry—a slow brightening through the trees, the first magpie call drifting in with the mist. The fire still smouldered from the night before, a thin curl of smoke rising into the pale light. Lisa sat on her rug, bare toes curling in the cool grass, notebook open beside her though she hadn't written a word.

Shay stretched, rolling her shoulders. "Feels like a waterfall day."

Lisa looked up from the mug warming her hands. "There's a waterfall?"

"More than one," Shay said, smiling. "But I know one that catches the sun in the afternoon. Perfect for a swim."

Willow was already halfway to her Kombi for a towel. David caught Lisa's eye and grinned. "If she says it's perfect, we should probably see for ourselves."

* * *

The road in wound rough and narrow, red dirt giving way to a shaded track that climbed into the hills. The air cooled as they rose—moist, sharp, carrying the scent of moss and wet bark. Sunlight flickered through the canopy like a moving spell.

Willow walked ahead, skirt swishing at her calves. Shay carried a basket filled with fruit, a loaf of Shelly's bread, and a jar of jam wrapped in cloth. Lisa stayed close to David, their conversation easy, both stealing the occasional glance toward Shay. Behind them, Gypsy hummed a slow tune—a rhythm threading through the trees.

Sometimes Lisa slowed just to watch how the group moved—colour and laughter drifting gently through the green.

They heard the waterfall before they saw it—a low murmur swelling into a roar. Then the trees opened, revealing an arc of white water spilling into a clear pool, sunlight catching the spray until it turned to shards of rainbow.

Willow dove first with a delighted shriek. Shay stepped in with unhurried grace, the splash cool and clean. Water caught Lisa's ankles as she followed, sending a shiver up her spine, but the moment she sank into the shallows she felt something shift—as though the land welcomed her back with a familiar touch. David waded in beside her, ducking under with a grin.

Lisa perched on a warm rock, water lapping at her feet, letting the moment settle. Willow's laughter carried over the fall's rumble. Shay flicked her hair from her face in a shining arc. David surfaced beside her, water streaming from his shoulders, eyes bright. Everything felt simpler here—sunlight, water, and the people who had become her home.

Afterwards they sprawled across sun-warmed rocks, sharing bread and jam, the sweetness cutting through the taste of river. Shay leaned back beside David, their shoulders brushing just enough to notice. Willow stretched out beside Lisa, tracing lazy shapes along her arm with a fingertip. Lisa didn't move away. She didn't want to.

The moment held its own quiet pulse—unspoken, weaving itself gently into the day.

By the time they walked back down the track, the sun had dipped low, turning the treetops to gold. Their clothes clung with river damp, the air warm against their skin. Lisa felt lit from within, as though the falls had rinsed something loose in her—a fear she hadn't realised she'd been carrying.

* * *

They reached camp as the last of the sunlight slipped behind the mountain. Towels hung from the Kombis like faded flags, dripping into the grass. Gypsy already had the fire going—a deep, steady burn. He didn't ask where they'd been; he only lifted his head with a quiet, knowing smile.

They gathered without planning to. Willow dropped beside Lisa, handing her the daisy chain she'd made that morning. Shay sat across from them beside David, the two of them sharing a plate of Shelly's damper. The day clung to their skin—a looseness in their shoulders, a shine in their hair.

Lisa's laughter came lighter. David leaned close to Shay; the fire caught in her eyes. Willow's fingers brushed Lisa's wrist, lingering without thought. The mountain loomed above, the river hummed behind, and the space between each of them felt warm enough to step into.

Gypsy's guitar threaded soft notes into the night. Shelly hummed while she strung beads in the firelight. Ryder's knife rasped steadily along a whetstone.

Lisa and Willow talked in low voices, laughter sparking between them. David and Shay traded stories about swimming spots, her hand brushing his arm as she gestured. Small moments seemed to glow larger under the flames.

The damper went around again, butter melting fast. Someone topped up mugs from the billy. Ash drifted into the night like lazy snow.

* * *

Morning came bright and simple. Bees hovered over Shelly's jar of sugar, rugs warmed in the sun, and the river murmured its constant tune. Willow attempted to teach Lisa a card game with more rules than reason. Shay sat nearby, threading cord through a carved shell. David repaired the handle of a camp stool, brow wrinkled in concentration.

The sound reached them first—tyres on gravel. Not a Kombi. Heavier.

It slowed.

A flash of white paint showed through the trees. A roof-mounted light. A patrol car. It crawled along the track above the river, pausing just long enough for the driver to scan the camp.

Lisa recognised him instantly.

Rand.

He didn't stop. Didn't speak. Just looked—a long, measuring stare—before rolling on, the sound fading into the bend.

Shay's hands stilled. David straightened. Lisa shifted unconsciously closer to Willow. Ryder muttered something under his breath and returned to his tools. Gypsy watched the road long after the car disappeared.

Some people passed and left nothing behind. Others took the air with them.

The day carried on, but everyone's rhythm tightened half a beat. Willow's laugh grew brighter. Shay's stories warmer. Lisa kept glancing toward the track. Rand didn't need to stop—he'd let them know he knew exactly where they were.

* * *

That night the fire was bigger than it needed to be. Not for warmth, but for light. For glow. For the way flames made the air move. After Rand's slow roll past, it felt like the right kind of answer.

Gypsy tuned his guitar in the firelight, thumb brushing the strings until they hummed awake. Ryder dragged over a heavy log to use as a drum, palms already working a beat from the grain. Shay strung lanterns between the Kombis, yellow pools flickering like tiny suns. Willow and Lisa spread rugs, laughter rising like sparks. Shelly worked a pot of stew, the smell warm and earthy.

The music began slow—a rolling tune everyone could follow. Then Gypsy shifted into something brighter. Willow pulled Lisa up. They spun barefoot in the firelight, skirts and hair flying. Shay joined, smiling, and even David let himself be tugged into the circle.

Lisa's eyes shone. Shay's laugh carried to the trees. David's gaze flicked between them, warm. Willow danced like light itself. Four threads in motion—distinct, but woven.

Ryder's beat deepened; Gypsy matched him. Someone shook a tambourine. The night leaned in. The cane fields carried the sound. The mountain answered with echo.

Stew was eaten on laps. Sweet tea passed from hand to hand. Someone added a splash of something stronger. Songs shifted shape—Dylan, Joni, half-remembered chords everyone knew in their bones.

By the time the fire settled to embers, the circle had drawn tight. Shay sat beside Lisa, shoulders pressed. Willow hummed softly from the grass. David's fingers picked out a slow run of notes on the spare guitar.

If Rand heard them from the road, he'd know they weren't hiding.

Some truths were better sung into the dark than whispered in the light.

35

The first thing Lisa noticed was the quiet.

Not the hollow kind that meant nothing was happening—the other kind, the kind that meant the day was holding something close to its chest.

The fire had burned down to a bed of soft grey ash, one ember still glowing faintly as if reluctant to let go. She wrapped a blanket around her shoulders and stepped out into the clearing. The grass was cool and wet beneath her feet. Mist from the river drifted low, silvering the air.

The butcherbirds sang first—bright, insistent—and the wrens followed, flitting in the shrubs like quick thoughts. High above, two kookaburras burst into their wild morning laughter and shook the quiet loose.

At the riverbank she crouched with her coffee. The surface caught the early light in slow, wavering lines. In the still pools she saw the reflections of branch-top nests swaying gently in the breeze. They looked like promises the day wasn't ready to keep.

Behind her, the camp was a scatter of sleeping shapes: Willow and Shay tangled in blankets on the same rug, hair spilling together like threads from the same spool; Shelly curled under her shawl; David half-buried in his swag, arm thrown wide as though chasing music even in sleep.

Shelly was the first to stir. She padded across the grass with her shawl pulled tight and crouched beside Lisa.

"Couldn't sleep?" she whispered.

Lisa smiled. "Didn't want to miss it."

They sat in companionable hush, watching the sun lift over the cane fields. Soon enough the trucks would rattle awake, but for now it was only birds, mist, and the quiet promise of another day.

* * *

By midday, camp had settled into the rhythm of a no-hurry day. Laundry flapped on the line. The river whispered behind the trees. The patch of shade beneath the tarp became their kitchen, dining room, and meeting place all at once.

Shelly had gone all out: still-warm bakery bread, thick slices of sharp cheese, and a jar of tomato chutney open in the middle of the tablecloth. Beside it sat a bowl of crisp lettuce, cucumber, and ripe tomatoes that smelled of sun and soil. Shay added handfuls of river mint and basil, turning the air sweet and green.

David poured milky tea into tin mugs. Willow loaded her plate, then passed it to Lisa so she could spread chutney across the bread. The knife rasped softly on the tin.

Conversation drifted: who'd nodded off first by the fire, whether the river was warm enough for swimming, whether Gypsy's guitar needed new strings or just sympathy. Willow stole a bite from Lisa's plate and earned a playful swat. Shay offered David the last slice of avocado; he accepted it with a grin.

When the food was gone, they lingered. The valley hummed around them—birdsong, the faint growl of cane trucks in the distance, the rustle of warm grass. Time matched the river's pace.

* * *

It was Willow who broke the stillness.

One moment she lay in the shade, eyes half-closed; the next she bounced to her feet.

"It's too warm to sit here," she declared. "River's calling."

Lisa followed without hesitation. Shay and David exchanged a single look—agreement, mischief—before rising after them.

The track to the river had become familiar, worn smooth by daily wandering. The water waited like an old friend—green, wide, and bright with sunlight.

Willow waded straight in, skirt darkening with every step. Lisa followed, squealing at the shock of cold. David dove forward in one clean stroke, surfacing with a grin and a spray that drenched both girls. Shay slipped into the water last, slow and sure, until the river reached her waist; then she glided forward with the ease of someone born to it.

Laughter scattered across the surface like tossed petals.

Willow splashed David; he retaliated with a wave that caught Lisa full in the chest. Her shriek dissolved into laughter as she lunged back at him. Shay surfaced beside them, sunlight running down her hair like liquid gold.

When they finally drifted to the shallows, they sprawled on the grass to dry. Lisa lay on her stomach beside Willow, tracing idle patterns in the damp blades. Shay sat with her knees drawn up, droplets catching the light on her arms. David lay back with his eyes closed, the rise and fall of his chest matching the river's rhythm.

Some afternoons were made of big moments. This one was made of nothing at all—and that was exactly why it would last.

* * *

By dusk their clothes still smelled faintly of the river, and the fire became an invitation again. Gypsy sat with his guitar across his knees, fingers brushing the strings. Ryder leaned back on his hands, eyes reflecting the flames. Chook perched on a log with a mug in hand and mischief already stirring.

Willow arrived last, hair damp, cheeks flushed from the climb. She dropped beside Lisa and pulled a blanket over their legs. Firelight sparked in her eyes.

"I've got one," she said. "A story. Not deep—just one that stuck."

She told them about a roadside carnival in Queensland—a Ferris wheel stalled high above a town full of blinking lights, a nameless boy who'd shared his sticky toffee apple, and a moment suspended so perfectly she hadn't wanted it to end.

"It felt like the world had paused just for us," she said softly. "And I knew I'd never see him again. Didn't even mind. It was perfect as it was."

Ryder snorted. "Sounds like you dodged a real winner."

Chook grinned. "Bet he still owes you the apple."

Willow tossed a cushion at him, laughing.

Lisa watched her, the fire shaping every word, every smile, into something she knew she'd remember.

Stories rolled on—Gypsy's protest-horse tale, Ryder's Newcastle misadventure, Chook's dubious railway carriage story. Laughter rippled through the clearing, warm as the fire itself.

Later, Shay turned to Gypsy. "Your turn."

He didn't speak. He just played—slow chords full of road and river and the ache of places left behind. One by one, the voices stilled.

The fire popped and sighed, sending sparks drifting into the dark like wandering stars.

Above them, the mountain's shadow stretched long and protective. Below, the river murmured, carrying their laughter downstream into the night.

36

S aturday began with good intentions.

Shelly wanted flour. Gypsy needed new strings. Willow wanted "just to see what's happening." Lisa simply wanted to go along.

Ryder had been quiet all morning but agreed to join them, saying he had "a mate to catch up with." Shay came too, more for the ride than any errand.

Murwillumbah's main street was already stirring by the time they rolled in. Utes angled outside the shops, kids chased each other past the bakery, and the air thickened with the smell of pies, coffee, and hot chips. Voices spilled from the pub's open doorway.

They split naturally into twos and threes: Shelly and Lisa heading for the grocer, Shay and Gypsy for the music shop, Ryder striding ahead alone, shoulders set in that deliberate way that meant purpose. He wore his Iron Chiefs vest openly—not flaunting it, but not hiding either.

A few locals noticed.

A few looked twice.

Most looked away.

* * *

The first hint of trouble came less than twenty minutes later.

Shay and Gypsy had just stepped out of the music shop, a packet of strings in hand, when raised voices cracked through the town's hum—the sharp, brittle edge of men about to forget themselves.

Outside the pub, a heavy-set man in an Iron Chiefs vest squared up to a wiry local in a checked shirt. Ryder stood between them, jaw clenched, one palm raised, trying to de-escalate before something snapped.

The local spat something harsh, leaning in too close. Someone near the door muttered, "Bloody longhairs. Think they own the place."

Shay felt the hairs lift at the back of her neck. Then she heard the controlled, clipped tone that tightened the air.

Rand.

He leaned against the verandah post, hat low, arms folded. He wasn't interfering. He wasn't stopping anything. He was watching.

Ryder's mate shoved past Shay as he stormed away. Ryder followed with that quiet, dangerous patience he used when he was holding himself together. He didn't look Rand's way—which told Shay more than words.

The pub's chatter resumed, shaky but functional, like a storm that spat rain without committing to thunder.

Shelly and Lisa appeared from the grocer, arms full of paper bags.

"What happened?" Shelly asked.

"Nothing," Ryder said—which meant everything.

They didn't linger. They loaded the Kombis quickly, movements clipped and purposeful. As they rolled out of town, curtains twitched.

Conversations paused mid-sentence. Faces turned openly toward them.

Rand's patrol car stayed angled under the verandah, but they all knew he'd memorised every one of them.

Some trouble passed like summer rain. Other trouble stayed. This felt like the second kind.

* * *

That night, the fire burned smaller than usual.

They gathered loosely—people seeking warmth more than conversation. Even the laughter came thin. Sparks lifted and died before reaching the branches.

Gypsy played a soft, uncertain tune. Shay sat close to Lisa, heads bent together. Willow perched opposite, picking at a loose thread on her skirt, her normal brightness dimmed.

Ryder leaned against the Kombi, arms folded, vest open, patches catching the light—his other life stitched visibly across his chest.

Shelly broke the heaviness, handing out slices of warm damper.

"Eat," she said—firm, kind.

It softened something. The air eased. Gypsy's tune steadied.

Lisa's laugh fluttered. Willow's followed, bright enough to crack the mood in half.

There were no stories that night. No dancing. Just the fire, sinking to embers while the valley folded itself around them.

37

Rain clung to the jacaranda branches like silver beads as they eased the last crates from the Kombi. The storm had broken overnight, but the valley still shimmered with its memory. The paddock felt soft underfoot, springy with new water, and the mountain loomed above them in a deep green hush.

Shelly coaxed a fire from damp kindling with quiet determination. Smoke wound upward in thin curls until the flames caught with a stubborn crackle. Minutes later the billy was strung up, steam carrying the first warm breath of the new camp.

Everyone settled without being told how.

Ryder kicked off his boots and leaned back against a fallen log, socks steaming in the cool air. Willow wrapped herself in a blanket and sat beside him, hair drying in soft waves. Lisa tucked her toes beneath David's leg; he shifted instinctively to keep them warm. Shay crossed her legs opposite them, mug cupped between her hands, firelight turning her eyes a soft amber.

Gypsy, grounded as ever, rested his guitar on his knee and strummed slow chords that settled the camp like dust after rain. The talk was thin and gentle — no stories yet, just the kind of conversation that moves the way a creek finds its own path.

Ryder suggested checking the tracks upstream once the ground dried. Willow declared she'd win every coloured bead in camp once the cards came out. Shay wondered about the old dairy they'd passed — fresh cream and milk. Lisa smiled without hiding it.

The rain had scattered them. This fire brought them back.

When the flames fell to a warm orange bed, Gypsy lifted his mug.

"Been a long few days," he said. "Let's call this our first real fire in Uki."

Mugs lifted.

Smoke drifted.

The paddock breathed them in.

* * *

Morning softened over the hilltops, gold threading through the jacaranda leaves. A rooster crowed like he owned the entire valley.

Shelly was already up, hair tied in a faded scarf the colour of ripe peaches, coaxing the coals back to life.

"Tea'll be ready in a tick," she said to the air, though her voice landed gently on Lisa's shoulder.

Willow stirred under her blanket. "Dreamt of frogs," she murmured.

Shay emerged barefoot and serene, tipping last night's rainwater into a bowl.

"Faces only," she warned as Ryder wandered toward it.

Gypsy came out rubbing sleep from his eyes, kissed the top of Shelly's head, and immediately launched into plans for the day: fishing, better tarp angles, the rumour of a swimming hole.

Lisa followed the smell of billy tea. David fell into step with her, hair still wild from sleep.

Breakfast unfolded in warm ripples — bread torn by hand, laughter rising, Willow fussing with a clothesline, Shay suggesting a path toward town.

"Every place has a rhythm," Gypsy said. "Let's go learn Uki's."

* * *

They walked into town like a loose tide — Shelly and Lisa up front, David and Shay behind, Willow drifting to watch jacaranda petals swirl under her bare feet. Ryder strode ahead alone, vest on, shoulders telling everyone he was simply passing through.

Uki greeted them quietly.

Weatherboard shopfronts, the smell of warm bread, a verandah that had held more stories than any fire. Locals paused — some curious, some cautious, none unfriendly.

Shelly bridged the gap first, stepping into the café and returning with bread under her arm.

"They said we're welcome for a cuppa," she said. "So long as we don't bring the whole circus."

Lisa laughed. Willow took that as a challenge.

They stopped at the general store to thank Mick for the paddock. He shook Gypsy's hand like he'd been expecting them.

"Keep the dogs out, don't leave rubbish, and spend a bit in town. That's the agreement."

On the way back they looped past the creek. Sunlight skimmed the water. The hills folded the valley around them like a gentle arm.

"Feels like we might belong here for a bit," Shay said.

No one argued.

* * *

By midday the field glowed — patches drying, patches soft, all of it holding the scent of warm grass and sun-washed rain. The camp rearranged itself into something home-shaped: laundry lines tight, a deeper fire pit, rugs drying at the edges of sunlight.

Gypsy leaned on a crate, picking soft chords. Ryder and David measured wood for a taller fire shelter, arguing amiably. Shay pulled rope through her hands, tying knots as easily as breathing. Willow scattered fresh wildflowers at the tarp poles because "colour keeps bad energy on its toes."

Lisa believed her.

Shelly passed warm damper around the circle, brushing flour from her hands like blessing dust.

The afternoon drifted easy and green. Not planning — just drying out.

The clothes.

The ground.

The hearts.

38

The sun climbed warm and honeyed by mid-morning, burning the last of the mist from the paddock. Uki felt different from the coast — gentler, greener, carrying warm grass instead of salt.

"We're basically living like it's December," Willow said, eyeing their mismatched skirts and smoky shirts. "If it stays this warm, we need summer clothes."

Shelly agreed with exaggerated despair. Shay simply nodded, amused.

So the four of them piled into Shelly's Kombi, its paint soft under a film of road dust, and rattled into town.

Uki's main street was a small miracle — bread, hand-painted signs, and a second-hand shop spilling onto the footpath like a rainbow had tripped over. Willow dove first, emerging with pale denim shorts. Lisa drifted toward a rack of soft cotton skirts, fingertips testing the sway. Shelly held up a floral singlet suspiciously.

"You reckon Gypsy would notice?"

Shay found deep green shorts that looked like they'd been waiting just for her — practical, soft, quietly beautiful.

The change rooms became theatre: curtains flapping, outfits swapped, laughter bouncing off the weatherboards. When Lisa stepped out in white shorts and a pale yellow singlet, the light turned her hair liquid gold.

"You'll break hearts," Willow said — and meant every word.

Lisa blushed and didn't put the outfit back.

They wandered into the lolly shop for mixed sweets, into the bakery for sourdough "for morale," and into a craft stall where Shay quietly bought a small carved unicorn and later slipped it into Lisa's palm with no explanation at all.

The drive back was slow, windows open, wind turning their hair to ribbons as the green folds of Uki wrapped around them.

The men had been busy.

Tarps taut. Fire pit deeper. Washing line straight as a spear.

Willow strutted her shorts like a catwalk queen. Ryder shook his head, smiling despite himself. Lisa spun once; David's grin chased her eyes away before she let it return. Shay changed without ceremony and let Gypsy's quiet nod be enough.

The afternoon stretched warm and loose.

Ryder and David took the tinny upriver, returning with two fish. Shay and Shelly cooked simply. Willow dragged Lisa into the tall grass to gather wildflowers for the tarp poles. Gypsy played something soft — half Dylan, half road.

By sunset, the camp smelled of herbs, warm fish, woodsmoke, and new beginnings.

Heat settled in the valley with a restless, summer-coming promise. Shay kept glancing upriver, drawn toward something the others couldn't quite feel.

"There's a place upstream," she said finally. "Locals call it Whian Whian Falls. If you've never been... you should."

It didn't take convincing.

The track wove close to the river, cool and dappled. The falls revealed themselves in a burst of white water pouring into a deep, clear pool. Light fractured through the spray like scattered glass.

Willow dived first with a wild laugh. Lisa waded in with a gasp — cold biting her legs before she slid under completely. David cannonballed in a great, soaking splash. Shay stepped in like she belonged to the water — slow, effortless, sure.

She surfaced beside Lisa, their arms brushing. Willow slung an arm around Shay's shoulders and whispered something that sent a warm flush rising along Lisa's neck.

David watched all three — not uncertain, just aware.

Nothing was spoken aloud. It didn't need to be.

Lisa didn't pull away when Willow's hand found hers beneath the water. Shay drifted close enough that their legs touched. David's eyes softened whenever he caught the small moments forming between them.

They stayed until shadows pooled along the rocks.

The climb out was slow — bare feet on warm stone, droplets catching gold in the last of the light. The walk home was quiet, but full.

Something had found its shape. Something none of them had named, but all of them could feel.

39

Morning poured over the valley like honey, turning the dew into tiny prisms across the paddock. Kombi doors stood open, enamel mugs steamed on crates, and from somewhere down Uki's main street a faint thread of music drifted up the hill — someone warming up a guitar long before the market crowds arrived.

Shelly had been up first, stacking baskets and knotting scarves around jars.

"We'll take whatever we can sell — macramé, bracelets, yesterday's bread. The rest is just for wandering."

Uki's market street was already a carnival.

Bunting sagged lazily overhead. Incense tangled with coffee. Cinnamon doughnuts puffed warm clouds through the crowd.

A busker eased into *Fire and Rain*, his soft voice slipping between stalls like water.

Shelly set up her table near the edge — macramé draped from an old ladder, jars nestled beside wildflowers Willow had gathered at sunrise.

Coins dropped easily into the tin. People walked away smiling, unsure whether they'd been sold to or welcomed.

Willow tried on a floppy straw hat and looped a string of glass beads around Lisa's neck.

"You're keeping those," she said with mock authority.

Lisa laughed, cheeks warm, her honey-gold hair catching the morning light so the beads glimmered like tiny stars.

Shay moved at her quiet pace, pausing at a timber carver's stall. She chose a small carved unicorn — smooth as river stone — and pressed it into Lisa's palm without explanation. Lisa slipped it instantly into her pocket, her thumb brushing the curved horn.

"Thank you," she whispered.

Shay only smiled — brief, soft, but warm enough to stay with her.

David appeared with second-hand books tucked under his arm. He held one out — a dog-eared poetry collection.

"For later," he said. "By the fire."

Something warm moved through Lisa's chest. Not new — just deeper.

By midday, the sun sat high. The market hummed with heat and chatter. They packed slowly, baskets lighter, pockets filled with small treasures — a carved unicorn, a necklace, a jar of chutney wrapped in paper.

The walk home was unhurried, the road shimmering, their limbs soft with good tiredness.

* * *

The heat eased into something gentler as they reached camp. Light slid between the gums, laying syrupy gold across the grass. The day exhaled.

Shoes came off. Skirts loosened. Laughter lingered like perfume from the market air.

Gypsy lay in the shade with his guitar across his lap, fingers drifting through warm, unhurried chords that stitched the camp together.

Ryder oiled his chain nearby, ears cocked toward the road the way some men listen to weather.

Willow stretched out in the grass, beads bright at her throat. Lisa sat cross-legged beside her, combing fingers through Willow's still-damp hair. The gesture looked casual; the way Willow's eyes closed said otherwise.

Across the clearing, David leaned on his elbows, watching Lisa — not possessive, just open. Present.

Shay sat beside him, close enough that their arms brushed whenever either shifted. She wasn't watching David. Her gaze followed Lisa instead.

When Lisa looked up and caught it, a small smile passed between them like shared sunlight.

Shelly moved through the glow like a quiet heartbeat — collecting mugs, laying a blanket over Ryder's shoulders without asking, resting a hand on Gypsy's back as his chords melted into James Taylor.

Down-valley, a car groaned along the dirt. Ryder's head lifted. Gypsy kept playing. The engine faded. The tension eased back into the grass.

Gold deepened. Shadows stretched. Gypsy's voice carried *Fire and Rain* across the camp, slow and steady.

Lisa tilted her head; Willow's hand slipped into hers. Shay listened, eyes soft as if remembering something she'd never told a soul.

Some afternoons weren't meant to end.

* * *

Night arrived smooth as velvet. The fire took the weight of the day, its glow rising in slow waves. The grass cooled; rosemary lingered on their hands from the craft stall.

Gypsy rolled a cigarette with deliberate care. Ryder leaned back, gaze fixed on the dark fringe of trees. Willow was halfway through a story about a stallholder who'd tried to sell her a goat when a figure stepped into the firelight.

Mick.

Hands deep in his pockets. Boots dusty. Eyes sweeping the circle before settling on Gypsy.

"Been down Murwillumbah way," he said quietly. "Rand's been busy. Shifted a few vans near the showgrounds. Didn't say much — just gave orders. Folk reckon he's makin' it clear he doesn't want your lot hanging about."

The fire cracked sharply. Silence tightened.

Gypsy struck a match, lit the cigarette, exhaled slow smoke.

"We're not in Murwillumbah."

"True," Mick said. "Word is he's looking further out. Thought you should know."

He tipped a small nod and stepped back into the dark.

Ryder was already on his feet, scanning the trees. Nothing — just insects and the river whispering its usual secrets.

David's hand found Lisa's beneath the blanket. Willow's smile thinned. Shay leaned closer to the fire, reading every shift of the coals.

"We're safe here," Gypsy said at last — steady, though the edge was there. "This land's not his. Just... keep your eyes open. And don't head into town alone."

Conversation returned slowly. Willow finished her goat story; Gypsy tossed in a dry punchline. Laughter rose — lighter than before, but still real.

Underneath it, something had changed.

It showed in the way Ryder stayed up long after the fire burned low, in the way Gypsy's eyes flicked to the shadows between chords, and in how they all sat a little closer —

their fire burning steady against the Uki dark.

40

Morning broke clear and soft, the kind of morning that forgets worry on purpose. Sunlight glanced off the river in long ripples, and mist clung low along the treeline before lifting in slow, silvery ribbons. One by one the valley's green folds revealed themselves, softened by promise.

Gypsy saw it before anyone else and made the day's plan with the ease of breathing.

"Let's take a roll through the valley," he said, brushing ash from his sleeve. "Not to town — the other way. See what's out there."

By mid-morning they were packing into the vehicles.

Gypsy took the Kombi with Shelly, Lisa, and Shay nestled among baskets and blankets. Ryder took David and Willow on the Harley, its familiar rumble echoing off the paddocks.

The road wound through sugarcane and grass as high as the bonnet — the fields shifting like green silk in the breeze. Weatherboard farmhouses blinked behind jacarandas: one verandah sagging, another held up by stubborn old posts.

Every few bends, the hills opened wide enough to glimpse Mount Warning in the distance, blue-grey and steady — a slanted guardian leaning back against the skyline.

They stopped at a roadside stall where mangoes were piled in a crate beside an honesty box nailed to a post. Jars of honey lined up like tiny suns. Shelly dropped coins into the tin; the clink echoed in the quiet.

Lisa and Willow argued cheerfully over the ripest mango until they were laughing too hard to care. Shay stood nearby, arms folded, breeze teasing the hem of her skirt. Her smile was quiet — a warm yes to the day without needing words.

* * *

Further along, Gypsy followed a whim and turned down a dirt track that curved through thick forest before opening onto a bend in the river. The water ran slow and green, a fallen gum stretching halfway across like a bridge abandoned mid-thought.

They sprawled along the bank, the air sweet with warm earth and fruit.

Mango juice ran down their wrists as they ate, sticky and bright. David skipped stones — one, two, three hops before they sank — and whooped loud enough to startle a magpie. Lisa tried, missed the water entirely, and collapsed into laughter until Shay came to her side, guiding her hand around a flatter stone.

The stones didn't go far. Lisa's smile did.

Willow watched them from her stomach, chin in her hands, hair bright as a flame in the sun. Upstream, Shelly rinsed cups and hummed to herself. Gypsy sat cross-legged sketching something half-formed — perhaps a better tarp setup, perhaps a stage for another fire-night.

It wasn't a day for decisions. It was a day for being — for letting the valley hold them in its wide, quiet way.

By midday they were back on the road, stopping at a macadamia farm where an elderly couple sold roasted nuts from a veranda. Shelly bought a bag for camp; Gypsy bought two "for scientific tasting"; Willow left with a jar of homemade jam gifted "for the pretty one."

Ryder stood beside the Harley, patched vest unmistakable. The old man didn't flinch — just nodded politely, as though bikies passed through every morning.

* * *

They rolled into camp in the late afternoon, the sky soft with pastels. The Kombi door slid open, spilling baskets of mangoes, honey, and macadamias onto the grass. The Harley clicked as it cooled, hot metal and dust mixing with the river air.

The day had loosened something in all of them.

The fire was lit early. Smoke curled through the fading light. Dinner came simple — rosemary potatoes, mango slices, macadamias roasted at the coals' edge.

Ryder sat at the fringe of the glow, stretching his leg, turning a spanner through his fingers though nothing needed fixing. His gaze drifted toward the treeline — habit more than fear. Rand's shadow hadn't followed them today, but some habits sit close to the skin.

Gypsy tuned his guitar, coaxing an easy rhythm that matched the unhurried beat of the day.

Willow lounged barefoot in the grass, plucking at a strand of beads. Every so often her gaze drifted to Lisa.

Lisa sat beside Shay, knees drawn up, hair falling over her shoulder. Shay leaned in to say something low, her hand brushing Lisa's knee with the kind of ease that comes from knowing she's welcome.

Lisa didn't pull away.

Across the fire, David watched — relaxed, open, accepting. When Lisa glanced his way, his smile curved gently. Shay saw it, met David's look with one of her own — not claiming, just acknowledging — before settling back into the warmth.

The fire popped, sparks spiralling upward.

Conversation drifted:

Shelly telling Ryder the macadamia couple had liked him. Willow teasing David about his "stone-skipping championship form." Gypsy humming beneath a melody that seemed to rise with the heat.

Lisa tilted her face to the firelight, her laugh warm and sure.

Something between the four of them shifted — not tangled, just deeper, threads weaving without needing names.

Shay's voice broke the quiet, low and steady.

"Some days the world feels wider than we can hold," she murmured, eyes on the fire. "And then nights like this happen — and it's small again. Just enough for everyone."

Gypsy nodded, not looking up from the strings. "That's why we build fires," he said. "To remind the night who we are."

The music rose a little, then settled again.

* * *

When the fire burned low, people drifted away — Ryder to his tent, Shelly to the Kombi, Gypsy last, covering the coals.

Shay and Lisa lingered, heads close, their voices soft. Willow brushed past on her way to her blankets, shoulder grazing Lisa's, a hidden smile tucked away. David waited until Lisa rose, then fell into step beside her.

Their silhouettes moved toward the riverbank together, quiet as the night itself.

Behind them, the fire cracked once more, sending a thin ribbon of smoke twisting toward the stars — the quiet signature of a day the valley would remember.

41

Morning idled into being, slow as a song without a chorus. Mist clung low over the river, and the smell of last night's fire lingered on blankets draped over chairs. Shay rinsed mugs in the shallows beside Lisa, both barefoot, their toes sinking into the cool mud. The camp breathed in a steady, lived-in rhythm — kettle on, ropes creaking, the river murmuring like it had more to say if anyone leaned close enough.

The peace broke before the sun cleared the ridge.

An engine coughed up the track, wheezed, then blasted the horn twice — and a third time, purely for effect. A battered Kombi rolled into view, one headlight wired in, paint dusted pale.

Chook leaned half out the window, hair wild, shirt unbuttoned, grinning like he'd outrun a story that might still be chasing him.

"Who's been missing me?" he called, not waiting for an answer as he parked crookedly and cut the engine. He was out before it stopped moving, bongo under one arm, a paper bag in the other.

Ryder rose from sharpening a knife, movements slow and eyes steady.

"Where've you been, Chook?"

"Oh, you know… here, there, and several other directions," Chook said, waving a hand as if excusing himself from a list nobody had asked for. He thumped the paper bag onto the table. "Brought breakfast. Doughnuts from Murwillumbah. Hot this morning."

Gypsy's gaze sharpened at the town's name.

"Murwillumbah?"

"Relax," Chook said, flicking his wrist. "In and out before Rand even noticed I was breathing his air. Saw him, though. Couple of blokes with him near the servo. Looked like he was getting new ideas — or running out of old ones."

The glance Gypsy shared with Ryder was quick and quiet — easy to miss unless you were watching. Lisa caught it. A tiny shift in the morning, rippling like a pebble dropped into still water.

Willow tore into the bag, sugar dusting her fingers as she handed a doughnut to Lisa.

"You bring trouble with these, Chook?" she asked, half-playful.

"Trouble follows me for the view," Chook said, tapping a rhythm on the bongo. "I don't have to carry it."

Shay walked up from the riverbank, eyes flicking over him as though measuring the wake he left, not just the man.

"You staying a while?"

"Long enough to remember why I like it here," he said, meeting her gaze without flinching. "And maybe long enough to make you miss me when I go."

* * *

Camp eased back into motion, but the air carried a new edge. Ryder kept Chook in his periphery. Gypsy asked more questions than usual about the town road. Lisa laughed a little too quickly when Chook tapped rhythms on the table, and David drifted closer as if drawn by instinct.

By afternoon, the unease had thinned into something else — a warm day, long shadows, the soft, rising promise of heat gathering across the valley.

Chook peeled sugar paper from another doughnut.

"They're saying Rand's got two more blokes working with him now. Saw 'em giving some poor bastard a hard time at the servo. Didn't look like a friendly chat."

Silence stretched thin. Ryder's jaw set. Shay leaned forward, elbows on knees. Willow twisted her beads. Lisa looked instinctively to Gypsy.

He had the guitar in his lap, fingers resting on strings that had stopped ringing. Firelight edged his features. He set the guitar aside.

"We should be concerned," he said calmly, "and we should remember what's true. We're together. We're welcome here. This land isn't his to take."

Then, with a sudden grin that struck like a match, he turned to Shelly.

"You know what we haven't done in far too long?"

Shelly narrowed her eyes. "What now?"

"This."

Gypsy stood, stripped off his shirt and flicked it to the grass. Boots off, belt undone — by the riverbank he was already down to nothing.

"Sunset swim!" he whooped, diving clean and sending a fan of golden spray into the air.

Willow seized Lisa's hand. Shoes vanished, clothes followed, and they hit the water seconds later, shrieks ringing like bells.

Shay set her hat on the grass, eyes glinting.

"You coming?" she asked — though she didn't wait. She stepped out of her shorts with unhurried ease and slipped beneath the surface like she belonged to the water.

David tugged off his shirt and ran in, grin loose and easy.

Chook wandered down, bongo still in hand, declared he'd "play them in," then cannonballed fully clothed, the drum tumbling safely onto the grass.

The river became its own celebration — splashes, shouts, arcs of water catching the last gold of the day. Shay floated on her back, hair drifting like ink. Willow surfaced beside Lisa, hands at her waist, both dissolving into laughter. David swam lazy circles, passing close to Shay once, then again — their eyes touching and drifting away like a quiet conversation.

* * *

When the sun finally slipped behind the ridge, bodies climbed out breathless and glowing, water clinging to skin. Towels were passed, clothes reclaimed. No one hurried. The plunge had done its work — smoothing sharp edges, dimming the sting of Rand's name.

Night rose without a plan. The fire caught easily, flames licking the dark. Gypsy played something bright and rolling. Chook found his groove. Willow moved first, hips finding the beat, hair tossing firelight. Lisa followed — shy for a heartbeat, then loosening into it. Shay stepped in like she'd been waiting for the right bar.

David clapped along from the edge, relaxed and content. When Lisa glanced at him through the flames, his smile deepened. Shay caught the exchange, gave him a look of her own, and the moment passed like a spark that knew where to land.

Songs slipped into stories. Chook told one about getting lost on the way to Nimbin; Ryder undercut it with a dry line that made it funnier.

Shelly handed out mugs of something warm. Sparks lifted into the night like tiny declarations:

we're here, we're here, we're here.

For a while, the world outside Uki was only a rumour — no Rand, no warnings, just faces in firelight, guitar and drum, the river offering its own small blessing.

When the last song faded, the quiet that followed was sweet and earned.

One by one they drifted — Ryder to his tent, Shelly to the Kombi, Gypsy last, covering the coals. Shay and Lisa lingered, their heads close, voices low. Willow brushed past on her way to her blankets, her shoulder grazing Lisa's, a smile tucked away. David waited until Lisa rose, then fell into step beside her.

They moved toward the riverbank together, quiet as the night itself.

The camp, warmed through, slept.

42

Dawn came slowly, as though the valley wanted to keep its dreams a little longer. Mist drifted above the river, and the fire pit held a pale cup of ash with a single dull coal breathing beneath it. Ryder was already awake, crouched beside his bike with a rag in hand, breath ghosting in the cool air. Every minute or so he glanced toward the track, then returned to the steady comfort of metal and familiar tasks.

Shelly emerged with the billy, scarf loose over her hair, moving with the calm of someone who had met too many early mornings to argue with them. Tea found its way into mugs, then into hands, and the camp grew itself awake.

Lisa came barefoot, hair sleep-soft, her new market shorts creased from being slept in. She wrapped her fingers around a warm mug and smiled when Shelly passed it over. Shay followed, boots unlaced, hat tucked beneath her arm, murmuring a gentle "morning" as she settled beside Lisa on the log. Their knees touched. Neither shifted.

David appeared from the far side of camp, stretching as he walked. His smile found Lisa first, softened, then lifted politely when she turned back to something Shay had said.

Willow surfaced last from a mound of blankets, yawning loud enough for the birds to answer, a blade of sugarcane grass tucked between her teeth. Her grin widened when her eyes landed on Lisa.

"Alive after last night?" she teased.

Only one person was missing.

Chook's bongo leaned against a chair as though it had wandered home without him.

Talk moved slowly — soft jokes about the swim, the dancing, the late laughter — but the ease was there, an afterglow that made people stand closer, pass things by hand, finish each other's half-started thoughts. When the tea was gone and the fire coaxed fully awake, Gypsy appeared shirtless and damp from the river. He took a long look at the circle and let a quiet, satisfied smile settle.

Whatever work he'd been doing here — naming it or not — was taking root.

* * *

By mid-morning he chose their direction the way he chose most things: by pointing.

"There," he said, vague but certain. "A ridge past the old tracks. You can see all the way to Mount Warning if the haze behaves."

They set out in a loose line. Rain from the week before had left the earth dark and springy beneath their feet. The bush smelled green — eucalypt, fern, the sweetness of sap. The trees opened now and then, offering teasing glimpses of the valley below.

Willow walked ahead with Ryder, interrogating him about every motorbike he'd ever owned. His answers were sparse, his humour bone-dry — which only made her laugh more.

Lisa and Shay kept pace together, conversation quiet, unhurried. David walked just behind them, eyes on the path and also not.

The final climb stole breath and speech alike. Then the trees fell away and they were on the ridge.

No one spoke.

Mount Warning rose in the distance — blue-grey and steady beneath a veil of haze. Below it, the valley unfurled — green folds, golden paddocks, cane fields drawn in long, dark lines. The occasional tin roof glinted where the sun found it. The river curled through everything like a silver thread that remembered every story.

Shay's hand rested lightly at the centre of Lisa's back. David stepped to her other side; the three of them framed against the expanse like a promise that didn't need naming.

Gypsy lowered himself onto a flat rock and produced a small flask from nowhere.

"Drink this in," he said.

Whether he meant the view or the rum, both were obeyed.

They lingered. Some wandered the ridge's edge, pointing out gullies and bends in the river. Ryder sat against a boulder, scanning the distance — not tense, just counting possibilities. Willow stood still for once, wind lifting her hair.

When the sun slipped a degree and shadows lengthened, they headed back down with steps that felt lighter, as though something heavy had been left behind on the ridge to keep watch.

* * *

Late afternoon brought the river back into view and the familiar sounds of camp — rope tapping Ryder's bike, enamel cups clinking, Shelly's knife steady against onions.

Evening came warm and clear. Shelly tended the cooking fire, rosemary scenting the air. Gypsy tuned his guitar as dusk gathered. Shay and Lisa spread a blanket by the river, rolling the hem between their fingers as they talked in low voices.

An engine approached up the track, slow and cautious.

Ryder stood, shoulders setting — then easing when Mick appeared in the passenger seat of a dusty van. When the doors opened, the air shifted in that way it does when history arrives wearing road dust and tired eyes.

Two young men and a woman climbed out, clothes creased and marked by travel.

The woman — Marla — had sunburn peeling across her nose. The taller man — Drew — wore a hand bandaged tight. The youngest — Sam — carried the hollow look of someone uprooted too many times in too few days.

Mick tipped his chin toward Gypsy.

"Sam, Drew, Marla. They were camped near the Murwillumbah showgrounds. Rand moved them on yesterday."

Tea appeared in mugs without anyone asking who needed it. Their story came out in gravelled pieces: Rand and two men before dawn, orders barked rather than spoken, accusations of loitering, littering, "bringing the wrong sort." No proof. No patience. Their camp torn down while the officers watched.

"Didn't matter we'd been there for weeks," Drew said, rubbing along the bandage. "Didn't matter we cleaned up after ourselves. Just wanted us gone."

Gypsy listened until their words ran out. Then he refilled their mugs and set the kettle back on the heat.

"You're welcome here," he said simply. "This land isn't his. Find a spot. We'll help you set up."

A glance passed between Gypsy and Mick — quiet, sure. Something settled that had been mist before.

This wasn't just hospitality anymore; it was a line drawn without chalk.

* * *

The circle widened that night.

Sam played a harmonica — soft at first, then with growing confidence. Drew found third harmonies in every song. Marla sat beside Shelly, slicing bread with hands that steadied halfway through the loaf. Chook's drumming slipped into the mix. Ryder's mouth remembered how to smile and nearly let it out. Willow danced barefoot, pulling Lisa into one song before Lisa drifted back to the log where Shay waited. They leaned shoulder to shoulder, the way people sit when the day surprises them in the right direction.

The fire threw its light further than usual, as if practising for something larger. No one said the word *sanctuary* — it would have felt too big, too bright — but they didn't need the word. They were making it, ember by ember, with food and music and the steady, stubborn act of telling strangers they could stay.

When the songs thinned to humming and quiet talk, the night settled clean around them. Beyond the trees, the river kept its silver secrets. In camp, faces softened. Unspoken plans shaped themselves: better windbreaks, more tarps, food runs in pairs, someone always watching the track at dawn.

Lisa watched the new arrivals — the way Marla's shoulders dropped when Shelly asked her opinion on the stew, the way Sam's laugh grew quicker with each song, the way Drew forgot the pain in his hand.

Something in her chest shifted, matching the fire's steady pulse.

Uki had tightened around them again. Not as a hiding place, but as a home that knew how to stand its ground.

43

Mist clung low over the river, turning the first light soft and blue. Gypsy found Mick at the edge of camp with his hands tucked into his jacket pockets, watching the water take its quiet time. Their breath showed pale in the cool, and the grass underfoot was wet enough to darken boots.

"Come for a walk," Gypsy said.

They took the narrow track behind the camp, weaving through gums and lantana until the ground lifted into an easy rise. From there the whole place revealed itself: the bend of the river, the scatter of vans and tarps, Shelly's small figure moving between the cooking fire and the Kombi, Ryder hunched at his bike with the patience of a man who believed in bolts. Beyond them, the valley rolled away in green and gold to the blue-grey wedge of Mount Warning.

"Good land," Gypsy murmured, more to the morning than to Mick. "Solid. Drains well. Enough open space for gardens... maybe a couple of sheds."

Mick glanced sideways. "Thinking of putting down roots?"

"Not for me," Gypsy replied. His gaze stayed on the camp. "For the ones who need it. You saw Sam, Drew, Marla last night. They won't be the last. Rand will keep pushing until there's nowhere left to go."

Mick was quiet a moment. "This place is private. No council sniffing around. But it's not mine."

"I know," Gypsy said. "But you've got the ear of the bloke who owns it. If he saw what we could make here — plant, build small, keep it clean and safe — he might back it. A place no one gets chased from. Not by Rand, not by anyone."

They walked on, dew silvering their boot edges. Gypsy pointed to a flat patch near the treeline. "Good for beds — pumpkins, beans, corn." He nodded to a higher shoulder of ground. "And up there, a lookout. Just in case."

Mick nudged a loose stone with his boot. "You'd have to keep order. Keep trouble out."

Gypsy's mouth tipped. "You've seen a camp when Shelly's watching the ledger and Ryder has the last word. Not much slips."

Below them, voices drifted up — Willow's laugh, Chook's half-awake bongo, Lisa calling something to Shay. The sun began to burn the mist off the water.

"You're serious," Mick said.

"Serious enough," Gypsy replied. "Not for me. For them. For whoever comes next."

Mick nodded slowly. "I'll talk to him. No promises. But I'll talk."

Gypsy clapped his shoulder, and they headed back down toward woodsmoke and the smell of frying bread, returning to a camp already shifting into motion.

    * * *

The morning warmed into the kind that promised heat by noon. Work found its rhythm without anyone naming it. Ryder strung a fresh line between trees for heavier tarps; David moved with him, rope coiling and pegs thudding into earth. Shay and Shelly sat near the fire with an enamel bowl between them, shelling beans in a soft, steady patter.

Sam, Drew, and Marla — still new enough to read the room before stepping fully into it — cleared ground near the edge: sticks and leaf litter into neat piles, a line of stones rolled to mark a path. Chook alternated between "supervising" with a lazy bongo and lifting things only when someone caught him not lifting them.

Gypsy drifted between jobs, offering a word here or a nod there, mostly letting people find what they were good at. The camp answered in kind: tarp lines tightened, the cooking space widened, paths tamped where feet already wanted to go. The work felt like planting — something invisible put into the ground to take shape later.

At the washing line, Lisa pinned up a blanket while Willow arrived with an armful of shirts. Their laughter was lower than usual, shared close. Shay called something over; Lisa waved back and didn't explain. A little later they vanished altogether, with the practised ease of people who knew where the trees made cover and where the riverbank curved out of sight. Those who noticed — Shay, Ryder, Shelly — smiled quietly and let it be.

By the time the sun tipped west, the camp had remade itself. Tarps stood taut and true. A new run of line turned the washing into a bright drying wall. A windbreak of branches braced the cooking space. Wildflowers — Willow's handiwork — were knotted along a rope like a promise no one had asked for but everyone liked. The newcomers' patch was cleared and ready.

Lisa and Willow reappeared with hair a little more rumpled than the work allowed and cheeks too warm for a mild day. Willow held a bunch of wildflowers as proof of a mission, tucking one behind Shelly's ear. Lisa slid in beside Shay to help with the last of the beans as if she'd never left.

When the tools were put aside, the group stepped back and looked at what they'd made.

It wasn't just a camp anymore.

It had edges, routes, purpose.

A place that held.

"Good work," Gypsy said. It didn't need more than that.

* * *

By late afternoon the river called them down without discussion. The light turned honey-thick, the surface catching it and throwing it back in broken coins. The walk over the cool grass eased sore legs; the air by the water had the sweet, clean smell of leaf and silt.

Ryder sat at the bank with his boots off, toes dug in, leaning on his hands as the current wrote itself past. David waded to his knees and dived, surfacing with the grin of someone who'd earned the swim.

Shay took the high log that bridged a shallow bend, hat tipped back, watching like she could read the river as easily as a room. Lisa trailed her fingers through the shallows, undecided, until Willow waded in with mock outrage at her hesitation, calling and coaxing until Lisa splashed in after her. When the cold caught Lisa's ankles, Willow's hands steadied her — more intention than necessity. Shay's smile shifted but stayed.

Shelly and Marla arrived last with a picnic — thick slices of bread, a jar of honey, a twist of warm roasted macadamias from the afternoon's work. Chook plonked beside them, bongo between his knees, tapping a rhythm so lazy it felt like the river was keeping time. Sam listened while Ryder talked about a long ride north; Drew stretched out and let the sun draw lines across his bandaged knuckles.

Lisa sank to her knees in the shallows and then to her waist, gasping at the cold and laughing because Willow saw it first. The water softened around shoulders and calves. Voices fell into an easy braid — small jokes, low talk, bread tearing, honey passed hand to hand.

The sun bled from gold to copper. Shadows stretched across the grass. Someone said they'd better think about fire, and no one moved. First stars arrived like shy guests.

They walked back in twos and threes, quiet, carrying the light tiredness that comes after building something and letting the river bless it.

* * *

Night came warm, holding the day's heat like a memory. The fire was big — not just for cooking but because the circle had widened. The newcomers had set their vans along the edge, shaping the light; faces glowed, conversation hummed.

Shelly's stew sent up thyme and garlic in slow waves. Chook anchored the talk with a low, easy beat; Mick leaned back in his chair, watching both the flames and the edges. When bowls emptied, Sam and Drew found a battered mandolin, tested a few notes, and then the songs opened up.

Willow rose first, beads swinging, hair threaded with firelight. Lisa joined her, shy for one beat only; their shadows leapt high on the trees. Shay watched with that private smile that held more thoughts than she ever said aloud. David clapped along opposite them, eyes finding, then yielding, then finding again.

The camp's heartbeat rose and fell — drum, mandolin, laughter — and everything beyond the gums felt distant and unimportant.

When the music eased to a hush, Gypsy leaned in, elbows on his knees.

"This," he said, letting his gaze travel the circle, "is why we're here. And why we're staying. Rand doesn't touch this place if we've anything to say about it."

Across the fire, Mick gave a firm nod.

Gypsy let a breath pass, then tipped the mood with a grin.

"But before we build any further — before we start putting real bones on the frame — we take a holiday. Surfers. A blow-out. One last run before the work begins proper."

A ripple moved through the group — Willow clapped; Chook whooped; even Ryder's mouth remembered how to grin. Lisa glanced at Shay; Shay lifted her brows like she could already feel the ocean on her skin.

"Surfers will wait," Gypsy said, hand sketching the circle. "But this — this could last."

Marla sat a little straighter. *Last* had weight she recognised — a camp that didn't vanish at dawn.

The music returned softer, leaving space for talk. Shelly and Marla traded recipes and gossip like they'd known each other longer than a day. Sam found a harmony that made everyone sound braver. Drew laughed at something Ryder said and forgot his hand hurt.

Willow leaned close to Lisa, said something that drew a warm laugh; Shay's eyes followed and softened. David passed along a mug, his fingers brushing for a breath longer than needed.

The fire burned on. Plans — soft, unnamed — took shape: more tarps, real garden beds, group runs into town, eyes on the track at first light.

Above them, the stars spread clear. Beyond the trees, the river turned and turned, carrying the day away.

Uki had tightened around them again — not as a hiding place, but as a home learning how to stand its ground.

And just ahead, somewhere in the shine of tomorrow, the ocean waited — one quick, bright exhale before they set their hands to the work they'd already begun.

44

The market was already humming when they rolled in — layered chatter, dogs tugging at leashes, the warm drag of hot bread threading through eucalyptus shade. Stalls bloomed with tie-dye and woven baskets, stacks of avocados, jars of golden honey catching the morning light like small suns.

They came as a group: Gypsy with Mick, Shelly beside him; Willow and Lisa walking in step; Shay with her hat tipped low against the sun. Sam and Drew were already scanning the food stalls. Marla paused to take a photo of a jacaranda spilling purple over half the square.

At first, the welcome held — the soft warmth some locals kept for familiar faces. A potter waved at Shelly; the bloke at the bread stall nodded. But not every gaze softened.

Four men stood near a ute stacked with crates — work boots, sunburnt forearms, the kind of narrowed look that wasn't curious and wasn't friendly. They didn't speak, but their small, deliberate shifts closer were like hawks tracing circles over a paddock.

"Don't like the vibe," Ryder murmured.

"Let it breathe," Gypsy answered, low and even. "We're here for mangoes, not trouble."

Lisa, Willow, and Shelly drifted toward a stall spilling with summer clothes — bright cotton skirts, singlets, cut-off shorts. The air held fabric dye and lemon from the soap-maker's table next door. Willow held a skirt against Lisa's waist and grinned.

"Perfect for the river."

One of the men from the ute stepped closer, pretending to browse.

"Don't you lot ever buy anything that isn't stitched by some stoner?" he said — not loud, but enough.

Shelly didn't look up. "Morning to you too."

"Not much of a morning when half the town's full of..." He gestured at bare feet, bangles, skirts. "Living for free. Using up what's ours."

Willow's smile dropped. "You don't know anything about us."

"I know enough," he said, closing the gap another half-step. "Passing through, leaving mess, thinking the world owes you."

David reached them before Shelly could answer — calm, solid. "That's enough. We're not here for a fight."

The man's lip curled. He shifted sideways — not quite toward David, but into the space Lisa occupied. His shoulder clipped her hard. She stumbled. The uneven ground caught her foot and dropped her. Her knees hit dirt.

"Lisa!"

Willow was on the ground in an instant, hands framing Lisa's face, searching her eyes. "You scared me." She kissed her — not playful, not teasing, just raw relief. "Don't do that again."

"I'm fine," Lisa whispered, wincing as she rose.

Shelly stepped in front of her, eyes fixed on the man. "You lay a hand on her again and you'll regret it." Her voice was low enough to stop him. Two of his mates shifted forward — until Ryder stepped into view, saying nothing, just existing like a wall built from denim and warning.

From the produce stall, an older woman pushed through. "That's enough, Kev," she snapped. A younger bloke from the coffee caravan joined her, hand firm on Kev's arm.

"You're done here."

The heat drained as the men backed off, muttering. The older woman turned to Shelly.

"Sorry, love. Not everyone's a fool, but the ones who are make the loudest noise."

"Appreciated," Shelly said.

They tightened their shape after that, moving through stalls without lingering. Willow stayed close enough for her hand to brush Lisa's arm — the quiet check, the still-here of it. By the time they reached the Kombi, the colours of the market felt washed, like the morning had been left too long in the sun.

Understanding settled quiet and deep: Uki was worth protecting, and they'd protect it together.

* * *

The ride home held mostly the road's low thrum. Willow sat pressed to Lisa's side, her hand warm on Lisa's knee, thumb drawing small, absent circles. Lisa kept saying she was fine, but her gaze stayed fixed on the blur of green along the verge.

Shelly rode shotgun with her head tipped just enough to watch the mirror. David's hands were steady on the wheel, though a pinch lived between his brows.

When they swung into the clearing, the sun was sliding toward afternoon, spilling gold through the paperbarks. Woodsmoke drifted from a half-built fire; Mick and Gypsy had dragged up a few river logs and gone back for more.

As they climbed out, Gypsy looked up and read the shape of them. "What happened?"

"Locals," Shelly said. Nothing more was needed.

Gypsy's jaw tightened, then eased. "Sit. Tea's on."

Lisa sank onto a blanket. Willow crouched to tuck a loose strand behind her ear.

"Still okay?"

"I'm fine," Lisa said again, softer. "You don't have to fuss."

"I do," Willow murmured. "You scared me."

Shay watched from a step back, not intruding, but the small flick of her eyes between them said she'd caught the weight of it.

By the fire, David sat beside Shelly. "It could've been worse," he said. "Ryder kept them from taking it further."

Ryder shrugged like it was weather. "They'll talk big down the pub tonight. Words. If they come up here…" He let the rest burn off in the smoke.

Mick leaned on his knees, scanning faces. "This land's yours as long as you want it. You don't run because a few loudmouths don't like the view."

"And if more come?" Gypsy asked. "If they keep pushing?"

Mick drew a breath. "Then maybe we make it more than a camp. Somewhere no one gets pushed off."

The fire popped, a thin ribbon of smoke rising like quiet punctuation.

By dusk, a soft pact had settled. Lisa's laugh returned in small bursts, then steadier ones — especially when Willow pressed a tin mug of tea into her hands and stayed close enough for their knees to touch. The market trouble had been contained, but it left its scuff marks. People watched one another a fraction more closely. Conversations drifted toward what-ifs and what-nexts.

Across the flames, something unspoken passed between Gypsy and Mick: Uki didn't need to be a stop. It could be a stand.

* * *

By the time the big fire chased the evening chill, everyone had gathered. The river logs Mick and Gypsy dragged up made a loose circle, bark still holding the river's damp. Smoke curled into the dark, a thread of mud-sweet beneath the wood.

The market was kilometres behind but not yet out of mind. Voices sat low at first, half-thoughts folded between spoonfuls of Shelly's stew.

"You handled it well," Mick said to Gypsy, boots planted wide. "Could've gone sideways."

"David and Shelly handled it," Gypsy said. "I kept the billy hot." He watched the flames a moment. "But if blokes like that are riled in town, it won't stop there. Rand's name will be in their mouths."

"This land isn't his," Mick said, drawing a rough line in the dirt with a stick. "Or anyone's to take." He sketched a quick, rough map. "Beds here. Tanks there. Windbreak along this line. A place that doesn't move when pushed."

Gypsy's mouth tugged. "Mayor of Uki. Never thought I'd trade the road for a title."

"You're not," Mick said. "You're laying the road down so others can walk it."

Across the circle, Willow, Lisa, and Shay had settled on one blanket, shoulders close. Firelight threaded Lisa's hair. When she leaned in to say something, Shay's eyes tracked her movement like it was the most natural thing in the world. Willow tucked a strand behind Lisa's ear, her fingers lingering.

"You sure you're alright?" Willow asked quietly.

Lisa nodded, a shy smile catching. "I told you, I'm fine."

"She's fine," Shay echoed, tipping her hat back. "But I think you liked having an excuse to hold her up."

Willow laughed, bright and soft. "Maybe I did." The look she gave Lisa pressed everything unspoken into the small space between breaths.

Ryder leaned back, gaze drifting toward Gypsy and Mick. "If we're making this a place worth defending," he said, "we'll need more than gardens."

"Trust," Shay called, tapping her knee. "And numbers."

Mick nodded. "Both."

Sparks lifted and fell. Someone passed mugs of billy tea; Gypsy coaxed a few low chords; Willow hummed the third; Shay kept the rhythm with a light tap. The river spoke just beyond the dark, the night folding close.

Whatever waited down in Murwillumbah could stay there a while. Here, the circle held. Here, the fire was theirs — and the plan, still only lines in dirt and glances across flame, felt real enough to take root by morning.

45

Dawn came slow, washing soft gold over the treetops and turning the river into thin ribbons of light. Camp held its breath with the low hiss of cooling embers and the rustle of someone shifting under a blanket. From Shelly's corner came the first drift of tea-scent, threading across the clearing like a promise.

By the fire, Gypsy and Mick hunched over the coals, two silhouettes breathing steam into the morning. They didn't speak at first. When they did, it was in the quiet voices of men who had already said the loud parts elsewhere.

"He's an old mate," Mick said, tapping a charred stick into the glow. "Owns the block up to the bend. Never minded people staying a few nights. But this — this is different."

"Different's fine if it's solid," Gypsy replied, rubbing a palm over his jaw. "You reckon he'll go for it?"

"If I tell him it's for the right people, and I vouch for who stays, he'll listen." Mick's breath came pale in the cool. "I'll ride over in a few days. Face to face."

"No council. No leases. Just a handshake?" Gypsy asked.

"A handshake still means something here," Mick said.

Shelly appeared with mugs, hair tangled from sleep, expression steady. "And if the handshake goes south?"

"Then we make the most of what we've got," Mick said simply.

That settled the morning.

* * *

By mid-morning the light had warmed, eating away the last of the mist. Lisa laced her sandals, last night's smoke clinging faintly to her shirt. Willow arrived with a grin that meant trouble or shopping — sometimes both.

"We're heading into town," Willow said. "Coming?"

Shay joined them at the edge of camp, hat tipped against the sun, moving with that calm assurance that always suggested she knew more than she let on. Mick needed to check a delivery. They tagged along — an oddly glamorous little crew.

Uki's main street sloped gently past weatherboards and hand-painted signs. The place noticed who passed, even when pretending not to. Coffee and warm bread scented the air. A dog barked twice — tidy punctuation marks in the morning.

Mick's shop sat on the corner, windows half-hidden behind racks of hats, enamel mugs, and canvas bags. Inside smelled of leather and dust, cool and familiar. Mick stood behind the counter, pencil tucked over his ear, counting boxes.

"Have a poke around," he said. "If anyone asks, you're helping me stock."

Lisa sorted tea towels by colour; Willow tried on every hat with theatrical flair; Shay leaned against the counter, discussing delivery routes with Mick. Outside, the street flowed with glances — some warm, some weighing.

A woman with sun-lined eyes came in for flour and salt. She smiled at Mick, nodded at Shay, then let her gaze rest a little longer on the girls than politeness required.

"You girls in for long?" she asked.

"Just helping a friend," Shay replied easily.

The woman nodded once. "Then help him well."

Not every look was kind. Two young men drifted past the window with sharp eyes and hollow laughs, their attention hitching too long on Lisa and Willow. It carried a flicker of the market day. It stayed in Lisa's shoulders, even as she folded the last towel.

When they stepped back into the sun, Lisa walked close to Willow without thinking. Shay took the other flank — silent, steady — like someone who had been handed the watch without being asked.

* * *

Back at camp, the sweet smell rising from Shelly's tin over the coals said damper before anyone lifted the lid. Mick's truck had gone chasing another supplier. Gypsy looked up as the three returned.

"How's town?" he asked.

Lisa thought of the woman's soft nod, the boys' sharp eyes, the way the street seemed to lean in and wait.

"Watching," she said. "Waiting to see which way the wind blows."

Evening settled warm and syrup-thick along the ridge. Ryder and Gypsy mended a tarp in quiet discussion. The scent of Shelly's stew curled around the clearing.

Tyres sounded on the track.

Mick's ute rolled in, tray rattling. He killed the engine and took one long breath — the kind that came from crossing something you couldn't uncross. Gypsy met him halfway; the others drifted closer.

"Well?" Gypsy asked.

Mick let a careful smile show. "He'll hear us out."

A breath went through the group — loosening spines, easing shoulders.

"He?" Ryder asked.

"George Harvey," Mick said. "Soft spot for me. Curious about you. Wants to know more before he says yes."

"What more?" Lisa asked.

"That you're not trouble," Mick replied. "You'll look after the land. Keep the river clean. Not turn it into a circus."

"Too late for that," Willow murmured, earning a gentle laugh.

"It's a good chance," Mick added. "Still a chance. I'll take him damper tomorrow. And that quince jam Shelly's been hiding."

Gypsy's eyes brightened — that far-off planning look he got when an idea started drawing bones around itself.

"And if he says yes?"

"If he says yes," Mick said, glancing around, "this is yours as long as you treat it right."

It landed. The air shifted. Lisa felt Shay's hand brush her forearm — *Here. In this. With you.* Willow's gaze softened. Even Ryder's clenched jaw eased.

The fire was lit large that night. Stew filled enamel bowls. Talk grew at the edges: garden beds, rainwater tanks, a small music stage under the melaleucas. No one said the word, but they felt it — sanctuary. A seed rooting deeper.

* * *

Mick left before dawn the next morning, ute rumbling toward Harvey's property with Shelly's damper wrapped in a tea towel and quince jam beside it.

While Gypsy waited for news, he and Shelly took the Kombi into town for rope and brackets. Rain from the night before left the road damp; the world smelled green.

Uki had shifted.

Two police cars sat nose to nose in the centre strip, doors open. Locals clustered around. Under the pub verandah, a man in cuffs stood stone-still. Gypsy recognised him — one of Ryder's old mates. His face was blank, but his eyes found Gypsy's across the street and held them as if passing a warning.

"Don't stop," Shelly murmured.

Gypsy veered down a side lane and parked behind the hardware. They were heading for the back door when it opened.

An older man in a washed-thin flannel jerked his chin. "Best come in and sit a spell."

Inside smelled of nails and timber oil. He shut the door quietly.

"They're looking for folk like you," he said. "Heard 'em asking where your camp is. That bloke in cuffs? Didn't do a thing wrong far as I saw."

"Rand's people?" Gypsy asked.

The man lifted one shoulder. "You didn't hear it from me. Keep to the back lanes on your way out."

Shelly thanked him. Her face stayed calm; her eyes didn't.

* * *

Back at camp, the river threw light like silver coins. Willow sat cross-legged, weaving dyed twine. Lisa rinsed mugs in the shallows. David wandered down with hands in his pockets, watching the way sunlight stitched through her hair.

"You think you'll be ready for Surfers?" he asked softly.

Lisa tipped water from a mug. "You're ready to leave?"

"I'm ready if you are. After the other day... you might want a change of air."

"I like it here." Her gaze drifted toward the hidden track. "But Surfers would be fun. Different."

"Would you want Willow along?" he asked. "Stay in the van a while?"

Lisa looked to where Willow's shoulders glowed in the light. "Would you mind?"

"I want you happy," he said.

A kookaburra cracked the moment, laughing sharp from the paperbarks. David reached for her hand. She let him take it.

* * *

By late afternoon, whispers of the cuffs incident moved through camp in a low current. Ryder's mouth tightened. No one asked what he'd do about it. Everyone knew he would — if Gypsy asked.

The sun dipped behind the ridge. Mick was still gone.

They heard him before they saw him — the ute's low growl coming up the track. Heads turned. The river hushed.

Ryder rose first. Gypsy stayed still, listening.

The ute rolled into the clearing, headlights washing the logs before cutting out. Mick climbed out, brushing dust from his shirt, scanning faces like he was counting them home.

"Long day," he said. "Worth it."

He dropped a hessian sack beside the fire and crouched.

"George Harvey's got no problem with you here. Likes the idea if it's done right. Says the land could use care. He's no fan of Rand. Reckons more eyes on this side of the river are better."

Relief moved through the group like a breath.

"And the 'if'?" Gypsy asked.

"You keep it tidy," Mick said. "No fights. No parties spilling into town. Grow something useful. Make it look like it belongs."

Shelly nodded. "We can do that."

Mick looked to Ryder. "Means your mates too."

Ryder didn't blink. "They won't be trouble. Not if they've got a reason to stay."

The river murmured. Sparks climbed and fell.

"Then maybe this isn't a stopover," Gypsy said quietly, his voice settling like something nailed to the air. "Maybe this is the start."

The ripple through the group wasn't noise — it was depth.

Willow's fingers brushed Lisa's knee. Shay's gaze lingered, warm. David watched the flames and thought of futures he hadn't voiced.

Mick pulled a dark bottle from the sack. "Worth a drink," he said.

Tin cups passed hand to hand. Plans — still unspoken — gathered shape: gardens, tanks, a music stage, eyes on the track at dawn.

Above them, stars brightened. The fire held its glow. The river kept its counsel.

And under their feet, the idea they'd carried quietly all day sank roots — deeper than any of them expected.

46

Late morning drifted easy through the camp — that quiet lull between chores when the air hummed with insects and the smell of sun-warmed earth. Gypsy was under the tarp, mending a frayed camp chair. Shelly knelt beside her herb pots, humming as she trimmed. Willow lay in the grass on her stomach with a sketchbook open, drawing shapes only she could see.

A low engine began climbing the track. Not the heavy growl of a work truck or the sharp whine of a ranger's ute — something lighter, unhurried, curious. Down by the river, Ryder straightened from the garden bed. Shay didn't move, but her eyes opened beneath the brim of her hat.

The ute rolled to a stop between the two signs. The driver leaned out the window, reading the red plank first:

PRIVATE PROPERTY — KEEP OUT

Then glanced at Shay's hopeful blue scrawl beneath it:

TRAVELLERS WELCOME :)

"Well," he said to the passenger, "which one are we meant to believe?"

Ryder walked toward them, slow and deliberate. "Depends who's asking."

The passenger gave a short laugh. "Just looking for somewhere to park a few nights. Heard the stories about this mob down by the river."

"That mob's us," Ryder said.

"Right," the driver replied, eyes flicking between the two signs again. "So which one applies?"

Shay rose from the grass and stepped beside Ryder.

"If you're here to share the fire, lend a hand, and keep the peace — you're welcome," she said, calm as the river behind her. "If not, the red one's the sign to read."

The passenger smirked, testing the air. "Bit of a mixed message, isn't it?"

"Not if you've got the right eyes," Shay replied.

For a breath, the moment held its own temperature — warm, taut, deciding. Then the driver's fingers curled on the wheel.

"We're moving on."

He backed the ute in a spray of gravel and disappeared down the track.

Ryder watched the dust settle. "That's the trouble with two signs. Gives blokes like that time to think they can play you."

"Or time to show us who they are before they get too close," Shay said, tipping her hat.

From under the tarp, Gypsy's voice drifted out.

"She's right. Better to know at the gate."

The tension eased — though not completely. People drifted back to their tasks, but the signs seemed to stand taller now: sentries on the edge of whatever the Sanctuary was becoming.

* * *

The afternoon deepened into gold. Down the track, Ryder worked at the post, adjusting bolts with the patient focus of a man who'd finally found something worth defending. The red letters of his sign caught the last of the sun; Shay's blue message glowed beneath it, softer but no less sure.

Loose windows rattled before the vehicles appeared: a green-and-gold Kombi with faded paint and a cream panel van with a surfboard tied to the roof. Two dust-trailed travellers eased up the track. The Kombi stopped first, the wiry driver giving a tentative nod.

Before Ryder could speak, Chook wandered into view with a mug in hand, bare feet powdered in dust.

"Stand back, mate," he announced. "Official welcoming committee. Mayor Gypsy appointed me this morning. Says it's the law."

Ryder raised a brow. "Mayor Gypsy?"

"Yep," Chook said solemnly. "Told me my people skills are unmatched. Second only to my spoon skills."

The Kombi driver chuckled. The woman leaning out of the panel van — bright-eyed, curious, sun-kissed — grinned at the exchange.

Chook stepped boldly into the centre of the track.

"Interview time. Question one: do you like soup?"

The driver blinked. "Soup...?"

"Question two," Chook went on, waving his mug, "how many pegs do you own?"

The woman laughed. "Pegs?"

"Forget that one. Final question: do you know what a Pegasus is? 'Cause I do."

The driver grinned. "We mostly just wanted to camp."

"And the soup?" Ryder said, half-teasing, half-testing.

"Love it," the driver replied.

Ryder's posture eased. Shay, coming up from the river, nodded at her blue sign.

"If you can handle him," she said, tilting her head at Chook, "you'll fit in fine."

The Kombi rolled forward, the panel van behind it. Chook marched ahead like a parade marshal, firing stray questions over his shoulder as he went.

Ryder watched them go, shaking his head.

"Your sign's gonna make my life hell."

Shay smiled, small and sure.

"My sign just made your job easier."

* * *

That evening, the new arrivals settled with the ease of people who knew how to join a circle without pushing at its walls. The Kombi driver introduced himself as Theo — a muso with a battered guitar and a smile shaped by too many sunsets. The woman from the panel van gave her name as Kirra — lively, sharp, with the grounded calm of someone who'd slept under enough open skies.

They brought energy like fresh air, and the camp absorbed it without effort.

Theo strummed gentle road songs while Kirra tapped a tambourine against her palm. When Gypsy asked, "What brought you down this way?" the two travellers exchanged a look that carried miles.

"We went to Byron first," Theo said. "Looking for your mob."

"Didn't find you," Kirra added, "but everyone was talking about you. Some said you were smart to get out before things got heavy. One bloke at the bakery said, 'If you're meant to find 'em, you will.' So... we kept going."

"Found a few markers along the way," Theo said, nodding toward the track. "That blue sign of yours helped."

Shay smiled. "Knew it would."

Rumours thickened with the dark — Byron camps broken up, police asking questions, Rand's name muttered like a warning. But none of it dulled the easy warmth of the fire circle forming around the night.

People laughed. Shared food. Shared stories. Shared songs. Theo's guitar carried the dark; Kirra's voice threaded through it in soft, sure harmony. Smoke curled upward, catching sparks as if the stars were listening.

By the time the fire sank to embers, the Sanctuary had grown by two more hearts — and the rumours from the highway had found their home.

They weren't just travellers anymore. They were the mob that didn't break.

47

The sun came up soft, dripping gold through the gum leaves. Mist clung low along the river, curling around ankles at the water's edge. A butcherbird's flute-bright call made the valley feel older than the people waking inside it.

Breakfast spread where it landed. Mugs warmed hands around the fire. Someone stretched under an awning. Theo sat cross-legged on an upturned crate, rolling a cigarette with patient fingers while Marla tore pieces from a warm slab of damper.

Shay handed Theo an enamel mug.

"So — what's really happening in Byron?"

Theo exhaled a thin ribbon of smoke. "Rand's name's everywhere. Didn't see him, but we saw what he leaves behind — camps broken up overnight, people drifting out with whatever they can grab."

Marla nodded. "It's not just beaches now. He's been knocking on shop doors — asking who's selling to hippies, who's letting them use the toilets. People are scared to look too friendly."

"That's new," Shelly murmured.

"In Mullum," Theo went on, "a bloke got pulled up for walking with a guitar. Called it a 'move along'. Looked more like a warning."

Ryder leaned forward on his knees. "What kind of warning?"

"That you're not wanted," Marla said simply. "Not anywhere he can reach."

Gypsy kept his eyes on the fire. "Which makes this place worth holding."

Mick strode in from the track, brushing dust from his palms. "Landowner's still warm to the idea. I'll get a word next week. But if Rand's sniffing around, we'll need more than a handshake."

Theo looked around the camp. "Word is — if Rand wants to find you, he will. But so will the right ones. We found you because someone wanted us to. That's something."

A quiet settled. Not fearful — thoughtful, like everyone was turning over the same idea.

Ryder broke it first. "Then we make sure the right ones keep finding us — and the wrong ones don't."

Shay smiled softly. "That's what the signs are for."

No one disagreed.

* * *

Work began without being named. Under the tarp, Mick, Gypsy and Ryder bent over a rough sketch of the camp, marking ideas with scrap wood and cooling mugs of coffee.

Mick tapped a dry rise of ground. "Soil's good here. Plant this patch and we'll feed ourselves through summer without running to town every week."

Ryder drew a slow line in the dirt. "And here — slow the track. Not a gate. Logs. Enough to make cars idle down so we meet them before they roll in."

"This isn't just about keeping Rand out," Gypsy said, stretching his arms behind his head. "It's about making this ours. A sanctuary. Somewhere people can stop running."

"Then we'd better help Harvey see it the same way," Mick replied.

They fell into rhythm — garden beds marked, a stronger cook shelter planned, sleeping areas settling into the natural windbreak. Even Ryder, who preferred nails to drawings, sketched a pattern that looked like something that could last.

* * *

Shay, Willow and Lisa took Mick's ute into town with the windows down, warm road dust spiralling behind them. The shopping list was short — fruit, bread, a handful of bolts for Gypsy's chair — but the errand mattered.

Being seen mattered.

The square hummed low and steady. A few stallholders waved — friendly, but careful not to show too much of it. Willow made straight for a stack of mangoes; Lisa followed, amused; Shay moved at her unhurried pace, taking in the looks and shifts.

Their bags were nearly full when a sharp whistle cut across the street. Two young blokes leaned on a ute, smirks ready.

Heat rose in Lisa's cheeks. Willow flashed a blinding grin and blew an exaggerated, glamorous kiss. The smirks cracked, then dissolved into awkward laughter.

Shay didn't speak. She simply looked — head tilted, gaze steady. A look that weighed a person and wrote the answer quietly.

The boys dropped their eyes first.

Lisa let out a surprised, shy laugh. Without meaning to, the trio had already moved into their shape — Willow's spark, Shay's calm, Lisa's softness — three corners of the same grounded circle.

"Come on," Shay said, tipping her hat. "We've better things to do than tutor the youth of Uki."

* * *

When they returned, stakes already marked out a broad rectangle where the garden would grow. Talk shifted easily — vegetables, mangoes, gate posts, whistles. Willow animated the story; Lisa rolled her eyes through smiles; Shay's amusement stayed in her eyes.

"Sounds like the town's still mostly with us," Gypsy said.

"For now," Mick replied. "Let's keep it that way."

The afternoon warmed again. Dust lifted in soft plumes. The Kombi returned from Murwillumbah with Theo's guitar case and Marla carrying a wrapped parcel.

"You should've let me send coins with you," Shelly said.

Theo shook his head. "We pulled our weight. Busked a bit. Not much, but enough to buy meat and a shirt or two."

Marla laughed. "Got a few stares. Friendly — but the kind that says people are talking."

"What kind of talking?" Gypsy asked.

"Rand," she said. "Two blokes at the butcher reckon he's sniffing further into the valley. Say it's only a matter of time before he pokes at Uki."

Theo added, "An old fella said the police asked about camps nearby. Didn't say your name — but he didn't have to."

The news moved through the camp like a slow ripple. Expected, but still cold on the skin.

* * *

David and Lisa slipped to the river while it settled. The water was cool and clear, stones smooth underfoot. Lisa waded out, then leaned back and floated, hair drifting around her.

David skimmed stones. "You want to leave here when we go to Surfers? Not come back?"

"Only if you want me to," she replied, eyes on the sky. "I like it here. Surfers will be different."

A small smile touched her lips. "Think Willow would fit in the Kombi with us?"

David laughed. "Willow fits anywhere she wants."

Upstream, Shay and Willow scrubbed clothes in the bend, skirts and singlets swirling in the shallows. Willow wrung a shirt out and slung it across a branch, hair sticking damp to her shoulders.

"You ever stay this long in one place?" she asked.

"Not lately," Shay said. "But this... feels needed."

* * *

Back near the firepit, Gypsy crouched with a stick, drawing rectangles and lines — paths, small huts, a shaded square.

"If Harvey says yes," he said to Ryder, "we'll put up two proper shelters. Tin roof. Weatherboards if town's got 'em spare. Dry when the rains hit."

Ryder nodded. "And a proper cool box. Fewer meat runs."

Gypsy grinned. "Now you're talking."

Night pooled across the ridge, warm and slow. The fire was fed thicker logs. Theo played until his fingers ached; Marla's voice threaded into the dark as if it had always belonged there. The news from Murwillumbah stayed close but didn't smother the evening.

The river murmured. Out on the track, the two signs — red warning, blue welcome — stood in the dark like twin truths side by side.

And the camp, wide-circled and warm, felt one quiet breath closer to becoming the place its people already believed it could be.

48

Uki woke to the hum of market day — utes and vans bumping into the gravel car park, stallholders calling greetings across the square, and the faint thump of a bass line from someone's portable speaker. The air was already warm, touched with frying onions, fresh bread, and the earthy lift of last night's rain steaming from the ground.

The Sanctuary folk arrived the way they always did: all at once, but never in a line.

Gypsy carried a box of carved trinkets, Shelly balanced baskets of macramé and beaded jewellery, and Lisa's arms overflowed with new woven belts. Shay and Willow trailed behind, chatting with a pair of locals who'd wandered over to ask where they'd come from.

By mid-morning their stall was a swirl of colour and movement. Lisa tied a bracelet around a child's wrist while Shelly haggled good--naturedly with a couple from Nimbin. Shay adjusted a hanging display so the sun caught the beads just right, coins chiming steadily into the tin. Across the way, Theo and Kirra had claimed a corner for music —

Theo with his guitar, Marla with a tambourine — and people drifted toward the rhythm like moths to light.

Then Chook appeared.

No one saw from where — one moment the space beside Marla was empty, the next it was full of Chook's wild energy and borrowed tambourine. He spun, stomped, and grinned like a man half-possessed, the crowd clapping along as if they'd known him for years.

By the third song he'd slipped into a full-blown performance, channelling Thomlin with arms thrown wide.

"Gather round, good folk of Uki!" he bellowed. "The road is long, the bread is warm, and the tambourine is your passport to joy!"

Laughter rolled through the square. Willow doubled over, half-delighted, half-panicked, and grabbed his arm.

"You're going to get us thrown out!"

"Thrown out?!" Chook gasped, hand to his chest. "No, my darling — I shall depart... in a flourish!"

He whirled away, tambourine rattling, cheers following him down the path.

* * *

The rest of the market unfolded in the same loose, sunlit rhythm. More travellers than usual drifted through — barefoot, sun-browned, guitar straps slung across backs, trading baskets of bread, jars of jam, patchwork quilts. Pot smoke curled unnoticed through the air. By late afternoon the Sanctuary's stall was half empty and the coin tin heavy.

Lisa leaned against Shelly, flushed and glowing. "We have to come back next week."

Shelly scanned the square — the lingering clusters, the newcomers setting up camp chairs, the familiar ones staying longer than they used to. "Feels like more are settling here. Not just us anymore."

Shay watched a young couple unloading a Kombi across the street. "Looks like Uki's on its own magical mystery tour."

For once, no one minded being swept along.

* * *

The drive back to the Sanctuary felt different — a small procession winding through the trees. A few new vans followed at a distance, curious to see where the laughter and music had come from. By the time the fire burned low that night, they'd joined the circle without fuss, passing bottles of ginger wine, sharing hand-rolled smokes, and settling in as easily as if they'd been expected.

Theo played the same tune he'd riffed at the market; the notes threaded with the smell of mango and woodsmoke. Chook, triumphant, retold the tale of his "performance", each version bigger than the last. People sprawled along logs, cross-legged on blankets, or down by the riverbank where the moon danced on the ripples.

Gypsy watched it for a while — the scatter of small groups, the murmur of overlapping conversations, the comfort of it all. It was loose, alive, exactly the kind of night he trusted most. And underneath, something settled into shape.

A plan.

He found Mick on the step of his van, a cup of tea steaming between his palms. Gypsy sat beside him, stretching long legs into the dirt.

"Mick," he said quietly. "I reckon it's time."

Mick raised an eyebrow. "Time for what?"

"Time to put it on paper. From Harland. Written approval. Not just to stay — to build. Maybe clear a small space. Six huts at most. Keep people dry when the rains come."

Mick took a long, considering sip. "You start putting up walls, Gypsy, you're talking about making rules."

"I don't want rules," Gypsy said quickly. "Just a rhythm. We promised no cars near the river, no oil in the water, fires only in the pit. If we set the tone early, it'll stay good. I've seen places go bad when no one bothered."

Mick's grin tilted wry. "You're talking like the man."

Gypsy smirked. "I don't want to be the man. But if wearing the hat means this place outlives us, I'll wear it for a while."

They sat in easy silence, listening to the laughter rising from the firelight. Willow's voice teased Chook; Shelly's laugh chimed warm; Shay leaned close to Lisa, both faces lit by the small, private glow of deepening friendship.

After a moment Mick nodded. "Alright. I'll see him tomorrow. If he's in a good mood, we'll have something written by week's end."

Gypsy exhaled, long and satisfied. "Good. I've got the shape of it in my head. And these people..."

He lifted a hand toward the firelight — the tribe, his tribe. "They're worth building for."

The sky deepened and stars opened above the ridge. The camp hummed soft around them — music, laughter, the murmur of the river. Something landed inside Gypsy, quiet and solid.

They'd given him a tribe. He'd give them a home.

49

The ute rolled into camp just after lunch, its engine note lifting heads from shade and work alike. Mick climbed down with a slow, easy smile — the kind that gave half the answer before he spoke.

"Well?" Gypsy called from the fire pit, a half-mended chair across his knees.

"We've got it," Mick said. "Harland's on board — so long as we keep to what we promised. No cars near the river, no big trees cut, and he wants a rough sketch of the clearing before a single post goes in."

A cheer rose around the circle. Theo struck a bright chord; Kirra rattled the tambourine in a triumphant flourish. Gypsy stood, rubbing his beard like he could already feel the shape of the place forming beneath his hands.

"Right then. We start tomorrow. Two main huts near the heart, quieter ones tucked back. A proper cooking shelter. Garden beds where the soil gets the first sun. People need space, not crowding. This isn't about walls — it's about the camp holding when the rains come."

Shay tipped her hat back, a warm, knowing smile touching the corner of her mouth. Willow was already whispering to Lisa about bead curtains and blankets. Ryder folded his arms and gave a curt nod.

"I'll peg the boundary," he said. "No wheels past the line."

"Good," Gypsy replied, "but don't scare off the right sort. Travellers who match the rhythm stay welcome."

The mood climbed like smoke through the gums. Jobs paired themselves off without instruction: Ryder hauling fallen limbs to the edge of the proposed clearing; Shay and Lisa walking the riverbend, marking safe water draws; Willow sorting market takings and peeling off coins for shared supplies. A few of the newer faces hovered nearby — offering hands, passing billy tea, fetching rope — easing into the shape of things without disturbing it.

By late afternoon the air smelled of sap, dust, and woodsmoke, humming with the sound of people who knew they were beginning something that could last.

* * *

Morning broke bright and sharp on the first day of the clearing. Mist lifted off the river in slow white ribbons as Gypsy stood with a stick in the dirt and a semicircle of listeners at his feet.

"Main huts here," he said, tracing lines with his boot. "Quieter huts under those gums. Cooking shelter on the lee side so the wind doesn't steal our heat. Three fire pits — not one big one every night. People need their own pockets."

Ryder hammered stakes while Mick ran twine between them. Shelly ferried buckets and bandannas, her steady hands keeping the workers cool. Axes and saws thudded through the clearing, though only deadfall came down; not a single living tree was touched. The work felt less like building and more like revealing something the land had already been holding.

The first fire-pit ring lasted five minutes before dissolving into play. Lisa leaned in with a stick to tidy the edge. Shay nudged her with a boot. Chaos bloomed. Lisa squealed, dodging through the dust, laughter spilling in bright bursts. Shay set her hat on a stump like a declaration of war and chased her until Lisa surrendered, breathless and glowing.

Across the clearing, Willow sprang onto Ryder's back without warning. He grunted, kept walking, and muttered something that made her bend double with laughter.

Theo strummed between tasks; Kirra tapped a tin can for rhythm. Chook wandered with his pocket knife and philosophy.

"Triangle fire pits," he declared to no one in particular. "Future of civilisation."

No one disagreed strongly enough to stop him.

By lunchtime the first corners of the Sanctuary had taken shape. A square of posts marked the cooking shelter. Two larger frames rose near the heart like the ribs of something waking. Three smaller frames waited in the shade for their woven walls. A wide circle of river stones promised the first hearth, with two more cleared and ready for kindling.

* * *

Two days later the rough plan lived in the ground.

Main huts: twin frames near the heart, one already thatched with plaited fronds — the storm shelter for people passing through. **Quiet huts:** three small frames under the big gums. Lisa and David had claimed one, threading a curtain of beads. Willow had the hut beside them but drifted between both as if gravity insisted. Shay claimed nothing and everything — sleeping wherever the night settled her. **Cooking shelter:** four posts and a sturdy roof frame under Mick's watch. Ryder had made the earth beneath it level and true. **Fire pits:**

river, heart, and back — each ringed in stone, each stacked with dry kindling.

Ryder carved markers — MAIN HUT, RIVER PIT — plain, sturdy. Later, beneath one of them, a little plank appeared with blue paint and a hand-drawn grin:

TRAVELLERS WELCOME

Shay's counterpoint to Ryder's hard-edged red **KEEP OUT** at the gate.

A boundary and an invitation. The Sanctuary in two signs.

People breathed easier. The unease of the week before eased to a steady watchfulness. Someone planted a herb bed; rosemary scented the shade. Tea mugs were swapped, stories shared, tools borrowed and returned with a nod.

Sunset draped gold across the river the first night the new fire pit was lit. Shay crouched low, coaxing the flame until it caught and held. The river whispered, cicadas rising in a soft, persistent choir.

Two logs formed a rough half-circle. Willow spread a blanket. Lisa curled her hands around a mug. David sat at her feet, leaning back on his palms, letting the light soak into him.

Further along, Theo tuned his guitar; Kirra tapped her tambourine. Ryder and Mick murmured over rafters. Shay lowered her hat as if coaxing sleep closer.

"Not bad for a first run," she murmured.

Someone said, "It feels closer here," and it did — the river gathering the world tight around them.

Lisa brushed Willow's shoulder; Willow laughed softly. David watched them with calm acceptance, learning something gentler about belonging. Theo slipped into a wandering tune. Conversation thinned to embers. The fire breathed in slow, steady pulses.

By the time the flames settled low, the river was a silver ribbon in the dark. One by one, people drifted toward the track — Lisa and Willow walking close, hands brushing; David a few steps behind, content; Shay wandering slow, eyes on the stars.

"This is the sort of night people spend their whole lives trying to return to," she said.

At the top of the rise, the glow of the main fire greeted them — laughter, mugs, Theo and Kirra weaving a tune, Chook's tambourine defiantly off-beat.

They stepped into the light like it had been waiting. Because it had.

The Sanctuary was no longer an idea. It was a shape in timber and grass, a promise in the dirt, a place choosing to become itself.

And this night — warm, bright, alive — felt less like a pause and more like the beginning of everything.

50

Morning unfolded soft and slow, first light slipping through gum leaves in thin gold threads. Mist clung low over the river, drifting into camp like it wasn't quite ready to leave the night behind.

A few early risers moved with the quiet ease of people who knew how to share space. Mick was already at the cooking shelter, the kettle hissing over coals. The scent of tea mingled with damp green earth.

Shay sat on a low log near the riverbank, hat tipped back, weaving a length of cord without looking — fingers working by instinct. She gave a slow, morning-true smile when the others wandered out, the kind that said she'd been awake long enough to know what sort of day it was going to be.

Lisa and Willow emerged barefoot, hair sleep-tangled, Willow talking with her hands while Lisa nodded through the last haze of dreams. David followed with three enamel mugs, passing them out before taking his own. Ryder stood beneath his red-letter sign — **PRIVATE**

PROPERTY – KEEP OUT — arms folded, eyes narrowed along the track as though expecting it to blink first.

Mick joined Gypsy by the fire.

"Heard Rand's been seen up Murwillumbah way again," he said quietly. "Asking who's camped out this side of the river."

Gypsy's easy grin thinned. "We won't panic. Just keep an ear to the ground."

Shay didn't lift her head. "We'll hear him before we see him."

Breakfast found its natural rhythm — toast browned on metal forks, slices of tomato, leftover eggs from the last market. Laughter rose easily, though underneath something had tightened. A thread pulled, but didn't snap.

* * *

Mid-morning brought the sound that shifted everything — the steady, deliberate rumble of an engine heading up the track.

A dusty Land Rover ute emerged through the trees. A blue heeler trotted beside it, tongue lolling. The man behind the wheel looked to be in his sixties — sun-cut, weather-carved — his hat held together by a strip of twine, the brim patched more times than remembered.

The camp went still. People straightened. Ryder folded his arms tighter. Gypsy and Mick stepped forward without speaking.

The man climbed down, boots scuffing dirt. His gaze swept the clearing — the huts, the neat lines, the small garden beds, the clean sweep of the river shining between trunks.

"You must be Mick," he said.

"That's me," Mick replied, offering his hand. "And this is Gypsy."

Harland — because there was no one else he could be — shook with a grip firm enough to settle dust.

"You've been busy," he said.

"We've got good hands," Gypsy replied.

Harland opened the ute's passenger door and pulled out a folded sheaf of papers, edges dirt-smudged from the drive.

"Let's make sure those hands have reason to stay steady."

Under the shade of a broad gum, the ute's bonnet became a desk. The camp drew closer — not crowding, just forming a quiet, hopeful circle around the three men.

Harland spoke in the voice of someone who understood the weight of both yes and no.

"Ten years," he said. "You can put up your huts. They stay on the land — no selling, no owning. No rent. No fees. Gardens are fine. If you've extra, drop some at my place."

He paused, meeting Gypsy's eyes with clean, uncompromised intent.

"Smoke what you want, but don't grow it. Don't trade it. I won't have this turning into trouble — for you or me."

Gypsy nodded once, slow and sure. "Fair terms."

Harland signed. Then Mick. Then Gypsy — careful strokes, as if carving the promise rather than writing it.

A heartbeat of silence held.

Then a ripple moved through the group — relief, awe, a quiet brightening that didn't need words.

Willow let out a triumphant whoop and grabbed Lisa, spinning her in a half-dance. Lisa laughed and folded into David's arms; his shoulders finally loosened, as though someone had cut a rope he'd been hauling for weeks. Chook clapped like he'd orchestrated the entire negotiation.

Shay's weaving paused mid-knot. She didn't cheer, but her slow nod radiated a pride that made the others feel it too.

* * *

Then came the moment that sealed it — not the signing, but what happened after.

One by one, almost unconsciously, they looked toward each other:

Lisa to Willow.

Willow to Shay.

Shay to Shelly.

Shelly to Mick.

Mick to Gypsy.

Small smiles. Quiet nods. A recognition shared.

They weren't just living here. They belonged.

Everyone smiled — except Ryder, who muttered, "'Bout bloody time," and kicked the dirt to hide the grin creeping up his cheek.

Harland folded the papers, whistled for his dog, and climbed into the ute.

"Keep it tidy," he said.

"We will," Mick replied.

The ute rumbled down the track, swallowed by trees.

The clearing rested in stillness — the engine fading, the lease in Mick's hands like a heartbeat. Gypsy inhaled slowly, grounding himself in the moment.

"We need a new sign," he said at last.

Shay raised an eyebrow. "Another one?"

"The Sanctuary."

Ryder groaned, already heading for the entrance. "Another bloody sign. Place'll end up looking like the Hume Highway."

Shay's smile warmed. "I think it fits."

And it did.

Perfectly.

As if the name had been waiting under bark and roots and riverwater — waiting for them to earn it.

And now,
finally,
they had.

51

By late afternoon, the mood in camp had turned loose and electric.

News had travelled faster than the river itself: they weren't just safe here — they belonged.

That truth lifted voices, lightened steps, and settled something bright in the air that felt a little like freedom.

Theo and Marla tuned their instruments beside the main fire pit, sharp twangs skipping across the clearing like sparks hunting places to land. Chook arrived beating a borrowed tambourine with missionary zeal, wearing a floppy felt hat that drooped over one eye like it was too tired to remember its own story.

Ryder set a crate of longnecks beside the kindling — Tooheys, Resch's — the bottles clinking like cutlery at a backyard wedding.

"Don't say I never bring anything," he muttered, already twisting off a cap.

A jar of plum wine made a slow, mischievous circuit — sweet, faintly dangerous. Willow took a swig, winced, and laughed. Lisa coughed into her wrist, then laughed harder. Someone sparked a joint; the sweet curl drifted through the clearing like incense from a church that worshipped rivers and gum trees.

Shay accepted her turn with a small nod, eyes tilted to the sky as the last blue washed into copper. She exhaled slow — like she was sending a quiet blessing to the first stars.

Music gathered around the fire. Theo and Marla's harmonies braided clean with Gypsy's guitar. Hands met the beat. Feet found their own. Voices rose into choruses like homing birds returning to a place they didn't know they'd missed.

Chook danced a wild, stomping jig until Shay launched her hat with sniper precision. It struck him square on the forehead. His theatrical, wounded bow set half the camp howling.

When the songs fell into a softer pocket, Gypsy stood — bottle lifted in the glow.

He didn't give a speech. He didn't need to.

"To the Sanctuary," he said.

The cheer cracked open something deep and golden. Bottles knocked. Arms slung over shoulders. Someone tried to start a chant that dissolved into more singing. Even Ryder — doing his evening watch near the entrance — let a grin slip before dragging his beer up to hide it.

"Bloody Sanctuary," he muttered. Not unhappily. Not even close.

The night widened — dancing in flame-flicker, quiet confessions at the river's edge, laughter with no sharp edges and no reason to stop.

For a few hours, it felt as if the world had made room for them — and liked what it saw.

* * *

Camp woke like a tide rolling in.

Smoke lifted from the main fire pit in lazy threads — part gum, part last night's herbs. Empty bottles stood in irregular ranks, catching the early sun like glass soldiers trying to remember their orders.

Lisa padded out of the van wearing one of David's shirts, hair mussed, smile soft and slow. The hem brushed her thighs as she stretched. She walked toward the water with a tin mug, still half-dream.

Down at the river, Willow knelt rinsing her hair, skirt hitched, morning sun warm on her shoulders.

"Morning, sunshine," she croaked, voice rough from plum wine and singing.

Shay passed with the last of the billy tea, apparently immune to smoke, wine, chaos, and sleep deprivation alike. She tipped her hat.

"You two drank like you were on shore leave," she teased, dry as the riverbed in drought.

Chook bellowed from somewhere behind them, holding a tambourine above his head like a captured relic.

"Whose bloody instrument is this? It's stolen my soul!"

Ryder groaned beneath his red-letter sign, muttering about locking every instrument in a shed and throwing away the key.

At the cooking shelter, Mick leaned close to Gypsy as he wiped down guitar strings.

"Bloke at the servo says strangers were asking where the music came from last night," he murmured. "Might be friends. Might not."

Gypsy's expression didn't shift, but his shoulders tightened. "Rand?"

"Could be," Mick said. "Word travels quicker than we do."

But even with the warning, the camp held its brightness.

Theo and Marla played soft, morning-gentle strings. Shelly browned bread in a pan with the kind of pride that comes from feeding people who matter. Willow braided Lisa's hair with slow, careful fingers. Shay, seated nearby, plaited another length of cord — the beginnings of a hanger for a sign the camp didn't know it needed yet.

Something had gone into the ground the night before. And it had taken root. Not loudly. Not with fanfare. But with certainty — the way a seed knows which way is down and which way is light.

52

Heat rose early, ripening metal and patience. Gypsy and Mick tied down a tray of hand saws, nail boxes, cut lengths of timber, a coil of rope, and a tin of paint.

"Want frames up before summer proper," Mick said, cinching a knot. "Shade's worth gold in January."

"And before Christmas," Gypsy added. "No one sleeping under stars unless they choose to."

The truck rattled toward Murwillumbah, dust unfurling behind it like a banner.

* * *

They took the ute into Uki at an easy pace — Lisa, Shay, and Willow with baskets and bare shoulders, sunlight loose in their hair. The square smelled of warm bread, orange peel, and rain steaming from the earth.

Six travellers leaned along the general-store rail — two women, four men, denim washed to memory, eyes bright from the road.

One pushed his fringe aside. "You know a bloke called Gypsy?"

Shay's smile stayed small. "We might."

A copper-haired girl stepped forward. "We heard there's a place by the river folk are calling the Sanctuary. We've been looking since Byron. People said if you find it, you'll know you're in the right place."

Willow tipped her head, grin slow and sharp. "You're in luck, darlings. We're heading that way."

She jerked her thumb toward David's kombi, parked crooked near the bakery. "Room for four easy."

Lisa shot her a look that carried no heat. "You can't keep volunteering his kombi."

"Can't I?" Willow said, already herding newcomers with a wink. "We're all going to Surfers soon. Good rehearsal for travelling cosy."

* * *

By the time Gypsy and Mick rolled back into camp with the hardware, the kombi was easing into the clearing with Willow riding shotgun, Lisa at the wheel, and the newcomers spilling out like kids at camp.

Gypsy met Shay's look. She lifted one shoulder. "Word's travelling," she said, as if reporting the weather.

Shelly drew a pot of stew closer to their swags without ceremony. The main fire threw light up the trunks; tea-tree sweetened the air. Theo dropped into a soft rhythm under the talk until Gypsy leaned forward, elbows on knees.

"You've found the Sanctuary," he said. "What's the road been like?"

Rowan — tall, tattered denim, voice rasped by dust — began. "Byron was beautiful. Cops sniffing around. We slept by the dunes and some bloke in a ute told us to move before we were made to. Same thing in Brunswick Heads."

Jessie, the copper-haired girl, took over. "At a roadhouse, two fellas talked about a cop in Murwillumbah — Rand. Sounds like he's set on clearing out anyone who doesn't fit his picture of 'local.'"

Ryder's jaw locked — a small, steady muscle ticking like a warning.

Jessie lowered her voice. "A bloke at a servo said there's a camp up here that looks after its own. Said, 'If you find Gypsy, tell him the world's getting smaller for people like you.'"

The words settled like ash — light, but weighty where they landed.

Willow chose that moment to snatch Chook's tambourine. "Well, if we're a sanctuary," she declared, "we should sound like one."

Theo lifted the tempo; Marla's honey-warm voice threaded through; palms found the beat.

The newcomers slipped into the circle as though they'd been expected all along.

* * *

From the track's mouth, you could see a new world stitching itself together.

Ryder's stark

PRIVATE PROPERTY — KEEP OUT

glared from the post, red paint sharp.

Nailed beneath it, cheerful and defiant, hung Shay's board:

Travellers Welcome :)

Someone had scratched a peace sign beside it. A daisy bloomed under the smile.

Two truths.

One story.

* * *

The track smelled of sawdust by the time camp came into view. In the main clearing, Gypsy and Mick crouched over a half-framed hut, arguing amiably about rafters. The steady thunk of hammer on nail kept a reliable rhythm.

Nearby, Rowan and Ryder split posts side by side — Rowan quick with jokes, Ryder answering with the kind of grunt that passed for approval. When Rowan managed a clean split, Ryder gave him a single curt nod — small, but real, a tiny spark of respect between two men who didn't waste words on friendship.

Along the gums, Shelly and Jessie worked in a patch of shade, a ply-and-crate bench between them. The hum of Shelly's hand-crank machine blended with Jessie's soft chatter.

A few paces away, Willow knelt with a paint tin, brushing the new doorframe sea-green. Lisa dipped her brush, then flicked a speck of colour at Willow.

Willow gasped in theatrical outrage. Lisa tried for innocence and failed, laughter bright on her lips.

Willow retaliated with a dab to her forearm, and for a moment they were children painting on summer concrete. Lisa's smile softened — private, glowing — a small memory she'd tuck away like a pressed flower.

Shay passed by, catching the scene, her mouth tipping in knowing amusement. Willow caught her watching and flashed a grin that said *oh, I know.*

Down the river path, Theo carried sloshing buckets while Marla padded behind him, guitar over her shoulder. Halfway to the bend, Chook had opened an impromptu lemon-tea stall on a crate.

"Cleans the soul," he promised, pouring steaming mugs like sacraments.

At the far edge, mown grass gave way to scrub where the first communal beds took shape. Shay worked a hoe with slow, even strokes, skirt knotted at the hip. Jessie suggested pumpkins along the borders, beans inside.

"Something quick," Shay said. "So people see we mean to stay."

Mick's truck tray sat open nearby, overflowing with seed sacks and lengths of cane for trellises.

* * *

By sundown, the frames had real form — four walls here, a roof beam there; a door hung on borrowed hinges that squeaked like a friendly bird.

Smoke drifted back toward camp.

Stew bubbled.

Bread was cut thick.

And Chook — in spectacular falsetto — performed what he insisted was Thomlin reciting poetry.

People ended the day sun-warmed and sweat-salted, smiling the way people do when something exists because their hands decided it would.

The Sanctuary wasn't a camp anymore. It was a village remembering its own name.

As bowls scraped clean and songs thinned to murmurs, Mick found Gypsy by the tool heap.

"Servo talk says strangers were listening last night," he said quietly. "Friends, maybe. Maybe not. If Rand wants to find us, he will."

Gypsy looked across the clearing — at the frames, at the braided hair, at painted doors, at the river pits glowing.

"At least the right ones are finding us too," he said. "And the wrong ones... they'll read the sign that applies to them."

Ryder rechecked both boards at the entrance, as though balance could be measured by eye. He ran his thumb over the smiley face and muttered,

"Too many bloody signs."

Shay stepped beside him, gaze on the track. "Just enough," she said. "So people know what we are before they step into the firelight."

He didn't argue.

The river moved in the dark, steady as breath. Somewhere beyond the ridge, a car door slammed and a dog barked twice — the world continuing, as it always does.

But here, the village gathered its warmth close and kept building.

53

The morning broke clean and gold, sunlight spilling through the gums as though it had been saving itself for this very day. The smell of fresh-cut timber clung to the clearing, threaded with sap and the faint ghost of last night's fire. Everywhere, colour and motion stirred.

The new huts stood proud — some brushed sea-green, others washed in sun-soft blues, and a few left bare so the warm grain caught the light like something alive. Narrow tracks had already worn themselves into the grass: river to firepit, hut to garden, garden to track.

Paths that only appear when a place stops being temporary.

Gypsy stood with a mug of tea, watching it all unfold like something he had once dreamed but never quite expected to touch.

* * *

Mid-morning brought a familiar hum from the track — not strangers, not wanderers following rumours, but Uki locals returning with easy smiles. Drawn by last night's music. Drawn by the glow of lanterns drifting up the ridge. Drawn by curiosity that didn't feel like suspicion.

Old Harry from the general store ambled in first, a bundle of newspaper for kindling under one arm and three battered paperbacks under the other.

"Thought you lot might like these," he said. "Music carried down the creek last night. Sounded like a good crowd."

Margaret from the bakery followed soon after, brushing flour from her cheek, offering a tray of still-warm buns.

"Too many hands here to be hungry," she declared. "And too many stories coming out of this valley not to drop in."

By late morning a pair of mechanics from the pub's darts team rolled up with a shy grin and a bag of old nails.

"Found these in the shed," one mumbled. "Figure you mob could use 'em more than we can."

No flourish, no fuss — just neighbours offering what they had.

And with every gesture, the Sanctuary sank deeper roots into the valley.

* * *

By midday the camp had relaxed into a soft, festival-warm rhythm. Someone laid a plank across two stumps for a makeshift table; Shelly draped a bright cloth over it without breaking conversation. Marla tuned her guitar while Theo followed with a companion rhythm on a tin.

The air tasted of bread, eucalyptus, sun-warmed grass... and something gentler.

Acceptance.

Ryder checked a new roof beam, nodding once when Rowan managed a clean split on the posts beside him. Willow passed him with a wink sharp enough to shave bark. He answered with a grunt that was, unmistakably, a laugh trying not to be seen.

Down by the river, Lisa and David chased each other into the warm current — her laughter bright and high, his low and surprised every time she outran him. Willow hummed nearby, toes in the shallows, while Shay perched cross-legged on a sun-warmed rock, guitar in her lap, watching it all with a quiet, contented awareness.

From the bank it shimmered:

the huts rising behind them,

music at the centre,

the river flickering with the afternoon's last gold.

The land felt like it had taken a long breath... and finally let it go.

* * *

By dusk, lanterns bloomed in doorways — soft pools of honey-light gathering under eaves. Someone pressed a cold beer into Gypsy's hand as he walked through the clearing, pausing every few steps to answer a question, admire a rafter, or simply listen to the low, happy hum of people building something together.

He stood by the firepit — the heart pit — where embers pulsed like a slow drumbeat. Across the circle, faces glowed in the gathering dark: Willow braiding Lisa's hair; David stacking kindling; Shay tuning a quiet chord; Shelly setting out bowls; Ryder fixing a hinge even now; newcomers laughing with old hands as though the line between them had never existed.

Gypsy lifted the bottle slightly — not a speech, just a moment.

Look what we've built.

The fire answered with a soft, rising crackle, and the night folded warmly around them.

The Sanctuary lived and breathed —

a place made,

a place claimed,
a place becoming itself with every step taken in its dust.
And no one needed to name it.
The valley already knew.

54

Mist clung low over the river the next morning, turning the clearing silver. The camp stirred slowly — the hiss of Shelly's kettle, Mick testing a hinge with the tap-tap of a hammer, Theo warming his fingers on quiet chords. Damp earth, eucalyptus, and the ghost of last night's smoke threaded the air.

Lisa stepped from the van barefoot, breath puffing in soft clouds. Down by the water, Shay sat on her usual log, hat tipped back, fingers braiding cord with the contented rhythm of someone utterly at home.

Behind them, the new huts glowed faintly in the early light — not new anymore, but lived in. A place taking on shape and memory.

Then Mick's ute rattled down the track.

It bounced to a stop in the centre of camp, dust curling around the tyres. Mick leaned out the window with a sheet of paper in hand, grin wide enough to break the morning open.

"Ten years," he said. "Signed and stamped. She reckons we're good sorts — so long as we keep our word."

For a heartbeat, no one moved.

Then Gypsy laughed — deep, unguarded — and took the document like it was breathing. He scanned the handwritten terms:

No owned houses. No selling huts. No growing or dealing — smoke if you must. Grow what you need. Share what you can. Keep the river clean.

"That's it?" Ryder asked, suspicious of anything simple.

"That's it," Mick said, dropping to the ground. "We're official."

Relief rippled like light over water.

Theo struck a bright chord. Shelly clapped Mick so hard his hat nearly went flying. Lisa felt something settle deep inside her — not just excitement, but belonging.

Gypsy lifted the paper again, eyes bright. "Then we're staying."

* * *

Later, Gypsy found Shay at the river, wringing a shirt against stone.

"We need another sign," he said.

Her eyebrow arched. "Another?"

He nodded, one corner of his mouth lifting. "The Sanctuary."

Shay held his gaze, something warm and certain moving between them. Then she smiled — small, steady.

"It fits."

Lisa caught the exchange from the washing line and felt warmth bloom in her chest as the name settled around the clearing like a bird finding its rightful branch.

By afternoon, **THE SANCTUARY** appeared in looping white letters across a slab of timber. Shay planted it just beyond Ryder's red-letter **KEEP OUT** sign and rested her palm against the post as though sealing a promise.

Even Ryder couldn't hide the ghost of a grin.

* * *

As word of the lease drifted through town, Uki faces trickled up the track again — not with offerings now, but with congratulations and easy curiosity.

Old Harry came for a cuppa. Margaret from the bakery arrived just to see the new sign. The publican's nephew leaned on the fencepost and said, "Reckon you'll put some heart back into this place."

No fuss. No ceremony. Just neighbours acknowledging something real.

By mid-afternoon, a long plank across two stumps had become a communal table. Music curled through the warm air. Bread, salad, and stew shared space with laughter. Lisa sat between Shay and Willow, a mug passed between them, shoulders brushing lightly.

Steady.

Peaceful.

Home.

* * *

The next dawn rose slow and bright, smoke lifting lazily from the fire pits. The Sanctuary felt settled now — rooted, sure of itself, as if it had always been here.

Then the sound came.

Low.

Heavy.

Wrong.

Engines on gravel.

Ryder froze mid-step. Shay's head lifted. Gypsy rose in one smooth motion.

Two police cars rolled into the clearing, tyres crunching over the quiet.

Rand stepped out — tall, broad, uniform crisp against the bush. Behind him, a younger officer hovered, notebook ready.

Ryder moved first. "You're not invited."

Rand ignored him, eyes sweeping the camp — the huts, the gardens, the washing line — lingering just long enough on Lisa to sour the air. Willow stepped closer, her smile tightening into something sharp.

"We've had reports," Rand said. "Overcrowding. Illegal crops. Damage to the riverbank."

"Rubbish," Mick replied, holding up the lease. "Ten-year agreement. Owner's blessing. You've no cause to be here."

Rand glanced at the paper but didn't touch it. "Agreements can change."

Gypsy stepped forward — calm, barefoot, steady. "Then you'll see there's nothing to change. We've got nothing to hide."

Rand's gaze flicked to the **TRAVELLERS WELCOME** sign. "You'll be attracting trouble with that."

Shay didn't blink. "We attract family."

The camp stood behind her — close but calm, silent but unshaken.

No threats. Just presence.

Rand weighed the moment, jaw twitching, then gestured to the younger officer. "Let's go."

They reversed out, gravel spitting.

* * *

Silence held them for a beat.

Then Chook struck the first absurd chord of a half-made-up victory song and the tension cracked like thin ice.

Lisa looked at Shay. Shay looked at Gypsy. Gypsy stirred the fire again — the same way he had at the beginning of everything.

"That's how you keep a home," Shay murmured.

And as lanterns lit one by one in the falling dusk, the Sanctuary breathed deeper.

They weren't giving it up.

Not now.

Not ever.

55

The sun hung low, bleeding gold across the gumtops, the heat still clinging to the grass. The camp sat quiet but charged — the kind of hush that settles after something has been won but nobody quite dares speak it aloud. The police cars were gone, yet their tyre marks still scored the edge of the clearing like claw marks from a world that had come too close.

Gypsy sat by the main fire, guitar across his knees, gaze fixed through the flames as though reading something only he could see. The earlier laughter had thinned to murmurs, soft as breath. When Shelly handed him a mug of tea, he didn't lift it — only gave her a small, sideways smile that meant something was forming.

"You know what we haven't done in too long?" he said.

Shelly squinted at him. "Oh no. I know that look."

"It's needed," he replied, rising, mischief already lighting his voice. "It's time."

He didn't explain. He didn't need to.

He walked toward the river, peeled off his shirt, and let it fall.

"Gypsy!" Shelly called — laughing but resigned.

He thumbed open his jeans, kicked them aside, and flung his shout over his shoulder:

"Sunset skinny dip!"

One bright ringing splash.

For a single stunned heartbeat, the camp held still.

Then Willow burst into wild laughter, stripped off her singlet in one motion, and tore barefoot toward the riverbank. Lisa covered her mouth in mock scandal, though delight shone behind her hands. Willow turned back, water to her waist, droplets catching the dying sun like sparks.

"Don't tell me you're shy now!"

Lisa hesitated only long enough to feel the tease land, then tugged her skirt free and sprinted, shrieking as the cold closed around her. She surfaced sputtering, Willow whooping beside her.

Up by the fire, Shay watched with a warm, secretive smile. Then she rose, moved with her slow, sure gait, set her hat neatly on the grass, and slipped her dress from one shoulder. She waded in unhurried, the river curling around her legs like silk. When she dipped beneath and came up laughing, the sound blended with dusk and water as though she belonged to both.

Soon the river was alive with splashes, shouts, and bright, reckless joy. Some swam bare, some half-dressed, some drifted on their backs beneath the bruised-pink sky. Chook climbed onto a half-sunken log, belting out a nonsense song until someone tipped him under and he resurfaced roaring.

Ryder stood on the bank, arms folded, trying — and failing — not to smile.

"Even warriors need a wash," Shay called.

He shook his head, but the grin betrayed him all the same.

* * *

The last of the sun slipped behind the ridge, painting the river in copper and rose. Lantern light pooled across the bank in small golden circles. Firelight reached the water like a flickering bridge, beckoning everyone home.

By the time the swimmers wandered back up the slope — dripping, breathless, wrapped in towels — night had settled in full. River-scent clung to skin. Someone swung the billy over the flames again, tin mugs waiting.

The big fire burned steady. Gypsy sat cross-legged, coaxing warm, wandering chords from his guitar. Shay settled beside him, humming a low counter-melody, her voice weaving through the crackling wood.

Willow leaned into Lisa, braiding her damp hair with slow, careful fingers. Their earlier laughter softened into something warm and private. People gathered as they always did — not in circles, but in loose constellations, drawn together by ease rather than arrangement. Firelight flickered over painted huts, over the Sanctuary sign at the track, over the shimmer of the river beyond.

For the first time, the place didn't look borrowed. It looked earned.

"Feels like we should mark it," Shay murmured.

Gypsy plucked a single bright note. "Already did," he said. "This is the mark."

A comfortable silence folded over them.

Then Willow stretched her legs toward the fire, mischief blooming like it always did.

"We need a trip," she declared. "A proper one. Not Uki. Not Mullum. Somewhere the air smells like salt and sugar cane."

She didn't keep them waiting.

"Surfers. Surfers Paradise."

Gypsy laughed. "You and paradise have a long history of trouble."

"Reconnaissance," Willow corrected solemnly. "Last time was reconnaissance."

Lisa leaned toward her, eyes bright. "What's it like?"

Willow's hands swept the air, painting neon. "Light everywhere. Music pouring from doorways. People dancing barefoot on midnight sand. Feels like the world might tip over — but somehow it doesn't."

Lisa smiled, wonder tugging at her mouth. "Sounds like another world."

Shay nodded. "Then maybe it's time we saw it."

Gypsy looked around the fire at his people and strummed once.

"All right. But this isn't a running-away trip. It's a celebration. We go because we can... because this place will still be here when we get back."

Mick lifted his mug. "I'll keep the home fires lit."

Ryder raised his chin. "And the gate shut."

Willow clapped, delighted. "Then it's settled! We'll take the kombi, the guitars, whoever fits. Surfers or bust!"

Shay smiled into the flames. "You'd better write us a song, Gypsy."

"It's already half written."

The fire cracked, sending sparks swirling upward like tiny, bright prayers. Someone began a tune; the camp joined in — soft at first, then strong, voices lifting into the dark like a ribbon of light.

It wasn't a song of defiance, nor a song of relief. It was gratitude.

For the river.

For the land.

For the fact that they had stood together — and were still standing.

* * *

By dawn, the camp was alive again. Mist curled over the river in pale ribbons, sunlight catching on timber, canvas, hair. Someone fried damper. Someone shook blankets. Sarongs hung in colourful, wet rows from the night before.

Willow perched on the back of David's kombi, legs swinging, calling out a list she was clearly inventing.

"Bathers — oh wait, none of us own any. Sarongs! Hats! Drums! Snacks! Mick's knife for mangoes—"

"Mick's knife stays here," Mick said without turning.

"Fine!" Willow grinned. "We'll slice mangoes with love!"

Lisa was already half inside the kombi, folding clothes into tidy stacks. David ducked in and out, handing things up to her, their rhythm easy as breath. Every so often, Lisa's eyes lingered on him — soft and warm.

Shay moved slower, collecting honey and lemons in her woven basket. "For tea," she said, tipping her hat to Lisa — a gesture carrying more than it looked.

Down by the track, Gypsy and Ryder crouched over a rough map scratched into the dirt.

"Plenty of wood stacked before we go," Gypsy said. "Food sorted. Fires tended. No cars near the river."

Ryder grunted. "And no trouble. Anyone starts it, they answer to me."

Gypsy chuckled. "That's what I like about you — consistency."

All around them, the Sanctuary shifted into readiness — tidy huts, packed baskets, earth swept clean. Anticipation sparked in the air: part sunlight, part horizon.

Lisa paused beside the kombi and looked back at their home — painted huts glowing in the morning light, smoke lifting gently from the cook pit, the Sanctuary sign catching the sun.

It was no longer just a camp.

It was home —

and the road ahead was waiting.

56

The sun stood barely a hand's width above the treeline when the clearing stirred with the soft chaos of departure. Tarps rolled, blankets folded, kettles hissed on last flames, and the smell of strong tea tangled with the bright tang of petrol. Dust hung suspended in the still morning air, scattering sunlight into flecks of gold.

Kombis and vans lined the track like colourful beads on a thread — Gypsy's painted beast at the front, David's sky-blue kombi tucked in behind, and Shay's canary-yellow Mini Moke bringing up the rear like a cheeky caboose. A handful of Uki locals wandered up to wave them off, while some of the older Sanctuary hands stood quietly behind, arms folded, offering approval without needing words.

Shelly drifted between the vehicles, slipping last-minute supplies into palms — a loaf of bread here, a jar of pickles there.

"Don't come back with sunburn worse than the fellas who forget their hats at the mill," she warned, though her smile softened every syllable.

Ryder leaned against his bike, chrome catching the rising sun. "Keep your noses clean," he rumbled. "If anyone asks, you're respectable citizens."

"That's a stretch," Willow called from the kombi roof, somehow already perched like she'd been born there.

Shay stood by the Moke, hat tipped back, her gaze travelling slowly across the camp as though taking an imprint she meant to carry with her. When her eyes found Lisa's, a soft, knowing smile passed between them — part blessing, part promise, a quiet thread of understanding.

Gypsy climbed into the driver's seat, leaned out the window, and whistled sharply enough to send kookaburras bursting into laughter.

"All right, my loves — Surfers awaits. Let's show 'em what sunshine looks like."

Engines coughed awake: Ryder's bike growling, the kombis thumping their friendly chug, the Moke buzzing bright and eager. A few locals clapped as the convoy rolled out. Shay touched the brim of her hat to the crooked **TRAVELLERS WELCOME** sign as they passed, its painted grin flashing them onward.

Behind them, the Sanctuary lay in soft morning gold — fires banked low, new huts standing like small sentinels, early risers moving through quiet routines. Cicadas called from the gums as if seeing them off.

* * *

The air stayed cool as they wound out of Uki. Gravel surrendered to bitumen, tyres humming a road-hungry tune. Gypsy led with Shelly beside him, rolling a cigarette one-handed. David's kombi followed, Lisa leaning in the open doorway with her knees tucked up, Willow beside her with an apple and a battered guitar. Behind them, Shay's Moke darted like a bright fish in the slipstream.

Sugarcane fields swayed like green waves. Farmers lifted slow hands as the painted vans passed.

Their first stop was a weathered highway café with fading Coca-Cola signs and a pie warmer older than Federation. The smell of pastry wrapped around them in rich, nostalgic comfort. Shay split a lamington with Lisa, while Willow pretended to be the waitress, taking outrageous mock orders until the entire café rattled with laughter.

Back on the road, the highway curved toward the river through Chinderah, then drifted into Tweed Heads — fish-and-chip shops, surfboards leaning against fences, the warm scent of frying oil drifting through open windows. They parked near the beach and ran barefoot across the sand, letting the salt wind whip wild fingers through their hair.

When they climbed back into the vans, the ocean breeze travelled with them — cool, salted, threaded with promise.

* * *

Coolangatta slipped by in a blur of pastel motels, fibro beach houses, and breeze-block cafés. The hills dipped toward the first glints of Surfers Paradise — a skyline part dream, part construction site: tall hotels catching the afternoon sun, low motels flashing **VACANCY** and **AIR CONDITIONED COMFORT** in flickering neon.

The air smelled of coconut oil, hot asphalt, and something sweet and electric that belonged entirely to summer.

They rolled down the main drag like a wandering carnival. Willow whooped from the kombi roof; Shay tapped her Moke's horn in a playful greeting; Gypsy cruised with one arm out the window, the picture of mischief. People turned to look — some amused, some charmed, others unsure whether they were witnessing a movement or a miracle.

The esplanade opened to the sea. Gypsy pulled into a strip of grass near the dunes, where the vans could rest side by side, their engines ticking as heat eased. Beyond the Norfolk pines, the Pacific shimmered like a scatter of silver coins.

Shoes vanished. Towels slung over shoulders. Laughter tumbled ahead of them as they ran for the water, sand hot beneath their feet. Willow hit the surf first, arms wide as if embracing the entire ocean.

Lisa followed, slower, wonder widening her eyes with every step.

Shay came last, steady and unhurried, the incoming waves painting gold across her ankles as though greeting her personally.

Lisa dove beneath a rolling wave and rose laughing, salt streaking her cheeks. Willow floated on her back, hair blooming like golden seaweed. Shay waded deeper until the world blurred into light and water.

Nearby, radios crackled, gulls squawked, kids yelled for footballs. A pop song drifted tinny on the breeze. The afternoon stretched warm and lazy around them.

They stayed until shadows stretched across the sand, their skin tasting of salt and summer, hair tangled by the ocean wind.

Walking back barefoot through the softening light, the scent of the sea clung to them like a promise —

Surfers was theirs now.

Body.

Heart.

Dream.

57

The salt dried on their skin as they walked up from the beach, hair curling in the warm evening air. Surfers Paradise was waking for the night — stretching, brightening, humming as if the whole town inhaled at dusk and exhaled in neon.

Lights blinked alive along the strip. The smell of grilled fish and hot chips drifted through open doorways. Laughter spilled across the warm breeze with an ease that felt almost tidal.

Willow spotted the café first — a low-slung turquoise place called *Sea Breeze*, its name painted in looping white cursive across the awning. Wicker chairs spilled onto the footpath, and sunburnt tourists clutched cold drinks like lifelines. A waitress in a chequered apron waved them toward two tables out the back, where conversation hummed beneath the hush of the tide on the other side of the fence.

They settled instinctively — Gypsy anchoring one end, Shay the other. The laminated menus curled at the corners but promised everything the road-worn craved: battered fish, prawn cutlets, crumbed whiting, thick milkshakes.

Lisa tucked her legs beneath her chair, settling between David and Willow, laughing at whatever mischief Willow whispered. Shay leaned over her menu, eyes warm.

"Prawn cutlets or crumbed whiting?" Shay asked.

Lisa grinned. "Both."

Shay smiled like she'd known before she even asked. "Thought so."

Cold lemon squash and beer landed on the tables, glasses sweating in the heat. Golden chips arrived in wire baskets, lemon wedges bright as tiny suns. The first bites silenced them, then softened into happy murmurs.

Gypsy launched into one of his Surfers tales — the early sixties, when the tallest building barely nudged ten storeys and the beaches still felt wild. Shelly rolled her eyes at his exaggerations, but the fondness tugging her cheek gave him away.

Two locals at the next table leaned over to ask where they'd come from. When Mick mentioned the Sanctuary, one man nodded slowly — as if hearing a rumour confirmed, half curiosity, half respect.

Dessert was communal chaos: pineapple fritters collapsing under melting ice-cream, plates passed hand to hand, elbows bumping.

Outside, the town brightened. Music drifted through streets shimmering with warmth and promise. Perfume and cigarette smoke replaced the day's sunscreen and salt.

Willow stood and brushed sand from her skirt. "I reckon this night's just getting started," she announced, eyes finding Lisa's.

Lisa's smile said she absolutely agreed.

* * *

They spilled into Cavill Avenue, the pavement still warm underfoot. Surfers throbbed with restless joy — exhaust, sea spray, coconut oil, all wrapped in neon light. Shop signs flashed like lures: *Paradise Arcade, Surfside Grill, The Playroom.*

Music poured from everywhere. A jukebox crooned Roy Orbison. A bar nearby shook with bass. A busker plucked soft folk chords beneath a streetlamp.

Willow wove through the crowd with Lisa at her heels; Shay followed with her hat tipped low and a slow, easy smile.

"It's like the beach decided to stay awake," Shay murmured.

Lisa laughed — because yes, that was exactly it.

They passed a man selling leather belts off a blanket, two girls in bell-bottoms harmonising for coins, and a tattooed bloke strolling with a cockatoo on his shoulder. Surfers held everyone: locals, tourists, drifters, dreamers — all sun-soaked and wide-eyed.

Above them, a live band thumped through an open stairway — loud, irresistible. Gypsy and Shelly exchanged a grin and headed toward it. The rest followed, swept up by colour and sound.

Inside, a four-piece band in flared trousers hammered out *Bad Moon Rising*, and the crowd moved as one — feet thudding, hair flying, everything alive.

Willow dragged David into the dance. Lisa hesitated half a breath before joining, letting the beat fold her into its pulse.

Shay watched her for a moment, then extended her hand. "Come on," she said gently.

Lisa stepped into the sway, the drums thumping through her ribs, the lights flickering red and gold across her damp curls. Bodies moved free of thought. The world narrowed to rhythm and warmth and the salt still drying on her skin.

When the song slowed, couples drifted together. For a quiet, suspended moment, Lisa met Shay's eyes in the half-light — soft, warm, steady. Something sweet and unspoken passed between them, a tender understanding without edges.

Then the music kicked back up, and the moment dissolved into laughter and motion.

They spilled back into the street, sweat cooling in the ocean breeze. A fire-twirler spun bright ribbons of flame near the foreshore. A silver-painted mime froze as coins clinked into his tin. Down by the dunes, the harmonising girls had gathered a bigger crowd, their voices lifting over the hush of the surf.

Willow linked arms with Lisa and twirled her once, mischief bright as moonlight. David bumped shoulders with them, all three glowing in the neon wash.

Behind them, Gypsy and Shelly wandered hand in hand, content in the quiet joy of it. Shay walked beside them, serene — as though the sea, the music, the night itself were exactly where she belonged.

Salt hung in the air. So did laughter. So did the warm, wordless possibility that comes only on nights where the world feels wide and open.

And as Surfers Paradise shimmered around them — loud, bright, alive — the night stretched toward dawn, held gently in their palms.

58

The first sound was the ocean — low, steady, insistent — slipping through half-open kombi windows before dawn had properly unstitched itself from the horizon. Warm air drifted in with it, carrying a soft salty damp that made everyone want to walk straight into the water.

Lisa woke first.

Barefoot and quiet, she crossed the road to the payphone near the corner store, a few coins pressed into her palm. The early light was cool enough that she folded her arms around herself as she dialled home.

The line clicked, and her mother's voice arrived warm, startled, relieved.

"Lisa! Where are you?"

"In Queensland — Surfers," Lisa said, leaning her shoulder against the glass. "The beach is amazing. You'd love it."

A pause followed — not awkward, simply full. Pride on one side. Longing on the other.

"We're so happy for you, love. But we miss you."

"I miss you too." She almost mentioned Willow's laughter echoing down Cavill Avenue, David floating in the surf like he'd left every worry under the water, Shay watching the waves like she understood them. But she held those close. "It's my birthday soon," she added.

Her mother brightened. "Eighteen! We'll be thinking of you."

Lisa smiled, though something in her chest tightened. She didn't say that no one here knew yet. She wanted to keep that thought small and warm — a secret cupped gently in both hands.

* * *

When she returned, the beach was waking.

Willow sat cross-legged on the kombi roof, sipping tea from a chipped mug, hair catching the morning light like spun honey. Down the sand, Shay was helping an older couple push a tinnie past the shore break, her laughter lifting clean across the water. David lay half-asleep inside the kombi, one arm behind his head, watching gulls bicker over scraps.

Willow lifted her mug when she saw Lisa. "Your turn for tea duty," she called, grin lingering just a little too long.

Lisa laughed, tossed her a wink, and ducked inside to put the billy on.

David sat up, stretching. "You excited for today?"

"Yeah," she said, handing him a cup.

He hesitated. "You want Willow to come with us when we head back?"

The tone tried for casual. The question did not.

Lisa paused, steam curling between them. "I just want everyone to be happy," she said softly. "And for now, I am."

David nodded, but when she stepped out of the kombi his eyes followed her — followed the way she looked up at Willow perched barefoot on the roof — and something in his jaw tightened.

* * *

By mid-morning, the sand was warm. They staked their patch just south of the lifesaver flags — Gypsy shirtless and cross-legged, rolling a cigarette; Shelly spreading a towel with brisk satisfaction; David hauling the esky down from the kombi roof.

Willow and Lisa went straight to the water, skirts tied high. The waves were small and playful, curling in with a hiss before collapsing into pale foam. Shay arrived later with her Akubra in one hand and a towel slung over her shoulder. She paused to watch them — Willow's laughter lifting bright over the surf, Lisa turning into it like she'd been waiting for the sound.

"That's not a holiday tide," Shay murmured as she settled beneath a pandanus tree.

Gypsy glanced up. "What do you see?"

Shay's smile was faint, knowing. "Love — or something close enough to be dangerous."

Out in the water, David splashed the girls until they teamed up to push him under. He surfaced grinning, but when Lisa instinctively reached for Willow's hand to drag her deeper, the shift — small, subtle — wasn't lost on Shay.

* * *

After sandwiches and sticky mangoes on the sand, they wandered the beach markets — stalls of woven baskets, tie-dyed singlets, jars of honey, carved wooden toys. Music drifted from every corner: a guitar under the shade of a banyan tree, a harmonica wandering between stalls. The whole place smelled of grilled corn, sweet pineapple, and sunscreen warmed by sun.

Lisa bought a string of wooden beads for a dollar and let them swing lazily from her fingers. Willow haggled for a pair of bright yellow shorts, declaring them "essential cultural attire." Shay found a dog-eared poetry book at a second-hand stall and turned the brittle pages slowly, as though listening for something inside them.

By late afternoon they were back on the sand. The sea had cooled, but it welcomed them in. David showed Lisa how to duck under waves without being pushed off her feet; Willow floated on her back with limbs star-wide; Shay waded until the shoreline blurred into shimmering light.

It was a day that asked nothing of them —

no building,

no thinking,

no standing guard.

Just sun, water, and the steady knowledge that the Sanctuary waited inland, warm and breathing.

* * *

As the sun melted toward the sea, the streets began to glow. Neon signs blinked to life. Shopfronts spilled coloured light across the pavement. Surfers shifted — as it always did — from the slow drift of day into the restless thrum of night.

Dinner was fish and chips wrapped in butcher's paper on the esplanade, gulls circling hopefully. A barefoot woman in a red skirt sang outside a café-turned-bar, her voice rich enough to still the conversations around her. Shay stopped, eyes closing briefly, letting the sound stitch itself into her.

Further along, four travellers lounged against a low retaining wall — Dan and Mick from Melbourne, Kieran from New Zealand, and Tessa from Sydney. They'd been camping rough for weeks, intrigued by rumours of "the hippie camp inland."

Gypsy only smiled. "Maybe we'll talk about that another day."

Music thickened the air as they wandered — Beatles from a jukebox, the Doors pounding from above, a harmonica drifting through lamplight. Willow tugged Lisa toward a doorway pulsing with coloured lights. David followed, pulled by rhythm and something he didn't want to name. Shay lingered a breath behind them, then stepped inside.

Inside, the band hammered out a bright, rolling tune. Willow spun Lisa in a loose ring of dancers, hair flying, faces bright. David moved with them, clapping off-beat, smiling despite whatever storm worked inside him. Shay leaned against the wall, beer in hand, eyes soft.

For a moment, everything was simple — music, movement, warmth.

A breath held between tides.

* * *

When they spilled back onto the street, the breeze had cooled. The ocean's breath rolled in with a quiet hush. Far off, a siren wailed — faint, harmless, a world away.

Here, the night was theirs — bright, uncontained, alive with possibility.

Just for now,

they were free.

59

Gypsy called the night early.

"Too much sun, too much beer," he declared with a grin as he kicked off his boots.

Shelly only laughed, tossing a blanket over both of them as they settled beside the vans with mugs of tea. Surfers buzzed softly around them — distant laughter, a low thrum of music, the steady hush of the sea — but for once they weren't in the centre of it. Tonight they were content to sit on the warm edge of the world and let the night move past without asking anything more of them.

The others kept the party alive.

The bar they found was open to the street, music spilling out every time the door swung wide. Barefoot, sweat-damp, hair wild from dancing, they moved as if the floor itself breathed beneath them. Willow bought tequila with lime wedges; Lisa tossed hers back in one go, coughing and laughing at the burn. Between songs they leaned into each other, Willow's hand warm at the small of Lisa's back, their rhythm syncing without effort. The outside world fell away like a dropped shawl.

David slipped out early, leaning against a lamppost outside, cigarette tip glowing in the salt breeze. A girl with sun-bleached hair stopped beside him, her laugh sharp and easy. She said she was heading south in the morning. When she asked if he wanted to walk the beach, he didn't think long.

Love felt too big to keep caged.

Maybe Lisa understood that.

Maybe he did too.

* * *

By the time Shay wandered back toward the vans, the streets had thinned into soft pockets of mist and quiet. A faint silver haze clung to the coast, smoothing the edges of shopfronts and lamps.

She found Lisa and Willow curled together on the kombi step, still warm from dancing, cheeks flushed, hair tangled from the night. Their laughter had softened to something gentler — private, glowing, familiar.

The kombi behind them was empty.

"David's not back?" Shay asked quietly.

Lisa shook her head. "Guess he found somewhere else to be."

Willow shrugged, her arm still draped around Lisa. "Guess that's the way it is."

No judgement.

No surprise.

Just truth spoken softly enough not to bruise.

Shay didn't push. She simply lowered herself beside them. Together they sat in the warm coastal dark, wrapped in unspoken things — freedom, understanding, and the delicate balance between them.

* * *

Morning arrived soft and gold, slipping through the kombi curtains and settling in warm pools across the sand. A delivery truck rattled somewhere up the street; gulls cried overhead; the sea whispered behind it all.

Lisa was already outside, barefoot, cradling a chipped mug of tea. Willow sat beside her, knees drawn up, hair a wild halo from sleep. Neither spoke — they didn't need to.

David appeared from the far end of the beach road, shirt half-buttoned, hair still damp with salt. He raised a hand in a casual wave, as though he'd simply gone for an early swim.

Lisa flicked her eyes toward him, then away. She sipped her tea.

"Morning," he said, voice easy but stretched thin.

"Morning," Willow echoed, expression unreadable — half-smirk, half-frown.

Shay joined them with her coffee, reading the shift in the air with one glance.

"We were talking about heading further up the coast one of these days," she said lightly.

David answered too quickly. "Yeah. Sounds good."

No one asked where he'd been.

No one needed to.

A new line had been drawn between them — subtle, but real.

* * *

Days blurred in Surfers.

Salt-sticky mornings, long swims, afternoons wandering cafés, nights glowing neon and wild. The sun bleached the edges of time until every day felt unbound.

Lisa moved differently now — not louder, not brighter, just... more certain. Like she'd stepped into herself without realising it.

David noticed.

He still shared her bed most nights, though Willow just as often slept curled at their feet. But since the night he hadn't returned, something in Lisa's gaze had changed. It wasn't anger. It wasn't hurt.

It was clarity.

One humid afternoon they sat beneath a pandanus tree. Shay wove a bracelet from scraps of hemp; Willow watched surfers carve the late-day waves; David leaned against the trunk, sipping lemonade. Lisa sat among them, knees drawn up, eyes on the glittering sea.

"It's my birthday soon," she said softly.

Willow rolled over, propping her chin on her hands. "When?"

"Next week. Eighteen."

Shay smiled. "Then we'll make it special — something you want, not just what we think you should."

David watched her quietly, something unreadable shifting behind his eyes.

Lisa only nodded, smiling to herself — small, certain, already knowing what she wanted... and who might be part of it.

60

The morning of her birthday rose warm and golden.

Willow was already perched on the kombi roof in cut-offs and one of David's singlets, hair wild, grin wicked with possibilities.

"Birthday girl!" she called, hopping down in a loose, catlike movement. "Eighteen! How's it feel?"

Lisa groaned. "Same as yesterday. Just sunnier."

Willow laughed, leaned in, and kissed her forehead. "We'll see what we can do about that."

David sat up inside the kombi, offering a small, careful smile. "Happy birthday, Lis."

He held out a paper bag.

Inside was a woven bracelet — shell beads threaded through bleached hemp.

"I made it in Uki," he said quietly. "Thought you might want something to keep."

"I love it," Lisa said, fastening it around her wrist.

When she looked up, Willow was framed in the doorway, sunlight catching in her hair, something unspoken simmering behind her eyes.

And Lisa felt it —

the tide shifting.

Gentle, but undeniable.

* * *

Surfers was already alive by the time they stepped into the heat of it. The main street hummed with tourists in board shorts and bikinis, shopkeepers sweeping doorways, the smell of frying bacon drifting through café windows.

They started at the markets — stalls heavy with shell jewellery, paisley skirts, hand-painted sarongs fluttering in the sea breeze. Willow found a rack of bright tropical prints and held a short skirt against Lisa's hips.

"Perfect," she said. "Try it."

Lisa laughed but let herself be tugged into the makeshift tent. When she stepped out, the skirt swung high on her thighs, catching the morning light with every small movement.

Willow's approval came as a slow, deliberate smile.

David's reaction was quieter — eyes pausing before flicking away, his hand tightening in his pocket. Lisa felt it, even if she didn't acknowledge it.

After lunch, she slipped away to the corner phone booth again, coins warm in her palm. She dialled home, heart thumping in a way it never did when she called from the road.

Her mother's voice arrived bright and familiar. "Happy birthday, darling!"

The sound wrapped around her like a hug. They talked about the weather, about Surfers — *Oh, we went there once in '58!* — and about how proud her parents were, even as they missed her terribly.

Lisa didn't mention Willow. She didn't mention David either —
only *the friends I'm with*.

When the coins ran out and the line clicked silent, she lingered a
moment longer in the glass box, watching the ocean through a smear
on the window.

She was further from home than she had ever been — and for the
first time she realised she might never fully return to the person she'd
been.

   * * *

They gathered on the beach as the sky turned coral and gold. Shay
had conjured a small cake from a bakery, candles stuck at odd angles.
Gypsy strummed a lazy tune while Chook poured cheap wine into
paper cups. Willow sat close, an arm warm around Lisa's shoulders,
laughing at something Shay said. David was across the circle talking
with Ryder, but his gaze drifted back again and again.

When the candles were lit, Lisa closed her eyes.

She made a wish she told no one —

not even Willow —

and blew them out.

Cheers rose. The wind carried the smoke out to sea, and for a
heartbeat it felt like the entire beach had joined in.

Later, as the night scattered them — Willow pulling Lisa into the
rush of music spilling from a beach bar, David drifting off with a
stranger near a fire, Shay walking the shoreline alone — the easy lines
between them blurred.

Free love was meant to be simple. But as Lisa spun barefoot in the
sand with Willow, laughing into her shoulder, the truth settled like salt
on skin:

Love — real love — always asked for something back.

   * * *

When the crowd thinned and the music softened to a distant hum, Shay wandered along the tide line. The sand was cool now, the moon throwing a silver road across the water that seemed to lead everywhere and nowhere at once.

Her hat swung from two fingers; her hair caught in the breeze.

She passed small fires ringed by travellers — guitars, laughter, the smell of woodsmoke and rum — until the shoreline quietened and the world narrowed to sea and starlight. She stopped to watch the foam curl around her toes, the surf whispering in its endless conversation with the land. The horizon shimmered where sky met water.

"It's easier to breathe here," she murmured, knowing Lisa would have understood if she were beside her. "Like the world's too distracted by its own beauty to bother you."

She lifted her face to the wind.

"Back at the Sanctuary you've got people to care for — things that tie you to the ground. But this..."

She breathed deep.

"This is just for you."

The waves slid in again, brushing her ankles, then slipped away. Shay wondered if they ever found one another again out there, or if they were destined to meet, collide, and drift apart.

The thought stayed with her long after she turned back toward the lights of Surfers — a quiet realisation that love, like the sea, was never still for long.

61

Willow pulled Lisa into the middle of a pulsing knot of dancers outside the bar, their bare feet kicking up sand, hands locking without thought. Music thundered from inside — a rolling, hypnotic rhythm that matched the sway of bodies around them. Lisa's laughter spilled over the beat as Willow spun her, and for a moment they were nothing but light and motion, lost to the rhythm and the warm, living night.

Farther along the strip, David drifted toward the darker end of the beach. Shay caught a glimpse of him speaking with a woman wearing a bright scarf and hoop earrings, their heads bowed close in easy conversation. By the time the music hit its peak, the pair had vanished into the tide of bodies and neon.

When Shay turned back toward the vans later, the noise of Cavill Avenue rose behind her — fires crackling, voices carrying, guitars weaving their way through the soundscape. And yet, as she walked, she felt she had left something unspoken down on that quiet stretch of sand.

Something patient.

Something waiting.

* * *

The sliding kombi door eased open, stirring Lisa from sleep. She shifted, feeling the warmth pressed against her side as Willow blinked awake. Streetlamps cast pale gold bands across the kombi ceiling, catching the spill of Willow's hair across the pillow.

David stepped inside, salt still clinging to his skin, shirt half-buttoned. He hesitated at the sight of them — bare shoulders, tangled limbs beneath the blanket, breaths slow and even with sleep.

Willow's lips curved into a soft, knowing smile. She lifted the edge of the blanket with two fingers.

"Get in," she murmured, voice low and warm. "She'll thank me later."

David's brows rose, but he didn't argue. He slipped beneath the blanket, warmth closing around him as he settled. Lisa murmured and turned toward him, her arm draping softly across his chest. Beneath the covers, Willow's hand found his — a gentle reassurance, or perhaps a quiet reminder that she understood the shape of this moment better than either of them.

Something flickered across her face — not jealousy, not possession.

A softer note.

Recognition.

A tenderness she wasn't yet naming.

David lay awake listening to the hum of the coastal night outside and the slower rhythm of their breathing within. It should have felt perfect. But in the quiet a question formed — how long could this hold, and where would each of them stand when the road eventually forked?

* * *

Dawn arrived slow and salted, light sliding through the narrow windows in soft bands. A bus groaned down the esplanade; gulls bickered overhead. Lisa stirred first. For a moment she didn't move — simply looking between David's sleeping face and Willow's arm looped lightly around her waist.

A quiet ache pulled at her — a tender, growing question she wasn't ready to touch. One that held both freedom and consequence.

Willow woke next, opening her eyes to meet Lisa's gaze without apology.

"Morning, beautiful," she murmured, her voice warm with sleep.

David yawned and stretched, smiling at both of them. "Beach before breakfast?"

It was an easy question, but the ache tugged again — faint but certain. She thought of home. Not with regret, but with a pull she hadn't felt in months.

They tumbled out of the kombi barefoot into morning heat thick with salt and sunscreen. Surfers was already awake — music drifting from shopfronts, surfboards tucked under arms, the beach stretching gold toward forever.

For now, the day was theirs. The bigger choices could wait.

* * *

By afternoon, the heat had melted into honeyed warmth. David was already out beyond the break, shoulders rising and dipping with the swell. Lisa spotted him instantly — a streak of movement against shimmering gold. She and Willow stood knee-deep in the shore break, cheering as he carved through a wave, water exploding around him.

"Show-off!" Willow shouted.

Lisa laughed, but her eyes held a glint of admiration she didn't bother hiding. Willow saw it, paused a heartbeat, then smiled — softer this time, understanding more than she said aloud.

Up on the higher sand, Shay stretched on a faded picnic blanket beside Gypsy, a paper bag of fresh rolls, cheese, and ripe peaches between them. They watched the trio through the veil of late sunlight, conversation drifting lazily — half words, half silence.

David hit the shallows, board under his arm, hair plastered to his forehead. Lisa ran to meet him, splashing water high into his chest. He retaliated, and soon Willow was in the fray, all three tangled in laughter and spray as the sun dipped low.

Farther down the beach, locals stacked driftwood into a rough pyramid. A lighter flicked; a thin thread of smoke rose into the pink sky. Word spread quickly. More people gathered — barefoot and sandy, still damp from the surf. A six-pack passed down the line. Someone strummed the first slow chords of a guitar.

They drifted toward the fire, the sand warm underfoot. Flames rose, casting everyone in flickering amber. A bag of hot chips made its way around, salt sticking to fingertips. The air filled with woodsmoke, sea salt, and the faint sweetness of someone's cigarette.

Lisa and Willow sat close on a worn blanket, knees brushing. Willow leaned into the contact, expression softening as she studied Lisa's face in the firelight — a brief, unguarded moment before her familiar spark reclaimed her features.

David leaned against an esky, talking with another surfer, but his gaze drifted back again and again toward the two of them in the glow.

A little further back, Gypsy stood alone watching the moonlit waves roll ashore. His thoughts drifted inland — to the Sanctuary, to the huts rising beneath the gums, to the fire pits and the smell of eucalyptus.

Something in him was shifting — a small, steady pull toward roots instead of roads.

He smiled to himself, the decision not yet spoken, but already true.

Behind him, laughter spilled down the beach on the warm wind. Gypsy turned toward the fire and walked into its glow, letting the light erase whatever shadows still lingered on his face.

62

The river moved slow that week, its surface broken only by the quick flash of a kingfisher's wings or the lazy drift of gum leaves. Each morning brought a pale mist curling through the trees, wrapping the Sanctuary in a soft veil. The half-finished huts rose out of it like something dreamed rather than built.

Mick stood at the cleared ground, hammer in hand, measuring twice before every nail. His steady, unhurried rhythm anchored the work crews. Even the wanderers — Quinn, Rowan, and a handful of newer drifters who usually floated from task to task — found themselves keeping pace beside him. The progress was real now: frames upright, rafters settling into place, roofs beginning to lift.

Along the treeline, Ryder patrolled at first light, boots scuffing through dew. His red-letter **PRIVATE PROPERTY** signs had already begun to weather, corners curling under sun and rain, but they still stood like sentinels. Just beside the gate leaned Shay's old **TRAV-ELLERS WELCOME** board, paint fading into a soft ghost of its original smile. Ryder had threatened three times to toss it into the fire, but each time his hand closed around its edge he heard Gypsy's easy voice:

Leave it be.

So he did.

Down near the lower fire pit, Chook held morning court — tambourine in hand, knees bouncing, a half-circle of listeners gathered as he launched into another rambling tale of Byron days. The story changed depending on the audience — some days he claimed he'd flown off a sand dune; others he insisted Willow had dragged him from "certain drowning" in ankle-deep water — but the laughter always carried clean across the clearing. It mingled with the rasp of saws, the thump of ladders, and the gentle percussion of hammers finding home.

Even the locals had begun to soften.

That morning the baker's wife dropped off a basket of day-old bread with only a shy nod. An hour later, the publican's son wandered in with two cartons of beer, muttering something about "neighbours helping neighbours." No one made a fuss. No speeches. But something eased — a tightness in the air since Rand's first visit loosening by a hair.

Not trust, not yet.

But the shape of it.

By mid-afternoon the Sanctuary had fallen into a rhythm as steady as the river. A few of the younger ones swam in the deep bend, their splashes drifting lazily across the water. Others tended the fresh garden beds, coaxing tender shoots from dark soil. Newcomers pitched tents at the far end of the clearing — cautious at first — but each night they edged a little closer to the fires as the camp's warmth pulled them in.

Nights were soft and long.

Music drifted from one fire pit to the next, guitars trading stories the way people did. Voices rose and fell in easy harmonies. Eucalyptus smoke threaded through the camp, settling into hair, clothes, and morning blankets like a familiar, comforting hand. Even the half-built huts seemed to glow in the firelight, as though the Sanctuary itself was beginning to believe in the shape it was becoming.

Still — in the quiet breath between songs — everyone felt the truth beneath the warmth.

Safety was a spell.

Temporary.

Fragile as mist over the river.

Out past the ridgeline, Senior Constable Rand was still prowling. Sighted in Murwillumbah. Seen hassling free campers near the showground. Asking pointed questions in the wrong tone. The Sanctuary had a lease now, inked and witnessed — a beginning — but paper alone never stopped a determined man from pushing through boundaries.

But tonight the air was calm. The fires burned steady. The river kept its slow, murmuring song.

For tonight, the Sanctuary held.

For tonight, it was enough.

63

Late morning set the footpaths shimmering as a salt breeze carried the faint echo of surf up from the beach. Cafés spilled music and frying-egg smells into the street; Surfers thrummed with that peculiar energy — part holiday, part hometown, part circus.

David peeled away with his board under his arm, promising to be "back when the tide's done spoiling me." Lisa watched him go, a small smile curving her mouth. When she glanced sideways, Willow was already watching her — a direct, knowing look that said more than any teasing remark could.

Shay found a patch of shade near the foreshore, sandals kicked into the grass, gaze on the bright chop of the water. Down at the tide line, Lisa and Willow settled on the sand with their knees drawn up, letting waves wash around them. Each time David caught a clean, glassy set, Willow nudged Lisa with a wicked little grin.

By late afternoon, driftwood gathered in quiet stacks. One spark became flame; the air thickened with sweet woodsmoke. Travellers, locals, and strangers folded into a loose circle. Guitars appeared. A bottle made the rounds. The glow caught faces and hair in a way that made everyone look like they belonged.

Gypsy paused at the edge of it all. In his mind: the riverbank, the half-finished huts, the hush of the Sanctuary under the gums. He let the image sit with him, steady and grounding, then turned back toward the fire, the light catching the rim of a smile. The road would bend him home soon enough. He felt it settling in his bones.

By nightfall the bonfire had quietened into a deep, steady glow. Couples drifted away; the lingerers without clocks stayed behind.

Lisa and Willow sat shoulder to shoulder on a woven blanket, toes buried in cool sand. Willow talked about a Thai beach she'd once seen only on a postcard; Lisa listened, tracing slow patterns in the sand between them. Across the fire, David sat cross-legged beside a sunburnt stranger, laughing at something half-muttered. Every now and then his gaze drifted back to Lisa — a taut little thread tugging across flames and darkness.

A little away from the circle, Shay cracked roasted peanuts, flicking the shells into the embers where they snapped and hissed. Her voice was quiet, certain, as she tipped her chin toward Lisa.

"She's already got one foot home," Shay said. "She just hasn't told herself yet."

"And Willow?" someone asked.

"Willow would follow if asked," Shay said with a faint, crooked smile. "That's not her usual way. Makes you wonder what she's found."

At the waterline, the moon laid a wide silver road across the sea. Gypsy stood with his hands in his pockets, tide brushing the toes of his boots. His thoughts drifted inland again — the firepits under the gums, the music, the hush of belonging. It didn't feel like a trap. It felt like a choice.

The fire burned low. The circle thinned. The streets behind them brightened, bars filling and emptying again in steady pulses of neon.

* * *

Near the vans, the night lay warm and close. The kombi still held the day's heat in its panels.

Lisa curled on one bench seat, a book half-closed in her lap. Willow sprawled along the opposite one, bare feet propped against the ply wall, brushing a lazy guitar string. When David slid the door shut behind him, the space pulled tighter around the three of them, charged yet familiar.

"Thought you might've stayed out all night," Willow murmured.

"Nah." David dropped down between them, shoulders loose from salt and surf. "Had enough ocean for one day."

Lisa smiled. "You always say that before sunrise."

He grinned, gaze lingering on her before flicking to Willow. "You two behave while I was gone?"

Willow threw Lisa a mock-innocent look. "We always behave. Don't we, Lis?"

"Not always," Lisa said, laughter soft in her throat.

They drifted through easy talk — surf breaks, odd souls in town, half-serious plans to keep following the coast just to see where the road ran out. David listened more than he spoke, eyes moving between them: the way Lisa's smile softened her whole face; the way Willow's hands carved the air when she spoke. Two different worlds sharing the same small space, and somehow he belonged to both.

Willow reached out and brushed a strand of hair from Lisa's cheek — a small gesture, almost casual. David caught the faint rise of colour in Lisa's face and felt something tighten in his chest.

The guitar's hum filled the silence. Outside, a jukebox rumbled up the street; gulls argued over bins; the sea kept its patient rhythm.

Inside, none of them hurried toward sleep.

* * *

Dawn arrived pale and silver. The beach lay empty except for a jogger and a lone fisherman cutting clean lines across the damp sand.

Lisa walked the tideline, sandals in hand, dress hem darkening each time the foam slid in around her ankles. The solitude felt good — needed.

She loved David. Loved the open road he'd shown her, the strangers-turned-family, the nights under stars. She loved Willow too — though that love was still taking shape, bright and strange as coloured glass. Beneath both, another pulse had begun rising: quieter, deeper, steady as breath.

Home. Not as escape, not as retreat —

but as the place that had shaped her.

She'd been calling more often.

Not for news — for the sound of being known.

A wave tugged at her feet, then slipped away. Lisa breathed in the salted light and turned back toward the vans.

Inside, the warmth of last night lingered.

David lay half-awake, one arm behind his head. Willow was curled against him, fingertips tracing slow circles along his ribs. Through a gap in the curtain they saw Lisa crossing the sand — hair blown wild, expression faraway.

"Looks like your girl's been thinking," Willow murmured.

Minutes later Lisa ducked inside, bringing the morning with her. Willow's hand stilled. Their eyes met — a brief, unguarded flash — before Willow broke it with a grin.

"Coffee?"

Lisa nodded, reaching for the kettle. The hiss of gas filled the cramped space; the light clink of mugs followed.

David propped himself on one elbow. "Might walk down the point after a surf," he said. "Clear my head."

"By yourself?" Lisa asked gently.

"Yeah. Just need a bit of air."

Willow's tone was easy, but her glance held a sharper truth beneath it. "You'll come back though, right?"

The kettle whistled. Lisa poured. The smell of coffee mingled with salt and warm canvas. They sat close, knees touching, gulls calling overhead as the town yawned awake.

For a few quiet minutes, all three were somewhere else —

David tracing a line back inland,

Lisa hearing her mother in the kitchen,

Willow holding a possibility that wasn't either/or.

The coffee cooled between their hands.

Outside, the day waited. Inside,

they lingered in that suspended space between love —

and whatever came next.

64

First light spilled soft and silver over the Pacific, washing the sand in pale pink. The air smelled fresher than the day before — less heat, more salt — as though the night had rinsed the coastline clean. A jogger traced the waterline; a fisherman cast from the shallows, his line flicking like a short, bright stroke of morning light.

Lisa walked barefoot where the waves curled and kissed the shore, her sandals dangling from one hand. It felt good to move alone, without anyone's rhythm beside hers.

She loved David — the way he'd opened this wild, wandering life to her. And she loved Willow too, in a different, dizzying way she still didn't fully understand. But beneath all of that, something quieter had begun to stir. She missed home — not as escape, not as retreat, but as a heartbeat she could still hear beneath the noise of the surf.

She pictured her parents at breakfast: her mother singing off-key with the radio, the kettle clattering on the stove, the familiar creak of

the front step. She'd been calling more often lately. Not for news —
just for the comfort of being known.

The tide wrapped cool fingers around her ankles, slipping away
again like a reminder that everything returns eventually. She watched
the foam slide in and out, patient and unhurried, then turned back
toward the vans where the curtains were still drawn and the morning
belonged only to her.

* * *

Inside the kombi, the air was warm and close with the softness of
sleep.

David lay on his back, one arm behind his head, features slack in the
quiet. Willow curled easily against him, her leg draped over his, hand
resting flat on his chest. She traced slow, idle circles there — careless
in gesture, deliberate in effect — though his breathing deepened with
every one.

"Morning," she murmured, soft enough not to wake him if he
wasn't ready.

He hummed, low and vague, eyes still shut.

Through a gap in the curtain, Willow saw Lisa walking up the
beach — dress hem wet, hair tousled by the breeze, eyes faraway with
the kind of thinking that had turned into feeling.

Willow's fingers stilled. For a heartbeat she simply watched her —
affection plain, curiosity rising, and something else too: that selfish
little tug that wanted to keep both of them close.

"Looks like your girl's been thinking," she whispered, though she
wasn't sure David heard.

Lisa ducked inside moments later, bringing with her the scent of
salt, sunlight, and something softer that changed the air. Willow's
gaze met hers over David — a brief, bright spark of understanding —
before she broke it with a grin.

"Coffee?"

Lisa nodded and moved to the tiny bench, matching kettle to flame with familiar hands. The hiss of gas filled the space.

David shifted onto his side, the blanket tangled low at his hips. He watched her as she moved about the van, his expression unreadable, breathing slow beneath Willow's resting hand.

Willow stretched like a cat, toes brushing David's leg before she rolled onto her back.

"Feels like it's going to be a scorcher," she said, looking up at the thin strip of brightening sky.

"Might be nice to find some shade later," Lisa replied.

David's voice was rough with sleep. "Thinking I might walk down the point after a surf. See what's there."

"By yourself?" Lisa asked gently.

He nodded. "Just need to stretch my legs."

Willow tilted her head, tone easy but edged with meaning. "You'll come back, though. Right?"

The kettle whistled softly. Lisa poured the water, the smell of coffee blooming warm and earthy through the van. She passed the mugs around and settled beside them.

They drank in a cocoon of small, unhurried sounds — surf in the distance, gulls waking overhead, coffee cooling in their hands. Knees brushed in the narrow space, bodies close though thoughts drifted far.

Each held a different horizon.

David traced the memory of the Sanctuary — river, smoke, the quiet pull of roots beginning to call him home. Lisa heard her mother's voice in the soft click of the spoon against her mug. Willow replayed the look in Lisa's eyes when she stepped through the door — the way it lingered, the way it meant something was shifting.

The morning was slow. The coffee strong. The silence honest.

Outside, Surfers Paradise began to stir. Inside, they sat with the quiet knowledge that each felt the tug of a different tide — none ready to name it, all aware it was coming.

65

David walked past the busy stretch of beach where kids carved trenches in wet sand and surfboards leaned neatly under the pandanus trees. The further he went, the quieter the coastline became — just the thump of waves folding against the rocks and the soft hiss of wind through saltgrass.

He stopped at the point, resting his arms on the low railing, watching long, even lines rise from the deep and glide toward shore. Out here he could finally hear himself think — no tangled feelings, no questions waiting for answers he didn't yet have.

But silence has a way of loosening what's held down.

He thought of the Sanctuary: eucalyptus smoke lifting through the gums, riverwater dark and patient, fire pits glowing like small, steady hearts. Surfers had its magic — bright, intoxicating, glittering — but it was the kind of magic you passed through, not the kind that held you.

Then Lisa. And Willow.

He smiled despite the tightness in his chest. Two different lights, both lodged somewhere deep. Lisa's soft trust. Willow's fearless spark. He didn't yet know the shape of what was forming between them — what was forming inside himself.

Only that it wouldn't stay balanced forever.

Sooner or later, the road would split.

He stayed until the tide began to turn, then headed back along the brightening sand, the day warming gently under his feet.

* * *

In a quiet Surfers side street, Gypsy and Shelly found a café with chipped tables and strong coffee served in heavy ceramic mugs. Gypsy lounged back, one ankle resting on his knee, watching the slow procession of holidaymakers drifting past.

"Feels like the wind's shifting," Shelly murmured, stirring sugar through her cup.

He didn't ask what she meant. "You see it too?"

She nodded. "Lisa's looking further away. Willow keeps trying to pull her closer. And David..." She tapped her spoon against the rim, soft metal on ceramic. "His body's here, but his heart's already upriver."

Gypsy gave a small, wistful smile. "That's the way of it. You can't hold people still if you want 'em to stay free."

"Doesn't make it easier to watch," she said.

"No," he agreed, gaze drifting to the thin slice of ocean between the buildings. "But that's why you make the most of the days you're given. Everything else becomes stories we tell ourselves later."

She reached across the table and squeezed his hand. They stayed like that for a time — two old souls reading the currents without trying to change their course.

* * *

David came up the road barefoot, board tucked under his arm, salt drying in a fine sheen across his shoulders. The kombi sat exactly where they'd parked it, curtains drawn, still in the morning heat.

He slowed.

The van shifted slightly — the gentlest sway, easy to miss unless you were looking for it.

He stopped. A faint, crooked smile tugged at his mouth.

He didn't need to guess.

Passing by casually, he caught a soft murmur through thin metal — Lisa's breathless laugh, Willow's lower, teasing reply, their voices blending into something intimate and warm. Something alive.

He leaned against the wall beside the surf shop, letting the sea breeze cool the last of the salt on his skin. He told himself he'd give it a few minutes — time for the air inside the kombi to settle, for whatever was unfolding in there to find its breath again.

Still, some part of him stayed tuned to the rhythm within — something stirring that wasn't jealousy and wasn't exactly peace either. Something older, quieter, like the first tug of a rip in the water.

He looked toward the horizon, where gulls rode the wind in slow, lazy circles.

The tide was turning. It always did.

66

The air inside the kombi was warm with salt and sun, the curtains breathing faintly each time the wind brushed past. Lisa sat cross-legged on the bed, trying — and failing — not to laugh at something Willow had just whispered.

Willow sat close, one knee touching hers, an arm draped along the back wall with deliberate ease. Her fingertips grazed Lisa's shoulder each time she leaned in, innocent only in posture, not intention. Her smile was slow and knowing.

"You think too much," she murmured. "Sometimes you just... do."

Lisa opened her mouth to reply, but the words tangled as Willow's hand slid down her arm, fingers threading gently through hers. She didn't pull away. Instead she let herself be drawn closer, until their knees aligned and their breaths mingled, the tiny space of the van humming like a struck guitar string.

When Willow kissed her, it wasn't rushed. It was chosen. A kiss that left room to stay or slip away.

Lisa stayed.

Her breath caught as Willow's hand moved to the small of her back, guiding her into the soft sway of the kombi. Willow's touch trailed a slow, careful path along her ribs, each movement stretching the silence between their heartbeats.

David flickered in the back of Lisa's thoughts — the steadiness of him, the anchor he carried without trying. Loving him didn't vanish here; that truth pressed closer, if anything, giving the moment a gentle ache beneath its brightness.

Willow eased back just enough for their foreheads to touch, her breath warm on Lisa's cheek.

"See?" she whispered. "Thinking less suits you."

Lisa exhaled — half-laughter, half-surrender. The van rocked gently with their shift of weight, and neither of them pretended not to feel it.

* * *

By nightfall the bonfire crackled in the salt-thick air, sparks spiralling into the dark. People settled in loose circles — strangers and familiar faces — passing bottles, sharing blankets, harmonising over a guitar that fought to keep tune.

Lisa and David sat close on the sand, their faces lit gold by the flames. Willow drifted toward them from the far side of the circle and folded herself down with that cat-like grace she wore as casually as a smile.

David's gaze lifted. A quiet, amused tilt shaped his mouth.

"I came by the van earlier," he said — soft, but threaded with meaning.

Lisa froze, heat rising in her cheeks. She drew a pattern in the sand to steady her hands, though they still trembled faintly.

Willow's grin curved slow and wicked. "You should've joined us," she said, her voice a warm invitation wrapped in mischief.

David's brows rose. His smile deepened. "Maybe later, then?"

Lisa gave a flustered laugh and swatted Willow's arm. "You're impossible."

"I'm delightful," Willow corrected. "Big difference."

She pushed herself to her feet. "I'll get us some beers."

When she slipped into the dark, the fire settled into a low, steady roar. Lisa curled closer to David, letting the warmth of him ease her breath.

"These moments will always stay with me," she murmured.

David kissed the top of her head, his lips lingering. "Mine too."

Willow returned with three longnecks, amber glass glowing in the firelight. She handed one to each of them and kept the last for herself.

"Here you go, lovers," she teased.

Lisa rolled her eyes and popped the cap against the esky. "You're terrible."

"I'm honest," Willow said, settling opposite them. She took a slow drink, eyes fixed on Lisa over the rim. "Besides... I think David already knows he missed a very good afternoon."

Lisa flushed deep. She hid behind her beer too late — David was already smirking.

"Do I?" he asked softly, the glint in his eyes betraying more questions than he voiced.

Willow leaned forward, her grin sharpening. "Oh, you do. And if you don't... maybe later we'll fix that."

Lisa laughed, half protest, half helplessness, and swatted Willow's knee. "Stop."

"Stopping isn't really my style," Willow said, laughter bright in the firelight.

David chuckled and pulled Lisa against him. The moment didn't need explaining; it settled between them warm and alive, like the fire they faced.

Willow watched them over the lip of her bottle, flames reflected in her eyes — mischief, affection, and something quieter — before she tipped her head back and let the rest remain unspoken.

67

The fire had burned low, settling into a bed of glowing embers. Sparks drifted upward into the warm night, rising as though they had somewhere else to be. Laughter rolled in gentle waves from scattered groups along the sand, breaking now and then for the strum of a guitar or the hush of a story told softly. Beyond the circle of light, the ocean whispered without pause — a steady breath no one could interrupt.

Lisa leaned into David, her head resting lightly on his shoulder, eyes half-closed. Across from them, Willow lounged with her legs stretched toward the heat, firelight catching in her hair. A ghost of a smile tugged at her mouth — the kind that knew this would be one of those nights, bright in memory long after the smoke faded.

Far down the beach, a couple danced barefoot in the shallows, their shadows wavering across the tide-washed sand.

When the fire finally collapsed inward, no one moved. They simply sat, letting the warmth sink deep, aware — even if they wouldn't say it — that the night was shifting beneath them. The best nights always passed quietly into something you carried long after morning.

* * *

By the time they stirred, the sun had warmed the sand to a soft burn. The kombi door stood open, letting in the salt breeze and the comforting mix of sunscreen, coffee, and last night's woodsmoke still clinging to clothes.

David sat on the kerb with a mug in hand, watching the surf roll in steady lines. He looked loose, rested — but every so often his gaze drifted south, following something only he could see.

Lisa padded over, barefoot and sun-kissed, a slice of watermelon in hand. She sat beside him, their knees brushing.

"You're quiet this morning," she said.

"Just thinking." He handed her the last of his coffee. She sipped, and neither spoke for a while.

Willow arrived next, sunglasses on, hair wild from sleep, carrying a brown paper bag fragrant with fresh bread.

"Breakfast, my darlings," she announced, tearing the loaf in half. She passed a piece to Lisa with a wink — pointed, but unspoken.

Across the road, Gypsy and Shelly sat beneath a café awning on a low stone wall. Two empty mugs rested between them. Gypsy spoke with slow, thoughtful gestures; Shelly listened, chin propped on her hands.

"They look serious," Lisa murmured.

"Probably planning something," David said.

Willow shrugged. "They're always planning something. That's why we get to be here."

A gull swooped low across the bitumen, chasing a scrap of food. Up the street, a busker tested his guitar. It was the kind of bright, open morning that felt like it could go anywhere — but beneath the warmth, something tugged gently. Quiet, but growing.

* * *

The fire on the beach that night was smaller, just a handful of people gathered beneath the moonlit waves. The crowd from the night before had drifted to pubs or spilled into the dark with their bottles and guitars.

Gypsy sat with his legs stretched toward the flames, a cigarette glowing between his fingers. Shelly rested her chin on her knees beside him. They had been silent a long time before she finally spoke.

"You've been thinking about the Sanctuary."

Gypsy didn't look surprised. "Always do. But lately..." He exhaled slowly. "It's like I can see it from here. The river. The gum trees. Feels like it's calling us back."

Shelly smiled softly. "Because it is. Lisa's looking homeward. David's drifting. Even Willow... well, she's watching Lisa more than anything else."

He hummed, a thoughtful sound. "This was always a holiday for them. A long one — but not the forever kind."

"And for us?" she asked.

Gypsy watched the distant line of the water, black under the moon. "The road's been long. Maybe it's time to build something that lasts longer than a season. The Sanctuary could be that. It already is, for some."

Shelly reached for his hand. "Wherever you go," she said, "I'm with you."

He flicked the cigarette into the fire, watching it disappear. "Then we'll go back soon. Before the wind changes completely."

They stayed there awhile, letting the waves break and the night hold them — two travellers already half on the road home.

* * *

Late morning carried the cheerful rattle of a canary-yellow Mini Moke climbing the street. Its sound arrived first, turning heads before the little car swung into view beside the kombi.

Shay was at the wheel, barefoot, one arm draped over the door. A paper bag of pastries sat on the passenger seat, still warm from a Burleigh bakery.

Willow spotted her and waved. "About time, wanderer!"

Lisa's smile widened before she even stood, shading her eyes against the glare. David straightened, the lazy grin he'd worn on good days finding its way back.

Shay killed the engine, leaving a surprising quiet in its wake. She lifted the pastry bag like a trophy.

"Breakfast for the late crowd."

Lisa peeked inside and laughed. "Still warm."

Willow tore into one instantly. "Tell us everything — and don't skip the good bits."

Shay leaned back against the Moke, her eyes glinting. "You'll just have to come see Burleigh for yourselves. Some places don't tell as well as they live."

Soon they formed a loose circle on the sand, pastries half gone, the surf whispering beyond them. Whatever distance had crept in over the past few days slipped away without effort — like the tide folding back to shore.

For a little while, the day felt whole again.

68

The afternoon settled over Surfers like warm honey — thick with light, soft with sea breeze. Someone had hauled a transistor radio down to the sand and propped it on a towel where the signal bent in and out with the wind.

The Beach Boys crooned *Wouldn't It Be Nice*, their harmonies weaving with the hush of the waves. Two barefoot kids danced uneven circles near the water before collapsing into the sand, shrieking with laughter.

Willow lounged on her elbows, sunnies tipped low, her toes buried in warm grit. Beside her, Lisa lay with a hat shading her eyes, a slow smile forming as the music washed over them. For a moment, nothing moved but surf and wind.

Then Jefferson Airplane's *Somebody to Love* burst through the static — Grace Slick's voice slicing clean through the lazy heat.

Shay stood on the first chord, grabbed Willow's hand with a grin. "Come on!"

They splashed into the shallows, dancing without rhythm, moving simply because the song refused to let a body stay still. Water lapped cool around their ankles, sunlight catching the spray each time they turned.

Further up the beach, David leaned against the driftwood log they'd dragged down earlier, dark glasses hiding his eyes. He tapped his fingers to the beat, watching the dancers, watching the girls sprawled on the sand — watching the whole scene as though trying to memorise every shifting piece before it changed.

When *America* by Simon & Garfunkel drifted from the radio, the mood softened, as if the song itself had lowered the sun.

Shay and Willow came up the sand, wet to the knees, and collapsed onto the blanket beside him.

Willow pulled off her sunglasses, eyes on the horizon. "Perfect song for the last page of a summer."

"Not the last page yet," Gypsy called as he and Shelly strolled back from the café — but his smile said she wasn't wrong.

Nobody rushed the moment. The waves folded over themselves with soft, endless patience. The sun slipped lower, lingering for one final breath before giving in to dusk.

* * *

By nightfall, the fire burned bright and steady — a warm heart in the sand with familiar and new faces gathered around it. A bottle of wine made its slow pilgrimage through the circle. Someone tuned a guitar. Stars pricked the sky just beyond the faint glow of town.

David sat close to the flames with Lisa tucked into his side, her head resting on his shoulder. Willow lounged opposite, one knee raised, idly plucking a guitar string between sips of beer, though her gaze drifted to Lisa more often than the fire.

Shay settled beside Gypsy and Shelly near the back, wrapped in the hum of hushed conversation.

Music found its own unhurried rhythm, folding around them like the night folding around the flames. Laughter came, but gentler now. Stories were told with longer pauses.

There wasn't a word for the feeling, but everyone sensed it: something was shifting.

Gypsy caught Shay's eye across the fire. She gave a tiny nod, as though both had heard the same subtle change in the wind.

Lisa lifted her head to study David's face in the glow. "These moments... they'll stay with me forever," she said — no tremor, just truth.

David kissed her hair, lingering. "Mine too."

No one spoke the ache aloud, but it rested in every chest. This golden, drifting chapter was beginning to close.

* * *

Morning came clear and blue, the heat of previous days rinsed away by a cool night breeze. The beach lay almost empty — long ribbons of untouched sand, a few early surfers carving clean lines, gulls picking through the tide's leftovers.

Gypsy and Shelly sat at a café table, the same one where their quiet talks had begun days earlier. This time, there was no circling.

"It's time," Gypsy said simply. He stirred his coffee once, set the spoon aside.

Shelly's eyes softened. "Not today."

"No," he agreed gently. "But soon. Before the season breaks — before the pull goes quiet. We go back while it still feels like ours."

She nodded, fingers curling around her mug. "You'll tell them?"

"Yeah. Enough to let it settle."

When they rejoined the others on the sand, the morning felt easy at first. Willow tossed a frisbee to David. Lisa sat cross-legged beside the kombi with her sketchbook open. Shay watched the surf from her blanket.

Gypsy waited for the lull.

"We'll be heading back to the Sanctuary soon," he said. "Not rushing — a few more days here — but the road's calling us home."

The words drifted over them like a subtle shift of wind.

Willow caught the frisbee and held it still, her grin faltering before she forced it back.

Lisa's pencil paused mid-line; her gaze went instinctively to the sea.

David's shoulders lowered — not disappointment, but recognition.

Shay looked at Gypsy and nodded once.

Shelly watched the group, calm as ever.

No one protested. No one panicked. But something tightened softly inside all of them.

They knew, now: these golden days were down to their final handful.

Whatever came next — the Sanctuary, the road, the choices waiting quietly in each of them — this place would remain imprinted on their hearts: the heat, the light, the wildness, the laughter, the nights that felt like they could last forever.

And maybe, in another life, they would.

69

The tide crept slowly toward their toes as Lisa and Willow sat apart from the others, just far enough down the sand to carve out their own quiet pocket of evening. Lisa had her knees drawn up, chin resting lightly against them, watching the foam slide up the beach, sigh, and fade back again.

"Feels different now," she said softly.

Willow lay on her side, propped on an elbow, eyes following the dying light across the water. "Because it is. We're counting down without a clock."

Lisa nodded, her teeth catching gently on her lip. "When we get back... I don't know what happens. David and I—"

Willow reached out and tugged a loose strand of hair until Lisa met her gaze. "Don't overthink it. What happens is what happens. You've got him. You've got me. And I'm not going anywhere unless you want me to."

Lisa's smile was small, shy, uncertain. "You make it sound simple."

"It *is* simple," Willow said, rolling onto her back and closing her eyes against the sinking sun. "Simple until we decide it's not."

The waves breathed their slow rhythm across the sand. Warm light brushed their skin as the last of the day slid behind the horizon. They didn't speak again for a long while.

Further down the shoreline, David wandered alone, leaving uneven footprints in the damp sand. Now and then he let a wave wrap around his ankles before stepping out of its reach. The thought of leaving Surfers didn't frighten him; it settled quietly in his chest like a truth he'd already accepted.

He'd miss the long days in the surf, the warmth on his back, the lazy rhythm of these weeks. But the Sanctuary called to him — the river, the gum trees, the hum of belonging waiting upriver.

He thought of Lisa. Then Willow. Then both of them — the strange, beautiful tangle they had woven together.

Whatever lay ahead, these weeks would stay with him always.

As the tide turned, brushing higher along the shore, he turned too, heading back toward the fires beginning to spark along the beach.

* * *

By nightfall, a single fire burned high — a beacon flame curling upward as though telling stories to the sky. The sand still held the day's heat. The air smelled of salt and woodsmoke. A battered tape deck sat on a driftwood crate, its speakers humming softly.

When the opening chords of *Suite: Judy Blue Eyes* spilled into the night, the whole circle seemed to lean closer.

David rose first, clapping in time, coaxing Lisa up from her blanket. She let him spin her once before Willow cut in with a laugh, catching Lisa's other hand so the three of them turned together in a loose, swaying knot beside the flames. Their shadows stretched long across the dunes, bending and folding with the music.

Shay watched for a moment before tugging Gypsy up by the hand. "You're not sitting this one out."

Gypsy's laugh rolled through the circle, warm as the fire. Shelly joined them, clapping to the beat, her hair bright in the shifting light. The guitars were bright and irresistible; bare feet stamped, hands clapped, voices rose and dissolved into the night.

Even Gypsy's easy shuffle drew cheers.

The fire's glow painted everyone gold — Lisa turning between David and Willow, Shay spinning beneath Gypsy's steady gaze, Shelly laughing into the night. For a moment it felt as though the very air was dancing.

Halfway through, the tempo softened. People folded back onto the sand, voices lowering into quiet murmurs as the harmonies drifted across them like smoke. It was a farewell song, whether anyone named it or not.

Lisa settled between David and Willow, her head resting on his shoulder while Willow traced slow shapes in the sand beside her. They didn't look at each other, but warmth glowed in the small space between them.

When the music lifted into its bright, tumbling Spanish ending, the circle revived — clapping, calling out half-remembered lyrics. Shay's laughter rose above it all. Gypsy threw his head back, still moving with her. For a heartbeat, the night felt infinite.

Then the tape clicked. The music stopped.

Silence settled — soft, full, deeply alive.

The fire crackled.

The sea breathed.

The night wrapped around them like a blanket.

No one spoke.

No one needed to.

The fire burned lower, painting their faces in gentle gold — faces they would carry with them when the wheels turned south. For the space of a song, and a little longer, it felt as though the world began and ended right here on this stretch of sand beneath the stars.

And everyone knew — without a word — that this was the last fire they would ever light in Surfers Paradise.

70

The horizon was already softening into gold when Lisa and Shay stepped onto the beach, the sand cool beneath their feet. They walked without hurry, the waves folding and unfolding beside them like a slow, steady breath. At first their hands brushed, nothing more — but somewhere along the way Shay's fingers found hers, warm and certain, as if they had always known how to fit.

The breeze carried the faint sweetness of pandanus and the clean salt of the night tide. Dawn kissed their skin with that tender warmth only morning can give. They didn't speak. They didn't need to. The road home waited beyond the headland, but for now the moment held them gently, letting each step leave its imprint on the sand before the sun claimed the day.

Up near the café, Gypsy and Shelly's kombi sat already packed, roof straps cinched across crates and blankets. They'd slipped into town for coffee, leaving the morning to anyone who still lingered between sea and sky.

Back at the other vans, curtains fluttered in the faint breeze. Earlier, they'd been still — then not so still. A shift on the tyres, a soft burst of laughter... a quiet intimacy no one would ever comment on. Some things lived kindly between the lines.

Lisa and Shay walked until the sun lifted clean above the horizon, spilling molten gold across the water. Shay stopped, squeezed Lisa's hand, and smiled out to sea. The moment brimmed with everything at once — reflection, excitement, fear, longing — braided together like waves just before they touched land.

* * *

By mid-morning, the street was alive again: surfboards under arms, kids darting between parked cars, sunscreen and frying bacon drifting on the warm air. The hush of dawn had sharpened into the bright, noisy clarity of a summer day.

Gypsy and Shelly's kombi was ready first, parked further down with its roof stacked high. They stood outside the café with empty mugs between them, speaking in quiet tones, morning sun softening their features.

Their own van looked nothing like ready — half-zipped bags, blankets spilling from the doorway, the lovable chaos of a life without walls. David leaned against the bumper smoking, gaze drifting between the surf and this loose, beautiful knot of people who had become something like family. Willow perched cross-legged on the bonnet, tapping a rhythm only she seemed to hear. Lisa sat on the kerb, sketchbook open, trying to draw the street as though she could keep it that way forever.

Shay arrived still tasting salt in her hair and helped stow the last of the cooking gear. They weren't rushing, but every movement carried that quiet weight — the subtle knowing that this was the last time they'd do anything here.

Gypsy wandered over, hat tipped back, Shelly beside him. "We'll make Byron by nightfall if we roll steady," he said — not a command, just a gentle marker in the sand.

No one argued. No one needed to. The truth was already settled behind their eyes.

When the vans were finally ready, the group lingered on the street. Hugs passed between them; promises half-serious, half-hopeful — *We'll meet here again next summer. I'll write. Don't disappear.*

Engines turned over one by one. The sound jarred after days of surf and song. Windows rolled down, arms lifted in lazy waves, and the convoy pulled away from the kerb.

In the rear-view, Surfers shrank quickly — the curve of the beach, the pale foreshore, the fire pits from last night cooling in the sand.

No one spoke much as the road opened ahead. There was too much to hold in the quiet: the salt on their skin, the glow of firelight, the tangled laughter in the dark, and the way this place had worked its way into all of them in ways they wouldn't understand until much later.

The wheels turned south. The Sanctuary waited.

The highway hummed beneath the tyres, the white line unspooling in a steady rhythm. Warm air poured through open windows, the scent of salt slowly giving way to gum and wattle — the smell of country reclaiming the edges of everything.

David drove without the radio, letting the rush of wind speak for him. Lisa sat beside him, one leg tucked under, sketchbook open but untouched. She watched the landscape slide by — green into gold, harsh glare into tree-shadow — and let her thoughts drift back to the beach, to the fire, to the way Willow's laughter felt wrapped in smoke and starlight.

In the back, Willow sprawled across blankets, hair whipping in the half-open breeze, fingers tapping the rhythm of a tune she carried but hadn't shared. Her gaze wandered somewhere far from the highway.

Shay followed in the Moke behind them, engine buzzing cheerfully along. She drove barefoot, sunglasses low, the road reflected in the dark curve of her lenses. "It'll feel different," she murmured — though she didn't yet know if she meant the Sanctuary, the road, or all of them.

Up ahead, Gypsy's kombi led the way. Shelly's scarf streamed from the passenger window like a wild little banner, dancing to the rhythm of the road. They hadn't said much since leaving Surfers. It was enough just to be moving again — the highway stretching out like a song they'd forgotten they loved.

By late afternoon, the forest would thicken. The river's breath would rise to greet them. Campfire smoke would curl into the cooling air.

Home was waiting. They simply didn't yet know how much had changed.

71

The road narrowed to gravel, trees leaning in overhead until the sunlight fractured into shifting shards across the windscreen. The tyres changed their song, crunching softly over stone. The scent of eucalyptus rose like a memory let loose.

Gypsy's kombi slowed ahead, brake lights flashing once before the turnoff. The rutted track welcomed them in, the forest drawing tighter with every metre.

Just before the bend, a new slab of timber appeared, wedged between two old fence posts. The lettering was carved deep and painted in weathered red:

THE SANCTUARY

Not polished.

Not perfect.

But solid. Rooted. A sign that declared the place as belonging — to its people and to whoever needed it most.

Off to the side, half-drowned in grass, Shay's old **TRAVELLERS WELCOME** board leaned stubbornly against a post, its paint faded to gentle ghosts of colour. Behind it, one of Ryder's **PRIVATE PROPERTY** signs glared from a gum trunk, corners curled from the weather.

David felt something loosen in his chest. Lisa leaned forward, smiling softly. Willow let out a low whistle.

"Look at us," she said. "A real address."

The track widened and the clearing opened before them.

The change hit all at once.

New tents dotted the edges — mismatched colours, handmade patches, tarps stretched carefully between trees. A larger hut stood near the riverbank, its pale fresh timber shining beside the older structures. Smoke curled from three separate fires, thick with the scent of stew and damp earth. A rope strung between two gums held shirts and sarongs fluttering lazily in the breeze. Someone laughed near the river.

Ryder strode out from between two huts, hammer in hand, swagger loose as if the place itself moved to his rhythm. Mick followed, brushing sawdust from his palms. Both wore the smiles men save for old friends — warm, relieved, but edged with new responsibility.

"About time," Ryder called, beard splitting in a grin. "We thought you'd gone soft up north."

Gypsy climbed down, stretching like a man arriving where he belonged. "Place looks good."

"Different," Mick added. "Lot more people since you left. You'll see."

Engines died. Doors swung open. Faces surfaced — some they knew, some they didn't. Curious eyes followed them, assessing, welcoming. The Sanctuary breathed around them, older and younger all at once.

They were home.

Whether they still fit... that was something the place — and each of them — would decide in its own time.

* * *

By dusk, firelight bathed the clearing in warm, shifting gold. Three fires burned bright, each ringed by its own constellation of people — some speaking low, others laughing loud enough to brush the treetops.

The smell of stew hung thick above the main pit, a big iron pot suspended over the flame. Damper made its slow journey around the circle until only crumbs remained. A harmonica line drifted lazily through the evening, bright and wandering.

The returning crew settled back without fanfare — blankets unfurled, mugs filled, bowls pressed into their hands by strangers who'd already become neighbours. The welcome was genuine, if different. New faces watched Gypsy with curiosity rather than instant recognition; the camp's rhythm had taken on Mick and Ryder's steadiness.

David sat with Lisa and Willow near the main fire, the three of them tucked beneath a shared blanket. The crackle of wood, the hum of voices, the rise and fall of music stirred memories of beaches, moonlit waves, and a different kind of closeness.

Lisa leaned into him, though her eyes roamed the camp, absorbing every detail. Willow watched the newcomers by the river, reading each body-language shift with her usual cat-like certainty, her toes nudging patterns into the sand.

Shay sat back from the fire, close enough for heat, far enough to see everything. She nudged Elara — ink-stained fingers, notebook balanced on her knee — and tilted her head toward a group gathered near the new hut.

"They've made it their home," Shay murmured.

Elara smiled softly. "And now we find our place in it again."

Across the flames, Gypsy and Shelly shared road stories to a half-circle of listeners. Ryder dropped down beside them with a steaming mug, his deep laugh rolling through the clearing as others drifted close to hear.

Stars surfaced slowly, one by one, in the high dark.

Despite the changes, the Sanctuary still held its heartbeat — voices mingling, firelight flickering across faces, music rising and settling like a tide. A place stitched together by smoke, food, and quiet understanding.

It was home.

But as the embers dimmed and conversations softened into murmurs, each of them felt the same truth rise like river mist:

The Sanctuary hadn't been waiting for them. It had grown. And now, they would need to grow with it.

72

Morning came slow, sunlight sifting through the canopy in thin gold lines. The camp was already stirring — someone chopping wood, voices drifting from the riverbank where a few people bathed, and the smell of tea and damper moving through the cool air like a welcome back.

Gypsy walked the perimeter with a mug in hand, Shelly beside him. The changes were impossible to miss. New tents and huts had appeared — some simple canvas, others sturdier with timber frames and patched corrugated iron. Along the main path, flower beds of marigolds, nasturtiums, and sunflowers leaned eagerly toward the light.

Near the centre stood a new structure — the craft hut. Rough-cut timber walls, a palm-thatch roof, and shelves lined with handmade goods: beaded necklaces, woven baskets, small carvings. A hand-painted sign beside the door read:

UKI MARKET FUND — DONATIONS WELCOME

Mick had explained it the night before. Anything made here went to Uki markets, the money returning as food, tools, and repairs.

"If you feel like it, you make something," he'd said. "If you don't, you don't. No one's counting."

David stood in the doorway now, running a hand over a half-finished macramé wall hanging.

"Feels different," he murmured to Lisa.

"Not bad different," she said — though her gaze drifted toward the road, as if measuring the distance to home.

Willow leaned against the post beside them, catching the look and tucking it away. "I could make things here," she said with a grin. "Bangles, maybe. Keep us in tea and biscuits."

A little way off, Elara sat beside a smaller morning fire, a battered leather notebook open on her lap. She'd been jotting scraps since they left Surfers — the colour of dawn on the water, overheard sentences, the way kombi curtains breathed with the wind. Her quiet smile suggested she approved of how the world looked in ink.

Gypsy paused in the middle of the clearing, taking it all in. The place had grown — stronger, busier — yet as he watched, it felt a little less his. Whether that was good or not, he couldn't yet tell.

For everyone else, the day was a gentle test: gauging new faces, finding where to sit, who to talk to, which fires held old rhythms and which held new ones. The river still sang, the fires still crackled — but the pulse had changed.

And for Lisa, the thought of home was no longer a distant hum. It was beginning to pulse steadily at the back of her mind.

* * *

The river was warm in the shallows, cool and dark where the bank fell away. After lunch, the old crew drifted down there — away from the noise of camp, toward familiar water.

Willow lay flat on a sun-baked rock, fingers trailing through the current. Lisa sat nearby with her skirt hitched up, dipping her feet. David, shirtless, stood knee-deep, splashing water across his shoulders.

Gypsy leaned against a fallen log, Shelly beside him, watching sunlight scatter across the surface.

"Place has grown," he said. "More people, more noise. Not a bad thing — just different."

"Some of them look like they've been here forever," David said. "Like they own it."

"They don't," Ryder called as he approached, boots crunching on the stones. He crouched to splash his face, then smirked. "And if they tried... well."

Gypsy shot him a half-warning look. "No choking anyone like a chicken, mate. This isn't that kind of place."

Ryder chuckled, settling back on his heels. "Just saying — no one's pushing you out while I'm around."

"What about Chook?" Willow asked, rolling onto her back. "Is he still here?"

"Was last week," Ryder said. "Took off north for a surf comp. Might be gone a month, might be gone a year. Wild—" he caught himself, grinning, "—character."

Lisa smiled faintly, remembering his stories, the chaos he carried like a breeze.

Gypsy skimmed a pebble across the water. "Any community worth keeping has to change," he said. "But we still hold the fire, not them."

The ripple-rings spread across the surface, catching the light. Everyone understood.

The Sanctuary was still theirs — but fitting back in would take time.

As the sun slipped low, shadows stretched across the clearing. Fires were already lit, each with its own gathering — some cooking, some sharing mugs, others deep in talk. Woodsmoke blended with roasted vegetables and the sharp, green scent of herbs from the new garden beds.

Shay moved through the clearing barefoot, damp grass cool beneath her toes. She tipped her hat forward against the pale glare, eyes drifting over the subtle changes — new huts, unfamiliar faces, flowerbeds brave in the late light.

A few heads lifted in greeting. *You're back; good.* But even in the warmth, she felt the shift deep in the soil.

She paused at the craft hut where Shelly sorted beadwork into a woven basket.

"Morning," Shelly said. "River still running smooth?"

"Always," Shay replied, though her gaze travelled across the camp again, thoughtful.

A quiet tremor ran through the place — not trouble, not yet — but change.

David sat near the main fire with Lisa and Willow, half-listening to a man in a broad hat explaining a water-catchment system. Lisa looked politely engaged. Willow did not.

Ryder sat alone to the side, sharpening a hatchet on a flat stone. New arrivals gave him a wide berth. Mick ladled out stew with steady, unhurried hands.

Gypsy and Shelly moved through the circles, their return noticed but not fussed over. Old faces brightened. New faces hesitated.

By the time the pots were scraped clean, the music had begun — guitar, hand drums, harmonica — drifting from fire to fire. Shay and Elara settled onto a blanket, firelight flickering across Shay's smile.

"It's still home," Shay murmured. "Just... a different home."

It was true. The Sanctuary was alive — maybe more alive than ever — but its rhythm wasn't theirs alone anymore. They would have to find their place again.

Behind them, the Sanctuary burned in full voice — fires snapping, guitars humming, laughter rolling through the clearing. Down by the river, everything softened into water sounds and the hiss of wind through casuarinas.

Shay sat cross-legged, Akubra tipped back, moonlight catching in her hair. The silence wasn't empty; it was a place to breathe.

Smoke drifted past her, rising toward stars half-obscured by branches.

* * *

At a smaller fire circle, Lisa and Willow had slipped into their own orbit.

Willow lay on her side, propped on one elbow, a strand of hair falling across her cheek. "So," she said with a slow grin, "you and me... we've been dancing around this, haven't we?"

Lisa poked the fire with a stick. "Dancing around what?"

"Oh don't play innocent." Willow's tone softened, though mischief glowed in her eyes. "We could stay a throuple — you, me, and David. After all..." she lifted her brows, wicked, "...he's pretty wonderful, if you know what I mean."

Lisa let out a helpless laugh. "Willow..."

"Oh, yes you do." Willow leaned closer. "You love him. I see it. And I'm not taking him from you." Her voice dipped, warm. "But you and I... we've got something too. A different spark."

Lisa shook her head, smiling despite herself. "You're impossible."

"Maybe," Willow said, flopping onto her back, "but I'm also right."

The fire popped, sparks spiralling upward.

* * *

Later, Lisa drifted toward the river and found Shay sitting alone, moon whitening her hair, firelit camp behind her.

Lisa settled beside her, folding her skirt beneath her legs.

"It feels different now," she murmured.

Shay nodded. "It is. It's their rhythm at the moment. We'll find our place in it again — just might take time."

Lisa watched the clearing where Willow teased a newcomer and David's laugh floated above the noise.

"I'm not sure where I fit anymore."

Shay turned gently toward her. "Lisa, you always find your place. You move with people, not away from them."

Lisa traced circles in the dirt with a twig, thoughtful.

David's laugh carried again, warm and familiar. Lisa's eyes flicked toward it, almost without thinking.

Shay noticed, but didn't call it out. She only nudged Lisa's arm.

"Whatever happens," she said softly, "you're not lost. You're just growing."

Lisa's breath eased, the tension slowly leaving her shoulders.

"I hope so."

"You will," Shay said simply.

Leaves shifted in the rising night breeze, carrying smoke and river mist through the clearing. Distant music rose, softened, rose again.

Lisa smiled — small, warm, aching and hopeful all at once.

"Me too."

73

Mist clung low over the river, the early light turning it silver. Somewhere deeper in camp a kettle whistled, followed by the soft clink of enamel mugs. Cool air lifted goosebumps — the kind that vanished as soon as the sun crested the treeline.

Lisa stepped from the van first, hair loose, jumper slipping off one shoulder. She paused on the top step, breathing in the smoke-and-damp-earth scent that made mornings here feel older than they were. Willow appeared a moment later, yawning as she wrapped a blanket around her shoulders. They shared a small smile — unspoken, steady — both carrying the weight of last night's conversations.

By the main fire, David stood with Gypsy, both gripping hot mugs, steam lifting into the mist. Their voices were low, the kind men slip into when the real thing sits beneath the words. Ryder passed behind them with a length of timber on his shoulder, nodding in greeting without breaking stride.

Shay walked up from the river track alone, the grass still wet beneath her bare feet. She tipped her hat forward against the pale morning glare, the smell of water and casuarinas clinging faintly to her skin. As she stepped into the clearing, a few heads lifted — brief, wordless acknowledgements.

You're back. Good.

Near the craft hut, Shelly sorted beadwork into a woven basket. She looked up, smiling warmly — the kind of smile that made mornings feel steady.

"River still running smooth?" she asked.

Shay nodded. "Always."

But her gaze drifted beyond Shelly — taking in the gardens, the fresh faces, the new tents rising like mushrooms after rain. The Sanctuary felt fuller now, thicker in the air. Not unfriendly... just changed. She breathed in woodsmoke and dew, feeling the subtle shift more clearly. This was still home, but the rhythm had a new beat, one she'd have to ease herself back into.

There was a current stirring beneath the morning hum — quiet but unmistakable. People cooked, built, tended fires; yet beneath the ordinary movement lay something deeper, a slow unravelling of the old rhythm. Choices were coming: who would stay, who would drift, and where the road might tug each of them next.

For now, breakfast called — fire-warmed bread, honey dripping from a tin, the first wandering guitar strum drifting through the mist. Laughter rose here and there, bright enough to lift the morning, but every one of them leaned ever so slightly toward the horizon.

* * *

Dew steamed off the grass as Gypsy stepped down from his kombi, enamel mug in hand, the metal tapping faintly against his silver rings. He didn't say where he was going — the slow loop he made through camp was familiar. Part habit. Part head-count. Part keeping a finger on the pulse.

The first stretch of camp was easy-going. A young couple stirred porridge in a battered billy while two barefoot kids chased each other between tents. But as Gypsy rounded the bend toward the new section, he slowed.

More tents. More tarps. More people than he'd seen here even a fortnight ago. They weren't drifting in anymore — they were arriving in clusters, some with bedrolls, some with bags, some with nothing but the clothes on their backs.

Near the old water barrel, four newcomers argued over whose turn it was to fetch from the river. At the woodpile, two unfamiliar men snapped branches off a live tree instead of using the neatly stacked split logs metres away.

"Morning," Gypsy offered as he passed.

They returned it, but their eyes were wary — measuring him, measuring this place, measuring their own place in it.

Further along, Shelly hung laundry beside one of the older women, their voices carried in fragments.

"...don't want trouble, but they're not pulling their weight..."

By the time Gypsy returned to the main fire, Ryder was already there sharpening a knife, each slow stroke whispering against the stone. Mick sat nearby, both hands wrapped around a mug as though warming them against a deeper chill than the morning's.

"How many now?" Gypsy asked, lowering himself onto an upturned crate.

Mick exhaled through his nose. "Fifty? Sixty? More every day."

"Some can pitch in, some can't," Ryder said without looking up. "Plenty don't even try. They see a fire and food and a roof of trees and think it just... happens."

Gypsy took a long sip of coffee, the heat grounding him. "How many more before this stops being a sanctuary and starts looking like a slum?"

"We're close now," Mick said quietly.

The knife rasped again — a quiet warning all on its own.

"Let it grow too fast," Ryder murmured, "and it'll eat itself from the inside. Or someone from the outside will come in and tear it down."

The three men sat in stillness, the fire snapping softly between them. Children's laughter drifted faintly from across camp, mixing with the sound of someone hammering fresh timber into place.

Gypsy finally set his mug down. "We'll think on it. No rash moves. But we need a plan before the river overruns its banks."

74

The valley air carried the scent of woodsmoke and frying bread long before they reached the market. By the time they rolled into Uki, the streets were already lined with stalls — larger, brighter, spilling into the side lanes like a festival that had outgrown itself overnight. Flags fluttered. Fabric tents billowed. Music drifted between the shopfronts, weaving with laughter and the steady hum of voices.

Gypsy parked the kombi on a patch of grass just beyond the main drag. They stepped out into the warmth, stretching after the drive as a fiddle and hand drum echoed through the morning bustle.

It was impossible to miss: the Sanctuary had changed the market. Familiar faces now manned stalls — beadwork, macramé, tie-dye, carved driftwood. Other free-campers had joined them too, creating a swirl of colour and texture. The crowd, bigger than ever, showed just how fast word travelled.

Shelly paused at a bread stall where the baker handed her a warm loaf.

"Place is booming," he said. "Must be all you lot. Hear your camp's filling up — not just your regulars anymore."

She smiled, but the comment stayed with her.

Near the musicians, an older man waved Gypsy over — sun-creased, sharp-eyed.

"Seen a lot of vans up your way lately," he said. "Good for some of us... but keep an eye on it. Too many people in one spot can sour quick."

Gypsy returned the smile, but the words lodged deep.

The morning spilled onward in a wash of colour — Lisa twirling in a flowing skirt while Willow lifted bangles to catch the light; Ryder filling a sack with vegetables; Shay testing a carved flute before handing over a few coins with an easy grin. Elara bought a small tin of ink and turned it in her hands like treasure.

By the time the sun tilted west, they'd gathered fruit, cloth and bread — and a handful of rumours to carry home.

Back at the kombi, the talk was light, but Gypsy's gaze stayed on the road, already counting how many more might follow the trail they'd unknowingly left.

* * *

The Sanctuary was lit in gold when they returned, the river throwing ribbons of reflected sunlight through the trees. Smoke curled from the cooking fires; the scent of stew mingled with the sweetness of fresh damper.

They unpacked without fuss — bread to Shelly's table, fruit to the shared crates, cloth to the craft hut. Others drifted toward the main fire, trying on new finds, laughing at Willow's wild bargaining stories.

Gypsy didn't sit straight away. He made a slow, familiar loop around the clearing, eyes tracking every corner before settling beside Ryder and Mick at a smaller fire.

"Markets are bigger than ever," he said.

Mick nodded. "Word's spreading."

"They know about us," Gypsy added. "Stallholders from as far as Nimbin. Even a few questions about how many live here now." His gaze narrowed. "Friendly enough — but watching."

Ryder tore bread with his hands. "Watching's fine. Better than acting. But that can turn fast."

Gypsy nodded slowly. "Every camp within a morning's drive is filling. People looking for somewhere like this."

"Not all of them know how to live like this," Mick said. "Some take more than they give."

A log cracked. From the main circle, Lisa's laughter carried — Willow leaning into her shoulder. Gypsy's expression softened, though the furrow in his brow did not.

"We'll need to talk soon," he said quietly. "Before someone else decides for us."

Ryder tossed the crust into the fire. "Whenever you're ready. Just don't wait too long."

The quiet that followed said the rest: keeping a place like this alive came with weight.

* * *

Word slipped through the camp all afternoon: Gypsy wanted everyone at the main fire after sundown.

By the time the sun dropped, the circle was full. Lanterns hung from branches, painting faces in warm gold and long shadow. Conversations softened as the fire popped and hissed.

Gypsy stood when the crowd settled. He didn't call for silence. It found him on its own.

"When I was a boy," he began, "there was a creek behind our house. In spring it ran so fast the banks gave way. We'd pile rocks and branches — whatever we had — to hold it steady. If we didn't, the creek kept widening until there was no path left. Water was still beautiful... but the land around it was gone."

He let the image breathe.

"We built this place because we wanted steady ground. A river that could run without washing us out. But the river's running faster now."

A murmur rolled through the circle.

A newcomer in a patched denim jacket leaned forward. "We heard this was a place that didn't shut people out. That's why we came."

"It still is," Gypsy said evenly. "But we can't let the water rise so high it takes the banks."

Ryder's voice carried from across the fire, blunt and steady. "If we keep growing like this, we'll have nothing left to share."

Old members nodded. Newcomers stiffened.

One of the early girls crossed her arms. "I'm not feeding people who won't lift a finger."

Gypsy raised a hand — not to silence, but to ease the current.

"We're not dividing this into us and them," he said. "We're working out how we stay *us*."

He stepped closer to the flames.

"What if new folk tell us what they can bring? Skills, hands, something for the gardens, shelters, firewood. And if the Sanctuary's full... we build a sister camp. Share the dream — don't choke it."

The circle stilled. A ripple of nods. A few thoughtful looks. A handful of wary ones.

But no one walked away.

Ryder grunted approval. Mick nodded once, already weighing options.

The river had been nudged back toward its banks — not settled yet, but flowing.

* * *

When the meeting ended, the circle loosened. Laughter rose again — quieter than before, but real.

The fire burned low, embers breathing orange into the dark. Most had already drifted back to their tents or vans, leaving only a handful around the glow.

Shay sat cross-legged, a mug cupped between her hands. Lisa leaned against David's shoulder, tired but calm. Willow stretched out beside them, tracing idle patterns in the sand with her finger. Elara sat a little behind, notebook balanced on her knees, pen poised but still.

"It went better than I thought," Shay murmured.

Lisa nodded. "Gypsy makes it feel safe. Like we're not losing anything — just rearranging."

David stared into the embers. "Some didn't like it. You could feel that too."

A couple of shapes lingered beyond the firelight — neither angry nor welcoming. Just watching. Measuring.

"They're not the type to leave quietly," Willow said under her breath.

Shay's gaze flicked toward the shadows. "No. They're not."

Lisa swallowed. "So what happens if—"

David cut in gently. "If they try anything, they'll learn quickly this place isn't as soft as it looks."

Shay's small smile held steel. "Exactly."

The fire cracked softly. Leaves rustled overhead. The river whispered beyond the dark.

Shay looked toward the water and added,

"Some people watch too closely... and forget they're being watched too."

75

It began as a low growl, deep and far away.

At first no one paid it much attention — a trick of wind through the hills, maybe, or the promise of an afternoon storm. But the sound didn't fade. It swelled, rolling in steady waves that seemed to come from all directions at once, echoing off the ridgelines.

Conversations thinned. People paused mid-task. Heads tilted skyward.

Blue. Clear, endless blue. Not a cloud in sight.

The rumble deepened — a heartbeat magnified — and unease rippled through the clearing. A couple of Uki locals visiting the Sanctuary exchanged puzzled glances. They knew this valley's storms.

This wasn't one of them.

By the kombi circle, Gypsy rose slowly, shading his eyes toward the southern track. Lisa and Shay looked up from the bracelets they were knotting. Mick stepped from the craft hut, wiping sawdust from his palms.

Ryder was already standing.

"Stay here," he said — calm, certain — and strode toward the track.

The sound grew until the ground itself seemed to hum. Children fell quiet. Someone let a pot burn. Even the birds stilled.

Then shapes broke through the heat shimmer — a line of chrome and leather, black tyres kicking up pale dust.

Motorcycles.

Dozens.

They came two by two, engines snarling low, sunlight flashing along polished tanks. Each jacket bore the same bold patch: an iron head-dress stitched in bright, unmistakable colours.

Iron Chiefs.

They didn't drift in; they arrived — moving like a single animal. They pulled into the clearing in disciplined rows, engines thundering before cutting in perfect unison.

Hot metal and oil drifted on the air.

When the last engine died, the silence rang loud enough to scatter birds from the treetops.

Off to one side, just beyond the old fire-pit stones, two figures lingered — the same watchers from the night before. Their faces stayed hidden beneath the trees. They watched the riders dismount, eyes narrowing, before slipping back into the shadows.

Ryder turned as Gypsy approached.

"Your idea?" Gypsy asked, one brow raised.

Ryder grinned — all teeth. "Sometimes you need to send a message. Hope we've got enough beer and weed."

Gypsy laughed and clapped his shoulder. "Welcome, brothers! Been a while..."

The Chiefs greeted him with nods and backslaps, unloading crates from saddlebags, shaking dust from their jackets. The camp exhaled — still buzzing, still unsure — but steadier now.

For the first time in weeks, the ground felt firm.

For now, the river had its banks again.

* * *

The clearing was alive before the first star blinked through the dusk.

Extra logs had been dragged to the main fire, and by nightfall the flames licked high, painting everyone in gold and ember-red. The scent of roasting vegetables mingled with smoke, sweet herbs, and the faint spice of rolled joints.

The Iron Chiefs moved through the crowd with quiet ease — not loud, not posturing, simply present. Laughing when laughter came, leaning in when stories softened. Boots and bare feet mixed on the dusty ground as though they'd always belonged together.

Ryder sat with his back to a log, bottle in hand, telling a story about crossing the Nullarbor in heat so fierce it made your teeth ache. Two of his brothers nodded at the right moments, grinning at the wrong ones.

Shay had found her place by the fire, hair lit copper as she strummed a borrowed twelve-string. Lisa sat close to David, their shoulders leaning together, swaying in time to a rhythm only they felt.

Beyond the firelight, at the edge where the trees began, those same faint silhouettes stood again.

Watching. Always watching.

One of the Chiefs — tall, rangy, a streak of silver in his hair — noticed them. He shifted, gaze steady, and gave the smallest nod.

Message received.

The music rolled on. Someone harmonised with Shay, voices twining like smoke. A bottle passed hand to hand. Every so often a Chief rose, stretched, and wandered the perimeter — effortless, instinctive, as natural as breathing.

By the time the moon was high, the fire felt like a living thing — hot, bright, pulling everyone closer. Whatever shadows lurked beyond the treeline, they didn't step into the circle tonight.

Tonight was for warmth. For laughter. For memories strong enough to stand against whatever storm was coming.

* * *

The sun rose clean and gold, washing the Sanctuary in a softness that made everything look gentler than it had under firelight. Smoke curled from the pit; enamel plates and bottle tops glinted among the dust.

Gypsy was up early, barefoot as always. He moved slowly through the clearing — not wandering, but checking a fenceline only he could see.

He nodded to two Chiefs still perched by the embers with mugs in hand and continued — past the kombi ring where the twins lay tangled in blankets, past laundry lines heavy with sarongs and patched jeans, past new garden beds where bean shoots reached for the light.

At first glance, the Sanctuary looked good. Alive. Thriving.

But the longer he walked, the more the seams showed.

Another half-dozen tents along the treeline — faces he didn't recognise. A second fire circle on the far riverbank that hadn't been there last week. Children he'd never seen racing barefoot through the long grass.

Down at the food store, he lifted a canvas flap and frowned: the sacks of rice and lentils were lower than they should've been this early in the week.

Mick found him there, chewing a strip of dried mango.

"Place is growing," he said. It wasn't praise.

"How many now?" Gypsy asked quietly.

"Hard to say. They're not coming in ones and twos anymore. They're turning up in clumps."

They walked toward the river where Ryder was oiling his chain. He looked up, met Gypsy's eye, and shrugged.

"Couldn't tell you how many more we can take before it starts feeling wrong — or before the locals start calling this a slum."

Gypsy didn't answer straight away. He watched a little girl carry water from the river, daisies braided into her hair, giggling as she stepped through the shallows.

"It's still good," he said at last. "Still what we meant it to be. But I've seen what happens when it tips."

Ryder nodded once. "Then maybe we make sure it doesn't."

Gypsy's gaze drifted toward the hills, where the track to Uki disappeared into green.

"Market's in a couple of days," he murmured. "We'll talk more after that."

From the craft hut came the steady tap of a hammer. Across the clearing, the Chiefs' laughter rolled warm and low.

It all looked, for now, like peace.

But Gypsy felt the shift — the season turning, the river rising, and something, somewhere, beginning to press hard against the banks.

76

The road to Uki was alive with colour — vans and wagons painted in wild swirls, battered utes rattling under crates of fruit and homemade bread, bicycles wobbling under baskets tied with fraying rope. By the time they reached town, the market had spilled beyond the usual square, flooding the side streets like a river that had slipped its banks.

It was bigger than any of them remembered. Twice as many stalls. Twice as many faces.

And not just locals — the clothes, hair, and accents told their own story. Other communities had come too, drawn by the same promise of freedom, trade, and something unnameable that lived in the valley air.

The Sanctuary's fingerprints were everywhere: Shelly's necklaces, Mick's carved spoons, the twins' woven mats, a basket of vegetables marked *From the River Garden*. People stopped to chat, smiling as though greeting old friends.

"You lot have put this town on the map," someone said.

"Heard it's getting busy up your way," someone else murmured —
light voice, curious eyes.

Gypsy smiled each time, but his gaze never stopped moving.

Willow was stacking jars of jam behind the stall when someone
called across the lane, "Hey, Willow! You still singing these days?"

Before she could answer, Shay slipped beside her, bright-eyed.

"Oh, she sings — and she's not escaping today."

"I'm working," Willow protested, but Shay was already guiding her
toward the makeshift stage beneath a pepper tree — little more than a
woven rug and an old guitar resting on a wooden crate.

Heads turned. A ripple through the crowd.

Someone handed Willow the guitar. Shay sat cross-legged beside
her and whispered, "Let's give them something true."

The first chords of *Turn! Turn! Turn!* drifted across the market —
soft, steady, sure. Shay's voice joined Willow's like it had been waiting
for its cue all morning, warm and low. They didn't look at one another;
the harmonies found each other easily, like they always had.

To everything (turn, turn, turn)...

At the back of the crowd, Gypsy watched with a half-smile. Ryder
stood beside him, arms folded, eyes scanning the flow of people with
quiet vigilance that never quite switched off.

When the last note faded, the silence held for a heartbeat — and
then applause rose, warm and real. Shay nudged Willow with a grin.

"Told you your voice carries."

Back at the stall, Lisa and Shelly clapped along, laughing. David had
his arm draped around Lisa's shoulders, though his eyes drifted over
the crowd — catching the same subtle shift Gypsy felt.

A little too much interest from strangers.

A few glances held a fraction too long.

A low murmur under the cheer.

It was a beautiful day — one of the best.

Yet beneath the warmth, something had turned.

Faint, but certain.

Like the first breeze before a storm.

* * *

By pack-up time, the baskets were light and the cash tin heavy. The mats had sold out. Shelly's necklaces were gone by midday. Only two jars of jam remained — apricot and plum — which Lisa insisted they keep for camp breakfasts.

Shay tipped the coins into a heap; Willow let them run through her fingers, laughing at the clink.

Mick crouched to count. "Eighty-three dollars and some shrapnel. Enough for flour, beans, maybe nails and paint."

Gypsy nodded. "It's more than money. It's how people see us now. Not just campers in the hills. Part of the valley."

Shay agreed. "Worth more than coins."

Still, the coins mattered. Market earnings fed the Sanctuary — food, fabric, tools, repairs. It wasn't much yet, but it felt steady. Like laying foundation stones without meaning to.

* * *

The walk back to the kombi was quieter.

Success lingered sweetly, but something tugged at Lisa's thoughts. David walked ahead with the jars clinking in a cloth bag. Willow kept pace beside her, sunlight catching fire in the golden strands of her hair.

"You've gone quiet," Willow said gently.

"Just thinking."

"That usually means trouble. Go on."

Lisa hesitated. "I've been feeling... homesick. More than I expected. I love it here — the Sanctuary, you, David — but part of me still thinks about going back."

Willow slowed, letting David drift ahead.

"You'd go back without us?"

Lisa's breath caught. "I don't want to lose either of you. That's what scares me. I don't even know if I could."

Willow's smile softened — smaller, truer. "Then that's the only bit that matters."

Lisa frowned. "What do you mean?"

"It means we stop trying to write the ending," Willow said, voice low and warm. "You stay while it feels right. If the road pulls you home, we figure it out then. One thing at a time, Lis."

Lisa's shoulders loosened. "I couldn't imagine not having you both in my life."

Willow bumped her hip lightly. "Good. Because you're stuck with us — at least for now."

Up ahead, David turned with a grin. "What's so funny?"

"Nothing!" Lisa called back — smiling still, though something tugged softly at her heart. She didn't know what the future held. Only that both of them were woven into her in ways she couldn't unravel without breaking something precious.

* * *

That night, the Sanctuary lay mostly quiet — the main fire reduced to glowing coals, soft guitar threads unravelling into the dark. Lisa had gone to help Shelly. Willow laughed somewhere across camp, her bright voice ringing through the trees.

David lay on the narrow van bed, arms behind his head, staring at the ceiling. He should've been exhausted, but the stillness just sharpened every thought he'd been trying to outrun.

Lisa — steady, kind, the one who'd leapt with him. She'd grown here. He loved her plainly.

Willow — wildfire wrapped in sun. Loud, fearless, impossible not to want. She sparked something in him he didn't have language for.

Two tethers, both tied deep.

He cared for them both. Memories with each lived under his skin. No regrets — just the quiet truth that whatever this was couldn't stay balanced forever.

Outside, Willow's laugh rose again, followed by Lisa's softer one.

A blessing and a bruise.

David closed his eyes and let the sound settle over him. Whatever came next, some part of him already mourned the moment they'd have to choose.

77

Two mornings later, Mick rattled his old Holden ute along the track to the Callahan homestead, dust rising in lazy curls behind him. He parked beside the wide verandah — a place that always smelled faintly of kerosene, saddle leather, and the ghosts of horses long since gone. Windchimes made from brass harness fittings clinked softly in the breeze.

Old Mr Callahan stood at the top step, mug of tea in hand.

"Mick! Thought you'd forgotten about me since that mob moved in down the end."

Mick grinned. "Couldn't forget you if I tried, mate. Actually—" he scrubbed a hand through his hair "—I'm here about them."

Callahan raised his brows. "Oh?"

"They've looked after the land," Mick said. "Better than anyone has in years. Gardens in. Rubbish cleared. Fences patched. But the camp's growing. We're running out of space. I was wondering if you'd lease 'em another patch — that bit past the creek you don't farm."

Callahan took a long sip, eyes drifting over the paddocks.

"That corner floods in a wet," he mused. "But if they build the ground up near the treeline, it'll hold."

He regarded Mick over the rim of his mug. "They'll need to keep it tidy. No rusting cars or half-finished shacks."

"They'll agree to that," Mick said without hesitation.

Callahan nodded slowly. "Alright then. They've been good tenants. I'll give 'em the creek side for a peppercorn rent. Just don't let it get out of hand. You know how these things go."

"I do," Mick replied — and he meant it.

* * *

By sunrise, the heat was already nudging at the edges of the day. Smoke drifted from half a dozen fires. Tents had shuffled closer in the night, ropes tangling like vines, and someone had lit a burner where it wasn't meant to be.

Gypsy strolled barefoot through the clearing, Shelly at his side. They didn't speak at first — the camp spoke for itself. Too many tents. Too many new faces. Too many quiet grumbles from the old hands.

Near the craft hut, Mick showed a pair of newcomers where to pitch their tent. Ryder leaned against a post, arms folded, watching everything like it was a slow-moving storm.

"How many more before this place tips over?" Gypsy asked quietly.

"Not many," Mick said. "Not if we want peace — or the coppers to keep thinking we're harmless oddballs instead of a slum."

Shay joined them, Akubra shading her eyes. "We set a number," she said simply. "Fifty. When one leaves, another can join. Until then, no more."

The idea landed like a stone in a deep pool — ripples moving outward through the clearing. Agreement. Doubt. Relief. A little fear.

"What if someone won't leave?" someone called from the hut.

Ryder's grin was slow and sharp. "Then I'll have a friendly word."

The laughter that followed softened the air but didn't erase the truth beneath it.

Gypsy nodded. "We'll talk to Callahan about more land and build up the creek paddock. But until then — fifty. And we look after what we've got."

It wasn't a speech. Just a truth settling into the bones of the Sanctuary.

* * *

Dusk melted gold across the trees. A fire lit early drew the camp together without a word spoken. Ryder arrived with a slab of beer; Mick with a basket of vegetables. Shay folded herself beside the flames, guitar resting across her knees.

A newcomer stepped into the glow with a fiddle. One slow note bent the night around it, then rose into a tune that felt like a shared road — long, dusty, and full of worn-in friendship. Voices joined it. Bare feet tapped the sand. Laughter unfurled like smoke.

The clearing pulsed like a living heart.

When the final note faded, the fire still burned high and faces glowed warm with heat and hope.

For a little while, no one thought about tents, or numbers, or limits. Only the simple miracle of fifty souls breathing in rhythm beneath the stars.

78

The storm didn't come from the sky.

It came up the track in a convoy of white and blue.

Engines broke the morning quiet. Magpies fell silent in the gums. Four police sedans and a paddy wagon rolled into the Sanctuary clearing, tyres crushing the damp rim of grass. Senior Constable Rand stepped out first, cap set hard, eyes flat as river stones. Eight officers fanned behind him, hands already resting on batons and holsters.

"Compliance check," Rand called, voice slicing the stillness. "Vehicles, knives, narcotics. Everyone stay where you are."

No warrant.

No complaint.

Just force.

Gypsy walked forward with Shelly, calm as a still pool.

"You're on leased land," he said evenly. "We're happy to talk."

Rand didn't look at him. He looked past him — to the ring of kombis, the craft hut, the Iron Chiefs by the cookfire, boots dusty, faces unreadable.

"Bikes first."

Two officers went straight for the Chiefs' machines, emptying saddlebags onto tarps: spanners, rags, plug tins, lube. One ran a hand along a sissy bar and smirked as though he'd uncovered a crime.

The Chiefs didn't react.

Ryder watched them all, arms folded, silent as iron.

At the kombi circle, another pair of officers began unzipping tents without asking. A boot snapped a guy rope; canvas sagged. A macramé wall hanging Lisa had left to dry was yanked down and dropped in the dirt.

Willow flinched, then steadied.

"Careful with that."

"Step back, love," a constable replied.

Lisa stepped forward anyway, lifting the macramé and shaking the grit loose. Rand saw it. He crooked a finger at the nearest officer.

"Move them on."

A hand clamped around Lisa's forearm — firm, not kind.

David was beside her in a heartbeat.

"Hands off," he said, low.

The constable loosened his grip, but didn't drop it. Rand watched long enough to leave a bruise without leaving a story.

"Cooperate and it's faster," he said, almost bored.

By the bikes, an officer tipped out a saddlebag and a sheathed camp knife dropped into the dust.

"Prohibited," he declared — though half the camp used the same blade for bread and rope.

"That's a camp knife," Ryder said. "You take mine, you take everyone's."

His smile held no humour. "Want to start at the kitchen fire?"

Two constables shifted closer, waiting for even the smallest rise of his hands.

Gypsy stepped between them, palms open.

"Ryder. Not worth it."

Ryder's jaw clenched. He stepped back.

The craft hut was next.

Two officers strode in, eyes on shelves instead of people.

Beaded necklaces hit the floor.

Carved spoons spilled from a toppled basket.

A baton poked the cash tin.

"Donations," Shelly said from the doorway. "Uki Market Fund."

"Paperwork?"

"On the wall," Mick said, pointing to a hand-painted sign. "Read it carefully if you need to."

The officer shut the tin harder than necessary.

Rand's sweep widened. He lingered on the Chiefs and picked his mark: a young rider with a split lip from some other life.

"Search."

Boots apart. Palms on the wagon. Pockets emptied.

Nothing on him.

Didn't matter.

The cuffs still came out.

"On what charge?" Gypsy asked.

"Defect to start with."

The wagon door clanged open.

The young Chief looked at Ryder.

Ryder didn't nod. Didn't blink.

"Don't make this a story," Shay whispered beside him.

"Already is," he replied.

Two more Chiefs were lined up and patted down. One had a penknife. One had nothing. It didn't change the choreography.

Across the clearing, the Sanctuary gathered — not closing in, but forming a ring of quiet, unspoken defiance.

"You're done here," Gypsy said at last. Calm. Steady. "You've seen what there is to see."

Rand didn't answer.

He stepped to the main fire, lifted the lid of the stew pot without asking. Steam hit his face.

He let the lid fall — not dropped, but enough to clang hard and slop broth into the coals.

The fire hissed.

Something small but ancient moved through the circle.

"Enough," a new voice said from the track.

Old Mr Callahan stood beside his ute, hat in hand, boots muddy from the creek road. He took in the opened tents, the upended baskets, the cuffs.

"They're here with my say-so," he said. "Lease is in order. If you've got a warrant, let's see it. If not, you're trespassing like anyone else."

A couple of locals had followed him in, drawn by the sound of police cars. One woman lifted a boxy camera and didn't bother to hide it.

Rand saw the lens.

Something flickered. Not fear — calculation.

"Wrap it," he told his officers.

It didn't end neat. It never did.

The young Chief still went in the wagon — "outstanding matter," Rand said, words so vague they echoed. Another rider got a defect notice. A third was told to push his bike to the road and "leave the grown-ups' traffic alone."

But the tents stayed up.

The stew stayed in the pot.

The macramé was rehung.

As they rolled out, Rand paused long enough to slide his window down.

"Fifty today," he said, eyes sweeping the clearing. "Sixty next week and it looks different."

He shut the window and drove off, blue and white shrinking down the track until the gums swallowed the sound.

Silence held.

Then the camp breathed again.

Shelly was already at Lisa's side, touching the angry red mark on her forearm.

"Cold cloth," she murmured.

Willow bent and began picking beads from the dust, one by one. Mick righted the basket of spoons. Ryder straightened a knocked-over water bucket no one else had noticed. Shay moved among the Chiefs, her voice soft.

"Eat first. Then we sort the paperwork."

By late afternoon, word had reached town: police at the Sanctuary; bikies searched; Callahan stepped in. By evening, a second rumour followed — something about a complaint up the chain, a senior man from Murwillumbah asking why a compliance check looked like intimidation.

No one at the Sanctuary celebrated.

They cooked.

They ate.

They swept the day out of the dust.

When the first stars appeared, Gypsy stood at the fire. He didn't make a speech. He lifted the lid, stirred, and served bowls until the pot was light.

"We hold the fire," he said at last. Soft. Final.

It was the last time they saw Rand.

Not by chance.

By change.

A transfer, they heard. Different district, different troubles. Happening sooner than later.

The Sanctuary didn't wait for details.

They had gardens to water.

New creekside to clear.

A cap to keep.

And a story the camp already knew by heart:

When thunder came on a clear blue day,

the banks held.

79

Morning came softly to the Sanctuary — not falling but seeping, sliding along canvas seams, catching on jars in the craft-hut window, warming the little tomatoes Shelly fussed over. Mist lifted slow from the hills as Gypsy walked the main path, hands tucked into his pockets, eyes taking in every tent, van and lean-to.

Rand's raid had left little visible damage now, but Gypsy knew the deeper bruises were still forming. He had always known the sound of this place — the clink of a billy, the rattle of Mick's tools, the laughter of kids at the river — but now new sounds layered over the old. More voices. More footsteps. More stories threading themselves into the weave.

He smiled as he passed people, nodded, even joked once or twice, but kept a quiet tally in his mind.

Love could stretch.

Food could stretch.

Peace... that was the one he wasn't sure had any give left.

* * *

Lisa sat on the craft-hut steps, knees drawn up, a cotton top slipping from one shoulder. She didn't look anything like the timid girl who'd first stepped onto Byron sands. She'd grown into her skin here — sun-browned, barefoot, her confidence easy and unforced. Yet something inside her was shifting, a restlessness she didn't want to name.

She loved David.

She loved Willow.

She loved this wild, ridiculous, impossible place.

But the small voice that remembered home — her mother humming by the kettle, her own bed with the window cracked to the summer night — was growing louder. She wondered, not for the first time, whether anyone would notice if she slipped away for a while... or whether the campfire stories would simply roll on without her.

* * *

David leaned against the kombi, arms folded as he watched two newcomers mend a torn tent flap with fishing line. The Sanctuary used to move slow, like an old river — familiar, steady, comforting. Now it felt as though the current was picking up, pulling everyone in directions they hadn't agreed on.

He thought of the surf in Byron, Lisa's laughter on the esplanade, Willow with her hair blown wild by the wind. He didn't know what he wanted — only that standing still wasn't working anymore.

* * *

Willow drifted past him barefoot, her skirt flashing green-blue like water. She winked — the kind of smile that said she knew a secret about you... and might tell it if you annoyed her enough. She loved the flood of life here: the chaos, the stories, the mess of people. This place made her feel bright and electric.

But when her gaze slid to Lisa, a small knot tightened beneath her ribs.

Would they all end up on separate roads?

Could she let that happen?

Probably.

Eventually.

Just not today.

* * *

Shay knelt beside Shelly in the garden, fingers deep in the cool earth as she tugged weeds from around the tomato plants. Her hat was tipped low against the sun, her laughter warm and bright. Shay could stay a year or leave tomorrow without regret — that was her way — but she found herself glancing toward Lisa and David more than she meant to, drawn by something she didn't intend to name.

* * *

Ryder sat on a cut stump sharpening a blade, movements slow and methodical. He'd been up since dawn patrolling the perimeter track — not because anyone had asked, but because his blood still hummed from Rand's stunt.

The Sanctuary had always been loose around the edges, but now the edges had edges.

Too many tents. Too many strangers with stories they didn't share.

A few faces from last night lingered near the treeline, watching rather than joining. Ryder filed their features away the way other men collected coins.

He wasn't worried — not yet.

But he felt it: the shift.

Camps didn't fall apart in storms.

They crumbled in the quiet weeks that followed.

* * *

By midday, the day had stretched its full length before them — each person moving through it with their own quiet reckonings, their own longings, their own small storms brewing beneath the ribs.

And for this moment — just this brief, bright moment — the Sanctuary still held.

80

The late-afternoon sun slanted through the gums, laying bars of gold across the Sanctuary. Most of the camp had settled into the lazy rhythm of evening chores, leaving the kombi quiet and breathing in the shade.

Inside, Willow stretched out on the mattress, loose-limbed and languid from a day spent drifting between sunlight and breeze. When David ducked through the door, she smiled as if she'd been waiting for him the whole time.

"Thought you'd forgotten me," she teased, patting the space beside her.

He sat, the kombi creaking its familiar reply. "Not a chance."

Their banter softened into the quiet, familiar pull between them — a kiss, a laugh, and then the warm hush that followed, the kind that settled instead of burned. For a while they simply breathed together, the world outside dulled to wind and birdsong.

"I'm heading off tomorrow," David said at last. "Just a few days. Surf trip."

Willow lifted a brow. "Running from me already?"

He brushed a thumb along her cheek. "Running towards some thinking space."

"Out on the water," she murmured. "Your kind of church."

"Something like that."

She rolled onto her side, tracing slow shapes on his arm. "And when you come back?"

He hesitated — a heartbeat too long. "Maybe... maybe I'll stay. Here."

Willow's grin softened, losing its mischief and finding something truer. "Then we'll see how much fire this little camp can handle."

* * *

Dawn carried the sea's breath up the valley. David strapped his board to the kombi roof, the morning air already tasting of salt. Willow leaned in the doorway, hair tousled, shirt hanging artfully crooked.

"You really think the waves will tell you what you want?" she asked.

"They usually do."

She tugged him closer by the sleeve and kissed him lightly — not to claim, just to tether. "Don't take too long to listen."

He left with a wave, the kombi rattling toward the coast until the gums swallowed the sound.

Without him, the Sanctuary felt quieter but not empty. Willow and Lisa slipped easily into each other's days — making tea, wandering the gardens, sharing the riverbank at sunset.

One afternoon they lay on a blanket near the water, the river flickering silver behind them.

"I love it here," Lisa said softly. "I love you. I love him. But sometimes I miss home. Mum. Dad. My bed. I feel... pulled in two directions."

Willow leaned back on her hands. "We keep circling this, you realise," she said gently. "You on the fault line between here and there."

Lisa huffed a quiet laugh. "Because I never actually do anything about it."

"You could have both," Willow went on. "Stay a trio. No rule says love has to pick a side."

Lisa blushed, smiling despite herself. "You make it sound simple."

"It is," Willow murmured. "You just decide whether you want to keep dancing... or walk off the floor."

They fell quiet as Gypsy's bongo rolled faintly through the trees, steady as a heartbeat.

* * *

That night, when the fire burned low, they stayed behind — one blanket, two shoulders touching. The embers pulsed red and gold, lighting Lisa's face in soft, uncertain glow.

"You really think this can last?" she whispered.

"Maybe not forever," Willow replied. "But it's real now."

She leaned in, slow and certain, her kiss tasting of woodsmoke and truth.

* * *

In the days that followed, they found small excuses to stay close — a swim downriver, a walk to Uki, an afternoon on the kombi roof tracing shapes in the clouds. Each moment stitched them tighter, even as thoughts of home hovered at the edges of Lisa's mind like a faint ache waiting to speak.

For now, though, the river ran warm, the sky stayed blue, and the world held them quietly in its hands while the question of what comes next waited just beyond the bend.

81

The kombi's engine announced him before the camp caught sight of him. Heads lifted from gardens and kettles as the afternoon softened into gold.

Lisa was threading beads beside Willow when the sound reached them. Willow's smile curved before Lisa could speak.

"He's back."

David stepped from the kombi with that slow, easy stride — sun-browned, salt-scented, carrying the ocean in his shoulders. He took in the Sanctuary as though he'd been gone months instead of days.

"Hey," he murmured, eyes finding Lisa first.

She hugged him — warm, certain. Willow rose more slowly, unreadable for a heartbeat... until her grin broke through.

"You look like you've been living on saltwater and servo pies."

"Guilty," he laughed.

They settled around the fire as the sky deepened. David spoke of dolphins rising through glassy surf; Lisa told him of the markets; Willow added the smaller stories Lisa didn't — lazy afternoons by the river, Shelly's tomatoes, the laughter drifting from the craft hut.

At one point, Lisa leaned into David's shoulder. Willow passed her a mug of tea. Their hands brushed.

The moment stretched — soft, fragile, full.

No one named it. They didn't have to.

* * *

Later, when the camp had thinned to embers and murmurs, Willow sat cross-legged by the dying fire, her mug warm between her palms. Usually she shimmered in firelight. Tonight she was gentler, folded inward.

She thought of David's steadiness. Lisa's softness. The way the two of them had carved space inside her without asking.

"Maybe I'm not as untethered as I thought," she murmured to herself.

Shay passed by and lifted a hand in greeting. Willow almost called her over. Almost.

Some truths needed to be held alone.

* * *

Back in the kombi, Lisa curled on the bed, hair spilling across her shoulders. She had been quiet all night. Willow leaned against the closed door, watching her with that uncanny mix of mischief and intuition.

"You've been off in your head," she said softly. "Want to let me in there?"

Lisa gave a small smile. "I've just been thinking."

"That's dangerous," Willow teased, sliding closer. "You start thinking too much, you might do something sensible."

"Maybe I've had enough wild."

Willow took her hand, thumb brushing soft patterns into her skin. "You thinking of going home?"

Lisa hesitated. "Part of me wants to. Part of me doesn't."

"What if I came with you?" Willow asked.

Lisa's breath caught. "You'd leave here?"

"If it meant not losing you? Yeah." Willow's smile shifted — gentler than her usual sparkle. "I'd miss this place. But I can find trouble anywhere."

She tipped Lisa's chin lightly.

"You and David... that's something real. But you and me... we're real too."

The air thickened, warm and uncertain.

Willow brushed a strand of hair from Lisa's cheek, letting her fingers linger.

"If you go," she whispered, "with or without me... you'll take a piece of me with you."

She pressed a kiss to Lisa's forehead and slipped out into the dark.

* * *

David's arm lay heavy across Lisa's waist that night, Willow's warmth still fading from the mattress. Lantern light flickered against the kombi wall. Lisa stared at the glow, Willow's words looping softly:

What if I came with you?

It had sounded playful. It wasn't.

David breathed steadily behind her. She pictured Willow outside by the fire — awake, thinking too much, same as she was.

Two heartbeats — both hers, both dangerous.

She closed her eyes and let the night cradle her confusion.

* * *

Morning spilled gently into the van, turning blankets pale gold. Lisa woke first — David behind her, Willow draped lazily across her legs. Gulls cried somewhere downriver. Warmth pooled in the soft, quiet space they shared.

For a long moment, she didn't move, letting the scene imprint: smoke on skin, salt in hair, the hush before decisions.

"Not a bad way to wake up," Willow murmured, voice rough with sleep.

David tightened his arm around Lisa's waist. She breathed deeply, trying to memorise everything.

They spilled out onto the sand, stretching into the morning. David poured three coffees. Willow tied her sarong with a grin that promised mischief. Lisa watched them both with a heart full and aching.

None of them mentioned that choices were coming. They didn't need to.

It was already there — in the way they touched, in the quickened laughter, in the glances that lingered a second longer than they had yesterday.

Lisa sipped her coffee and thought:

This will be a memory that stays with me forever.

82

Ryder moved through the Sanctuary the way a man takes the temperature of a place — slow, loose, seeing everything without ever looking like he was watching. The late-afternoon air held woodsmoke, eucalyptus, and the faint tang of curry bubbling over someone's fire.

The Sanctuary was thick with life now. More vans. More tarps. More fires than the last time he'd traced this same loop. Not bad — not yet — but right up against full.

He passed the craft hut, solid these days instead of the sagging tarp it once had been. A half-dozen people worked inside: sanding spoons, knotting twine, jars of market coins catching the sun like treasure. Good. It meant the camp could feed itself if it had to.

Mick was in the garden, showing a couple of newcomers how to weave twine between stakes so the tomatoes didn't snap. He caught Ryder's eye and gave a tiny shake of his head — nothing urgent, but the clear sign that the work still wasn't being shared evenly.

Farther along, Shay's old sign clung to a gum tree:

Tread soft — the earth remembers.

The paint had faded under months of sun, but the words still hung in the air. Ryder huffed a quiet laugh. That was Shay — simple truths that stuck to your ribs.

Down by the creek, Lisa and Willow lay stretched on a blanket, hair tangled by the wind. Something Lisa said made Willow laugh — her hand brushing Lisa's arm in that casual, dangerous way. David wandered up, hair wet from the river, and sat beside them. Willow's foot pressed lightly against his leg; Lisa didn't move away, though something in her gaze drifted far beyond the water.

Ryder clocked the three of them without judgement. People tangled how they tangled. But he knew the look of a thread stretched close to snapping.

At the firepit, Gypsy and Shelly talked in low tones, scanning the camp as they spoke — listening to the place as closely as the people. Shelly's hand rested on Gypsy's arm. The ease between them softened the moment.

Near the Sanctuary entrance, Mick's handiwork stood tall:

THE SANCTUARY — RESPECT THE LAND, RESPECT EACH OTHER.

The letters were carved deep, oiled dark, built to last.

Ryder paused, thumb brushing over the timber grain.

He liked what they'd built. Liked the bones of it.

But the air had shifted — the way it does before a storm forms, even when the sky is spotless blue.

Two people arguing near the creek. Someone packing too slowly. A new arrival sitting apart, arms crossed, eyes watchful.

Yeah. Something was moving.

He'd find out what soon enough.

* * *

Mist clung low to the trees the next morning, muffling sound until it felt like it rose from underwater. Ryder leaned against Mick's sign, smoking the first rollie of the day as the Sanctuary woke one sound at a time — a guitar strumming, the cough of a cold kombi engine, a billy rattling on a grate.

Movement near the veg patch caught his eye.

Two of the new blokes — hair still shaped by army barbers — were pulling up carrots, onions, even a couple of small pumpkins.

Not harvesting for the camp. Hoarding.

He dropped the cigarette and walked over.

"Mornin'," he said easily.

One froze. The other kept yanking onions until Ryder's shadow swallowed him.

"We were just takin' what we needed," the taller one muttered.

"That's the deal," Ryder replied. "Everyone takes what they need. But they put back too."

He jerked his chin toward the craft hut where Shelly's laughter drifted through the canvas.

"You fellas planning on that part?"

Something muttered about not owing anyone.

Ryder stepped closer, the faded Iron Chiefs patch catching the dim morning light.

"This place works because no one thinks they're above the rest. You wanna eat? Plant. Fix something. Chop wood. Or—" he paused, letting silence lean in, "pack up and find somewhere else."

The shorter man nudged the other. The onions and carrots were shoved back — roughly, but returned — and they walked off muttering.

Ryder watched them go. They'd either pitch in now or be gone inside a week.

Gypsy wandered over moments later, coffee steaming. "Handled?"

"Yeah. Little spotfire."

Gypsy followed Ryder's gaze across the camp — kids laughing by the creek, tie-dye fluttering on washing lines, breakfast smoke drifting from half a dozen fires.

"Balance," he murmured. "Always balance."

Ryder didn't answer, but he agreed.

This — not the cops, not the storms — this was what decided whether the Sanctuary thrived or cracked.

* * *

Lisa had been carrying something quiet in her chest for days — showing in the way she lingered near the gardens or stood at the fire's edge instead of joining in. That morning she slipped from the van while David and Willow still slept tangled in blankets.

She walked to the big gum at the clearing's edge — the place she always came to when she needed her own thoughts. The bark was rough beneath her fingers, grounding her more than the soil underfoot.

Shay's voice drifted through memory:

You can love something and still have to let it go.

She hadn't wanted to believe it then. Now she finally understood.

She loved them both. Loved this place. But home had been calling quietly — the smell of rain on asphalt, her mum's laugh, her dad handing her a cup of tea. Not loudly, but always.

The truth settled like a stone finally stopping its roll.

Willow's voice broke the quiet.

"Thought I'd find you here."

She crossed the dew-wet grass barefoot, wrapped in a throw, hair loose. She lowered herself beside Lisa, their legs brushing.

"You've been different," Willow said softly. "I can feel it."

Lisa swallowed. "I think... I'm going home, Will."

"Home as in a visit?"

"I don't know when I'd be back."

Willow let out a cracked, soft laugh. "You'd leave me with David on my own? I'd kill him. He can't handle me without you."

Lisa smiled despite the ache. "Maybe that's the point."

Willow reached for her hand, thumb tracing a slow circle.

"Then we make the most of what's left. Promise?"

"I promise."

For the first time, the decision felt less like goodbye and more like truth.

* * *

When Lisa walked back toward the van, Willow stayed beneath the gum, breath slow, heart louder than she liked. She wrapped the throw tighter and watched the camp move — Shay by the fire, Ryder talking to Mick, Gypsy laughing near the craft hut.

She'd always been the drifter, the spark, the one who could slip away without leaving shadows.

But this place — these people — had become something else.

And Lisa was the thread holding it all together.

She wasn't ready to let that thread break.

By the time Willow stood, brushing dew from her legs, she knew the truth without argument:

When Lisa left, she would leave too.

Backpack slung over one shoulder. Grinning like she'd talked herself into another wild plan.

Except this one didn't feel wild. It felt inevitable.

She looked toward the van where Lisa spoke quietly with David, sunlight catching in her hair.

A small, steady calm settled in Willow's chest.

Wherever you go, Lis... I'm coming too.

83

The kombi's engine rumbled up the track just as late-afternoon sun slipped into gold. Heads lifted from kettles and craftwork. Lisa looked up from her beadwork beside Willow, and Willow's grin arrived before the words did.

"He's back."

David stepped out with that easy, sun-browned stride, hair still tasting of salt, breath carrying the sea. Lisa hugged him soft and sure; Willow rose slower, expression unreadable — until her smile broke through.

"You look like you've been living on saltwater and servo pies."

"Not far off," he laughed, ruffling his hair.

They moved toward the fire as the Sanctuary settled into its evening rhythm. David talked about dolphins rising through the waves; Lisa told him about the markets; Willow filled in the smaller stories Lisa didn't — quiet jokes, lazy afternoons, moments that felt like their own secret language.

At one point Lisa leaned against David's shoulder while Willow passed her a mug of tea. Their hands brushed.

The moment stretched — soft, fragile, full.

No one named it. They didn't have to.

* * *

When most of the camp had drifted to sleep, Willow stayed by the embers, cross-legged, staring into the low orange glow. The fire usually made her sparkle; tonight she was quieter, softer.

She thought of David's steady warmth. Lisa's gentle gravity. The way these two had unknowingly carved themselves into her.

"Maybe I'm not as untethered as I thought," she whispered.

Shay passed behind her, raising a hand in silent greeting. Willow almost called her over. Almost.

Some truths needed to be held alone.

* * *

Back in the kombi, Lisa curled under the soft lamplight, hair spilling across her shoulders. Willow leaned against the door.

"You've been in your head all night," Willow murmured. "Want to let me in?"

Lisa managed a small smile. "I've just been thinking."

"Dangerous habit," Willow teased, sliding closer. "You think too much, you'll do something sensible."

"Maybe I've had enough wild."

Willow reached for her hand, brushing her thumb across Lisa's knuckles. "You miss home."

Lisa exhaled. "Sometimes. Mum. Dad. My room. My old life." She hesitated. "But leaving here... leaving you... leaving David..."

"Hey." Willow cupped her cheek, gentle. "Nothing lasts by pretending it isn't changing."

Lisa leaned into the touch without thinking — the quietest con-
fession.

Later, when Willow slipped out into the dark, lantern glow catching the warmth still on her cheeks, Lisa whispered into the quiet:

"I don't know what to do."

The night didn't answer. But something inside her shifted.

* * *

By morning, something small and invisible had changed — not
love, not connection, but the breath between them.

And the Sanctuary, always listening, felt it too.

84

The firepit was a ring of soft coals when Ryder settled on the nearest log with a mug of tea, warming his hands. The Sanctuary stirred the way he liked — slow, unhurried, honest. A kettle hissed. Kids whispered conspiratorially behind the tool shed.

The kombi door creaked.

David stepped out barefoot, hair rebellious from sleep. Lisa followed, brushing her eyes; Willow stretched behind her like she'd been poured from sunlight. They shared a quiet smile — gentle, heavy, threaded with something unspoken.

David tipped his chin toward the track to the beach. Lisa hesitated for the smallest heartbeat, then nodded. Willow fell into step with them.

Ryder watched their silhouettes fade between the dunes.

That wasn't a walk.

That was a turning.

* * *

The beach was empty except for the hush of the tide and the lonely cry of a gull drifting above the headland. They walked until the sounds of camp disappeared, leaving only the sea breathing in slow, patient rhythm.

David stopped first, curling his toes into the sand.

"I'm thinking about staying," he said quietly. "This place... breathes right for me."

Lisa didn't look at him; she watched the shoreline. "I'm going home."

She said it cleanly — not to hurt him, not to force a reaction, but because truth doesn't soften when spoken in salt air.

Willow's head snapped toward her. "You'd leave me here?" A joke in tone — a crack in the middle.

"I don't want to leave either of you," Lisa whispered. "But something's been pulling me. My parents. My old life. I can't ignore it anymore."

Willow crossed her arms, then let them fall.

"If you go... maybe I go too."

She kicked a ridge of sand.

"But if I stay, I get stuck with him, and honestly?" She flicked her eyes to David. "He can't handle me without you."

It broke the tension — a laugh, small but real — but didn't change the gravity beneath it.

They stood in a wavering triangle on the sand, breathing the same salted air, knowing the world they'd built together was beginning to tilt.

* * *

Back at camp, Shay sat by the fading embers, Akubra tipped low. Ryder joined her.

"You heading out?" he asked.

She nodded. "Feels like time."

"For how long?"

"A week. A month. A year." She shrugged. "When the wind says go."

He smiled, though something pulled behind it. "Door's open."

She bumped her shoulder gently against his. "You know I always find my way back."

They watched the morning unfold like a quiet farewell.

* * *

Later, Willow found Lisa at the water tank. Lisa's fingers dripped clear lines through the dust.

"Hey," Willow murmured.

Lisa turned. "Hey."

Willow stepped close — too close for it to be casual — and tucked a strand of hair behind Lisa's ear.

"No dancing around it," Willow whispered. "If you go home... I'm not staying without you. I thought I could. I can't. Losing you feels worse than losing this place." She gestured at the Sanctuary. "Worse than losing him."

Lisa's breath caught. "And David?"

Willow swallowed. "I love him. But he isn't you."

They leaned their foreheads together — breath shared, truth shared, nothing else needed.

"You're not asking me to choose," Lisa whispered.

"No," Willow said softly. "I'm telling you mine."

* * *

David saw them on the walk back — Willow's hand cupping Lisa's cheek, Lisa leaning into the touch with unguarded tenderness. Something tightened inside him.

Not anger.

Not jealousy.

Something quieter.

Something sad.

He had always known they weren't just his.

* * *

That night, smoke rising in thin threads from scattered fires, the three of them sat inside the van. They lay close without touching — breath warm, decisions waiting.

Lisa drew a breath. "I'm going home. Soon."

David closed his eyes. Willow inhaled sharply.

Willow straightened. "Then I'm coming with you."

David leaned forward, elbows on his knees. He wasn't ready to lose them — not the laughter, not the shared mornings, not the gentle tangle of limbs that made everything feel less like chaos and more like living.

But he wouldn't ask them to stay.

Willow reached for Lisa's hand. Their fingers wove together instinctively.

"You're not going alone," Willow said.

Lisa's eyes shimmered. "I wasn't sure you'd want to."

"Are you kidding?" Willow huffed. "I'm not letting him have you all to himself in Sydney." She jerked a thumb at David.

He laughed — small, real — and for a moment the tension cracked.

They didn't talk about what came after. They didn't need to.

The goodbye had already begun.

85

The sun rose slow and golden, spilling warmth across the Sanctuary as if it knew it had to try harder today.

Inside the van, morning light drifted across loosened blankets and sleepy limbs. Willow's leg rested across Lisa's hips; David's arm draped over both of them in heavy warmth. Lisa stirred first, cheek brushing Willow's hand; Willow's thumb traced a lazy circle along her ribs. David's fingers slipped through Lisa's hair.

No one spoke.

Silence held the shape of them tenderly.

Some part of each of them already knew:

They would never wake like this again.

* * *

The Sanctuary hummed with late-morning life — mugs clinking, a guitar tuning, children racing barefoot toward the river. Gypsy waved them over to breakfast with a grin.

"Eat before you disappear into your little love bubble again," he teased.

Around the table, it almost felt normal. Shelly passed warm bread; Ryder nodded at David with something close to respect; Chook pressed a painted stone into Lisa's hand "so the city doesn't make you boring."

The day moved in small perfect pieces.

Lisa strung bunting across the craft hut. David caught one last surf. Willow lay in the grass weaving bracelets, humming something soft and defiant.

A few newcomers came to offer blessings.

"Won't be the same without you," someone said.

Lisa felt the truth settle inside her ribs.

* * *

In the craft hut, Lisa wrote a letter home — crossing out more words than she kept. Shelly read it with soft eyes.

"They'll be proud," she said. "Not because you left. Because you chose when to come back."

Lisa sealed the envelope before her courage slipped.

* * *

By the veg patch, David found Gypsy turning soil.

"I'm going with them," David said quietly. "Sydney first. Then... see where the road leads."

Gypsy didn't look surprised. "Good. You've given this place strength. It'll be here when you wander back."

Something steady settled in David's chest.

* * *

Willow packed like a storm — velvet flares, sarongs, bracelets everywhere. Shay helped her fold it into order.

"You sure about city life?" Shay asked.

"No," Willow said truthfully. "But I'm sure about her."

"That'll do," Shay murmured, pulling her into a tight hug.

* * *

By dusk the kombi was ready — blankets rolled, bread packed, Shelly's mystery parcel tucked safely away. Ryder slapped the side of the van.

"She'll get you there," he said. "Just listen when she complains."

Lisa laughed, but the sound wavered.

* * *

That night the Sanctuary gathered around a gentle fire — no speeches, no ceremony. Just warmth. Just presence.

Shay sang something low and wordless. Conversations rose and fell like tidewater.

David sat with an arm around each woman, firelight reflected in their eyes.

The embers sighed inward.

The night held them softly.

Tomorrow would be packing.

The next day, leaving.

Tonight —

they were still here.

Still held.

Still part of the Sanctuary's living, breathing heart.

A last night to belong.

86

Mist clung low across the Sanctuary, drifting between tents and trees as though trying to hold the night in place a little longer. A kookaburra cracked open the silence, insisting morning had arrived whether anyone was ready for it or not.

Lisa stepped from the van barefoot, arms wrapped lightly around herself. Willow followed with a blanket draped over her shoulders, hair still tangled from sleep. David came last, carrying the kettle and three chipped mugs as if tea might slow the turning of the clock.

They sat together on the kombi's back step, not speaking, letting the mist thin and lift around them. The quiet wasn't awkward; it was the kind of silence that holds everything words can't.

When the camp finally stirred, people came in small clusters — no ceremony, no speeches, just soft goodbyes offered by those who had woven themselves into their days.

Shelly pressed a warm paper bag into Lisa's hands. "Something to remind you of here."

Ryder clapped David on the shoulder — firm, grounded. "Safe roads, mate."

Chook demanded a postcard from "wherever the hell you end up next," then wandered off with a theatrical sigh, as if their departure were an inconvenience he alone would bear.

Shay held Lisa for a long, steady moment. Her hands were warm at Lisa's back, her breath soft with understanding. When they parted, Shay's smile was gentle, private, threaded with a truth she didn't bother to speak aloud.

"The road changes you," she murmured. "Don't be afraid to let it."

A few more hugs. A few final nods. A few quiet looks that said everything that didn't need to be said.

The bags were loaded. The van door shut with a hollow, decisive click.

When the tyres rolled over the track, the Sanctuary gathered behind them — familiar faces, hands raised, fading slowly in the rear-view mirror until the trees swallowed them whole.

For the first few kilometres, none of them spoke. The hum of the engine filled the space between them, steady as a heartbeat.

It wasn't until the highway opened ahead, long and straight and full of promise, that Willow finally whispered — still staring forward —

"Well… guess it's just us now."

Lisa reached for her hand. "Yeah," she murmured. "Just us."

David nodded, eyes fixed on the road unfurling before them. Whatever came next had already begun.

* * *

Back at the Sanctuary, morning slipped back into rhythm. Fires smoked. Children raced barefoot between tents. The craft hut swung open, spilling colour and chatter into the clearing.

Shay watched the dust trail fade to nothing, then stepped back and let a small, sly smile tug at her mouth — the kind that meant she already knew her own road was shifting.

Without another word, she turned toward the beach track. Eucalyptus stirred in her wake as she disappeared into the trees.

The Sanctuary exhaled.

New stories waited.

And those who remained stepped quietly into them.

87

The dust of the kombi had not yet settled when the Sanctuary felt the absence.

It wasn't quiet — not truly. Breakfast fires still crackled, kettles hissed, and children tore barefoot through the grass the way they always had. Someone tuned a guitar near the craft hut; someone else laughed through an argument about whose turn it was to fetch water.

But beneath it all, something had shifted.

As though three silhouettes had been gently lifted out of the morning light, leaving their outlines stitched into the air.

A macramé cord drifted in the breeze beside the craft hut, still smelling faintly of the oil from Lisa's fingertips. The blankets where Willow sprawled most afternoons were still warm from the night before. And the dunes carried the ghost of David's laughter — scattered by the wind the moment it rose.

Shay felt it most.

She stood beneath the big gum near the gardens, arms folded, gaze soft but somewhere far beyond the clearing. She didn't look toward the track. She didn't need to. She could feel the empty space where the kombi had been — not sharp, just steady, like a tide that had receded more than expected.

Shelly wandered over and stopped beside her. They didn't touch at first. They just breathed the same cool morning air.

"Strange, isn't it?" Shelly murmured. "How the whole place feels... thinner."

Shay nodded, swallowing before she spoke. "They were part of the rhythm. The fire's still burning, but..."

She let the words trail off.

"But it sounds different," Shelly finished for her.

A kookaburra cracked into laughter down by the river — loud, ridiculous — as if trying to stitch humour back into the morning. It didn't quite work, but the effort was noted.

Shay lowered herself onto the log by the garden beds, elbows resting on her knees. After a moment, Shelly sat beside her, their hips a finger's breadth apart.

"Do you think they'll come back?" Shay asked quietly.

Shelly considered. "People who love this place always find their way home. Might not be next month. Might not be next year. But the Sanctuary has its own kind of gravity."

A small, crooked smile pulled at Shay's mouth — softening her whole face.

Her gaze drifted across the clearing. A few tomato vines were still tied with Lisa's careful knots. Willow's leather bracelets dangled from a low branch, catching sunlight in tiny glints. David's footprints near the water tank were already softening at the edges.

"Funny," Shay said. "I always thought I'd be the one to leave first."

Shelly's smile turned knowing.

"You still will. Roads don't stop calling someone like you."

Shay breathed out slowly.

"Not today."

Shelly reached for her hand at last, their fingers linking with a quiet, natural ease. No declarations. No need for any.

When someone called her name from the cookfire, Shelly rose, letting go only at the final moment.

"Come on," she said softly. "Let's see if this place can still hum without them."

Shay stayed a heartbeat longer, watching shards of sunlight sift through the trees. The Sanctuary didn't look broken. It looked... expectant. Like a place waiting for its next chapter to begin.

She stood, brushing red dust from her legs. Her hair caught the morning light, turning the ends gold. As she walked toward the centre of camp, the breeze shifted, carrying the faintest trace of sandalwood and salt — memories still warm from bodies that had slept tangled together only yesterday.

She didn't turn toward the track.

She didn't need to.

People leave.

People return.

The Sanctuary endures.

The fire would be tended.

The gardens would grow.

New stories would take root in the soil left behind.

And somewhere on the long road, three hearts were already carrying this place with them — tucked soft behind the ribs, where the best memories live.

The Sanctuary exhaled.

And the day continued.

88

The sun had barely slipped behind the rooftops when Lisa excused herself from the lounge room, leaving her parents absorbed in *Bandstand*. As she stepped into her bedroom, Colleen Hewett's new song **"Day by Day"** drifted from the radio — warm, bright, threaded with memory.

The first chords pulled her straight back to the Sanctuary: drifting smoke, river mist, dawn laughter, and the faces she still carried like small, glowing lanterns.

Shay. Gypsy. Shelly. Ryder.

And, always — David and Willow.

The ache came first. Then the smile that always followed.

She settled on her bed, one leg tucked beneath her, hugging a cushion as the chorus unfurled. *Day by day* — that was exactly how she'd lived up there. How she'd learned to breathe.

From beneath the bed she drew a carved wooden box — the one Gypsy and Shelly had hidden inside the Kombi for her to find later.

Foot-long, brass clasp, hand-carved lid. A parting gift that felt more like a promise.

Inside lay a folded note.

* * *

To beautiful Lisa,

You arrived like a precious new rose into our family at Ourimbah.

We are grateful to have watched you grow and bloom — elegant, mature, adding beauty everywhere you walked.

We will miss you.

Our home is your home, wherever we meet.

Don't forget us.

Love, Gypsy and Shelly.

* * *

Her breath caught as she smoothed the paper flat. Beneath it lay small keepsakes from her time on the road — a feather, a painted bead, a scrap of tie-dye, a tiny jar of river sand. At the bottom she found the woven bracelet David had made for her eighteenth. She held it gently, a single tear warming her cheek.

Her parents loved her — unquestionably, fiercely — but the Sanctuary had loved her differently. Freely. In ways she could never fully explain.

She lay back against her pillows, smiling through the ache, wondering where they all were now.

* * *

Thailand — Pattaya Coast

The long-tail boat's engine rattled into silence as Somchai lifted the propeller from the water. Light catch today, but enough. As the boat drifted toward shore, he spotted the big white *farang* barreling down the beach, arms flailing like a runaway child.

"Sawasdee krup!" Chook shouted, waving both hands.

Somchai sighed, smiling. Pattaya saw many foreigners these days, but this one — loud, eager, bright as a misplaced bird — helped unload the catch each morning, bought a fish, and bowed like a monk at the temple.

Chook hugged him, paid double for a single mackerel, and bounded off across the sand singing something indecipherable.

"Crazy white man," Somchai muttered fondly.

But he smiled all the while.

* * *

Somewhere Inland — A Concrete Cell

Ryder leaned against the cold wall, rolling a smoke with the precision of a man who'd learned patience the hard way.

"You got papers?" he asked.

The bloke opposite handed him a packet. Ryder sealed the edge, struck a match.

"Jim," the man offered, extending a hand.

Ryder clasped it — firm, not cruel. "Ryder."

"What're you in for?"

"They say I killed a cop." Ryder took a long drag. "Didn't. Wanted to. Never got the chance."

Jim stiffened. Ryder half-smiled.

"Name was Rand. Bully. Hurt good people. I stomped him more than once, but he was breathing when I left. Someone else finished the job. Wish I knew who — I'd buy 'em a beer."

Ash drifted to the floor.

"I lived at a place called the Sanctuary," he said. "Karma's made this my new home."

A steady look.

"Don't make it yours."

* * *

Sydney — Bondi

Willow stood naked at the window of a Bondi flat, the morning sun turning her skin to honey while Billy Thorpe blasted from the radio. She belted the chorus with zero shame.

"Willow!" Max groaned, wrestling into his jeans. "You want us kicked out?"

"A little fun never hurt anyone," she grinned, bouncing onto the bed.

"It's not fun! You flirted with my sister, Mum won't talk to me, the neighbours hate us — you're doing my head in."

"Let's take a trip," she teased.

"Willow, I'm serious. You need to leave."

Her smile faltered. "Where would I go?"

"Back to your boyfriend — David, wasn't it? He didn't want you either, you freak."

She flinched, masked it with a smirk.

"Takes one to know one."

The door slammed.

Silence fell, heavy and sharp.

Two hours later she stood at Central Station with a ticket in hand.

"Train to Murwillumbah?"

"Two p.m. sharp," the porter said.

She tucked the ticket into her skirt, grin lifting, bright and reckless.

"Home," she murmured. "I'm coming home."

* * *

The Sanctuary

Shelly handed Gypsy a mug of coffee — one of the new clay ones a recent arrival had fired. She still preferred her chipped favourite, but the community's hands were everywhere now: the butter dish, the painted stools, the woven blinds.

The Sanctuary hummed. Forty-nine residents.

"One more and we're full," Shelly said.

"I'll keep a place open," Gypsy replied. "Feels like one of ours is coming home soon."

Shelly nudged him. "You getting psychic now?"

He chuckled. "Wouldn't that be something. Funny how the ones you least expect change everything."

Just then, **David** wandered up from the garden beds.

"Smells good," he said. "Any spare?"

Shelly passed him a plate. "Sit down before you fall down."

They ate as guitars drifted through the trees and the river whispered beyond them.

Gypsy paused mid-bite.

"You hear that?"

"Hear what?" David asked.

"Thought I heard a didgeridoo."

They listened.

The forest held its breath.

"Mad as a cut snake," Shelly said, swatting him. "Eat."

Gypsy smiled — but the feeling lingered, settling deep as a footprint in soft earth.

* * *

Shay — Somewhere on the Coast

Shay perched on the bonnet of her yellow Moke, watching the sunset pour gold and purple across the sky — a horizon caught between two colours, much like her.

Pinned to the visor was a photo: her, Lisa, and David at the Uki markets. She brushed her fingertips over it, kissed them lightly, then turned the key.

The engine purred.

The road waited.

* * *

Sydney — Home

Lisa slid the wooden box back beneath her bed and wandered into the lounge room. Her parents sat shoulder to shoulder on the couch, Donny Osmond's voice floating from the television.

"Your favourite's on!" her father called.

She slipped between them, resting her head on her mother's shoulder.

"This one doesn't seem like you, Lis," her mother teased gently.

"It does," Lisa murmured. "It's not about the song. It's about knowing I was loved."

Her parents exchanged a look — protective, relieved, still unsure.

Lisa closed her eyes as the chorus softened through the room like a memory exhaled.

"I'm great," she whispered. "Everything's exactly where it should be. I'm sure of it."

* * *

And somewhere far away —

on beaches,

roads,

riverbanks,

and in places both broken and beautiful —

the people who had loved her, and whom she had loved just as fiercely, stepped into new sunsets and fresh beginnings.

None of them had left each other.

Not really.

Some stories don't end.

They simply move into the next light.

Mark Wisnewski is an Australian storyteller who writes across genres, from crime fiction to contemporary drama. He lives on the Gold Coast with his dog Buddy and his partner Rae, where he divides his time between writing, reading, and planning their next adventure together.

https://markwisnewski.net

Hunter's Moon - A Blaire Hunter Crime Novel

When a young woman is found dead in a quiet Sydney suburb, Detective Blaire Hunter is called to a scene that feels wrong from the first step inside. The body is staged. The injuries don't match the room. And the evidence — what little there is — feels arranged rather than discovered.

Blaire's instincts tell her this isn't a crime of opportunity. It's deliberate. Controlled. Personal.

As she digs deeper, the case begins to echo patterns she's seen before — patterns tied to an older investigation that still haunts her career and her sleep. The more she uncovers, the more she realises someone has been watching her work, anticipating her moves, and shaping the narrative around her.

With departmental pressure rising, a partner she can't fully trust, and a killer who understands procedure as well as she does, Blaire is forced to confront not only the truth behind the victim's final hours, but the shadows in her own past that this case is dragging back into the light.

Hunter's Moon is a tense, atmospheric crime thriller set in Sydney's coastal and inner-city streets — a story about control, buried histories, and the cost of seeing what others miss.